Mrs Nobody

Amanda Miles

Miles and Miles Publishing

Book Cover Design by ebooklaunch.com

A CIP catalogue record for this book is available from the British Library.

ISBN: 978-1-9999383-1-4

www.amandamilesauthor.com

For all the strong women it was a honour to know and love

Leah Hill, Laura Thornton, Estelle Cuthbert, Dani Stephens, Brigid Corcoran and Jill Neale.

Foreword - A fictional true story

The Association of Finnish Architects hired Alvar Aalto to rebuild the town of Rovaniemi, which the Germans had destroyed in 1945. Alvar began rebuilding the city with single housing units designed for the Lapland climate. His plan expanded beyond the city in the 1950s and included hydroelectric plants built on the rivers of Lapland. He also commissioned impact assessments on the environment, indigenous Sami, reindeer herds, water basins and microclimate. Nobody in the world had ever devised such a plan.

In June 1950, Eleanor Roosevelt visited Rovaniemi, as a representative of the United Nations, to see post war rebuilding efforts. Officials built the Polar Circle Cabin at a point where Finland met the Arctic circle, to impress the former First Lady of the United States. Here, guests could buy a cup of coffee and send a postcard from the new post office. Eleanor Roosevelt wrote in her diary, "It had been opened for our coming so that I might mail the first letter home from the Arctic Circle...addressed to the President of the United States." It was one of the first attempts to create an attraction in this part of Finland.

But what about the story of Father Christmas? The locals believe Santa's true home is found at a mysterious site in Finnish Lapland called Ear Mountain and Rovaniemi plays the role of Santa Claus's public face to ensure his identity remains a secret.

These facts were the inspiration for the book.

Chapter 1

London, 2009

There is nothing more satisfactory than making a list and checking it twice. Sitting in the back of the taxi on my way to the studio, I open my notebook. My latest list is growing faster than I can delete and all points needed to be allocated by yesterday. I should be looking at the questions the production team gave me, but this feels more important.

- 12 conifer trees. Contact Green Garden Design Company.
- 10 new signposts—decorated with red and green crystals.
- 8 kg bags of mincemeat. New Nigella recipe to try out.
- 5 gold chandeliers for foyer. Give to Nic to source.
- 4 seasonal waiting staff needed. Chase HR.
- 3 quotes for reindeer feed needed.
- 2 new ovens for the kitchen.

All I need now is a partridge *in a pear tree. I wonder if the production team would like to hear this?*

My handbag beeps again. I close my notebook and search for my phone nestled at the bottom. I left home twenty-four hours ago and already have 226 emails, 56 text messages and 7 missed calls, most of them from Nic, who's been trying to contact me since this morning. Reading my emails makes me queasy, so I stare out of the window instead.

The taxi slows and I see people's faces up close, a strange mix of weariness and excitement. Not surprising, considering the time of year. There are more pensive looks than frivolous ones, weighed down by more than their shopping bags. It always makes me sad to see partners or parents frantically searching for that one illusive gift for that one special day, when it's the other 364 days of the year that are important. I suppose we never understand until it's too late.

"Sorry about the traffic, love." The cabbie's thick cockney accent fills the back of the taxi. "Always worse at Christmas. I hope you're not gonna be late."

"No, it's fine. I left myself plenty of time. And I need to make some calls, anyway."

I hold my phone up in the air and dial Nic's number. A familiar voice answers, desperate to talk about the new problems: the kennels need a proper clean, some of the village sleds are broken, the elves' post office costumes have not turned up and most of the new tree lights are not working.

Nothing unusual then. "Nic. Take a breath. It will all be fine." I can physically hear her take in a lung full of air and breathe out. "Speak to Krystoff about involving the guests in a Husky experience, to include the cleaning. Ring maintenance and ask for Fred. If you collect all the broken sleds, he will fix them by lunchtime and check the lights. Ask Lisa if she will drive to Rovaniemi to pick up the costumes. Now anything else?— I'm fine, stop worrying— I'm doing the right thing."

The cabbie pulls up outside a grey concrete building, which looks more like an old asylum hospital than a television studio.

"Perfect, thank you. How much do I owe?" I go through my purse, not recognising many of the notes now. A lot has changed since I was last here.

"It's all taken care of. The studio has paid." And then, as an afterthought, he says, "Are you famous, then?"

I laugh and catch him looking at me through the rear-view mirror.

"Excuse my asking, love, but the studios don't normally pay out unless you're famous."

"Well, I'm not famous and you won't know who I am. No one ever does. But that might be about to change."

He scratches his head and looks more confused than ever, but I can't explain now. I tell him this as I step out of the warm cab and into the first signs of a cold snap. I don't bother fastening the gold buttons on my coat. Five degrees is positively balmy compared to home.

***

The security guard at the studio door is most helpful. He looks confused at first, as most people are when they see me, but he behaves professionally and leads me to the reception area. The receptionist takes my coat and walks to the coat stand. I watch her feel the luxurious velvet and open the thick white fur collar, trying to see the manufacturer's label inside which is not there.

"Made to order, dear, I'm afraid." Poor thing turns as red as my coat. I really shouldn't say anything. But then that's always been my problem.

She hangs it up before saying, "Could you come with me, please?"

I follow behind, admiring her patent high-heeled shoes that click-clack down the corridor. I can't remember the last time I wore any kind of heel. We reach a door that says 'Make Up' in gold capital letters. How lovely it would be if there were rooms like this in real life. Rooms where people could apologise for things they've said and done. A room full of nice smells where you could talk, a room that left you feeling and looking better than when you walked in. Inside the room are four black leather chairs, each positioned in front of an oval mirror with spotlights either side.

"Miranda will do your make-up. She'll take years off you!" She shuts the door and I look at Miranda.

"If that's the case, you must work with magic." I laugh.

"No, I don't, but I heard you do?"

I laugh again, more restrained, as I'm not sure what I can say at this point. I was told by the booker of the show that I had to keep this secret.

Another secret. Not a problem. I'm used to keeping secrets.

Half an hour later and Miranda has indeed worked her magic. I scrutinise her work. Gone are the dark circles and my eyes are more prominent than my wrinkles. My pale skin has a golden sheen, not too St Tropez, but enough to make me look like I've had a holiday, which is definitely not the case. I admire my reflection. I look good. I'm beginning to like this television idea. Maybe this interview wasn't such a bad idea of mine? I'm distracted from my thoughts by a gentle request from the studio director to be on set in ten minutes. Jessica, another young girl from the production team, smiles and asks if I need anything before we go through the questions. I assure her I have gone through the questions.

"I'm sure you have," replies Jessica, "but it helps to go through them again. In case you dry up."

Many things have dried up recently; my skin, my hair, my libido, but my ability to talk is not one of them. Jessica doesn't look like she would understand. Too young.

"We are ready for you on set now. Please be careful of the wires on the floor," says one member of the camera crew and they usher me to the side, where I see the presenter Anna Grey sitting bolt upright on a dark blue sofa, her legs tucked to one side and pieces of paper in her hands.

"Don't forget, you have one hour left to enter our competition to win £10,000," says Ms Grey, beaming at the camera. She swivels to face a different direction, a different camera. "And coming up, my next guest is the wife of one of the most famous men in the world. Who is she? All will be revealed after the break."

I smooth down my hair and adjust my skirt. And then I feel it. The heat rising from my chest, up my throat and into my head. I try to swallow the flickering, but it turns into a flame, then a furnace.

Please dear Lord, no. Not now. A flush is the last thing I need.

Jessica is standing next to me, clipboard in hand. Perfect. Before she can say anything, I seize it and begin fanning my face and panting. She looks at me like I'm insane, which I must admit is happening more and more these days.

"Are you okay?" she asks.

Early menopause is hell. I want to tell her but just nod instead, the heat thankfully subsiding. A short one today. Jessica removes the clipboard from my clenched fists and points to where I should sit. Before I move, I wipe the back of my neck and the river of sweat running down my cleavage with my handkerchief.

After stepping over the multiple cables strewn across the floor, I sit on the velvet chair opposite Anna Grey. I can't help staring. She is exquisite, beautiful features with killer cheekbones.

"How lovely to meet you?" Her eyes scan me up and down, and she smiles with approval. Then she notices me staring at her. "What? Do I have lipstick on my teeth?" She shouts: "Make up!"

"No!" I say over her high shrills. "I was admiring your face." She looks a similar age, but without the crevice of wrinkles and furrowed brow. I must assume her life and the weather have not been as extreme as mine. She doesn't say anything. I clear my throat. "How are you?"

"Right, I think we are nearly ready," she says, ignoring me. "Jessica has gone through the questions with you?"

"Yes." *A one syllable answer is all* you're *getting.*

Ms Grey launches into presenter's speech, mistaking my shortness for nervousness. "There's nothing to worry about. I will lead you into each question and if I feel it needs expanding, I will ask you to tell us more. If you repeat an answer, I will cut in and change direction with a different question. Do you understand?"

I nod. This is her show. I understand people like her.

The lights dim, apart from the bright spotlights shining on our faces. I hear a voice counting down in the darkness, then an introductory jingle playing in the background.

"Welcome back," says Ms Grey, smiling animatedly at the camera. Watching her, I now understand the term 'making love to the camera'. "I am joined by Chrissie Connor. Not a name you would know, but you will know of her husband."

Flashing her white teeth, she turns to me. "Chrissie. Can you tell us who you are?"

Memories of the show *Stars in their Eyes* flash before me. "Tonight, Mathew, I'm going to be—"

"Isn't that the ultimate question?" It was a question I'd been asking myself a great deal recently. "Do any of us know who we really are?"

Ms Grey's face drops, just like my Aunt Joyce when she had a stroke. She clears her throat and asks again, "Yes, that is a much larger question that we won't be able to answer on today's programme."

I note the emphasis on 'won't'.

"But please tell us who you are?"

As she leans in, demanding an answer, I smell her perfume. Cedar and spruce. An earthy, woody smell. Home. I take a deep breath. "Well, there were lots of names for my husband. Kris Kringle, Santa Claus, Father Christmas, sometimes St Nick, but that is definitely taking a name too far."

A few of the backstage crew laugh. Ms Grey doesn't.

"But I don't have any names. I am just the wife of Father Christmas."

Ms Grey does her best, astonished look, although I think it would have been more effective if she'd been told Harrods were doing a half-price sale. "Father Christmas? The real Father Christmas. Not the imitation ones we see in department stores, but the one who lives at the North Pole?"

I furrow my brow, not sure what she means.

She leans over her papers. "We have younger viewers who might not understand," she whispers.

Of course, those Santas. The overweight, older men wearing red costumes and white, dirty polyester beards that have never seen a washing machine for fear of falling apart.

"Yes, but it's Lapland, not the North Pole."

She glares at me.

"Better transport systems," I explain apologetically.

Some of the crew giggle. Ms Grey does not.

This is not going well.

"And how long have you been, Mrs Christmas?"

"I've been married— for fourteen years, and was Mrs Christmas for six of those." I smile.

Ms Grey doesn't smile.

You think it's a gimmick. A whimsical half hour slot to fill in between the real people you interview. I wonder if you'll be convinced by the time I finish.

"The entire world knows of Father Christmas but his wife—" She contemplates for a few seconds. "I know nothing about her."

"That's not unusual. We never hear about the wives of famous men. How many women have been responsible for their husband's greatness but never acknowledged? Maybe *War and Peace* would not have been one of the finest works of literature if Mrs Tolstoy hadn't copied and edited it seven times by candlelight from Mr Tolstoy's written notes. Maybe Mr George Washington would not have been President of the United States without Mrs Washington's wealth. And maybe we would have lost World War Two if Mrs Churchill hadn't been her husband's closest confidante. These women helped change the course of history, yet we don't even know their first names."

Ms Grey looks me in the eye for the first time since we started this interview.

You're interested now.

"So," she says with a long pause, emphasising it is time. Time to talk.

Time to tell the story. "How does your story begin?"

The beginning. When was that? I suppose it must be when I met Daniel.

Chapter 2

Majorca, Spain 1990

It was the first time I'd ever been abroad. Before this, there had been holidays in caravan parks with grandparents. Playing cards, with Nan dressed in her underwear, for most of the day and sleepless nights due to Granddad's snoring, but this was different.

Now I was standing under a neon sign next to my best friends, with the scent of aftershave, beer, and vomit wafting in the warm air. The place was amazing, and it came alive at night.

"Let's go in here," shouted Lisa, five tickets in her hand from the ticket seller with the colourful, braided hair.

We walked down the red carpet of 'Chaplin's' nightclub. As the door opened, I don't know what hit me first: the music at 500 decibels or the heat. It was electric. Crowds of gyrating bodies, pushing against one another, moving in time with the pulsing music like a can of worms writhing in and out of each other, blind to their surroundings.

Paula pushed to the front of the bar and ordered. The rest of us squeezed into a tight corner near the toilet, not the most pleasant but a space at least. Four vodka mules later, I felt amazing. I felt confident, making eye contact with boys, instead of staring at the floor.

"What is wrong with these leggings?" Rebecca shouted over the loud thumping bass, turning her head round to see her bottom, like a puppy chasing its tail. "It's my knickers. It must be my knickers. Chris, is it my knickers? Chris, you're not even looking?"

No. I wasn't looking. I was staring, mouth open, at the boy crossing the dance floor. Rebecca dug me in the ribs to get my attention, but it didn't work. I was busy trying to act casual, but nerves overwhelmed me, and my eyes found the floor. A pair of psychedelic trainers walked into my peripheral view. Very striking. As were the red socks that poked out the top. My eyes continued moving upwards, taking in the skinny blue Levi's and tight white t-shirt until I reached a pair of hazel eyes. He smiled. I melted. It was all very 'Jackie' magazine photo story perfect. Dark-haired, sun kissed skin. A perfect Spanish boy.

"Hi. Can I buy you a drink?" he said, in a clipped Northern accent.

Not Spanish. Shame. What did he say again? Concentrate Chrissie. "Vodka and lemonade, please?" *Sounds more sophisticated than a vodka mule.*

He turned and walked to the bar, which was now three people deep. It would take him at least ten minutes to get a drink.

I should have gone with him, so we could carry on talking.

The music is so loud he wouldn't hear you.

Maybe that would be a good thing.

Here I go again. Internally arguing. My devil and angel sat conspicuously on my shoulders. The girls' whoops stopped me from going any further down the rabbit hole.

"He's lovely," said Lisa, staring in his direction but primarily at his bottom.

"Well done you," cooed Nerys. "He seems nice."

"She doesn't need nice," shouted Paula over the music. "She needs a good shag."

The girls gathered round, deciding now I had a bite, I would need help reeling in the catch and each of them had a piece of advice.

"Remember to lick your lips when he's talking to you," said Paula. "They like that."

"And keep looking around you as though you're not listening. Keep him keen," said Lisa.

"And push your boobs out," said Rebecca demonstrating with her own ample chest. "You might even want to graze them against him."

"Flick your hair back and laugh when he says something funny," said Nerys.

Although I wasn't sure that any of this was good advice, I needed all the help I could get. I would have liked to clarify the running order of all these tips, but he was back, drinks in hand, looking very pleased with himself.

"There you go. Gin and tonic."

"Oh!" I looked down at the glass. I could never drink gin.

"Everything okay?" he asked, watching my every move.

I don't like gin.

Don't make him walk away.

But I don't like gin.

But you like him, so just drink it.

"Yes," I answered, swallowing the contents in one go. He smiled, pleased with my reaction, and told me what he'd been up to.

He was funny. Really funny and I liked listening to him. Then I remembered what the girls said. I laughed and flicked my hair back. Unfortunately, it caught him in the eye. I couldn't apologise enough. I was so embarrassed.

With one eye closed, he asked, "How long are you here for?"

"A few more hours yet, I hope."

He looks puzzled.

He meant here in Majorca, not in the bar. You're such an idiot.

I tried to lick my lips but my tongue got stuck on my cherry lipstick so I pushed my boobs out, hoping he wouldn't notice the gunk I was now trying to get off my teeth. It seemed to do the trick. But he kept on staring, which felt rude.

"What have you got down there?"

"Cheeky," I said in my sexiest voice, which somehow sounded like a cross between Dolly Parton and Danny la Rue.

"It's just you seem to have something stuck." He pointed at my cleavage.

I glanced down to see the toilet paper I used to pad out my bra, creeping its way upward and over the top of my cleavage.

I'm such an idiot. How do I get out of this?

"Er, us girls need to keep some tissue in case they run out in the toilets. You men wouldn't know what that's like."

It will do. It's better than the truth. I need a distraction. Make him think I'm not interested.

I looked around me.

"Are you looking for someone?"

No. I just want to nestle my face in your chest.

"What are you looking at?" He sounded annoyed.

"Er, nothing."

I can't tell him. Bloody Paula ! He won't even look at me now. You should never have listened to the girls.

His face was so close to mine, I could smell his soapy aftershave. I tried to give him a seductive look, but it was more Dracula than Madonna.

This is hopeless. I'm hopeless. I didn't know what to do, so I grabbed his face and kissed him. At first it surprised him, but then he leaned in and, with his left hand, put his fingers around my neck and drew me to him. He was good at this. We continued, oblivious to the music and the chants from my friends jeering in the background. He stopped for a minute and looked into my eyes. Then he kissed the top of my lip, the side of my mouth, and down my neck. With my eyes still closed, my head raised automatically as if on autopilot, and he made his way round my neck with soft, fluttery kisses.

He stopped. "I don't even know your name."

My cheeks were flushed. Being spontaneous was hot. "It's Chrissie."

"As in 'Brinkley', the supermodel. You two could be sisters."

It was cheesy, but I liked he was trying so hard. He was still just a boy trying to impress a girl.

"I'm Daniel."

"Nice to meet you, Daniel." And it genuinely was.

Half an hour later, after a lot more kissing, Lisa interrupted us. "Paula has thrown up and Rebecca needs her bed, so we're going. You can stay though." She smiled at Daniel and winked at me.

I looked at Rebecca and Nerys dragging Paula by the arms, struggling to get her upright. Then I looked at Daniel. "It's okay. I'll help."

Disappointment was painted all over Daniel's face. "I thought we could go somewhere else. Somewhere quieter?"

He looks so sad.

You're going home tomorrow.

But I want him to like me.

You're going home tomorrow.

"I'm sorry, Daniel, I—"

"That's fine. I get it. Have a nice life." He walked off.

I was taken aback by his reaction. It was so childish. But what did it matter? I'd never see him again.

***

But I did see him again, about a year later, in my local pub. I was sitting at a table with the girls on an ordinary Friday night after work. I didn't recognise him at first as he had his back to me. But there was something about those broad shoulders, stretched into a tight-fitting blue shirt. He stood talking to a girl. When he angled his body to get a better position, he saw me. I smiled. He didn't.

He can't see me.

He can see you.

It's dark in here.

He can see you.

He turned and glanced at me before he bent over this girl and kissed her. I knew I shouldn't be watching, but I couldn't take my eyes off them. He kissed her lips, her cheeks, her forehead, then her neck. Just like he did with me. It was as if he was doing it on purpose, trying to make me jealous.

What an idiot! I'm never jealous. I wasn't even jealous when Simon le Bon married Yasmin and he was plastered all over my bedroom wall.

I tore my eyes away and looked around at the groups of men dressed in shirts and ties, enjoying the end of week drinks, knowing there was no work tomorrow.

It was my turn to get the drinks, so I walked to the bar and a group of men who were standing to the left of this humiliating show. I smiled at one guy who seemed keen to talk to me.

A laugh with a hair flick, as he talked about his dull job. Not funny, but Daniel didn't know that. Move in closer with cleavage visible due to undoing of buttons on shirt, no toilet paper on show this time. Licking lips but the whole time staring at Daniel. *You're being weird.*

The bloke I was with didn't care and tried to kiss me. *Crap! This wasn't what I wanted. What do I do now?* Just then I felt my hand being grabbed, and I was pulled through into the arms of Daniel.

"What are you doing here?" We both said at the same time.

Daniel stared at me so intently, my legs felt like jelly.

"I was saving you from making a big mistake." It looked like he was smirking.

"I don't need saving." I shook his hand off mine.

"You did. He was going to kiss you, and he's not your type."

"How do you know?"

He laughed. "I thought you needed my help." He scratched behind his left ear before folding his arms across his chest.

"I didn't," I whispered, so quietly even lip readers would have struggled to work it out.

He didn't say anything. I couldn't say anything.

"As you said, you don't need me."

How old is he? Ten.

He was silent. Sulking.

I'm glad you're here. I want to keep talking to you. I couldn't open my mouth.

"Do you want me to go?"

No. "Do what you like."

So, he left. Pushing past the groups of lads, he disappeared into the belly of the bar.

Why didn't I tell him to stay? I'm so stupid.

No, he's stupid because he didn't realise that you wanted him to stay.

"What the hell!" said Lisa, struggling to carry the drinks in her hands. "I thought you were going to get it on, but instead, you stood there arguing like a married couple. What is with you two?"

I couldn't explain it. I hadn't seen him for a year, yet he made me feel so many emotions. He was childish and demanding, confident and self-assured and I couldn't get enough. He was like a drug I had to have.

As we sat at our table I tried to listen to the girls' conversations, but I couldn't concentrate. *What was he doing here? Did he work here now? Had he been here the whole time, and I'd never noticed?* Every time I saw a glimpse of a blue shirt or heard a laugh, I looked up, thinking it was him. I went to the toilet so often in my quest to see him that Rebecca asked if I had cystitis. It was all too much.

"I'm going," I announced over the cacophony of voices. The girls pleaded for me to stay, but it was no use. I needed to escape so I could stop thinking about him. I stepped outside, the cool air a welcome release.

"Where are you going?"

I didn't need to turn around. His scent tickled more than my nose.

"I'm going home."

The next thing I knew, he was holding my neck again and kissing me full on the mouth, his tongue exploring, tickling my tongue. I felt it again. The fluttering rising from my groin heating through my body like lava flowing up and out of the volcano.

He stopped and looked at me, still holding my neck in between his hands. "The thing is, I can't get you out of my head."

I feel the same.

I didn't know what was going to happen, but I knew one thing. This boy was going to change my life.

Chapter 3

London, 1993

Being five years older than me, Daniel was more worldly wise. I had little experience of life and relationships, but he was patient and kind and helped me discover things about myself I never knew. We had a similar sense of humour and always agreed on which number the contestant should choose on *Blind Date*. We loved Bohemian Rhapsody, were grateful the Gulf War had ended and continued to debate whether a Jaffa Cake was a cake or a biscuit.

We talked about everything. Our dreams, our future, our fears, our past. I moaned about my awful life with my controlling and condescending mother, and Daniel told me how his parents had died in a car accident when he was sixteen, leaving him orphaned. He had no siblings and no extended family. But he had worked hard, gone to university and now had a great job in a private finance department.

I was a secretary and I loved it. My job wasn't as glamorous, but I loved organising people and stationary cupboards. And I was good at it. I wasn't academic and never encouraged to see what I might achieve. Know your place. My mother's favourite words. She believed a woman's place was in the home. I was happy to go along with it when I was living at home but being with Daniel made me feel more independent and I realised I wanted more. Daniel was much more confident than me, and he encouraged me to ask for a pay rise, which I got, much to my surprise. His support made me feel valued in a way I'd never known before, and I couldn't get enough of him.

When I first told mum I'd met someone, she knew this was different. No boyfriend had ever met my parents before, and she insisted on him coming round to the house. On his first visit, as he got out of the car, she gave her appraisal while looking out the window.

"He hasn't cleaned his shoes, shame. He could have worn a jacket. He has nice hair though. I like a man with a good head of hair." She looked over at my dad, sat in his armchair, the light from the window bouncing off his bald head.

Mum was right. He had the most gorgeous hair. Boy band hair. Thick and wavy, slightly longer at the front than the back.

After the appropriate time had elapsed, Mum opened the door and held her arms out towards him, smiling as if he was her prodigal long-lost son. He obliged and acted the role brilliantly, ignoring me while he focused on winning my parents' approval, charming them the way only Daniel could. He didn't need to worry. They always loved him. My family was dysfunctional, but I had one and Daniel surprisingly wanted to be a part of it.

About a year later, we decided to move in together. The practicalities were straight forward. Telling my mother wasn't.

"Mark my words, you two will be married before we know it," said Mum. We were sitting on the sofa in the lounge, Daniel and I squeezed together like conjoined twins, with mum at the other end and dad in his armchair.

"Sit up straight, Chrissie. You have a spine for a reason."

I knew this was a bad idea.

"I don't approve of you living in sin. You should get married. It's the proper thing to do." Her Catholic Irish roots were deeply ingrained.

"Mum," I said, a little too loud. My cheeks were burning. Although Daniel was becoming more used to her behaviour I was still embarrassed. Daniel noticed, scratched behind his ear, and looked to my dad for assistance.

"Did you see the Rover's match yesterday?" said Dad, his answer to any religious comment. "I don't think it was a penalty. Harries had crossed—"

"Now is not the time to be talking about inconsequential things like football. We have more important things to discuss. Like how we are going to explain that our daughter delights in deriding her parents by living with her boyfriend?" She made the sign of the cross, an act to ward off the demons that must now possess my soul.

Dad rolled his eyes at Daniel and me. I stifled a giggle. Mum stared at Dad.

"I saw that, Robert. It's not helpful. Just like you." She turned her attention to Daniel. "I will pray for you both. I'm sure the rest of the congregation would too, but I don't want them knowing that my daughter disobeys her parents and her faith."

Jesus, Mary, and Joseph. I clenched Daniel's hand so hard he winced.

"Mary." Daniel's calm and confident voice got her attention. "You know we don't want to do anything that upsets you or him." He looked up at the ceiling, addressing God directly. "It's just that for now, Chrissie and I are happy to get to know one another before making the truly enormous and reverent act of marriage. With one in three marriages ending in divorce, we want to make sure we are not one of those statistics."

The word *divorce* made mum cross herself three times.

He continued, my mother in the palm of his hands. "And if God is love and we love one another, then surely we are honouring him in our union."

I had to give it to Daniel. He was very good at talking someone round, making them see his argument and them agreeing it was the right one.

Mum smiled and reached out to stroke Daniel's hand. He could do no wrong in her eyes. Unlike me. I always seemed to upset her, no matter what I did. I was an easy child and compliant, but I never felt I did the right thing or acted the right way with mum. Mum was complicated, dad always said.

"So, for now, we are not getting married. We want to live together first. We think we will be happy doing it this way."

"Of course. I understand." She patted his hand in complete agreement.

He was great with people and had a way with words I admired. My shyness made it difficult to say what I really thought or wanted. I let others make decisions. Looking back, I could see I'd always done this. The nervous child, happy to stay in the background and let others shine. I didn't have anything to say. Nothing of importance. I was happy, a young girl starting life with a man she loved, and life was great. But a year later, he got a new job. And that's when everything changed.

***

I knew Daniel was excited about something as soon as he came into the room.

"And where is my lovely wife?" His voice louder than the pop music playing on the radio. He had a massive bouquet of my favourite white lilies, which he thrust into my arms before wrapping his arms around me, squeezing me tight like an accordion and planting a massive kiss on my lips which made a sucking noise as he came up for air.

"You're in a good mood." I laid the flowers on the kitchen worktop. The silver foil wrapping bounced light onto Daniel's face, like a spotlight on the quiz show *Mastermind*.

"I've got a new job, Chrissie." The room went dark.

"And your specialist subject is?"

"My new job," he answered.

"Okay, you have two minutes to answer questions about your new job. What job is it?"

"Executive assistant."

"Correct. What does executive assistant mean?"

"I am basically the right-hand man to the boss."

"Correct. Does that mean if your boss is ill, you take his place?"

"No. That's the deputy."

"Correct. So, what is your role?"

"I'm there to answer all the bosses' emails and correspondence, write his board notes, attend board meetings and organise anything he needs."

"Correct. So, you're basically his secretary?"

Daniel huffs. "No. I'm an executive assistant. He has a secretary for all the other stuff."

"Correct. It sounds like you're his secretary."

"Well, I'm not. You don't understand."

"Correct. Is it more money?"

"Yes, it's more money, but it's more about the opportunities."

"Correct. So, when do you start this job?"

"Three months' time."

"Three months?"

"Correct.

"And where is the job?"

Daniel paused. "Lapland."

"Lapland?"

"Correct."

"Is that an actual place?"

"Correct."

I was confused now. "But isn't Lapland miles away?"

"Correct."

"We won't be able to see our family and friends?"

"Correct. Well, no, not correct. You'll still be able to see them, but not as often."

"Where will we live? What will I do?"

Just then the phone rang, and he went to answer it.

"I've started, so I'll finish!" I demanded, wanting him, needing him to explain.

He stared. "Pass. I don't know all the answers yet, but we will work it out."

Daniel answered the phone as I washed the plates in the sink, trying to make sense of it. *Lapland? I thought it was made up. Where is it? And what do you do in Lapland?* All I knew was that it was cold. And there was nothing there except snow. *Do people actually live in Lapland?*

This wasn't like Daniel. He wouldn't move somewhere without knowing all the details. Daniel thought things through. He took his time with important decisions. He was considered, measured, reasonable. When we first moved in together, he made a spreadsheet of our income and likely expenditures. He discussed making savings. Did we really need the branded cereal when shops' own brand chocolate puffs were just the same? Cycling to work would save us pounds, financially and physically. No gym membership for us.

Maybe he's worried about money?

He hasn't mentioned it.

Have I been spending too much?

It seems a long way to go for a job.

I dried my hands and looked up into the living room across the way. Daniel had finished on the phone and was now looking at his computer, elbows on the table, his hands supporting his head, rubbing the scar behind his left ear. He always did this when he was thinking or worrying.

"Look at how beautiful it is," he said, turning the screen to face me as I entered the room.

I had to admit he was right. The snow looked so white and plump, like a new feather duvet. And there were Christmas trees everywhere. It reminded me of the pine tree Dad bought every year and wedged into the corner of our small lounge. The branches poked you whenever you tried to squeeze past, and its needles, caught upright in the pile carpet, stabbed your feet so you looked like you were walking on a bed of hot coals.

Daniel turned and saw me smiling. "I know this move will be the best thing we've ever done."

I stopped smiling. "Er, no. I wasn't smiling because of that."

"Imagine us curled up in front of a log fire eating marshmallows," he went on.

I sat down next to him. "Can you get marshmallows there?"

"Of course you can, silly," he said confidently. "I assume you can. You must be able to. It's the same as here. It's not outer space."

"Daniel, I've been thinking and I—"

Daniel swiveled round in his chair to face me. "I know this seems sudden, but just imagine us in another country, in a bigger house—"

"I don't need a bigger house," I whispered. My heart was pounding. "I think you have been worried that I want more than I do, and I don't."

Daniel turned back to the computer.

"I'm happy here with you. I love you and I love our life."

He didn't say anything, so I continued to talk to the back of his head. "Please, can we just carry on as we are?" I leaned over and kissed him on his cheek.

"I have to take this job."

What? Did I not explain clearly enough?

"Chrissie, this is an enormous opportunity for me, and I'd be a fool not to take it."

For you, and 'you'd' be a fool. There's no talk of me in there. "But it's not what I want."

"Maybe not now, but you'll change your mind."

"I'm not sure I will."

"Chrissie, I want a job I'm passionate about."

"But can't you have that here?"

"No." He stared at me as if trying to see inside my head. "I've tried. I've tried to do what you want, live where you want, but I need to do this."

Live where I want? Do what I want? Did I decide that? Daniel never said anything. Until now. Tears were pooling in my eyes.

"Wouldn't you like a new adventure?"

No. I'm happy here. The tears, like an overfilled bath, found their way down the side of my face.

Daniel took me in his arms. "Please don't cry. I want you to be happy."

"What about my job?"

He kissed my forehead. "I don't know, but I do know you don't need to worry. I'll be working so you can just enjoy yourself. Take up a new hobby? You're always saying you'd like to be more spontaneous."

This was not what I had in mind. I was thinking more of booking a last-minute mini break or trying the Chinese takeaway near the University. Moving to Lapland was life changing, not spontaneous.

"Have I ever made you do anything for me?"

I tried to think of something, anything, but couldn't.

He edged me slightly away from him but kept hold of both my hands. "I have to take this job, and I want you to come with me. I love you, but I have to do this."

His hazel eyes were serious. This was serious. But I had a choice, I told myself. I didn't have to go with him. It would be hard, but I could live without him, find someone new. I tried to picture it. Imagine my life without Daniel. I sighed. Who was I trying to kid? Living without Daniel would be like living on Mars. I wouldn't be able to breathe.

"Oh, and this is important, Chrissie," he said. "You can't tell anyone, but the person I'm working for is Father Christmas."

Chapter 4

Father Christmas! The revelation that Daniel wanted us to move was difficult, but to discover his job was working for some made up character who pretended to deliver presents to children sent my mind into overdrive. I spent a sleepless night tossing and turning, going over everything that had been said and everything that hadn't. It was as if I'd gone to bed and, when I woke, the person next to me had morphed into someone I didn't recognise. *Who is he? Is he an actual elf?*

"This is all very secretive," Lisa said. "Why can't you tell us?"

I was with the girls at a restaurant for our monthly night out. They knew Daniel had a new job and we were moving, but that was all.

"I'm sorry, but I can't. Daniel signed this confidentiality clause in his contract, which forbids him from saying anything."

"Yes, but it doesn't stop you," said Paula, picking up her glass of wine. "We're your best mates."

The strain of keeping this all secret was too much. I burst into tears.

Lisa dabbed at my eyes with a paper tissue. "Why are you doing this, then?" she asked quietly.

"Because it's an amazing opportunity."

"And?"

"Because it's a promotion with more money."

"And?"

"He is so ambitious I couldn't stop him if I tried."

"And?"

"Because I love him."

"And there we have it. You're doing this because you love him and want to spend your life with him. You can't do that living hundreds of miles apart?"

"Try thousands." I sniffed, using the tissue to blow my nose.

The girls all turned and handed over five-pound notes to Rebecca. "Told you it was far," she said, collecting the money and putting it in her purse.

I laughed. "What else are you betting on?"

"Daniel's job," Lisa said. "Nerys thinks it's MI5, Rebecca thinks it's something to do with the Middle East and Paula thinks it's working for someone famous, like Simon Cowell's personal accountant."

They stared at me, waiting for my answer.

"I'm sorry. I can't say anything."

They were all quiet. After what seemed like five minutes, Lisa spoke, "If you can't tell us where it is, could you show us? Point to a map? Or charades? You mime and we'll guess. You're not breaking any confidentiality clause if you're not actually saying anything, are you?"

She had a point. I put my glass of wine down on the table, stood, and put one finger in the air.

"One word," everyone shouted.

I sat and pointed to my lap.

"Legs!" said Lisa.

"Thighs!" said Paula.

"Fanny!" screeched Rebecca.

They all burst out laughing. I shook my head while still trying to show it was my lap. I grabbed Lisa and made her sit on me. It didn't have the desired effect.

"Sitting on someone? What? I don't understand."

"Lesbian," shouted Nerys, oblivious to the spectacle we were creating.

"Amsterdam," said Paula. "It's all about fannies there!"

"I know, I know," cried Rebecca, who couldn't contain her excitement. "Lap dancing!"

I jumped up and pointed to Rebecca while Lisa fell to the floor in a heap. The girls all looked at one another.

Lisa pulled herself up with the help of the table. “What? Daniel is going to do lap dancing?”

“No! I didn’t think it would be this hard to guess. Think of a country.”

“No talking,” Paula said.

Rebecca waved her hand. “I know, I know! Las Vegas. Capital of lap dancing.”

I clapped my hands over my eyes and shook my head, aware of all the other diners who were watching our show. “Go back to the first thing you said, ` I shouted.

“You’re not supposed to talk,” Paula corrected until she saw Lisa glare at her. “I was only saying.”

“Lap dancing?” said Rebecca.

I nodded and showed them with my hands that they had to shorten the word.

“Lap?” said Lisa.

I nodded furiously. The girls all stopped laughing and looked at Lisa. Then they looked at me.

“Lapland?” Rebecca almost whispered it, not sure if this was a real guess.

“Finally!” I said, collapsing in my chair, which creaked under my weight. It was so good to hear it out loud.

“Lapland?” Rebecca repeated, with the same confused expression she had when she found out Bobby Ewing was not dead, and it had all been a dream.

“Is that an actual place?” Lisa said, looking at the rest of the girls.

“Of course. Father Christmas lives there,” I said.

The girls’ eyes darted around each other before they rested on me.

They think I’m crazy. Of course, they do. It sounds crazy.

“Does he? I thought he lived at the North Pole,” Nerys said jokingly.

“No. That’s a myth,” I said. And then I laughed, a little too loudly.

I think I should stop drinking. "Maybe we should order some food."

Everyone agreed and quietly looked at their menus, occasionally glancing over the top at each other. Silence.

Lisa closed her menu with a snap and looked across the table. "So why the secrecy? What is Daniel doing in Lapland?"

Just tell them. Maybe it won't sound that crazy.

I took a deep breath. "We're going to Lapland because Daniel is working for Father Christmas." I closed my eyes, afraid to witness the girls' expressions.

"Father Christmas?" said Paula.

I squinted my eyes open a little. They sat there with quizzical looks and furred eyebrows.

How do I explain? Here goes. I told them everything I knew, which, even after research, was not a lot. "The word 'Lapland' applies to the northern region of Finland, but it actually covers the extreme northern area of Sweden, Norway, and even a part of Russia."

Pleased with myself for remembering those facts I then told them about the snowy landscape, the snowy climate, the snowy temperature... freezing because of the snow, and that there is a lot to do in the snow: husky rides, snow shooing, skiing, and seeing Father Christmas.

"Oh, I get it now," Paula said, relief flooding her face. "Daniel got a job arranging Santa visits?"

"Yes, I know," said Rebecca. "I took my niece to one of those last year. " She sat smiling, confident she now understood.

She did not. None of them did.

"It's not that Father Christmas or that place." Their smiles all disappeared, and the frowns reappeared. "This is the real Father Christmas." They looked at me as if I'd told them I had cancer. Disbelief clouded their faces. "I know it sounds crazy."

So, I explained how Father Christmas was a real person chosen by the Company XMAS, which was an acronym for Ten Miles Across Snow. His role as CEO was to organise the making, distributing, and delivering of Christmas presents to children around the world with the use of technology.

"They have offices, giant distribution and storage warehouses, workshops, and hundreds of people on the payroll. Father Christmas is a normal man who works for the Company. So, in theory, anyone could be Father Christmas. And before you ask..." although I wasn't sure any of them would as they all looked stoned, "he doesn't wear a red suit and he doesn't do the deliveries. That's a myth too."

They looked at each other like they were following a fly.

Eventually Lisa said, "So Daniel is working for this man?"

"Yes."

"And he's working in an office?" said Lisa.

"Yes."

"And he could be Father Christmas one day?" said Rebecca.

"I suppose so." *I haven't thought about that. I know Daniel is ambitious, but the top job?*

"But does he have to grow a white beard? Daniel's not very good at growing a beard," said Paula.

I tried to make myself heard above all the hysterical laughing. Eventually, they stopped. "There are no white beards. Everyone is like you and me."

"But what about the elves?" said Nerys.

They all started laughing uncontrollably. In an out-of-body experience, I looked at my friends, remembering all the happy times. I would miss them terribly.

"We're going to miss you, Chrissie." I could tell Lisa was trying to hold back the tears. "But it's a chance to experience something different. We're not all that lucky," she paused, "and I think it will be the best thing that's ever happened to you."

"I know, it's just—" I didn't have to finish the sentence. They knew. We stood in an octopus huddle, arms laced through one another's, heads resting on shoulders. I took a photo in my mind. Something to hold on to when the dark days came.

The next day I told my parents.

"You must be so proud." My mother sat bolt upright, hands in lap, her glazed eyes looking at my dad. He was sitting in his chair opposite the television, staring at a blank screen.

I just told you we are moving miles away and Daniel made this decision without considering me and you think I must be proud?

My eyes go dizzy following the swirly grey and white pattern on the carpet.

"You said he's going to be working for someone important. They must trust he will do a good job. And he's ambitious and hardworking. I admire him for that." She glanced over at Dad, one eyebrow raised. "And more money? You'll be able to have a bigger house than here and more of the benefits with a larger salary. Maybe a cleaner?"

The epitome of my mother's ambitions for me: a cleaner.

"We're also getting married." I heard her moving her rosary beads through her fingers, muttering some chant under her breath.

She thinks I'm pregnant. "I'm not pregnant."

Her chanting turned to prayer and sounds of 'praise be'.

"Daniel said it's the Company's idea. They prefer couples to be married."

"A Winter wedding, how lovely. Very sensible too. I like the sound of this company. Robert, did you hear that? Your daughter is getting married. Maybe you could wear a good suit. For once." I caught Dad's eye as he half smiled at me. It was clear I had interrupted something.

"Daniel said we will have to move soon, so it will be a small wedding?"

"Very sensible. It's a waste of money."

I wasn't sure what reaction I was expecting, but I hoped she might disagree. My parent's wedding was small, as they couldn't afford a grand affair, and she'd never forgiven my dad.

"Anyway," I said as Mum stopped glaring at Dad and looked back at me. "I'm worried about what I'm going to do?"

She looked at me, surprised. "What you're going to do? What do you mean?"

"My job, my work? Daniel said it will be fine, but I'm not sure what type of job I'll be able to get in Lapland. Daniel said I should wait and see what opportunities there are when we get there, but I'm concerned about me and my career. *I've noticed a lot of these sentences have started with 'Daniel said'.*

Mum ran the rosary beads through her fingers. "A career. What career? You are a secretary. It's not exactly working for the government, is it?"

Very supportive! "But I need a career, a job. I need to make friends, build a network around me."

"You won't have time for that?"

I must have looked like a bulldog, a scrunched-up, confused face, cocked to one side. "Why not?"

Without taking a breath, she said, "You will look after the house. You will look after Daniel. You will do your duty as a wife so he can provide for you and the children."

There was not a line out of place on her face. It was all a matter of fact.

But I don't know if I want that or want children. Not yet anyway.

I looked over at Dad, who was staring blankly at the television screen.

Say something. Anything. Back me up.

He didn't say a word, but I couldn't say anything either. Mum used to control my life. I think it was why I enjoyed being a secretary. In the office, I took charge. I organised the daily routine, made the decisions, solved the problems. Leaving home enabled me to be independent. But that's changed, and now it feels my life is being mapped out by Daniel and his dreams. I have moved from one controlling parent to another. Only this time it's my future husband. And it scares me.

Chapter 5

I handed in my notice at work, a place I'd worked since leaving school, and began organising my wedding. It wasn't the wedding I dreamed of as it was such short notice, but it was a wedding, so I was no longer 'sinful' in my mother's eyes.

I was mostly looking forward to the honeymoon. Somewhere romantic, somewhere warm, just the two of us. And it would give us time together before he started his new job.

Daniel came home from work early so we could discuss it. He cleared some space on the kitchen table, moving the dirty plates to one side of the sink so he could open up his new computer. "I thought it might be sensible to have the honeymoon in Lapland, so we can acclimatise. What do you think?"

I was surprised. I thought he would want to go somewhere different than where we were going to live. I didn't understand, but Daniel convinced me it was the right thing to do. Fortunately, I had done my homework on Lapland and knew it could be romantic: roaring fires, curling up under fur blankets, having massages and saunas together.

"There are lots of outdoor activities to do, like hiking and fishing." Daniel's words ripped my daydream apart.

Oh! Not romantic.

Daniel looked down at me. "But there are other things. I read about a new annual competition that happens in Finland. It's called 'Wife Carrying'. Lots of newlyweds do it as part of their honeymoon. Doesn't that sound like fun?"

Is he joking?

"And you get to wear your wedding dress again."

A race? In a wedding dress? In a cold country. Fun!

"It's a proper sport."

Great! My honeymoon is a sport. I don't know what to say. "Is there a prize?" *Great retort, Chrissie.*

Daniel went quiet before answering, "The wife's weight in beer."

It sounded like something from the Middle Ages, and my opinion didn't change when Daniel showed me on his computer what he meant. There were a variety of pictures of half-naked men and women, the women in a fireman's lift position, buttocks proudly pointing to the sky as the men pulled agonising faces. The only smiling faces I saw were those who had got to the finish line. Obviously grateful they would never have to do this again. Unless they remarried.

I wonder what Finland's divorce statistics are like.

"I also have to leave sooner than I thought."

What?

"I need to be there just after the wedding."

How long have you known about this? "What about me?"

"It's okay. The delay is convenient since the house isn't ready yet."

A good thing. Nothing about this is good. We were moving to a secret place, so secret, you couldn't find a 'Christmas town' brochure or book. It wasn't in a guidebook 'Top towns for completely starting your lives over from scratch'. There was more information about living on the moon than living there. What I knew you could write on the back of a small post-it note. I knew the temperature. I knew there was snow. I knew there were reindeer. I knew there were cold winters, and I knew it took a long time to get there. Apart from all that, I knew nothing.

And neither did Daniel. I was filled with questions and doubts and had no one to talk to except for him. He pretended he knew all the answers, but he was as much in the dark as me. Whenever he tried to ask something, the Company always told him they would explain when he got there, and it didn't bother him because he was busy. He had his job to think about. He was already receiving mountains of documents to read, and taking phone calls with management. I had nothing to do except pack and think.

"Where are you going to stay?"

"Don't worry. The company will provide a flat for me until you arrive."

"So that means I'll have to pack the house and travel there by myself?" My voice quivered as I tried not to cry.

Daniel put his arms around me. "I know, but the company will sort out the removal and they will make sure you arrive safely. They have worked it all out. You have nothing to worry about."

I buried my face in his shoulder, glad he couldn't see me. *Nothing to worry about? Is he kidding?* He made it sound so simple, which, for him, it was. He knew what he'd be doing. He was excited, enthralled by this move and new job. He could think of nothing else. Neither could I, but for different reasons. But I loved Daniel more than I had ever loved another person, and I trusted him. It would be okay. Wouldn't it?

***

Time moved quickly. Before I had time to sing *Driving There for Christmas*, (I'd deliberately changed 'home' to 'there' to make me more excited about moving—it didn't work) Daniel was off to the airport in a chauffeured car, courtesy of the Company.

Packing boxes filled with my life stood in the corner of every room like statues signaling the past. Photo albums and frames. Wedding dinner plates and bowls wrapped in newspaper. My Jilly Cooper books stacked next to Jane Austen. Daniel's science fiction next to his business books.

The house was quiet except for the sound of the grandfather clock in the hall. You never normally heard the arm swinging because of Daniel's fondness for having the television on at full volume, but now in the silence it struck loud and clear. The noise ominous, shaming me. *Tut, tut. Daniel gone. I'll be next. What have I done?*

The mother-of-pearl clock face twinkled, reminding me it was too late to think about that now. I had accepted, taken up my orders, like a person devoting themselves to God. I was leaving all my worldly goods and old life behind me to start a new one.

Packing was difficult. Upstairs on the bed was a selection of clothes I thought would be suitable for Finland. I consulted the recent list in my notebook.

- 3 roll neck woolly jumpers, one with reindeer on. (I want to fit in)
- 10 pairs of thermal vests and leggings (It's freezing so essential, although they are very unsexy, and I don't want Daniel to see me in them)
- 4 t-shirts (Apparently there is some sun)
- 3 pairs of jeans (I decided against my favourite ripped pair, as the holes would only make me colder)
- 2 pairs of corduroy trousers (I didn't want to buy these, but the shop assistant convinced me they were warm, and I would regret it)
- 1 ski jacket (Another essential)
- 1 blazer (Probably not useful, but if I go for a job, it will be more professional than the reindeer jumper)
- 1 duffle coat (Paddington Bear is my hero)
- 2 pairs of trainers (One for exercising, although I'm not sure there is a gym or that I will do any exercise)
- 1 pair of hiking boots (Daniel said I had to buy these. I'm

wondering if Daniel really knows me at all?)

- 1 pair of snow boots

The snow boots, hiking boots, and ski jacket had been recent purchases. Daniel didn't think my duffle coat would be warm enough, but I loved it. Paddington and I had a lot in common, although I hoped I would be collected when I arrived at the station.

I couldn't look at the clothes anymore, so went downstairs to make a cup of tea. I could smell Daniel's aftershave on my mug. He always put too much on in the morning, and the residue on his hands would linger on the breakfast things long after breakfast was over. It was too much. The tears fell and they didn't stop. Moving house was one thing, but this move was more than that. It was moving country, moving climates, moving lives.

Chapter 6

TV studio, London, 2009

"Mrs Connor. Are you ready?" Ms Grey's voice pulls me from my daydream back to reality. And the reality is I must now explain to Ms Grey and the thousands of viewers watching what Lapland was really like.

The makeup artist is fussing over Ms Grey, who is sitting on the sofa like one of those living statues, not blinking, no rise or fall to her chest to show she is breathing. She reminds me of someone I can't place. It will come back to me. My recall, like my skin, is not what it once was, although bringing up memories from years ago is easy today.

I nod at Ms Grey, her replenished eye shadow shimmering under the lights. The lights dim.

"Welcome back, Chrissie Christmas. Those early days must have been difficult. You were a young woman in a new and unknown country, not speaking the language. A stranger to the environment. And your husband, I presume, was busy with his new job. So, what was it like?"

After each fact, I nod and smile. Ms Grey smiles in anticipation. Like everyone in the studio, they want to hear about this beautiful place. This unknown, almost mythical place to most people around the world.

"Yes, it was difficult at first with its unfamiliar language and customs, but the scenery is breath-taking, the community friendly, the houses and streets idyllic. Imagine a thousand Christmas cards rolled into one warm and welcoming environment."

Ms Grey is delighted with this answer and invites me to embellish. I'm enjoying myself as I weave this magical land on air. It all sounds so enchanting, this Lapland we all have a mental image of. Shame it wasn't anything like that.

Lapland, September 1995

After landing at the airport in Rovaniemi, the capital of Lapland, I walked to a desk with bright neon lights and pictures of people all smiling next to giant snow-covered trees. Opposite me with a large rectangular comedy name badge attached to their shirt, which I couldn't read, was a man who insisted on speaking to me in Finnish. In the end, we used the international language of hand signalling and facial expressions to help explain where I needed to go next.

Staring out the window on the bus, like an excitable puppy, I saw the first glimpse of Lapland. I knew there would be snow, but I had underestimated how much. A thick carpet of snow lay on the ground. Tall trees carried it on their shoulders. It drenched the buildings and roofs like smooth white icing on a wedding cake. And it was dark, really dark, yet it was only three o'clock in the afternoon.

We slowed down, and the driver motioned this was my stop. As I approached the door, it swung open automatically.

I don't know what hit me first: the realisation this was the beginning of my new life, or the weather. The freezing air wrapped around me like Snow White, an embalmed mummy in her glass coffin. But this wasn't cold. This was a temperature I didn't understand. My body stopped working like a windup toy running out of momentum. I stopped moving and couldn't put one foot in front of the other. I was literally frozen to the spot.

Using hand gestures and an ever-increasing voice volume, the driver communicated it was time to disembark. It took all my power to will my legs to move and step outside. Was this how Buzz Aldrin felt when he stepped onto the moon?

After ten seconds, I decided Buzz definitely had the better experience. I stepped out into a street. A normal street, which could be anywhere. Of all the images I had in my mind, this was not one of them. It was frankly disappointing.

The silence was interrupted by a low-level hum. I turned to see a strange contraption, neither car nor tram pulling up next to me. The roof opened and out stepped a man dressed in black.

"Hello, Mrs Connor. Welcome. I hope you had a pleasant trip. My name is Luc."

Luc looked at me with the bluest eyes I had ever seen. His hair almost as white as the snow. *An alien life force from another planet.*

"Hello Luc. Do you know..."

"I will be your guide this afternoon."

"Yes, good but I—"

"It is a brief trip to the accommodation which we will go to presently."

"But I've just arrived and—"

"Yes. Therefore, I am taking to your accommodation presently."

He's not listening. I'm not sure if he's human or a robot?

"Please get into the ski dog."

What?

He pointed to the contraption he had arrived in. On closer inspection it looked like a skidoo I had seen once in a film.

"But Daniel? Where is he?"

"Daniel? Oh, you mean Mr Connor. He had to stay in the office."

I was silent. *After travelling all this way, Daniel isn't here to meet me.*

"Don't worry, Mrs Connor. Mr Connor told me to show you your house and get you acquainted with everything. Please." He pointed to the unusual transport.

I couldn't believe Daniel wasn't here. I knew he'd be busy, but he could have taken ten minutes out of his day to make sure I was okay. I wiped my tears with a tissue I'd found at the bottom of my coat pocket. It had fluff attached, which floated up my nose and made me sneeze.

"Terveydeksi!" said Luc.

I don't know what you're talking about, but I'm trying my best here.

After a quick journey, we stopped. It was a suburban street typical of any new build development in England but with less thought and less character. I was warm inside the skidoo and in no rush to step into the freezing cold. I looked out at the row of houses lit by security lighting, bright and artificial.

"This is your house," said Luc." Number 120. C Block. Management level."

I looked up at the grey box. It was more 'Cell Block' than C block. Prison decor. Nothing to get excited about.

One night, before Daniel left for Lapland, he had read out some descriptions of the type of houses we might live in. I had imagined pretty, quirky cottages with sleigh bells for doorbells and brightly painted arched front doors covered in ivy. Cottages of varied sizes, with a small front garden festooned with holly bushes. *Wouldn't everyone?*

"I know you want to choose a house for yourself, but it's not how it's done," he told. "The company owns all the accommodation there. It's not like going to an ordinary town."

I know. You've told me plenty of times.

"If you like the description of any the houses, we can ask for more information."

I don't like any of them.

"What about this one? This has four good-sized bedrooms, a large kitchen and a utility room. You said you've always wanted a utility room," he proudly stated, as if he'd just solved all my worries in one go.

I didn't know what to say so, I figured it was probably better to wait to see for myself.

And now here I was, seeing for myself. And it wasn't any better.

Chapter 7

I followed Luc down a long, cleared path. Snow piled up either side of the path, large mounds that looked like mini hills disguising what lay underneath. I looked up at the house, cold and still under the moonlight. Grey stones wrapped themselves around the frame of the black metal door, as if they were holding up the house or stopping it from escaping. Or maybe it was the square box-like shape of the house? All I knew was it wasn't very inviting. There were no twinkling fairy lights adorning the front door or a row of icicle lights hanging from the roof. There was no lit-up reindeer or snowman in the front garden. There were no trees, no flowers, no foliage of any kind. Even a small window box would have helped to break up the cold, grey slab that was now my home.

"No keys needed," said Luc. "You control everything."

If only that were true!

"Your voice, your fingerprints, and your eye retina. To open the door, you look here." Luc pointed to a round spy hole to the right of the door frame. "Or speak here." He pointed to a small rectangular grid, made of tiny holes, to the left of the frame. "Which would you like to try?"

Neither. I want to go home.

"Voice commands or finger keypads activate everything here. It makes life easy." He saw my face and continued. "You will get used to it and will wonder how you lived without it."

He'd obviously never seen me try to pay my utility bills over the phone using the automated function. It never ended well. I didn't know why, but the computer never recognised the digits I'd call out on my bank card. And now he was telling me I'd have to use the same process to get my lights to come on, get the oven to work or open the door. We were going to live in the dark, starve or live outside at this rate.

Luc gave me the 'walk and talk' tour of the house, explaining room after room and applauding it all for the simplicity and use of technology, and all the while I felt like a sleepwalker desperate to sleep but compelled to keep moving. The only room that woke me from my slumber was the sauna. An actual wood panelled room with seating. The only time I had seen one of these was in television shows. Now here it was, in our house.

"Many Finns believe saunas provide healing for the mind and body," said Luc proudly.

If this is the case, I will be in here most of the time.

"This is end of our tour. If you need anything, please ring for assistance."

The only thing I need is Daniel.

Saying his name started the waterfall of tears that had been threatening to fall ever since I arrived. Luc, oblivious to my distress, got back into the ski thing and drove off leaving me slumped against the front door on the floor, my coat wrapped around me like an invisibility cloak. I wanted to disappear. I didn't understand what was happening. And why Daniel wasn't here. Where was he?

You need him, and he's not here.

He's at work.

He's at work because it's more important to him.

He has an important job.

It's more important than you.

I continued to howl. Eventually, after a good ten minutes, my sobbing was reduced to occasional heaves of the chest that came in threes and my nose was bright red. *Rudolph would be proud.*

Suddenly the front door opened. *Oh no, it's Luc again.* I closed my eyes, like a young child assuming they'd now be invisible.

There stood Daniel, holding flowers and a bottle of champagne, his mouth and eyes wide open, staring in disbelief. "What the—Chrissie what's the matter?"

I jumped up, forcing my way into the space between the flowers and champagne as Daniel tried to wrap his arms around me while holding the said objects. "Wait. Let me put these down, " he said, making his way into the kitchen with me still clinging to his body like a chimpanzee on its mother.

He loosened my grip and held my shoulders, bending slightly so he could look into my eyes. "Chrissie, what's the matter?"

"I— can't— find— any— tissues?" My sentence broken by sobs.

"What do you need the tissues for? Are you bleeding?" He pushed me away slightly so he could examine me.

"It's— for— my— nose."

He reached into his back pocket and pulled out a neatly folded white cotton handkerchief and wiped my eyes.

"What is going on, Chrissie? I don't understand."

Of course, he didn't understand. I didn't really understand it myself. Why was I upset?

He wanted this new job more than he wanted to stay where we were.

He made us leave our home, family and friends.

He came here without me and made me travel by myself.

He wasn't even here when I arrived.

I realised then it was the last point that had upset me.

"Where were you?"

Daniel frowned. "Didn't Luc meet you at the station?"

"Yes, he did but—"

He looked annoyed. "I told him to tell you I had a meeting."

"Yes, he did but—"

He looked puzzled. "Oh! Didn't he show you around the house while you were waiting for me?"

"Yes, he did but—"

"Was there a problem with the journey?"

"No, not that." My voice lowered with each answer.

"Were there any problems?" Daniel's voice rose with each answer.

"No, it was all fine."

"So, what's the matter?" Daniel's forehead was a mass of furrows.

"I don't know," I said and burst into tears again.

Daniel pulled me towards him into his arms. I could hear him heave a heavy sigh as he hugged me. "Chrissie. Everything is going to be okay. I know you're sad about leaving and it's all scary and new, but this is going to be the best thing we've ever done. I promise."

I wish I felt the same way he did. I knew he wanted us to have a better life, but I felt it was a long way to come for a job. I knew there were advantages, but all I could see were the negatives. We both knew he'd have to work longer hours. They would want their pound of flesh for what they were paying him. And it was so bloody cold.

"Honestly, Chrissie. This place is amazing. I've never known a place to work so efficiently, and I don't just mean my workplace. The whole town is the same. They have thought of everything, from how we use energy in our homes and our communication network to travel, medical health, education, and the economy. It's the healthiest place I've ever seen. Everyone grows in prosperity and wellbeing in this town."

His excitement was infectious. He sounded credible. He continued talking about the number of ways they control the traffic, the weather, the emergency services. It seemed they had thought of everything. But the more he spoke, the more apprehensive I became. And I couldn't get it out of my head. *There seems to be a lot of control in Christmas Town.*

Chapter 8

By the end of the week, I had a grip on my emotions and the household chores. I organised downstairs, reorganising the fridge with food which was mostly recognisable, and what wasn't, like the purple potatoes, I shoved to the back for another day.

Our own furniture hadn't arrived yet and nobody could tell us exactly when it would turn up. Daniel promised we could get some furniture from a new Swedish furniture store called Ikea. The name sounded so glamorous. I imagined Greta Garbo spread out on a purple velvet chaise long, surrounded by exquisite cushions, but we would have to wait until Daniel had the time to travel to the nearest store. Until then, we would make do with the starter package the Company provided: a firm mattress, a couple of chairs, a table and crockery and cutlery. No fancy cushions and no bookcases or shelves. So, I visualised where I thought the bookcases would go and promptly dumped a box of books there. It would do until we had the proper furniture.

"How was your day?" Daniel asked, putting his laptop on the kitchen table next to him.

"Okay. I've unpacked the clothes, finally understand the voice control for the lights and worked out the oven. Ta da!" I announced as I laid two bowls of pasta on the table. "Dinner is served."

"You're a good wife," he said. He lifted a huge forkful, smiling at his food rather than me. He opened the laptop.

I carried on talking as I sat down opposite him, hoping he would join in. "I'm excited about the new resident's course next week. Should be fun."

They'd invited all new residents onto a weeklong programme to get acclimatised, or so the blurb said on the shiny A4 brochure each of us received when we arrived 'to welcome the new guest'. That's what they called us, guests. It made it sound like a holiday.

Daniel continued staring at the laptop screen.

"On the first day, there's a special guest speaker," I said. "Do you know who the guest speaker is?"

Silence. I asked again.

He looked up. "What guest speaker?"

"That's what I'm asking. The special guest. Will it be the same person you had?"

He treated me to a blank expression, tomato sauce hanging from his lips. "I never saw a special guest."

"What? But you must have had this meeting three weeks ago when you arrived?" I put my fork and spoon down and looked at Daniel across the table.

Daniel didn't stop eating. Through mouthfuls of pasta, he answered, "No."

I folded my arms. "Why not? I thought this was something everyone attended?"

"No. Not everyone."

"Why not?"

"Not needed."

"But won't you be doing the course too?"

"No."

"Why not?"

"I'm management."

"What does that mean?"

"I don't have to."

"Why not?"

"I go to work."

I was now very confused and getting annoyed with his inability to expand beyond four syllables.

"What's the matter?"

Another four syllables! "Why do I have to do this course and you don't have to?"

He put his cutlery down neatly on the side of his plate. "Because I have to go to work."

"But I'm working. I have things to do."

"It's not the same."

"Why isn't it?"

"Because I am trying to learn the business, and it doesn't allow me time to take in the sights and ask questions about when the shops are open."

I can't believe you just said that. "So, you're more important than me."

"Oh, Chrissie. Don't be silly. That's not what I meant."

"So, I'm silly now."

"You know what I meant. I can't believe we're arguing about this."

I can.

"Look, all I know is this course is for every new family that arrives here, and they expect at least one person to attend." His voice was flat.

"So, because I don't have a job and have so much time on my hands, it must be me?"

I watched Daniel take a deep breath, deciding if what he wanted to say would be the right thing to say.

"Yes."

I was silent, staring at the specks of tomato sauce Daniel had peppered on the table. He reached for my hands and lowered his voice. "I thought you'd like to go. You get to find out where everything is, get to know who's who and how everything works. You also meet other people who are new, like you."

That's true, but you're new too. "What about you?"

"I'm meeting new people every day in work, and this gives you an opportunity to do the same. That's good, isn't it?" Finishing his dinner, he closed his laptop and stood up.

I had to admit, I already thought this course was a great idea. Everyone was in the same position, and you could ask those awkward, stupid questions. But I wasn't going to admit it to Daniel.

"I suppose so," I said, sounding like a sulky teenager. *How do you always argue, so it looks like you're right all along?*

"So, you're okay?"

I nodded, but I wasn't. That night, I couldn't sleep. I held onto the argument and my side of the bed, which kept me awake. Daniel was fast asleep as soon as hid head hit the pillow.

Chapter 9

The next day, just like ET, I phoned home. I'd been putting it off because I knew I'd get upset. I was lonely and miserable, but I didn't want anyone to know. I also desperately needed to talk to someone I knew and who knew me. I pressed the numbers carefully into the dial, praying I didn't make a mistake and would need to start from the beginning.

After what seemed like a minute of ring tone, Mum answered.

"Hello. 475632."

"Hi Mum."

There was a pause. "Chrissie? Is that you?"

"Yes, Mum." Her voice pulled me back into her world. I gulped down air to stop my voice from breaking.

"Chrissie?"

"Yes, Mum. Can you hear me?" I spoke louder down the phone.

"ROBERT!" Mum shrieked down the phone, not raising her mouth from the mouthpiece. "It's Chrissie, I think. She sounds different."

"It is me, Mum." *Who else is it likely to be?*

"Yes, now I know it's you. I can hear the tone."

Of course, she can. Thank God, she can't see me rolling my eyes.

"Stop rolling your eyes!"

I looked down at the mouthpiece. *How can she see me?*

"Did you hear me, Robert? You know I don't like it."

She means Dad. I forgot about him now getting all the unwanted attention.

"Let Chrissie talk," I heard him say in the background. "The phone call is probably costing a fortune."

"It's okay. The Company pay the phone bill."

"Really?" answered mum. "In that case, you should phone more often." She paused. "I mean, we haven't heard from you since you arrived. And I think you should phone us at least every week."

I just want to talk, and you're giving me a lecture.

"So, what's the weather like?"

Don't you want to know how I am? Not the bloody weather! "Freezing. It's minus eight degrees today."

"I hope you're keeping warm, love," said Dad. "Extra layers and don't skimp on the logs for the fire."

I looked around the magnolia room with no fire in sight. I didn't think it was necessary to tell him any differently.

"How's Daniel?" said Mum. "Working hard, I assume."

"Yes, he is. I've hardly seen him."

In the week since I'd arrived, he was out of the house before I woke up, and I was in bed when he came home.

Mum didn't say anything and changed the subject. "And what is the house like? Does it have all the mod cons? Not like here."

I glanced around at the beige box I lived in. Every room the same colour. No pictures, no colour. A cold, stark space devoid of clutter and life. "It doesn't feel like home."

"Give it time. Once you reorganise and decorate, it will feel better. And you'll meet new people too."

"I haven't met anyone yet except for Luc. It's too cold to stand outside."

"What an unusual name? Luc." She pronounced it out loud as if she were French. "He sounds nice."

"He just showed me round the house."

"Showed you round the house? What service! Very impressive."

I didn't say anything. Couldn't, in case I upset her.

"I must say, it's a very good line. Isn't it a very good line, Robert?"

"Yes, it's a good line," he mumbled.

"And it's all so different here, what with the language and the weather and I don't have any friends and Daniel—"

"You can hear so clearly."

Can you? "Mum, did you hear what I said?"

"I heard," she said quickly. "Chrissie, this is an amazing opportunity. You don't know how lucky you are. If I'd have had such a chance to live in another country, experience a different life—"

She trailed off, although at first, I wasn't sure if it was the very good line.

I swallowed the lump in my throat. "I know and I am trying, it's just—"

"Love, if you ever want to come home, you only have to say."

"Don't tell her that, Robert. It doesn't help." Mum's voice came hurtling down the very good line. Loud and clear.

My voice wobbled now. I was homesick, which seemed ironic when I used to feel sick being at home. "I'd better go." There was nothing more to say. It was clear mum didn't sympathise with my situation and she would not give me what I needed to hear.

"Lovely to hear from you and send Daniel our love." She paused. "You'll call next week?" Mum's voice was searching, unsure. Something I'd never heard before.

"Yes, I'll call again next week." Maybe she was feeling lonely now I'd left?

"Good. Make sure it's on Sunday and after mass. God comes first."

And there she was again. The voice I knew.

Chapter 10

After a week of cleaning, cooking and sorting the house, I was looking forward to meeting actual people, and the Residents course. The Welcome Meeting began at ten o'clock, and congregating in the hall outside the meeting room were four other women—although I wasn't sure about one of them. She was wearing a grey trouser suit with a white shirt and very manly shoes. Brogues or something. And her black hair was slicked back with what looked like gel. But then she may have had the same problem I had with unruly hair. The cold, I assumed.

Getting dressed that morning was difficult. Outside was freezing, minus ten degrees, but inside was warm. Finding the right balance was tricky, but I had decided on a check skirt, black jumper, and boots. As we walked into a small room with a large table in the middle, I wondered if I'd made the right decision. The room was very warm, and there was a slight tang of something unsavoury in the air.

"Come on in, ladies," boomed a rather large and jovial gentleman with an American accent, who seemed genuinely delighted we were there. We spread ourselves around the U-shaped table facing the front of the room, where there was a projector hanging down from the ceiling.

"My name is Jim Handsome."

A few of the girls chuckled.

Recognising the irony, Jim said, "I know, I know. A fitting name indeed for someone of my good looks. Wouldn't you agree, ladies?"

Maybe not.

The chuckles died down and we all politely nodded, joining in with his joke.

"It's lovely to see you all this morning. I'm really looking forward to getting to know each and every one of you a little better."

I don't know if it was the way he said this as the buttons on his wool suit bulged at the waistline, or the way his ruddy whiskered cheeks sat above his fleshy jowls, but he reminded me of a certain type of uncle who was not really your uncle—and definitely the type you didn't want to know you better.

To my right, a woman with dark hair tutted under her breath. The rest all looked down at the desks in front, avoiding eye contact.

"This morning is very informal and a chance for you to ask questions and see around the place. In the afternoon there will be more of a—" He paused, and I could swear he raised his grey eyebrows as he said, "—hands on activity." The way he said it made me feel queasy. Either that, or the smell I noticed when I walked in was getting stronger.

"We're going to begin with a film and then you can ask questions. Lower lights." The room went dark. The screen lit up, and what looked like a town map appeared.

"This is Christmas Town." He raised his arm, pointing up at the screen and the entire room inhaled a wave of body odour that made everyone gasp and move back in their seats.

"It's quite something, isn't it?" said Jim, mistaking the audience's reaction for amazement. We continued holding our breath for long periods of time, pretending we had colds using handkerchiefs to block the stench as Jim explained the history of Christmas Town.

"This area was developed in the late 19th century with the agreement of fourteen European governments. The area was chosen because of its sparse population, lack of urbanisation, no real manufacturing industries, and no cash economy. First, it was a market town with trade being set up to import and export local goods, to mask the actual nature of the work which was happening here." He paused. "I hope it's not too complicated for you all to understand?"

The dark-haired girl tutted again. The rest of us shook our heads, afraid to open our mouths or take our handkerchiefs away from our noses.

"The industrial revolution of the 19th century had produced a generation of incredibly wealthy businessmen and philanthropists in many countries who wanted to invest in new ideas."

"And I bet they could make a shitload of money out of it too," whispered the attractive, dark-haired woman to no-one in particular.

"After the First and Second World War, more countries joined the syndicate, all looking for some way to move forward after the horror of war. It began with one small company who worked with wood. They manufactured pieces of furniture and ultimately turned to children's toys. This company established the first network of companies bound by their common goal to bring pleasure and happiness to children."

He is so condescending.

"The crafting of the gifts and delivery was only one part of the industry."

"I wonder what else they discovered they could do to make money?" It was the dark-haired woman again.

I wonder why you're here.

"Due to the nature of the project and the secrecy involved, they realised they would need to house and educate the offspring of their workers. This led to a housing development and an academic program that produced a growing pool of highly educated workers, who were hired by the local companies here. This helped to maintain this secret project. But times have changed and some of the younger people want to leave. This has left a shortage in many of our teams, so we outsourced. Which is the reason you ladies are here. They have chosen your husbands to work for the Company because of their skills and experience. You must be very proud."

"Extremely!" said Miss Opinionated, staring at Jim. The others echoed her sentiments, but not quite in the same way. Her comment seemed to unnerve him, and he looked uncomfortable. But it could also have been because of his belt-straining stomach.

“Any questions?” Jim asked at the end of the screening.

We all looked at one another, willing everyone to remain silent so we could escape. Jim encouraged us to get a coffee and some fresh air, although encouragement was not needed. We fled like wasps from a disturbed nest, not knowing where we were going, only glad to get out of there.

Chapter 11

The coffee bar was bright and airy and had a delightful aroma of freshly brewed coffee. There was a man pouring out coffees behind the counter, wearing a beige uniform of top and trousers. His grey hair slicked back, not a strand out of place. His name badge said 'Bert'. We all picked up a cup and stood round in a circle.

"I needed this," said a very thin and immaculately dressed woman. She was a little older than me and spoke quickly in a French accent. "What was that man thinking? The smell was hideous. I think we should say something or complain to management at least. Even though we all have name badges on, it seems right to introduce ourselves. I'm Nicole. Pleased to meet you all."

"I don't think we should say anything," said a girl with the most angelic face I've ever seen. "He can't help it and it might upset him. I'm Savannah."

"You can help it. Daily ablutions and deodorant are all you need. It would also help if he lost weight. Toni Tucker." She nodded after introducing herself, like a private detective or FBI agent. I half expected her to get out a police badge.

"It's not always that simple," said Katrina. "We know nothing about him... Katrina. " Her voice got quieter the more she spoke, and I struggled to hear her.

"Her name's Savannah, not Katrina," said Toni, quick to point out the fact.

Katrina looked like a baby giraffe who had just seen a predator. She whispered, “I know. My name is Katrina.”

Toni stared. “Oh! I see. Speak up next time.” She looked at me. “Who are you?”

“Chrissie,” I said quickly and clearly, a little afraid she would shout at me too.

“And I’m Alex.”

Miss Opinionated. She doesn’t hold back.

“It’s nice to meet you all,” she continued. “Maybe we could ask Jim if we could have the tour after our coffee, so we don’t have to sit in that room?”

“Yes, I agree,” said Toni. “Shall I tell him? He’ll probably appreciate my directness.”

Alex and I caught each other’s eyes across the circle.

“Yes, you do that.” I coughed to stifle the giggle forming. “Where is everyone from?”

Katrina and her husband, Kaarl, had been the first to arrive in Christmas Town. They were Scandinavian, and Kaarl was working in the accountancy department.

Nicole shifted her weight from one foot to the other, unable to stand still. She was French and married to an engineer who was helping build a new wing of the building which housed all the technology.

“It’s all very top secret,” she gushed before telling us all about it. “They are trying to develop technology to help with the speed at which they can travel, exploring issues of hyperbolic travel, the structure of atoms and their transformation in unique ecosystems.”

She’d lost me after hyperbolic. I didn’t know what she was talking about, but it impressed me.

“You seem to understand a great deal,” said Alex. Her tone seemed disingenuous, but no-one else seemed to notice.

“I should do. I’m a physicist and engineer, with a degree in Atoms and a PhD in Molecular Structure.”

Not what I was expecting or any of the others, judging by their stunned reaction.

"What about the rest of you?" she asked.

Toni slicked back her hair. "I ran a large shipping firm back home in Kansas. Well, — I ran it before my husband took over. It was my father's business. He wanted a son to carry it on, but none of my brothers were interested, so I took it on."

That explains the clothes.

"But you were running it?" Alex said, clearly impressed.

"I was always interested in the business, but Dad thought it was better if Brandon, my husband, took over once he'd learnt the business."

"So, why have you moved here?" asked Savannah.

"The Company had a position in logistics."

She looked like she wanted to say something else, but deliberately stopped.

What else were you going to say?

"So, what do you do?" asked Alex.

Toni looked confused. "I already told you."

"No, I meant here. What is your job here? Are you helping in logistics?"

"I don't have a job." She looked down at the floor. "Brandon has talked about us having kids."

"Me too," said Savannah and Katrina at the same time. They smiled at one another. "Maybe we would all get pregnant at the same time? Wouldn't that be fun?"

Really? I glanced around the group. Alex looked horrified. *I'm not the only one then.*

"Might be time for us to go back," Katrina said, pointing to her watch.

"You're right," answered Toni. "I have set a timer for 11.15, and it is now 11.14 and 34 seconds precisely." Toni strode off, persuading Katrina and Savannah to do the same.

"She's a funny one, isn't she?" said Alex when we strolled down the corridor by ourselves. Neither of us were in a rush to go back into the room with Jim.

I laughed, slightly nervous with this woman with loud opinions. “What does your husband do?”

“He’s a lawyer. Well, we both are. We met at Harvard Law school. He has a job in the legal department. There are a lot of legal contracts because of the secrecy of this operation.”

“And are you going to be working there, too?”

“Apparently not.” The sarcasm reverberated up the corridor.

What was that about?

“Anyway, enough about me. What about you, Chrissie?”

“My husband, Daniel, works for the CEO.” Saying it aloud to a stranger sounded impressive.

“Interesting. He’ll get to see it all.” There was a tinge to her voice, which sounded suspicious. “But what about you? What will you do, or are you having kids like the rest of them?”

I was saved from answering as Jim appeared in the corridor and beckoned us to hurry back into the room.

Chapter 12

We walked tentatively into the meeting room, where someone had thankfully opened a window and placed a couple of bowls of potpourri on the tables. Jim was leaning with one hand on the desk at the front of the room and the other on his hip.

Here's a little teapot, small and stout.

"Come on in, ladies." He looked us up and down as we entered. "We will have a tour of the premises soon, but I want to hand out these folders first. This is for you," he said, standing over Katrina. "What's your name, darling? I can't quite see your name badge," blatantly staring at Katrina's chest. "Poor eyesight."

Alex looked over at me, shaking her head. After Jim finished handing out the folders and staring at some part of our anatomy, he went through the documents.

"Now, some of this stuff won't be very interesting for you little ladies, but it's important, so we must go through it. There are some pretty pictures and colourful brochures in here, so it's not all bad."

Alex's sighs were more audible than ever, not that Jim noticed. He wiped his sweaty forehead with the back of his hand, then onto his trousers before holding up a white piece of A4 paper, exposing the dark sweat stains under his arms.

"This is an important document. You will find it at the beginning of your folder. Could you all take it out please and read it carefully? You will need to sign it at the bottom where it says signature."

It was a confidentiality agreement, stating whatever we saw or heard in Christmas Town was not to be shared with anyone outside of Christmas Town. Basically, it was *Fight Club* rules. The first rule of Christmas Town is you do not talk about Christmas Town. The second rule of Christmas Town is you DO NOT talk about Christmas Town.

"Excuse me, Jim," Savannah said, raising her hand. "Does this mean I can't talk to my parents about where I live?"

He laughed before saying, "Of course not. You can talk about your house and the weather and your friends."

"Anything else?" asked Alex, her eyes narrowed.

"Of course. There are lots of things you can talk about." He wiped his hand on his forehead again.

"Can we talk about this building?" asked Savannah.

"No."

"Can I talk about my husband's job?" Katrina asked.

"No."

"Can I explain the setup here?" asked Toni.

"No."

"Can I talk about the ski dogs?" Nicole chipped in.

Jim paused for a moment. "No, er, yes, maybe?"

"Can I tell them I had to sign a confidentiality agreement?" asked Alex, holding the paper in the air.

We all laughed. All except for Jim, his forehead shiny with sweat dripping down his jowls.

"Look, ladies. This is just a formality. You will still have lots to talk about. We know you ladies like to talk." He laughed. We did not.

"Does everyone have to sign this?" asked Alex.

"Yes. Even your husbands will have signed it when they started their jobs."

"And what happens if we refuse to sign it?" said Alex.

"You won't." He smiled.

"But what if we do?"

"Look— I think you're getting all worked up for nothing. Maybe it's the time of the month and you're not feeling agreeable, but you will sign it because if you don't, you will have to leave."

My mouth fell open, and it wasn't because of the leaving comment. *The arrogance of this man.*

Toni spoke next. "So, you are saying this is a legal agreement and everyone must sign, or we won't be allowed to stay?"

"Correct, sonny."

Alex, having read it the most, picked up her pen and signed. "It's legal. They have us over the proverbial barrel."

So, we did the same and signed a deal with the devil. Jim went through the rest of the documents, which were mostly about the company, the ten men who started the company, the company board of directors, the company mission and vision plan and several pages containing numbers and percentages.

"You probably won't understand these last few pages, as it's all about the company figures, expenditure, capital, income, growth. That kind of thing. Not as interesting as your lovely figures."

I feel sick.

"Ladies. Now you will have a tour of the campus and Christmas Town."

Just then, the man from the coffee bar appeared. He wasn't wearing the uniform anymore. He was now smartly dressed in a navy suit and white shirt. His hair was still immaculate.

"This is Bert and he will escort you," said Jim. "You'll need to go soon before it gets dark."

Before it gets dark? I looked at my watch. It was only midday. *This place is weird.*

TV studio, 2009

"What an amazing description! You can tell you lived there for a long time," gushes Ms Grey.

The picture I'm painting for her and the audience is not an accurate reflection of Christmas Town. I can't tell how awful Jim was. I can't tell her how it snowed so much you couldn't get outside your house or didn't want to, and I can't tell her how lonely I was.

In those early weeks and months, the relentless pace of Daniel's working hours continued. He was keen to show everyone, especially his boss, he was indispensable, but it meant he was always at work. I was always at home with nothing to do, a prisoner of my own making. Apart from the new women I met on the Welcome Week, none of the neighbours had introduced themselves or even said hello when I ventured out and braved the elements. There were no social engagements or welcome gatherings. Everyone kept to themselves, which made you isolated. I didn't want to phone my friends as I didn't want them to know how awful this place was, and was afraid to say I'd made a mistake. I missed everyone back home. I missed my old life. And with Daniel working such long hours, I missed him, missed us. I couldn't tell Ms Grey or the viewers any of this. Christmas Town back then was not good.

I look at Ms Grey. Her recently applied lipstick has worn a little at the edges as her mouth stretches to accommodate her exaggerated smiles. She seems to be enjoying herself, which makes me feel slightly better. I'm not sure if she believes me yet, but it is reassuring.

"Could you tell us now about where Daniel worked? I'm sure our viewers would love to hear all about Father Christmas's workshop and the elves who make the toys."

What a lovely idea but seeing where Daniel worked for the first time couldn't have been more different.

Chapter 13

None of us had seen the grounds of Christmas Town. When watching the film, we realised they built the houses on the outskirts, with Christmas Town in the middle. We bandaged our bodies like Egyptian mummies in scarves, hats, gloves, and coats stuffed with down and boarded what looked like a cross between a tram and a sleigh. I sat next to Alex, excited to see where Daniel worked. Bert was sat up front in the driver's seat.

"I wonder what they will actually show us," said Alex.

"Everything, I assume," said Toni, leaning over from the seat behind, eavesdropping on our conversation.

"Don't bank on it," said Alex.

"But we signed the confidentiality agreement."

"It won't be that simple," replied Alex. "They are under no obligation to share anything with us."

Toni sat back down quietly in her seat.

"Ladies," Bert announced. "Please make sure your lap seat belt is fastened. The transport we are using today is an old-fashioned version of the newer Ski Dogs you all arrived in. Although the Company prides itself on its technological advancements, they kept these as a reminder of the past and how far we have come. This Ski Dog will follow guided tracks laid under the surface of the snow, whereas the newer Ski Dogs follow GPS routes and do not need tracks."

We came to the end of the building, where we turned onto a track along a path that curved around the bottom of a line of tall, bushy

Christmas trees signposting our route: giants wearing emerald, green evening gowns with white fur trims. The snow fell again. Large, engineered snowflakes ended their journey on my coat, lightly landing, layering, covering. I wrapped my scarf more tightly around my neck and further up around my mouth and nose. It was quiet. Nobody spoke. We were all transfixed by the beauty of the scenery and conserving energy to keep warm. The metal feet, skimming the snow, were the only sound you could hear. There were no animal noises, no birds, no human voices, none of the obvious sounds of life. Still. Except for us moving further towards the belly of Christmas Town.

The snow twinkled; ice diamonds buried just under the surface. Breathing in the cold air sent a rush up your nostrils and your chest burned slightly, but it smelt so clean. Detoxing, cleaning out my nasal passages, my windpipe and my lungs from traffic fumes and tobacco smoke.

"This, ladies, is Christmas Town," said Bert.

We sat at the top of a road looking down a gentle gradient into the heart of the town, sitting on a low level of flat land. From here, you could see a cluster of small buildings in the middle of one large circular building broken up at regular intervals, like a clock.

"It looks like a spaceship," said Katrina.

She was right. A spaceship right here in Lapland. It was so strange.

"And so much bigger than I thought it was going to be," said Alex.

As we continued down to the lower level, I kept looking around. It wasn't for small green people. Something seemed odd, but I couldn't work out what. The ski dog slowed down at a checkpoint. A man in a small wooden hut came out as we approached. Bert showed him some papers, and they waved us through.

"For security, we have to have people monitoring the area, and all visitors must be escorted in," explained Bert.

We continued along the path in silence.

Just then, Alex jumped up, almost knocking me off my seat. "There's no snow. Something was bothering me about this place."

"She's right," said Savannah. "Look behind us."

We turned to the back. A white blanket of snow covered the path all the way to the checkpoint. It looked like winter. But when you turned to the front, you were in the middle of England in the Summer. It was like leaving Narnia through the wardrobe.

Bert smiled, seeing our confused faces. "Don't worry. It's all perfectly explainable."

"Of course it is," Alex muttered under her breath, only loud enough for me to hear.

We slowed at the bottom of some wide concrete steps. At the top of the steps were enormous pieces of glass encased by rings of polished metal. They overhung the glass like an awning, providing shade. The metal reflected the surroundings, so it blended into the area.

Nicole was practically salivating. "This is amazing. Amazing! This building is quite something. I've not seen anything like this, and I saw some things during my career."

"I'm scared," said Katrina.

She wasn't the only one.

"Don't worry," said Savannah, putting an arm around her. "It's only a building."

"Not just any building," said Bert. He smiled as if he had a secret. He led us through two giant glass doors which opened and closed without making a sound.

We all looked at one another.

"I didn't hear anything. How is it possible? Magic?" Savannah asked.

Bert laughed. "There is no magic in Christmas Town."

How sad!

"It's all engineering."

"Which is a kind of magic," said Nicole, beaming at Bert.

Although Nicole looked like a child in a sweet shop, I felt sad. It didn't seem right that the heart of the Christmas empire had no magic. Either realistically or figuratively.

"Machinery housed underground operates the doors, which is why there is no sound. All very simple and perfectly explainable."

There it was again. That repetitive phrase. A car pulled up alongside us and two things struck me: it was very large, large enough to seat ten people and there was no driver. We all looked at each other, afraid to voice what we were all thinking.

"This is our transport for the tour."

"Why can't we walk?" Katrina asked, a grimace on her face reflecting her feelings on the 'no driver' situation.

"Believe me, you'll be glad after half an hour. This site is enormous, and you just won't see everything in the time we have. This building, which we have affectionately named The Ring, is one million square feet. Its circumference is nearly a quarter of a mile, and it is not attached to the ground."

Our reaction was like someone shouting 'mouse'. We automatically looked down at the polished concrete floor, hopping on our feet one at a time.

Bert laughed again. It was obvious he had seen this reaction before. "Don't worry. It's perfectly safe. The building rests on hundreds of huge stainless-steel saucers instead of the actual ground, so it's protected in all kinds of weather."

We reluctantly got into the car being driven by a computer program, which seemed safer than hovering above the ground. The car moved off at a fast pace, and I was grateful I had checked my seat belt three times. "Over two hundred engineers and other employees work in this building, which has its own electricity supply, powered by a hydroelectric plant built on the Kemi River," Bert said. "It is also the world's largest ventilated building using thermal generated power, so no heating or air conditioning, making it environmentally friendly."

This was impressive. Everyone talked about looking after the environment, but I'd never seen it done on such a large scale. I could see why Daniel wanted to work here. As we drove up each long corridor we saw rooms, similar in size, with men in white coats looking at materials and toys. Some were stood, some sat and some lay on the floor. A huge track, like an obstacle course, stood in the middle of the room.

"What is that track for?" Alex asked.

"So the engineers can test out their theories and ideas before manufacturing the toys. They like to get a child's experience," said Bert.

Strange! I wonder why they don't just use children to test them.

We sped past several other rooms at speed fortunately as they all looked the same, each a cream colour with at least four men in suits sitting at a wooden desk. Bert explained these men were the accountants, the finance teams, the logistic teams, the marketing teams, the advertising teams, and the PR teams.

"The other offices house the upper scale of workers, including the board members and Father Christmas himself, Donald Pittman. A very important man."

That's where Daniel is. I wonder what Donald Pittman is like?

"We won't be able to go up, I'm afraid. They have very important jobs, as I'm sure you understand."

How many times have I heard this?

On the other side of the ring was a huge greenhouse, featuring a variety of trees.

"What is this?" Savannah asked.

"Many of our toys are wood, although other man-made materials are now used. With technology advancements, the trees grown initially for the manufacturing of the toys are now used for the development of the forest area off the main building. It does, of course, act as a reminder to everyone working here about the origins of the Company."

They seem to have thought of everything.

"Ladies, the question you asked earlier about the weather?" said Bert.

We all sat up.

"The Company realised with such a huge production that they needed to be protected from the elements, which can be very harsh here. Mr Petersonton came up with an engineering solution to revolutionise the business."

"Who's Mr Petersonton?" Toni was writing notes in a small black book.

"He was a brilliant engineer here at Christmas Town. He realised the weather was the major factor in delays in manufacturing and production. So, he devised an all-weather building, with a roof system which could open and close to protect everything and everyone underneath. This roof system extends all the way out to the perimeter of the area where we first entered Christmas Town. That is why there was no snow once you entered."

We all stared upwards. You couldn't see anything. Just the sky.

Bert smiled at our puzzled expressions. "You can't see it because it's invisible."

We must have looked like five goldfish, mouths open, trying to see the invisible roof above our heads.

"They covered the roof with a material which is invisible to the naked eye. This simply means you take the light on one side of the object and transmit it on the other, so you don't see the object, in this case the roof, in between."

"Like a cloaking device," shouted Nicole, clearly delighted she could talk about this subject. "I read about this technology years ago, although at the time I thought they would use it in the military to hide war planes and so forth."

Bert's patriotism was infectious. I couldn't believe I was living in such a cutting-edge town and Daniel was working for such an elite and forward-thinking company. It was amazing. *So why do I feel disappointed?*

This place existed in my childhood imagination until, at ten years of age, Johny Gibbon announced in class Father Christmas did not exist and it was actually our parents who put the presents under the tree. It crushed me in the same way as discovering George Michael was gay. I knew it was probably true, but I didn't want to accept it.

Finding out this place was real had stirred up my childhood fantasy, and I envisioned a magical place, full of snow, colourful and quirky buildings and maybe a few elves for good measure. But it was nothing like that. In fact, it was the antithesis of Christmas.

As we made our way back to the Welcome centre, I stared at the shops which made up the rest of Christmas Town. The path was flanked by three or four shops on each side. Dark wooden fronts with no sign of what they were selling inside. They wouldn't have looked out of place at the O.K. Corral. Dusty, creaky desolate buildings, with a biting wind whistling through the street. There was no character, no personality, no life. This was Christmas Town and yet there was nothing to signify Christmas existed here at all.

Chapter 14

Daniel had finally finished working for the night and came to join me under a blanket on the sofa. He was holding something small in his hand. "So, what do you think?"

I held the blanket up for him. "You were right. It's the most unbelievable place I have ever seen."

Daniel looked disappointed and stared down at his hand. "No, I meant this." He held it up for me to get a better look. Another new gadget the company had given him, which he hadn't put down since he got home. It made a beeping noise.

"It's a Nokia 365. It's the first of its kind. A proper mobile phone. It's so small compared to cordless phones and I can use it everywhere. I could speak to someone walking down the street."

Why would you want to? It's too cold to get your hands out. "Yes, amazing." I heard myself saying a little too assertively.

He looked up.

You're not happy.

"This is very exciting. We are one of the first companies to use them. They are so forward thinking." He stared at the phone again. "Okay. I get it. You're not interested."

"I am interested." *Not really. Let's change the subject.* "I saw your workplace, which was exciting."

I watched Daniel puff up like a proud dad. *Happy again.*

"But it's not very Christmassy."

Like a meerkat, his face dropped at the same time his head popped up. “Christmassy? What were you expecting?”

Was this a trick question? “Er, what everyone expects. Snow, colourful lights, people dressed up in costume?”

“I told you this was a modern, technologically advanced company.” His phone beeped.

“I know it’s just I thought—“

“What? Santa sat on a chair in the middle of the office surrounded by workers who look like elves.”

“No, of course not.” *Yes, I did. Father Christmas surrounded by elves and maybe a computer.* “What I mean is the building and all the technology. It was amazing.” *You’re still annoyed. Let’s try a different tack.* “Nicole was impressed.”

Daniel looked down at his phone. “I’m glad someone was. Who’s Nicole?”

“One of the new girls I met today. I’m impressed too. It’s just—“

Daniel looked up from the phone. “I said it was a big deal. But you didn’t believe me, eh?” His phone beeped again.

“No, it’s not that,” I said, trying to catch his eye and becoming slightly annoyed with the constant beeping coming from his new pet. “I did believe you.” *I didn’t. Not really.* “It’s just I thought it would be on a smaller scale.” *I thought you were exaggerating.*

Daniel was silent, staring at his phone.

“The companies you’ve worked for before haven’t been so big and because it was to do with Christmas, I thought it would be more like a toy store.”

“A toy store!” Daniel screwed up his mouth.

“No, sorry. I meant a toy— factory?” Daniel’s brow furrowed. He was getting cross. “No, I mean an emporium?” I said, adding quietly, “You know what I mean.”

“Do you have any idea what I do?”

I hate it when you ask me this. “Yes, of course I do.” *Something to do with looking at numbers and working out difficult sums?*

Daniel sighed. “I suppose you think I look at numbers all day and work out difficult sums?"

Damn! You're good. Add clairvoyant to your skillset.

"I am the executive assistant to the Chief of Christmas, Donald Pittman. The boss of a company which is worth millions of pounds, employs hundreds of staff and is one of the biggest secrets in the world."

"I know," I said, slightly bored with where this conversation was going.

"You obviously don't!"

I do. But I don't know what you actually do.

"I look after the man who runs this company. I write his speeches. I put together the board papers. I take notes, find out stuff, have the answers when he asks or when someone asks him something." He was breathing hard, as if he'd just been for a run.

"I'm sorry. I don't know what you do because you never tell me anything. You always say it's boring, or it's complicated, or I won't understand." My voice wobbled, my lower eyelids filling with water like a paddling pool.

"Okay. Maybe I don't explain, but when I come home, I just want to relax and forget about work, not talk about what I've done, which *is* boring and complicated, and you probably wouldn't understand." He sighed. "Look, Chrissie. I promise I will talk to you more about the job, the interesting parts anyway, but can we please drop this?" He took the wineglass I'd been clutching to my chest for the last five minutes and put it on the coffee table. He put his arms out and pulled me towards him.

"I do love you, and I know this is difficult for you. Much harder than it is for me."

At least you recognise that.

"Come on. Tell me about your day. Who did you meet?" Daniel placed his phone down and turned to face me.

He's trying. "Well, we started off with a presentation by Jim Handsome."

"Jim! He's a funny bloke, isn't he?"

Really! "I suppose so, bit creepy, though."

"Creepy? Jim?"

"Well, it was the way he looked at us."

"How did he look at you?"

"Most of the time, he was looking at our boobs."

"Oh, Jim's harmless. Very easy going and amiable. That's why they use him for the introductions."

"I'm not sure I'd want him as the face of the Company."

"He's not the face of the Company, and you're being too sensitive."

I'm not. "I'm just surprised."

"Why? What introduction would you have preferred?"

"Just someone who focused on our questions and not our body parts."

"Did he not answer your questions?"

"Well, yes, but—"

"Was he entertaining?"

"I suppose so."

"There you are then. He did his job. The rest is all banter."

Banter! "He also slapped me on the bum when I bent down." I wasn't going to say anything about this, but Daniel's reaction annoyed me.

"What? Why were you bending down?"

"I was picking up the papers he'd dropped in front of me."

"And what did he say?"

"He said thank you."

"There you are then. It's fine. It's his sense of humour, that's all."

Why are you sticking up for Jim?

"Oh, come on, Chrissie. You weren't bothered, were you?"

Yes. "Well, no but—"

"He's only having a laugh. It will be something else tomorrow."

And that's the point. It does bother me, and why doesn't it bother you?

"At least you've learnt your lesson. Don't bend down in front of Jim Handsome again."

Not the answer I wanted to hear.

"What else did you do?"

I'm not sure I want to tell you now, but I don't want to argue. Count to three. "I met some interesting people on the course."

"Oh, yeah. Who?"

"There was Nicole, who I mentioned earlier, and Alex, who I think I'm going to get on with very well."

"Why?"

"I don't know. Just a feeling."

"That's nice," said Daniel, looking at his phone again.

You're not listening. "She's a lawyer, you know," I said purposely.

"That's nice." Daniel repeated.

Still not listening. "But she's not sure if she will carry on working as a lawyer here."

"That's nice."

"Daniel! You're not listening?"

He looked up.

"I said, it's a shame she won't be able to continue to be a lawyer."

"Her husband works, I assume?"

"Yes. He's a lawyer too."

"That's okay then. He'll be working."

"And what is she supposed to do?"

He sighed. "Maybe a hobby? Coffee with friends. Just like you."

I looked over at Daniel. "What? What do you mean? Like me. I thought I would get a job and work too."

"Did you?"

I did. I do. I don't want to be like my mother. I thought you understood.

"And what job will you do?" He was staring as if this was completely new to him.

"I don't know. I haven't thought about it properly. I—"

"Maybe you should have before you got here."

"But whenever I tried to talk to you about this, you always said we'd have to wait until I got here."

"I assumed you meant a volunteer role."

"Why would you think that?"

"Because you don't need to work, and I thought you would start a family soon, too."

What? We've never had that conversation. I took a breath. "Well, we need to talk about this, but what about after I've had a baby?" I tried to sound more assertive.

He took my hand and, lowering his voice, said, "And who's going to look after it, silly? You don't have any family here to help, so you're going to be busy. Too busy to have a job as well."

Tears rolled down my face. He was right. I didn't have a choice, and I never realised. *How stupid am I.*

"Don't cry." He pulled me into his embrace. "I love you Chrissie. Everything will be okay."

Will it? Burrowing my head in his chest, I breathed in the familiar scent of soap, comforted, until I felt a buzzing on my back. Bloody Nokia 365.

Chapter 15

"I thought you were going to phone after mass on Sunday." My mother's voice, confused as to why someone would do something different from what they had agreed.

What my mother didn't realise was that I was desperate to speak to someone. I was so lonely. Daniel didn't understand or have time to listen. I didn't yet know the new women properly, and I didn't want to call my friends back home as I knew I would get upset and then they would be upset. So, I phoned home, foolishly thinking Mum might offer some sympathy. They never did anything after six except watch soaps and argue. Surely, they would welcome the distraction by their daughter, now living thousands of miles away.

"I'm sorry," I said, hoping the apology would soften her.

"I have a schedule and I like to keep to it."

Maybe not.

"I'll need to record the programme I was watching now and it's difficult." I heard her shout to dad. "Robert, record this. And see if you can get it right this time." She cleared her throat with a small cough. "So, what is the emergency?"

"No emergency. Just wanted to talk."

"Okay. So, what have you done today?"

"I hoovered the lounge and cleaned the downstairs bathroom. I've still got lots to do with unpacking and sorting the house out." I tried to be upbeat. I didn't want to sound like I was moaning.

"Anything else?"

No, nothing else, because this is my life now. Housework, cleaning, cooking. And I think I've made a mistake in coming here.

"Are you okay? Is there a problem? What is the matter, Chrissie? You're scaring me."

I didn't know what to say. "Daniel wants to start a family."

"My darling. That's wonderful news."

Not the reaction I'm looking for. "It's just— I didn't think— I didn't think we'd be thinking this yet. It's too soon. I've just arrived."

"I think it's sensible." She was unemotional. "You don't have to work. You can concentrate on rearing a family."

Like a cow. "Maybe one day, but not just yet."

"Why not? What are you going to do instead?" Mum made it sound so simple.

"I'd like to get a job?"

"What job?"

"I don't know." The truth is I've never known. I was a good secretary but it wasn't my dream job, but then no-one ever asked me what I wanted to do and I had never thought about it. "I'd like to live a little first."

"Don't be silly. Children don't stop you living."

"Yes, but you have to put them first and you can't go out unless you have someone to watch them, and I don't have any family here to help me, so I'd be doing it all by myself because Daniel won't be helping." I knew I was sounding pathetic. Mum was silent. Why did I think she would understand? Not Mary. She was put on the earth to raise a child, just like her namesake. 'If it's good enough for the mother of God' she would tell me and anyone else who would listen, and often those who didn't want to.

"You're upset, Chrissie, and now you're upsetting me. Don't you want me to have grandchildren?" She sniffled down the phone. I imagined her dabbing at her eyes with her crisp white linen handkerchief she would have ready for such occasions. "And the thing is — it might not happen for a while, and you don't want to be wasting your window of opportunity."

How many times have I heard about my ticking fertile clock? And it felt more like a bomb than a clock.

Mum sighed into the receiver. "I've never told you this, but your dad and I—" She swallowed so hard I could hear the lump roll down the phone line. "We waited a long time to have you. There were the beginnings of life, but they never stayed." Her voice trailed off.

Miscarriages. She never told me.

"And it wasn't because I wanted a life first." Her voice was hard again, the voice I knew well.

"Eventually, God granted me a child and I have never forgotten how fortunate I was."

I may have been a miracle, but I never felt like a miracle. If anything, it was the opposite. A feeling I was never good enough, and everything was my fault or dad's.

"What your mum is trying to say—"

"I can speak for myself, Robert," she hissed. "What I'm saying is, you never know what life has in store for you, and you might end up disappointed."

I didn't know if she was talking about her own life or mine.

"Take every opportunity while you can."

This conversation was not the one I thought I would have, or the one Mum thought she was having, but it was probably the one I needed. She was right. I had to stop feeling sorry for myself and throw myself into this new life. Getting pregnant was not on my 'to do' list, but making friends and getting a job was.

TV studio, 2009

"So, the elves are a big part of the workforce?" Ms Grey emphasises 'are', ensuring everyone realises she knew this all along. "It's very interesting to learn the elves are professional carpenters. And the workplace— I can almost smell the wood and candy sticks and the baking of the mince pies."

Ms Grey is accepting some of these newer inventions of mine. I hold back on describing the Ring and the technology. Some things have to be kept secret if the new place is to benefit.

She continues. "With Daniel working such long hours, what did you do to pass the time?"

Pass the time? Interesting choice of words.

Thinking back to those years, I remembered the list of what I wanted to do, or, rather, what I didn't want to do.

- I don't want to work with children.
- I don't want to work with animals.
- I don't want to stay at home.

Well, one out of three wasn't bad, I suppose.

"And I'm sure our listeners would love to hear about the other people who live and work at Christmas Town?" said Ms Grey, nudging my knee to get on with it.

This part is easy. I spent most of my time with other people.

Chapter 16

The day after the tour, I woke up looking forward to what lay ahead. Today would be more of a practical 'hands on' day unlike yesterday, which finished with a 'special' guest speaker who turned out to be an old employee of the Company, now formally retired and obviously bored. Someone in their wisdom had thought that people newly arrived in Christmas Town would enjoy listening to an old man drone on about how he single-handedly saved Christmas one year by finding a supplier of a special type of glue they couldn't manufacture on site. He also waffled on and constantly praised the Company, obviously grateful to come out of retirement.

I wanted to know the other women better. We were all outsiders, and who better to help than those who understood what you were going through?

We huddled around in a circle at the entrance to the *Welcome* building.

"Here we are again," said Katrina, in her gentle voice. She looked at each of us briefly.

"Of course, we are," interjected Toni. "We were told to report at zero nine hundred hours with three basic ingredients we use for cooking."

Katrina looked down at the floor again. Toni and Katrina were behaving exactly as they'd done yesterday.

These two are interesting. One who seems to know everything, and one who is afraid to.

The first part of the day was to be a cookery demonstration, using a unique ingredient.

"I brought spices and rice. I'm not sure they have curry houses in Christmas Town," said Katrina, looking up at Toni.

"That's affirmative," said Toni. "When I was researching the area, I didn't see any Indian restaurants."

"No Indians!" shrieked Nicole. "No one told me that."

No one told us anything.

"I brought tomatoes, courgettes, and onions," said Savannah. "I'm a vegetarian. I'm helping the planet, you know."

I know you're annoying.

"I didn't bring anything," said Alex proudly. "I don't cook."

Everyone stared at Alex. I wasn't sure if it was in admiration or confusion.

"Who does the cooking in your house?" asked Nicole.

"Rikkard."

None of us said anything, but we were all thinking the same thing.

"What? It's exactly what women do: work and cook."

You're right, but I don't know any men that do.

"Maybe he should have come to this workshop?" said Toni.

Something's bothering Toni.

"It's fine," said Alex, ignoring Toni's comment. "He'll just improvise. He's very good."

"Ladies. Do come in," said a familiar voice. It was Bert again. He was wearing a shirt with an apron in the front.

"Do they not have any other employees here except Bert?" said Alex. "I'm getting worried that Bert is actually Father Christmas, and next time we see him he'll have a long white beard."

I laughed out loud, and everyone turned to face me.

Bert glared. "Please stand by a station."

We were in a typical Home Economics classroom, except the kitchen was much nicer. Toni and Savannah rushed to the front: one a soldier ready for her orders, the other wanting to be teacher's pet. The rest of us took our time spreading ourselves out. Alex headed straight to the back table and beckoned me to follow.

"Welcome. The company knows it's a difficult for women when you move. To help this transition, they thought a cookery lesson would help you feel that life is still normal. We all love food. And cooking for your husbands and sharing food with friends can bring such pleasure."

Alex tutted. I rolled my eyes.

Bert didn't seem to notice. "This morning we will make a dish with the ingredients you brought, and the magic ingredient that we use a lot of in our cooking here."

"I don't cook," Alex blurted out, "so what shall I do?"

"This is very unusual and not something we have come across before," said Bert. "I will speak to my Line Manager, but maybe you could share a station with someone else."

Alex came over and stood next to me.

"I'm assuming you cook?" Bert stared at me, a serious look on his face.

"Yes, I do."

Bert's face relaxed. "Good. Let's continue. Any ideas what the special ingredient is we use here in Christmas Town?"

"Is it a preserve? I thought with the weather you might harvest a certain fruit, then store it over the Winter, or maybe into the Spring when the weather is warmer. Oh, but then it doesn't warm up here until much later in the year, does it?"

Nicole spoke so rapidly I had trouble keeping up with her.

"No."

Savannah had her hand up and was waving it frantically at Bert. He nodded in her direction. "Is it a plant?"

"No. It's a type of meat."

Savannah's face fell.

Meat? I hadn't seen any animals here so far.

"Does the animal live here?" Toni asked.

"Yes. We breed them for this purpose."

"It's not Rudolph, is it?" said Alex, laughing at her own joke.

"Rudolph?" said Bert. He looked puzzled. "Oh, you mean Father Christmas and Rudolph being the only reindeer that everyone remembers. You are correct. It's reindeer meat."

There was an outpouring of distasteful noises.

"Oh, ladies. Don't be silly. It's still meat, just like beef and lamb. You eat those meats, don't you?"

"Actually no, I don't, I'm a vegetarian," said Savannah, who'd turned a slight shade of green.

Bert looked confused, turning away from Savannah to address the rest of us. "Let's continue with the lesson."

Alex watched as I rolled the mince into patties to make beef burgers or deer burgers. "What do you think of Toni?"

I looked over at her station. She was distracted at that moment by Bert, who insisted that Toni was cooking her reindeer steaks on too high a heat, while Toni insisted he was incorrect and that she and her husband liked their meat tough.

"She's nice."

Alex raised an eyebrow. "Nice? Interesting. Not an adjective I would have used. I think there's a story there." Alex was sampling the sherry wine, one of the cupboard ingredients we could use. "Yuk! Too sweet." She put the bottle down and picked up something pickling in a jar.

"What do you mean?"

"From what she's said so far, I don't believe she was happy to leave her dad's business."

"She said it was a great opportunity?"

"Yes, but for whom? She was obviously running the business and her husband, what's he called?"

"Brandon."

"Brandon had an inferior role, but somehow he's the one working for the logistics team here. She strikes me as being ambitious. Doesn't make sense."

"Maybe. Maybe not." I continued to squeeze the cold mince in my hand.

"Did you do that?"

I stopped rolling the patty in my hand, unnerved by Alex's directness. "Do what?"

"Did you give up a good job so your husband could work here?"

"No," I laughed.

"What's so funny?" Alex was staring at me, her curiosity aroused.

Oops. I didn't mean to be so obvious. If I tell her the truth, I'm going to sound so lame.

"No. He was the one with the good job and prospects. I was just a secretary."

"Just a secretary? Don't be so hard on yourself. Were you a good secretary?"

No one has ever asked me this before. "I think so. Yes. They were going to promote me before we came here, so I must have been doing a good job."

"Yes, you were, but you never found out how good because you had to move because of his career."

She's right, but I can't say that. "Is that what you did?"

Alex put the pickle jar down firmly on the table. "No. I didn't."

I froze, slightly scared by her angry tone.

"We made a deal."

"A deal?"

"Yes. Rikkard said he would go travelling around the world with me after a few years of working in the corporate world. When this job came up, he was so excited and, to be honest, I'd not seen him that excited about anything for a while, so I agreed. It made economic sense too. We don't have a mortgage here, our living costs are low, there are no restaurants or proper shops, so we won't be spending our money—"

There was a loud crash over at Nicole's station.

"Did you say there are no shops?" asked Nicole, now standing in a puddle of water from the jug she had just dropped.

Bert spoke as he mopped up the water on the floor. "Of course, there are shops here," he said.

"Really?" said Nicole, who looked like a patient who'd finally received good news.

"Yes. We have shops that sell many foods and handy gadgets for the home, like this potato peeler." He picked up the peeler from the table and brandished it aloft as though it was Merlin's sword.

"There are shops. I went today," said Savannah. "Not for the meat, obviously." She directed this at Toni. "They don't look like shops. They're more like large sheds with boxes piled high inside. There's a fruit and vegetable shop, a butcher, a bakery, a DIY shop, a newsagent, and a small supermarket."

Nicole looked like a Pierrot clown with an actual real tear.

"There was also a clothing store."

"And?" asked Nicole, her face lit up in anticipation that everything was okay, that there was at least one high-end fashion store.

"Some interesting Christmas jumper designs but mainly thermals, scarves and gloves."

Nicole shook her head. "No proper shops. Alain never told me that, he would have told me, he should have told me, he knows how much I like to shop. He's always finding the empty bags and boxes I hide when I come back from a shopping trip. It's a little game we play. He likes to pretend he's annoyed, but secretly I know he likes it." Nicole slumped over her station, her hands on her head. "My life is over."

Katrina walked over to Nicole and put her arms around her. "It will be okay. We will find some shops." She looked around the room, beseeching us to offer more knowledge of the retail market in Christmas Town.

"The shops are rubbish," said Alex, who seemed to delight in informing everyone how awful this place was.

She was right, though. Christmas Town had little to offer in the way of retail, which seemed so antiquated and so different to the Ring, and I couldn't work out why. Did the residents not want to go shopping? Did they do their shopping somewhere else? And if so, why weren't the people who ran Christmas Town not bothered?

Nobody knew what else to say, so Bert told us we could go for lunch early. Savannah just stared at her dish, which didn't include reindeer. She had refused to add it, so had effectively made ratatouille, much to Bert's annoyance. I piled my deer burgers on a plate and covered them with foil.

"That was interesting," said Alex, who waited until all the girls had left the room.

I shrugged my shoulders.

"If the only thing she has to look forward to is shopping, then it doesn't say much about her life or marriage."

"I'm not sure you can comment. You've only just met her," I responded quickly.

"I was only saying," Alex said, responding just as quickly.

Crap! I've upset the only person I've spoken to properly since I've arrived. "What I mean is— we know nothing about her or her life before she came here."

"What you mean is, I shouldn't judge and be more sympathetic. Fair enough. I've always been quick to judge. I think you'll be a good influence on me."

I think I've made a friend.

Chapter 17

After lunch, we had our first Finnish lesson. The company encouraged us to learn to speak the language, although it seemed most people spoke English. There was also a written test to become a citizen of Christmas Town.

Daniel told me it would be easy, which was easy for him to say, as he didn't have to take the test. No man did. Self-improvement, it seemed, was just for the women. I wondered what that said about the men. Could they not be improved? Or was it because the men were busy and the women had nothing to do?

"What was all that about?" said Savannah as we sat at a table in the cafe. "I didn't understand a word and I'm quite good at languages."

"Do you speak any other languages, then?" Alex asked.

"Er, no. But I was pretty good at French in school." Her cheeks flushed as she avoided Alex's gaze.

"I wouldn't worry," said Toni. "Finnish is one of the hardest languages to learn, so it's going to take us a while to get the basics, except maybe for Nicole. French people are usually good at languages."

Nicole was motionless, her eyes glassy, staring dead ahead. She hadn't uttered a word since the cookery lesson.

"I was thinking," said Alex, "maybe it would be a nice idea to all meet up? I don't know about you, but Richard comes home late, and the evenings are so long. I'd like to go out and get a drink."

"That's a great idea," chipped in Toni. "But where can we go? They don't have any bars here."

"There is a pub." Katrina said this so quietly we all had to lean in, unsure we had heard her properly.

"That's incorrect," corrected Toni. "I've studied the plan of this town and there is definitely no pub."

"There is," Katrina said, a little louder this time. "Kaarl told me."

"How does he know?" I asked.

"Because he's been there." Katrina's voice grew louder, becoming more confident with each answer.

"Rikkard hasn't told me about a pub." Alex looked annoyed.

Daniel hasn't told me either.

"Sorry, but there is a pub." Katrina sat bolt upright, looking at each of us. 'Kaarl doesn't lie."

I believe you. "Where is it?"

"That's just it," Katrina explained. "It's not here. It's over there." She pointed toward the Ring.

"The main building we visited that we had to be escorted into?" Savannah said.

"Yes."

"So, how do we get into the pub? Does Bert have to go with us?" asked Alex.

My mind was whirring now. *Does he serve behind the bar too?*

"We can't go. It's just for the employees."

Nicole finally broke her silence. "We're not allowed into the pub? No shopping and now this. My life really is over." She struggled to keep from crying, though little sobs escaped periodically.

Toni had been unusually quiet. When she spoke, she was calm and methodical. "Let's go over this one more time. There is a pub, but it's in the main building."

Katrina nodded.

"Our husbands have been or will be likely to go sometime soon, but we are not allowed because we are not employees."

Katrina nodded again.

"There are no other pubs or bars outside of the Ring?"

One more nod.

"So, the only way we can frequent these places is to become an employee ourselves?"

"Yes," agreed Katrina.

"But we can't," said Savannah.

"Why not?" asked Alex. "I'm not saying I want to be an employee, but if I want to work, I should be able to. Right?"

"Wrong," answered Savannah. "Did you not see the set up?"

"Massive building, rooms full of men doing stuff," said Alex.

"Correct," said Toni. "And that's the issue, isn't it?"

What issue? I'm completely lost.

"The rooms were full of men. There were no women."

Crap! She's right.

"Maybe it was just on that day?" said Alex. "There must be women working in a big organisation like that?"

Katrina shook her head. "Kaarl and I had a long conversation about it before we moved. The Company only employs men. The women are expected to do the caregiving, look after the homes, cook, clean, and have babies. They are not encouraged to work outside the home."

"That explains it," said Toni under her breath, clearly talking about something else.

"It sounds like somewhere from the 1950s. This can't be true. Not in 1995." Alex pushed her chair back. "I can't believe Rikkard didn't tell me any of this."

Although the Company prided itself on modern technology and visionary ideals, it also wanted to keep things the way they used to be with regards good old-fashioned values and home life. We sat in silence, contemplating what this meant for us all. I couldn't get my head around it.

Did Daniel know this? Why didn't he tell me, and what have I agreed to?

Chapter 18

Daniel was home from work later than usual.

"Sorry, babe, but there was a meeting and it droned on." He extended the last word over three seconds and the smell of beer permeated the space between us.

Have you had a drink? Have you been to the pub Katrina told me about earlier? "What happened then?" I said, trying to act normal but placing the plates firmly down on the dining table.

"Yum! Homemade burgers and chips," said Daniel, popping a chip in his mouth, oblivious to my vexation.

Avoidance tactics.

He picked up the burger next. "Did you make these on the course?"

"Yes."

Daniel opened his mouth to bite into it.

"They're reindeer burgers."

He hesitated at the word reindeer, before taking a bite. "These are good. Who knew Rudolph could be so tasty? Did everyone make these?"

"No. We could make what we wanted as long as we included the reindeer meat," I said, wiping my chin where the juice had spilled down it. "Savannah didn't, but then she's a vegetarian."

"A hippy, more like."

"Don't be so judgmental."

"Don't be so sensitive. Those veggies are all a bit off the wall, aren't they? Do things differently."

"Savannah's fine. She just doesn't eat meat."

Daniel continued eating. "So, how did it go today? No bum groping, I hope?" He laughed.

I didn't. *Don't react. Find out about the pub.* "The cookery lesson was fun, and I got to know the other wives better. But there was one strange thing." I paused, selecting my words carefully. "We didn't see any women working at the Ring. That's not normal, is it?"

Please tell me I'm being silly and of course women work there.

I studied his face carefully for any sign of discomfort. Daniel only nodded and carried on eating. He wiped his last chip around his plate, mopping up the excess tomato sauce. "That was lovely, Chrissie. I enjoyed that. You can make that again."

"Well, is it?"

"Is it what?"

Are you being facetious now? "Is it normal? Do women work for the company?"

"There are women," he answered.

Thank God. I knew Katrina must be wrong.

"There's a few." Daniel looked down at his empty plate. "About ten."

I'm confused. "But how many people work for the company?"

"What area?"

"What do you mean?"

He huffed as if bored by the conversation. "Most of the employees work in the main building and some work at the entrance building where you had your cookery lesson."

"How many women work in the main building?" I asked.

"None." He said it as calmly as if he was telling me how many cups of coffee he'd drunk that day. "Look. I've got work to do. Do you have any more questions?"

Yes, I have more questions, but you have stopped listening.

I shook my head. He walked to the living room, leaving his empty plate on the table.

As I packed the dishwasher, I kept thinking about what the girls said and why hadn't Daniel told me. I mean this was huge, yet Daniel acted like it wasn't. I made a cup of tea for him and took into the living room. A peace offering I hoped would help me get some answers.

"I don't want to fall out over this," I said, putting the cup down on the coffee table.

"Neither do I," he said as he pulled me down next to him. "Chrissie, I know this is all new to you, but it's new to me too. I don't have all the answers, and some of the answers won't be what you want to hear."

I nestled under his chin. "It's just that, this place, as amazing as it is with its technology, seems a little old-fashioned with regards women." Now I'd started, so I had to get this out. "I thought I would get a job." He was quiet, which was reassuring, so I continued. "Maybe get a job working in the main building? I have my secretarial skills and I'm sure I could be an asset to the company."

"No, Chrissie. That won't happen."

I sat up. "Why? I don't understand."

He looked away. "Women aren't allowed. They made the decision years ago."

"They?"

"The Company."

"But it's unfair."

"I know, but it's to protect women."

This made me sit up. *Protect women. How?*

He sighed. "The company decided it was more productive to have women and men separated. The men are less distracted. It's an ideal situation."

I've never considered myself a feminist, but I was finding this very difficult to listen to, especially coming from Daniel. Women were a distraction. Men could work more efficiently without these distractions. I was wondering if I had travelled back in time when I journeyed here.

He pulled my stiff body into his arms. "This place isn't perfect, and things will change in time, but for now, this is the best opportunity I have to make my way up the corporate ladder."

I replayed the sentence in my head. *Where was I in all of this?*

I didn't say anything, I couldn't. I was grappling not only with what Daniel had just told me, but that he must have known all along. How could he do this? How long had he known? He was working more hours, spending more time away from home, and now he was keeping things from me. I didn't recognise him anymore.

Chapter 19

Lapland, October 1995

As working was not an option, I busied myself learning the dos and don't's of Christmas Town. In the Winter months, which lasted over half the year, we were surrounded by deep snow, and it wasn't easy getting around unless you could ski or use snowshoes.

The Company, keen to ensure all newcomers were competent, kindly organised ski lessons. They encouraged the wives to be as independent as possible, which seemed ironic when it was clear they wanted the women to stay at home.

"I won't be able to do it," I said, as we sat one evening watching a documentary about winter sports. Daniel thought seeing some people skiing would help me.

"How do you know you won't be able to?"

"I just do."

"Don't be so negative? This is an amazing opportunity."

He wouldn't understand. He excelled at every sport he ever tried. Nothing was too difficult for Daniel.

"Can you ski?" I realised it was a question I'd never asked him. He paused.

"Yes, I can."

Of course, you can.

"It was only a school trip, but I know the basics."

Of course, you do.

"I'll still need lessons though, because it was a long time ago."

I bet you will be brilliant as you are with everything.

"Chrissie, you'll be fine."

I doubt it. "I'll try."

"Good girl. I knew you wouldn't let me down."

I frowned. *Why is this about you?*

***

The next weekend, Daniel and I were standing with the instructor and three other people in our beginner group, waiting for the lesson to begin. I was already hot and bothered. Getting dressed for skiing was an experience and no-one had prepared me for the horror of putting ski boots on. The assistant who sold us our boots made it look easy as he undid the silver buckles on the side of the boot, moved the hard plastic tongue to one side so the foot could slide down easily into place. I questioned the tightness of the fitting but was told a snug fit was important in making the skis move. I asked him if it mattered if I couldn't move my toes. He laughed, finding me funny. I didn't find it funny.

"Welcome. My name is Johan and I glad to be your instructor." He spoke each syllable deliberately, slowly, and loud, like my Nan used to speak to any foreign person she met.

"First, skis on, then we do exercises, to warm up. Follow me." Johan jumped onto his skis, the bindings snapping like a crocodile at the back of his feet.

I tried to balance daintily on one foot, difficult in these heavy space type moon boots, as I picked up my other foot to step into the bindings. My arms swayed like tree branches as I attempted to stay upright. Johan moved his arms in large circles across his body like a windmill. Then he squatted up and down on the spot, his brightly coloured all in one ski suit making embarrassing noises. I was nervous and couldn't stop giggling. Johan didn't notice. He swung his leg out in front and behind while using his ski pole to balance. My leg was so heavy I could hardly lift it off the floor.

"Good. Second, we go here. Magic carpet. Follow me." He pointed to a large piece of plastic flooring which moved slowly up a slope.

Daniel strode off confidently. It didn't look like he was even wearing skis. Whereas I shuffled along to the strange contraption, an inch at a time. When I reached the magic carpet, I breathed out, relieved to have finally made it.

As the carpet did its job and carried us up the slope, I looked around me. The scenery was breath-taking. An army of forest green conifer trees surrounded us, and the snow stretched out as far as the eye could see. There wasn't a cloud in the sky and everywhere was still, like a piece of art. I felt silly. Maybe I'd been worrying over nothing.

At the top, we faced Johan, who stood on the lip of the slope.

"Third, we go down here. On our skis. I show you how. Then you try. Put skis like this." Johan moved his skis together so only the tops touched. "This is snow plough. You go down like this. Squat a little, yes, then point skis together and lean forwards. Push legs out more to go slowly, together to go faster."

We did as we were told. This was okay.

"Now, follow me."

Daniel went first, followed by all the other keen students. I casually walked to the edge of the slope and looked over the top.

Oh, my good god! Where am I? This isn't the same slope we have just come up. This is a mountain. A cross between a Heidi and James Bond kind of mountain. "I can't do it."

"Come down," Johan shouted.

"I can't," He obviously hadn't heard me.

"Come down."

Is he deaf? I can't come down.

"Come down now, please!"

"Come on, Chrissie. It's easy," said Daniel from the safety of flat ground. I took a deep breath and edged closer to the top of the slope. The phrase 'going over the top' had new meaning for me, and I knew what it must have been like for soldiers during the war. Okay, slightly different scenarios, but for me, still just as scary.

You can do this. You'll be fine. You can do this.

I looked down the mountain again. Daniel was at the bottom cheering. Johan was leaning on his pole, lighting up a cigarette. So much for instruction.

I leant forward and forced my legs apart, so the top of the skis turned in. This helped to slow me down, which was reassuring. Feeling braver, I pulled my legs in a little, but almost immediately felt myself going faster. I panicked and pushed my legs apart again. I continued with my legs apart, but they got wider and wider all the way down. By the time I reached the bottom, my legs were so wide I was almost doing the splits. Johan was not impressed.

"What is wrong?"

"Sorry, but I was scared."

"Why?"

"The mountain was a lot bigger than I thought it would be."

"This is not a mountain. Look." He pointed to the gentle slope next to the escalator.

"No. We didn't come down that slope. We came down a mountain." I said the word 'mountain' slowly as he obviously didn't understand. "Much steeper."

"No. Look."

I looked back at the slope. *Is this the same one? But it looks so different from the top.* This was so embarrassing, especially when I saw a young child race down in three seconds.

"You'll be better next time. Yes?"

Next time? I'd been so elated that I had got down without breaking my neck I hadn't thought about doing it again.

"Franz Klammer would have nothing to worry about with you."

Daniel chortled while Johan made smoke rings in the air.

Even in this cold, I could feel my face heat. This was humiliating, and I knew it wouldn't get any better.

"Don't worry about him," Daniel said. "You did it. But maybe you'd be better at cross-country skiing?"

Are you joking?

Chapter 20

As expected, Daniel was an excellent skier and quickly moved to a more experienced group. I stayed in the beginner group, persevering and went out practising with the other wives who didn't mind me tagging along and holding them up, unlike Daniel.

"I would just undo your boots if I were you. Don't take them off completely or you won't get them back on," said Toni, who I found out was a very proficient skier. We were sitting in a wooden hut decked out in sauna type panelling, next to the beginner's ski area. I did as she said, luxuriating in the feeling of release and freedom from pain all at once.

"That's better," said Savannah, agreeing with me as she rubbed her shins.

"I'm actually not feeling anything," said Toni. "I acclimatised before I got here by putting weights around my ankles and placing stones near the top of my socks. Seems to have worked."

"Was that necessary?" asked Alex, applying an extra coating of lip balm.

"I always feel it's better to be prepared."

"Were you a girl guide?" asked Nicole.

"No. I was a scout."

"But you're a girl?" Nicole's eyebrows locked together in one straight line across her eyes.

"Yes, but there were three boys in our house and Dad thought it best if we all did the same thing. Saved on uniform and logistics with travel."

I looked at her as she spoke. She'd used this speech before.

Nicole looked deeply concerned by this revelation and was about to speak when Savannah placed a tray on the table. "I got everyone a hot chocolate."

We leaned in and picked up a mug, grateful for the refreshment. No one spoke for the first few minutes as we nursed our mugs, warming our hands.

"It's hard work, but I enjoyed that," said Alex, breaking the silence first.

"I agree," said Savannah.

First time for everything.

"The scenery is amazing—and that air!"

Although I wasn't enjoying the skiing, because of the number of falls and general lack of natural ability, the air was exhilarating and smelt so clean.

"Brandon and I have been skiing before, but the air still takes my breath away," said Toni.

"Where did you ski?" asked Savannah.

"Brandon's parents have a place in Canada, so we go there during the winter months."

I can't imagine my parents skiing. My mother would hate to get messy, and Dad would never leave his armchair.

"I'm not sure I'd want to go away with Rikkard's parents," said Alex. "Too controlling."

"Nor me. Alain's parents are difficult most of the time, always demanding to see him or speak to him. They've even accused me of not passing on messages like it's my fault that he hasn't phoned them back. But really, it's because he doesn't want to speak to them." Nicole waved her hands around almost as fast as she spoke.

"I get on okay with my in-laws," said Katrina. "They're actually very nice."

That makes sense. You are one of the nicest people I've ever met.

"Me too," said Toni. "Although they treat me like a girl."

"But you are a girl," said Nicole, screwing up her face in confusion for the second time that day.

"I know it's just they think only boys can do certain things and that girls should be feminine and dainty, and I'm neither."

"I guess I'm lucky then, as Daniel doesn't have any parents."

Four pairs of eyes sought mine. "What happened?" asked Katrina.

"They died when he was young. They were in a car crash and only he survived."

"How terrible," said Katrina, who was near to tears.

"It was a long time ago. He's fine now."

This wasn't quite true, but I didn't know any of them that well yet. A fractured skull left him with loss of hearing and a large scar behind his left ear. He still had nightmares. Those who didn't know him thought he was driven. I knew this was a fear of being caught by the past he had escaped in the car, all those years ago.

"I forgot to tell you, but Alain said he would ask at the Company if they were recruiting any engineers. After we saw The Ring, I was so excited I couldn't stop talking about it and thought it would be amazing to work in an environment like that with the resources and technology they had," said Nicole at one hundred miles an hour, her face animated imagining her life working there.

"And are they?" asked Katrina.

"Are they what?" said Nicole, coming out of her daydream.

"Recruiting?"

Her face fell. "Er, no. Not at the moment, but Alain said it could change in the next few months after the year's end. I hope so, because Alain is absolutely loving working there. He's never seen a place so well resourced and the importance they put on innovation is very rare. They really want you to use your imagination and think outside the box."

"Well, maybe they could use their imagination and think outside the box of men." Alex slammed her mug down, causing Katrina to jump. "Sorry, girls. I'm not normally like this. But my brain is dead and I need a job. A proper job."

I know what you mean.

"I'm happy being at home," said Savannah.

"Fair enough. That's your choice," Alex said quickly, her voice bitter. Savannah looked down at her mug. Alex turned to Nicole. "I know Alain said that they might recruit soon, but I don't believe it. I don't think the Company would ever recruit a woman if they could choose a man instead."

Toni, who hadn't said a word during this conversation, forcibly pushed her chair back, causing poor Katrina to jump again. "I need to go to the restroom." She got up and marched to the door, which wasn't easy with ski boots on.

"Was it something I said?" asked Alex.

"Probably," replied Savannah.

As I listened to the girls debate the pros and cons of working, and Alex's theory of male dominance at Christmas Town, Toni returned to the table and slumped into her chair. "Brandon stole my job."

All of us stared, confused at what she was saying.

"I don't understand," said Nicole. It was the shortest sentence I'd ever heard Nicole utter.

"He stole my job." She took a deep breath as we waited in silence for her to continue. "Dad's business was doing well, and Brandon got more involved, which was fine until he took over. I'd been doing the job a long time, and it annoyed me. Especially that my dad would let him. One day, we were arguing about it and he said it was easy for me because my dad gave me the business. It hurt. He didn't know how hard it was for me in the beginning and how hard I had to work to get some respect. I was angry, so the next day I saw an advert for a logistics manager for a large corporation and applied. I had an interview over the phone and they offered me the job."

"So, what happened?" asked Alex.

"They found out Toni was a woman and retracted the offer."

"Oh. They thought you were a man," said Nicole out loud, as if she suddenly understood why they would have thought so. "I'm sure the clothes didn't help."

I made a face at Nicole not to say anymore and turned to Toni. "So, what happened next?"

"Brandon said it was an opportunity not to turn down, and we should say there had been a mistake, that he had put my name on the form instead of his own."

"And they believed it?" asked Savannah.

"Yes. They seemed relieved that it had just been a typo and asked him to start straight away."

"Won't they realise they've made a mistake when he turns up?" said Katrina.

"The board recruited me—" Her face dropped. "Him, but they won't be working with him on a day-to-day business. They won't know."

Alex huffed. "Well, they will if Brandon can't do the job?"

"He's thought of this. He's already said he will need my help."

"And you're happy to go along with this?" It was clear from Alex's tone she was not happy just being told this.

"He's my husband. I know I won't actually be going into work, but I'll be helping Brandon to. We'll be partners."

They sounded more like Brandon's words than Toni's. Toni would do the job and Brandon would get the credit.

Suddenly Toni straightened up and looked around the table. "I shouldn't have said anything. Brandon told me to keep it a secret."

Another secret.

"It's okay, we won't say anything. Will we?" said Katrina. Everyone nodded in agreement. "Us girls have to stick together."

Nicole put her three fingers up next to her shoulder. "Scouts honour!" And we all burst out laughing except for poor Toni, who had no idea what we were laughing at.

Chapter 21

Later that evening, I tried talking to Daniel about the conversation with the girls.

"It's the old boy network, Chrissie. I'm not saying it's right. I'm saying it's how it is." He pushed a tendril of hair away from my eyes. "I hate seeing you look so sad."

I'm not sad. I'm annoyed and confused. "It's just—"

"I know. It's not what you thought, is it? I mean, my job is amazing and I'm learning so much, but you need something to do, too."

Finally, the penny has dropped.

"Maybe you could work at the entrance building?" He paused. "Or in the shop?"

No. The penny is still firmly lodged. "I was thinking—"

"Or maybe at the medical centre. You're very good with people and you're always watching those medical programmes on television."

Great! I can be a doctor after watching sixty episodes of ER.

"I'm trying, Chrissie. You could suggest something instead of screwing your face up like you're chewing a wasp."

I'm not. I'm frustrated. Why can't you see this? "I know you are and I'm grateful for your help but—"

"You're lucky, you don't have to get a job. I wish I had the time to take up a new hobby."

And I wish you wouldn't keep interrupting. "But you have the dream job, and I don't have—"

"I don't have a dream job." His voice was hard. "I have a job that is very demanding and a boss who—“ He was going to add something, but the shutters came down over his eyes and he left me in the dark once more.

“You know what I mean. You have a career path to follow. I don’t have a path. I don’t even have a first step.”

“So, what would you like to do?”

I’ve been thinking about this for days. “Maybe writing?”

“Writing? Writing what?”

“I don’t know. Some magazine articles or short stories?”

“But you were a secretary. You wrote what other people said.”

Thank you, Daniel. Very supportive. “I have written other things.”

“What have you written then?”

“Well, nothing, but I used to write short stories in school. I was pretty good.”

“I’m not sure that some short stories in school will make you the next Stephen King.”

You are so condescending. “I know that. It was just an idea. Maybe I could write some articles about Christmas Town?”

“You can’t write about Christmas Town. It’s top secret.”

How many times have I heard this? And I don’t understand why you are so defensive whenever I mention Christmas Town.

“But I’d be writing for the residents who already live here. Maybe I could write a travel piece, something about what it’s like to live here and what we could do to improve it?”

“Improve it? How can you make it any better? You have the top of the range—“

I stopped listening. It was another propaganda broadcast through Daniel, the mouthpiece of Christmas Town. I twirled my hair through my fingers.

“I’m trying to help.”

You’re not helping. But now you think you are the injured party.

It didn’t make any difference whether Daniel agreed. Besides what he thought, there were several obstacles in my way.

1. I wasn't sure I'd be able to write any articles. I mean, it looked quite easy. What's hard about writing words?

2. Daniel was right when he said I always wrote other people's words. Writing my own would be a challenge.

3. The Company would have to agree.

I felt despondent already, and I hadn't even written anything.

Although I let Daniel believe I would think of other ideas, the writing one seemed like a good fit. Researching the area and the people who lived here would make me feel connected to the community. I hoped Daniel would see the benefits, but he was busy protecting the Company. From what, I had no idea.

"I think it's a bad idea." My mother's response when I broached the conversation on Sunday with my parents at the allotted time.

"But I thought it would be interesting and get me more involved," I suggested.

"But why? You need to be involved in Daniel's life. You have to organise the house and make Daniel's life as easy as possible so he can do his job to the best of his ability. How is he? Still working hard, I presume?"

Yes, he was working hard, but he loved it. Being the executive assistant meant he was the second person to know everything. It was exciting. I didn't think it was asking too much to want the same thing.

"But I'd like to work too." I whispered this down the phone. She would never understand.

"You do work, love," said Dad, contributing to the conversation. "All that cooking and cleaning. I'm sure Daniel appreciates it."

"Shame you never appreciated me when I was doing it."

"Don't start, Mary. All I'm saying is that I know looking after a home is a full-time job, but if you'd like to do something different now, go for it."

"Thanks, dad." I was in shock. This was the longest dad had spoken for in ages. Even more than at my wedding. Emboldened by his support, I continued, "I think it would be interesting to use my skills outside of the home and be able to tell Daniel about my day without referencing housework. I don't want to be one of those wives who has nothing to say."

Mum was silent. Dad rushed into a conversation about the weather. A wind blowing through a gap by the front door made me shiver. I attributed it to the cold, but it could have been the thought of my mother's life. Either way, it made me certain that acquiring a job was essential for my happiness.

***

The day it finally happened began like every other day for the past twelve weeks: clearing the front path of snow. A daily job required of all residents to ensure the height of the snow on paths did not exceed twenty centimetres. Another Company rule. Shovelling the snow, draped in layers of clothes and thermal protective gloves, I turned to see a woman walking tentatively up my path.

"Hello. Can I help you?" I asked, now realising the woman was pregnant.

"Hi. I'm Mia," she said, offering me a leaflet. It was a picture of a very pregnant looking Mia pointing in front of her with the words in a speech bubble above, 'Your street needs you!'

She explained how all the residents of Christmas Town attended a neighbourhood community meeting every month to discuss 'important issues' that concerned them, and she wrote up the minutes.

"It's all getting a bit much being eight months pregnant." She put her two hands round the base of her stomach to support the protruding bulge. "I'm so big and tired. I need someone to take over, but so far, no one has. I was hoping this might embarrass someone into volunteering."

"I'll do it," I said, before I'd even realised what I was saying.

At first Mia looked relieved, but then her face fell. "But you're new and you don't know anybody, and nobody knows you and it isn't fair to make you do it when there are so many who could volunteer. And it's not paid."

"Is anyone likely to do it?"

"No."

"There you are then. I'm happy to do it."

"Are you sure?"

"I was a secretary, so the job will be easy, and I'd love to meet more of the neighbours. I'm going stir crazy here just doing housework."

"Okay then, the job is yours. Congratulations." She handed the leaflets over. "And your first job is to deliver these. The meeting details are all on there." She smiled, looking more relaxed than when she first approached. "Thanks, Chrissie. That's a load off my mind, and considering the load I'm carrying, I'm grateful."

I waved goodbye on the doorstep.

My first job. Not a new career or even getting paid, but it's a start.

Chapter 22

After another week of sorting, cooking, and cleaning, I was bored out of my mind and relieved when Alex suggested we should all meet up at her house. On Friday evening we sat around Alex's kitchen table, continuing conversations and discussing whether it was better to clean the windows with newspaper or a cloth.

"A beer anyone?" asked Alex. She held up a red bottle that looked more like cough mixture than a drink.

"The best that Christmas Town offers?" I laughed.

"Actually. No. We got this from a large supermarket about twenty kilometres away."

"You left Christmas Town?" asked Nicole, a shocked look spreading across her face.

"Yes. You can leave, you know. You're not a prisoner."

Aren't we?

"That is correct," stated Toni, "but the Company prefers you to stay at the town and purchase goods from them directly."

"The company like a lot of things," replied Alex.

Like men working and women staying at home.

Toni turned her gaze on the rest of us. "It's better for the economy of the town if we buy here rather than going to outside sources."

"Yes, but they really need to improve the choices on offer. The shops are abysmal," said Savannah. "But I do agree with supporting the local community, and when you are in a different country, you should try the local foods and delicacies."

"Like reindeer, you mean?" said Alex, who was busy opening another bottle of beer.

Savannah's cheeks reddened. She took a swig of her beer, ignoring Alex.

Alex continued, oblivious to Savannah's discomfort or intentionally trying to upset her. I couldn't tell which. "They eat some weird stuff here. Moose? I mean Moose? Isn't it brown and hairy? And they eat whales."

"In fairness, I think it's only some parts of the country that eat whale meat and that's because of location and tradition," said Katrina, trying to use her calm voice to diffuse whatever was bubbling up inside Alex.

"Tradition. Yes! I've been hearing that word a lot recently. 'Alex, it's tradition. It's what they've always done.' Well, I don't care what they've always done."

Toni jumped in again. "The Company here is very traditional. They have old-fashioned values and encourage a different way of living, and if that involves eating different foods and living a different way, then I can only endorse it."

"Well, you and the company can shove it up your arse." Alex swallowed the last of her beer. "And that's what I told Rikkard when he said the same."

Like a chain smoker, she opened another bottle before the one she was drinking was finished. "Anyone else?"

We all declined. The beer was potent and had the desired effect on Alex.

"These are actually quite tasty," she slurred, dipping her hand into a bowl of chubby peanuts. "Another purchase from the supermarket, reindeer flavour."

Savannah's hand, which hovered over the bowl, swiftly returned to her side.

"You, okay?" I asked. I was feeling uncomfortable and, judging by everyone else's downward glances, was not the only one.

"Yes, of course. What's not to love living in Christmas Town? A fabulous house, these tasty snacks and lots of beer. But only if you buy it and drink it at home. Who needs to go to a pub like everyone else in the world?"

We were silent, awkwardly playing with the glasses in our hands.

"Maybe we could do something about that?" *Did that just come out of my mouth?*

"Like what? Tell the big bosses that the women need more than cookery and fancy Finnish lessons?"

"Yes." *What am I saying?*

Everyone was silent.

"The Company makes the rules," said Alex. "Have done for over a century. They won't listen to us. They've made it perfectly clear."

"I'm sorry, Chrissie, but Alex is correct," said Toni.

The only thing to me that is perfectly clear is how easily everyone here is willing to just accept what is happening. This is going to be our home for the next how many years, so shouldn't we try to make it better?

Nobody speaks, not even Nicole.

"We could try."

"How?" said Alex. She swigged another large mouthful of beer. She was angry. With me or something else, I wasn't sure. "I don't know..." This was so hard.

"That's the problem. We are the minority here. Our opinions are not wanted or valued."

I wanted to tell them about meeting Mia and going to the resident meetings, but was worried that Alex would see it as trivial. Her opinion seemed to bother me the most, yet as I looked at her slumped over the kitchen worktop, she appeared to be the one who was most vulnerable, lost and insecure.

"I've got a job."

Alex sat bolt upright and looked at me expectantly.

"Really?" asked Savannah. "I thought we couldn't get jobs here."

"That's affirmative," replied Toni, who looked very sad. This night was as dark as the sky outside.

"Don't get too excited, but I met a local who asked if I would take the notes at the next Home Watch meeting."

Alex slammed her head back down on the worktop with a huff.

"What's the Home Watch meeting?" asked Katrina, genuinely interested unlike Alex.

"Once a month the residents all meet to discuss issues and problems with the neighbourhood."

Nicole pulled a face. "So, it's not a social event, just another opportunity for some people to moan. But I suppose some people always moan about everything and at least they have an outlet for it. Not sure it will be the most exciting of meetings though? Are you sure you want to do this, Chrissie?"

After hearing her view, I wasn't sure it was a good idea, but it was too late to say no now. And it was at least a chance to speak up. "I know it doesn't sound very appealing, but this could be our opportunity to tell everyone that there could be another way. A way to include everyone in the community."

Alex sat up. "You're very naive, Chrissie. A residents meeting is just that. For the residents. It won't affect the Company. They won't listen to what you have to say."

I looked around at the other girls. "It's worth a try, isn't it?"

Toni, Nic, Katrina and Savannah all smiled but stayed silent. I had a lot of convincing to do if anything was going to change.

Alex shook her head. "My husband has decided he wants a family."

"That's wonderful news," said Katrina, reading the situation wrong. "Isn't it?" she added on seeing our faces.

"Wonderful news, if that's what you both wanted before you left to come to a place that insists on good old-fashioned values where mummy stays at home with baby while Daddy goes to work."

I put my bottle down. "What happened?"

She rubbed her eyes, smearing mascara onto her cheeks. "He doesn't want to go travelling anymore. He wants to stay here."

"He might change his mind again," said Toni gently.

"Maybe." She didn't sound convinced. "But in the meantime, it doesn't change the situation. I thought I'd be working, but that's not possible."

I knew exactly what she meant. Before moving to Christmas Town, I thought Father Christmas was a lovely story told to children, and men and women were equal. After arriving here, I wasn't sure what I believed in, and I didn't know what to think. But at least the Home Watch meeting would get me out of the house.

Chapter 23

On the last Friday of the month, I stood in the doorway of the Chairman's house where the meetings were held. A petite woman who kept pushing her glasses up the bridge of her nose greeted me. She did it five times while apologising for the house.

"Do excuse the flaky paintwork." She pointed out a couple of patches on the hallway wall. "I've been meaning to paint this hallway for the last year."

"And be careful of the loose door handle." She jiggled it. "I've been meaning to get it fixed." Despite the loose handle, she opened the door into the main living room and with a flourish introduced her husband. "This is Gerrard."

Gerrard was standing behind lines of chairs. As I stepped towards him, he seemed to grow taller, as though he was being inflated like a full-sized man balloon. He put one arm out to the side and bowed. His wife still had her arm out, as if she was a magician's assistant signalling the end of a trick. I nearly clapped but decided it wouldn't be the best idea I've ever had.

"Hello," I said instead.

"Welcome," boomed Gerrard. He was large in stature, with a stomach to match. He held out his hand. His firm handshake, while looking straight into my eyes, drained what confidence I thought I had.

"Mia told me you are taking over from her. Thank goodness. She could pop at any moment."

I could say the same about you.

"You ladies get so large when you're pregnant."

What's your excuse?

"Remember how big you were, Valma, when you were pregnant with Henri? The size of a whale. I didn't think you would ever be slim again."

Valma smiled, not responding to her husband's comments. "So dear, I hear you've just arrived?"

I've been here for two months. I was just about to say this when the doorbell rang.

"I'm sorry," said Valma, walking off to the front door.

Apologising again.

"So, Chrissie. I assume Mia has filled you in on what your role is here?"

Alone, with Gerrard staring at me as if I was a newly discovered species made me mute. I nodded.

"I hope you have good listening skills. It's important to write what is actually said, not what you think they are saying or, God forbid, your opinion. You understand? I want to see these notes before they go to the Company committee to make sure they are accurate."

He was serious. I thought this was a local community meeting, not a meeting of MI5. Thankfully, people walked into the room, and I sat at the back of the room. Gerrard had made it clear I was to be in the background.

Considering it was a neighbourhood meeting, it wasn't very welcoming. Most people ignored me when they walked in, except for one. She scuttled in, like a beetle, silent, head down, making no effort to converse with anybody. Sitting on the opposite side of the room, she looked up, her eyes narrowing and brow furrowing when she saw me. I looked at my notepad and doodled in the top right-hand corner. After ten seconds, I wondered if she was still looking. I moved my eyes up while keeping my head down in a swift Action Man movement. I hoped she wouldn't notice.

She did. She was still staring.

It was very disconcerting, so I looked round at the other residents. They were all women.

"Let's begin," said Gerrard. "Item one on the agenda."

I don't get introduced. Not important enough.

All the residents placed a copy of the agenda—which I'd typed and delivered to their houses—in front of them.

"Lighting. Some residents have turned off the security lighting controls and are hanging up fairy lights outside their home and in their gardens."

I giggled. People turned to look at me, so I pretended I was clearing my throat. I assumed item one would be about lighting in the street, which is not great. The streetlights are operated automatically and very bright. Whenever someone arrives in the street, everyone knows about it. I half expect to hear sirens and dogs barking when they come on, alerting us that a prisoner has escaped.

"We must remind everyone they are not to touch the controls," said Gerrard. "We set them to the most optimum setting for the safety of the neighbourhood."

"Do you have a problem with security?" The words tumbled out of my mouth. Not something I was expecting to do, and judging by the stunned faces around me, not something I should have done.

There was silence. None of the residents said anything.

"No, we do not," said Gerrard firmly. "Precisely because we have state-of-the-art lighting."

His eyes burnt into mine. I looked down quickly, pretending to doodle something very important in my notebook.

"Item two. Fencing."

"Was there— ever a problem?"

I looked up to see who had braved to ask this. It was the beetle lady.

"No." Gerrard's mouth twitched, and he pulled down on the braces he was wearing. "There has never been a problem with burglaries, but the Company were afraid there might be if the lighting wasn't adequate enough."

"Adequate enough? I think you could see our street from space." Some of the other residents joined in. The rest all sat hushed, moving their heads from one direction to the other like spectators at a tennis match.

"If you have a concern or complaint, you must fill in the Company complaint form. This is not the forum for airing grievances."

Isn't it? What are the meetings for?

"Item two." Gerrard was forthright in his manner, and everyone fell into line. "Fencing. Some residents are painting their fences different colours to the approved standard colours. Please, can you inform myself or Valma if you see this in the neighbourhood, or indeed inform the guilty party what the correct colours are?"

Interesting. Spying and now snitching. This wasn't what I was expecting.

This time, nobody said anything. And nobody said anything for the rest of the meeting. Gerrard went through the agenda, which, as far as I could see, was a list of everything the residents were doing wrong and needed to be corrected on. It wasn't a Home Watch meeting to discuss how to help the community. It felt more like 'Big Brother is watching you'.

The meeting finished exactly on time with no discussions or debates, just Gerrard telling everyone what to do, who to spy on and how to inform the 'people on high'. And no one stayed to say hello or ask who I was. I thought the meetings would help to feel I belonged. Now I wasn't sure if I wanted to.

I put my notes in my bag as Gerrard approached.

"Can you have the minutes ready for next week, please? And a word of advice—" He leant in closer. His aftershave was musky and cloying, strangling my nasal passages.

"You are here to take notes, not give your opinion."

"I only asked a question," I said quietly, not making eye contact.

"One too many. I'm not sure this is going to work out."

"Sorry?"

"I think Mia was too hasty in recruiting you."

"I thought no one else would volunteer." I was almost whispering now.

He coughed over my sentence. "You don't know how things work around here. That's not your fault. I think it would be better if we let someone who is aware of the customs take over. Thank you for helping today and remember to drop those notes off next week." He walked over to the last few remaining residents.

Great! Fired from my first job.

***

Valma was saying goodbye to some people. As she opened the front door, we were treated to a blast of icy air. With the door firmly shut, she turned to me.

"Thank you for coming and for volunteering to take the notes. I didn't think we'd find anyone. Poor Mia had been trying to offload it ever since she found out she was pregnant."

"No one spoke to me except for you and Gerrard. Have I done something wrong?"

"Don't take it personally. We all keep to ourselves here. Always have done. Partly the weather and partly the fact there is no social life in Christmas Town. When they get to know you, they'll open up more."

Will they? "The meetings? Not the most interesting, are they?"

Valma laughed. "I'm sorry. Not much happens here. We're not very good when the weather is like this." I nodded. It was difficult leaving a warm house when it was so cold and dark. I could understand now why animals hibernate.

"But to be fair, there's not much to do in Christmas Town."

"That's why I said I'd take notes. My husband is working at the Ring and apart from the skiing, language lessons and coffee, I do nothing except for housework. My brain is going to mush."

"I don't think I've used my brain properly in years."

"Did you work?"

"Yes. I was in marketing. Worked for a local company before we came here—" She paused before saying softly, "I loved it."

"Why didn't you get a job here?"

She pushed her glasses back up the bridge of her nose. "You know, I used to ask myself that question all the time. In fact, I used to ask a lot of questions when I first got here."

"What happened?"

"There were no jobs for women, and that was that."

So, it's always been like this. "But it's not fair. The men work, but they don't allow women to?"

"Women can work," Valma corrected me, "but you can't do the jobs the men do. It's a boys' club."

"But it's not right, is it?" I whispered. *Please agree with me. I need someone to agree with me.*

"No, it isn't. I'm not even sure it's legal."

Hallelujah. My delight was short-lived.

"But it's the way it is and always has been. Look, we're not prisoners. And we can't complain about our lifestyle. We live in nice big houses, in a safe environment."

You're right, but it doesn't feel right. I must ask Alex about the legality of all of this.

"But when you asked that question in the meeting, it reminded me of when I used to ask the 'why' question."

"And why don't you now?"

"Because no one else ever questioned anything. I thought it was just me, but now there's you." She smiled at me.

"My mouth gets me into trouble."

"I think it's your brain, not your mouth, that causes the trouble." We both laughed. "It's been very nice meeting you, Chrissie. You certainly livened up a normally dull meeting."

"I'm not sure Gerrard agrees with you. He doesn't want me to take the notes anymore."

Valma sighed while shaking her head. "Oh, dear. That is a shame. I hoped he would see it's time for a change."

Change yes. But how? We could debate the need for longer shopping hours and rubbish collection days, but I wasn't sure if we would ever make the patriarchal system operating in Christmas Town an agenda item.

"You can't take anything Gerrard says personally. He'll have forgotten by the next meeting. He's only upset because of how he left the Company."

"Oh? I thought he was retired."

Valma smiled. "Yes, he is. But they made him retire."

"What did Gerrard do then?"

"Oh, didn't you know? He was Father Christmas."

Chapter 24

TV studio, 2009

"See you after the break." Ms Grey stares at the camera, checking the light is out before yawning.

She's bored. The information I'm giving is not entertaining enough.

"It's been interesting to hear about your new friends, but you haven't really explained what you did apart from the Finnish and skiing. We want to hear about you being Mrs Claus and Daniel being Father Christmas." She stares at my face, looking for acknowledgement.

She's right. This is what the audience wants.

"Yes, I will, but a great deal happened before then."

"Well, unless it's going to entertain the audience, could you skip to that part, please?"

That told me.

"Let's start with Daniel's job and what it was like to work for Father Christmas."

This will be difficult to explain.

"I imagine him surrounded by presents, ribbon and wrapping paper, ordering the elves around." Ms Grey smiles, her teeth dazzling.

If only it was. "Something like that."

"Can you give our viewers an example, then?"

I pause. A feeling of disloyalty hits me like a wave.

How can I tell the children watching what Father Christmas was really like?

Ms Grey makes that face again. I decide to tell a mixture of truth and fable, which will keep some of the worse facts hidden, and hopefully explain how hard a job it was.

The lights dim and the producer shouts out, "And we're back in five, four, three..."

"So, Mrs Christmas, what was it like to work for Father Christmas?" Her smile encouraging me to tell all.

"When we first arrived, the hours were long and there were many a night when Daniel worked until midnight, had a few hours' sleep and was out the door again before six o'clock in the morning. Being Father Christmas's right-hand man meant he had lots of jobs." *And all the jobs his boss didn't want to do.*

"Did he have to clean the sleigh or feed the reindeer?"

That would have been easier.

"Being Father Christmas is like being the captain of a ship. It's his job to steer it in the right direction, oversee the information about weather predictions and any other issues that would affect the ship. Being Father Christmas's right-hand man means you do all the practical jobs to ensure Father Christmas can do his. This might mean keeping awake all night to make sure the captain doesn't fall asleep, checking weather reports and resolving any maintenance works. You don't have to fix the ship, but it's your job to let the engineers know if there is a problem and when it is resolved. And you must be available all the time."

This analogy made it easier to understand the job, although it didn't make my life easier.

Lapland, December 1995

Working at Christmas Town was all-consuming. Daniel worked every day. Even Sundays. They made it easy to work every day, and they made it easy to get in touch with you, as Daniel illustrated one evening after dinner using his new work gadget.

"You can email, page someone, put your calendar on there and reminders. It has the time and the date and you can set alarms." Daniel was holding this thing gently, gazing lovingly at it.

It was called a Blackberry. The Company was trialling the prototype before they launched it into the world. It was a palm-sized black gadget, and from the moment he received it, it was either next to him or in his hand. He thought it was the best invention since television. I remember being quite jealous of this tiny thing my husband held close to him and was constantly looking at.

"It's like a desk that you can put in your pocket. It has everything you need."

Why would you want to put a desk in your pocket?

"But the most amazing thing is the instant messaging."

"What's that?" I was trying to read my book, not really interested in this new contraption.

"I can send a message to someone straight away."

"Isn't that what an email does?"

"You don't understand. Look." He shoved the screen under my nose, then tapped out some message on a mini keyboard at the bottom.

"Hi Tim. Let's meet on Friday 9.30am. Daniel."

"Isn't that the same as email?" I looked over his shoulder as he stared at the small screen.

"No. Watch. I have just sent this message. Now we wait." He was holding this thing, one hand under the other, like he was about to receive the sacrament in church.

Just then, the Blackberry beeped.

"Tim replied." He read out the answer. "'Okay. Tim'. Isn't that amazing?" Daniel gazed at the screen like a teenager staring at their idol or school crush.

Riveting. "Er, yes. Amazing."

"You don't understand."

Apparently not.

"This will change the way we do business. Now we can send and receive information instantly."

"Can't you just phone them?"

Daniel didn't answer. He carried on staring at his 'precious', gently caressing it in his hands. If Daniel's reaction was anything to go by, Gollum would definitely want one of these.

"Sorry but I don't see what all the fuss is about. It means your boss can contact you all the time now?"

He frowned, not liking my reaction but also probably knowing I was right.

"I will mainly use it at work but it won't interrupt your busy schedule if that's what you're worried about." He glanced down at my book.

"I wasn't. I was thinking of you. Now they will contact you at whatever time of day."

He stopped a moment, as if registering what I said. "Don't you worry. It won't be like that."

But it was exactly like that. Whenever he was at home, he was always tapping on it. It was his own personal Game Boy. Not such exciting colours or content but in his hands the whole time, his thumbs following a Jane Fonda workout. When God gave us opposable thumbs, I'm not sure this is what he envisioned for the human race.

When he got out of bed in the morning, it was the first thing he picked up. When he sat down, it perched next to him like a lapdog and when he went to bed, it came too. When Princess Diana said there were three people in her marriage, I knew what she meant. Only the third person in our marriage was whoever Daniel was corresponding with. And it crept into our weekends.

One Saturday evening while we were watching television, it made a beeping sound. Daniel looked at it straight away, as he always did, and jumped up off the sofa.

"What's the matter?"

"Sorry, love." Daniel had already collected his bag and coat before I realised he was serious. "I'll be back as soon as I can."

"What? You're going out now? Why?"

"The Boss needs me." The door shut behind him.

I had to wait until after midnight when Daniel arrived home to hear what had happened.

***

Donald Pittman, also known as Father Christmas, was the CEO of the company. He was due to speak at a charity event in the town of Sinetta, twenty kilometres away. These events made good business sense. The charity helped raise money for disadvantaged children and the Company were direct recipients of this cash.

Someone had foolishly forgotten Donald's special suit needed collecting from the dry cleaners at the Ring, and it was now Daniel's problem to solve. This was his job. Correcting other people's mistakes and taking care of Donald. His strategy was to contact security at the Ring to open the shop, retrieve the suit and take it to Donald, who would be waiting at the train station.

All went well and Daniel handed the suit over just before seven o'clock. Donald then decided it would be beneficial to go through his speech again and, as the train would leave in five minutes, it would be better if they both went to the event.

"You're here now, so you might as well. Ho, ho, ho!"

Daniel wrote all of Donald's speeches. And as they had practiced it all day yesterday, Daniel knew it off by heart.

"It's an honour to be here tonight—" began Donald. "Blah, blah, blah— This charity which helps disadvantaged children is close to my heart. Ha. Not likely. Can't stand kids. Any kids disadvantaged or not. They're all the bloody same. Annoying. Not sure about the next line, Daniel. Sounds insincere. We don't want to give them the wrong impression, do we? Thought you would have noticed that."

Daniel listened as Donald continued to read and criticise, even though he had read this speech a dozen times before now and not mentioned it. Daniel continued to edit the speech and Donald continued to dislike everything Daniel came up with.

"Think my line is better. I should have written the thing myself. Would have done a better job. Ho, ho, ho!"

Daniel wanted to remind him of how he always said this, but still insisted on Daniel writing it. A car picked them up from the station, which gave Donald another reason to moan as the car was too hot and too small. Donald insisted Daniel rode up front with the driver, so he had more room.

Once they arrived at the venue, Daniel watched Donald's mood change. The scowl vanished and a broad grin replaced the pursed lips. Donald dumped his overcoats on Daniel and loudly announced his own arrival to the welcome committee inside the doorway. Daniel thought he should have been an actor instead of Father Christmas. It would have been more believable.

As Donald worked the room, first Daniel went to the cloakroom and then to the bar to get Donald's drink. Whiskey with just a splash of coke and definitely no ice. Donald had to have a glass in his hand within two minutes of arriving or he shouted out, oblivious to all the people within earshot and the embarrassment he caused.

"Where's my—" began Donald as Daniel slipped the glass into his hand. With Donald safely surrounded by his fan club, he went to check the sound system, the microphone, and speakers. Donald didn't tolerate feedback of any sort.

"Can you make sure the volume is correct before you hand him the microphone?" Daniel was busy going through the list of requirements with the room manager. "He doesn't like to press any buttons once it's in his hand."

The manager frowned.

Daniel explained. "It distracts him. Stops the flow of the speech."

The manager nodded, now understanding.

"And please make sure the room doesn't get any hotter than eighteen degrees. If it's too hot, he gets distracted. Stops the flow of the speech." The manager nodded, writing all the additional notes.

"And make sure he has his whiskey drink here on the podium next to him. Make sure it's on the left though, as he likes to use his right hand to dramatise the speech."

"Is there anything else?"

"Yes. Make sure the air conditioning in the room doesn't go above fifteen decibels, and that it's not blowing anywhere near him. It distracts him—"

"And stops the flow of the speech. Yes, I understand."

Under Daniel's instructions, the room manager and a waiter dragged the podium to a different area, which would be more suited to Donald's needs. Then he spoke to the organiser to go through the schedule once again, ensuring Donald was indeed the major act and not on first or last. Then it was back to Donald with another drink and some food to encourage him to eat. Donald accepted the drink but swatted the food away with his other hand.

"No time, Daniel. You should have given it to me earlier," he said quietly so no one except Daniel could hear.

Daniel stepped back from the group that Donald was winning over and looked on from a safe distance. He was like a bodyguard, continually scanning the area for danger. Although, for Daniel, the danger was Donald himself. It never surprised Daniel how amiable and charismatic Donald was with a crowd. He was a natural crowd pleaser, funny and engaging. Different to the man Daniel knew.

Donald decided he could get as drunk as he liked after his speech. Daniel would be there to get him home. Daniel had nothing to eat or drink all night. The perks of being the 'right hand' man.

After Daniel finished telling me what had happened, he undressed.

"I'm so sorry," I said. "It doesn't sound like it was much fun." I sensed Daniel hadn't told me all the story regarding Donald's behaviour. It seemed to me he defended his master like a loyal dog.

"At least the Company will benefit from the extra money," he grunted. He put his phone next to the bed and got under the duvet.

Poor Daniel. He was always thinking of how the business would benefit, but what about how he could benefit? “I know how we could have some fun now?” I said, snuggling up to him, my hand roaming down his body.

“Sorry, love. I’m so tired. I’m not up for anything else tonight.” He rolled over onto his side, away from me.

I tried not to be upset. He was tired. Of course, he just wanted to sleep. I watched him close his eyes. Just then, his Blackberry beeped. He sat bolt upright and started tapping on the screen. I turned over.

So not up for anything unless it’s work.

Chapter 25

When I woke the next morning, the bed was empty and cold where Daniel had been. He must have left early, as it was still only six o'clock. This used to upset me when we first arrived. We could go for days without seeing one another, weeks without talking. Now there was just a dull ache when he was gone. I was becoming used to it.

There was no organised activity today, and I had cleaned the house so many times this week I was running out of cleaning products. I didn't want to be alone all day in the house, so I thought a day out might help as I hadn't ventured outside of Christmas Town yet. Daniel kept promising we would travel when he had some free time, but it hadn't happened, and I was realising it might never happen.

Rovaniemi was what the locals called the capital of Lapland, and it was only about ten kilometres away, so a good place to visit. The train to Rovaniemi pulled up to the tiny, five-metre-long platform I was clinging to. Not encouraging for visitors, but that was the idea. There was nothing about this stop that would make one want to get off. It was a minor road with no signage. I half expected to see one of those signs you see in old horror movies 'Enter if you dare' next to an image of skull and crossbones. It was also difficult to get on at this stop, as I discovered when I tried to hurdle the step of the train and nearly ended up in the ditch under the track.

Nobody else got on. I walked through the deserted carriage, trailers from *Murder on the Orient Express* playing in my mind, which wasn't helpful. I sat down and looked out of the window. April brought a little more sunlight, and now it forced itself through the gap in the clouds, creating short blue shadows on the creamy snow. Next to the snow-dusted trees travelled a group of reindeers, each of them pulling a sleigh with a man sitting inside. Where were they going? What were they doing? I was smiling now. All negative thoughts gone.

It wasn't long before the train arrived at Rovaniemi, and it could not have been more different to Christmas Town. Stretched ahead of me were rows of colourful shops, all lit up with fairy lights and decorated with hanging icicles, Father Christmas ornaments and reindeer figures. The snow was still deep in places, pushed up the side of the shops, but the pavements were clear and you could walk easily up and down the streets.

People with red cheeks and smiling faces bustled along, enjoying the act of shopping. I thought of Nicole and how much she would enjoy this. I caught a reflection of myself beaming in a shop window. I'd missed this. The atmosphere. It felt real. The first real thing since arriving. Christmas Town was sterile. Everything organised, structured, empty. This town, with its flimsy bright lights and fake character figures, was real. It wasn't trying to be something it wasn't.

Every shop window I passed was full of colour and character, like being in Willy Wonka's chocolate factory. Candied peel in rainbow colours arranged in plastic tubs. Cinnamon and cherries, nutmeg and lemon all competing in the small space for your attention.

"Would you like to try?" asked the man behind the counter, in his almost perfect English accent.

He held out an orange cloudberry coconut ice he swore tasted like the heavens. And it did. Cold, fruity, sweet, and moist. The next shop had colourful lights and signs and a Santa figure standing outside. All the shops were adorned with Santa figures, some lit up, some blown up, some with signs attached to them, and some holding lanterns or sacks. And there were reindeer everywhere I looked. Reindeer statues, pictures, biscuits, cakes, bread, people dressed as reindeer and reindeer pulling sleighs.

The shops in Christmas Town were nothing like this. They were more like sheds. No windows, just large brown stable doors, small and cold with cobwebs decorating each corner. One dirty fluorescent tube stuck to the ceiling, illuminated the boxes of vegetables and baskets of bread you got to choose from. Everything was brown and dull.

My nose twitched as a burst of coffee drifted by. Bitter, sweet coffee smell so strong I could almost taste the roasted beans on my tongue. Where was it coming from? I followed my nose to a shop, its windows misted up with condensation.

In this coffee shop, years before Starbucks arrived in the UK, was an array of sweet treats in the glass cabinet next to the counter. Rows of doughnuts and almond cakes shaped like small towers topped with a dollop of raspberry jam. Deep fried funnel cake and cream buns with icing sugar sprinkled like snow. There was only one chocolate desert which looked like a chocolate pudding. I pointed to it, afraid to use any Finnish vocabulary just yet, as my pronunciation was terrible.

"Mammi," said the girl behind the counter, understanding my reticence. "Very good. A traditional dish. Would you like some?"

I nodded and took my coffee and dessert over to the only empty table in the shop. The pudding was warm, which I wasn't expecting, and my spoon got stuck in the middle of the dense, sticky mound. I sucked my spoon. The sweetness of the molasses cut through the intense chocolate flavour and made me feel like I was a child again, scraping the bowl to get every last lick of chocolate. It was good. Daniel would love it. The girl boxed up two cold puddings for me to take away.

Stepping back onto the train to Christmas Town, I felt different: more alive, excited. I was here in Lapland. The place where Father Christmas lives. A place of snow and reindeers, beautiful skies, and amazing scenery.

On my journey home, I squeezed into one of the few seats left. I smiled at the elderly couple holding hands opposite me, and wondered if Daniel and I would do this one day.

Somewhere in the carriage, I heard a sneeze and automatically said

'Terveydeksi'. I was surprised when I heard a reply, 'Kintos'. It seemed they could understand me, after all.

Looking out of the window, I saw how amazing this place was. The sky changed colour more times than I changed my clothes. Now it looked black, but the more I stared, the more it altered. It was now almost navy and shiny, then it became lighter with waves of light azure blue, weaving in and out.

The vast array of stars on display against this colourful background was mesmerising. It was a dazzling show of who's who in Hollywood at some award ceremony. Some stars were petite, turning from side to side just a little to show us their silver glow outfits. Then there were the bold, bright stars. The stars who didn't need to do anything. The stars of the show. They just stood there, confident in themselves, knowing that you couldn't take your eyes off them, even for a second. And then the darker, brooding stars. The ones who don't really want to show up. They preferred to stay in the background.

As the train pulled into Christmas Town, my happy feelings quickly disintegrated. Where were the pretty lights? Where were the reindeer and the animals? Where were the people? Where were the fires, the warmth, the life?

Christmas was supposed to be about magic and excitement and the Christmas spirit, yet Christmas Town was none of these things. This town had no life in it, no magic, and definitely no spirit. If I was going to change the way I felt about being here, Christmas Town had to change, too. We both needed a makeover. But what could I do to change a town that had been like this for a hundred years?

Chapter 26

Living in a country, with a different climate, culture and surroundings is hard, but I was learning—more through necessity than choice. I did a lot of things by myself now, as Daniel was never around and, when he was, he was exhausted. And having time on my hands meant I had time to think, mainly about what I could do to change Christmas Town. But this was complicated, so I decided to start small. Having stared at the plain, boring beige walls in my house for the last few months, I decided they needed revamping, but we weren't supposed to decorate. No house could be different, another of the company's stupid rules, but it was often overlooked. Out of sight, out of mind.

This last month, Alex had kept herself busy decorating her house and had somehow filled her days and the hole inside her she'd been carrying around like a handbag since she'd arrived. After our last get together, I'd been spending more time with Alex. I realised she needed it more than I did.

"Honestly, it's easy once you know how," Alex explained as she filled a bucket with warm soapy water. "Preparation is key."

Alex encouraged me to decorate and ignore the rules. It made her feel better about herself to defy the Company and she was keen to recruit me to the dark side too. She unrolled a wallpaper that wasn't too difficult to hang or to take off if it became necessary. We washed down the magnolia walls as I told her about the conversation I had with Valma.

"It's not legal, is it? Women not working, I mean?"

Alex sighed. "No, it isn't." She shook her head when she saw my eager smile. "Don't get excited, kiddo. There's not much we can do except take them to court, and no one is going to do that. And before you say anything, you need money to take a big company to court and our husbands are all working for the company. I've talked this over with Rikkard. It's just not possible."

"But it's not right. It makes me so mad we didn't know what we were getting into."

Alex squeezed my arm. "I know. Me too. But what's the alternative? Our husbands are not going to want to leave. It's all so exciting for them. So, we either get divorced or put up with it, for now." She held the wallpaper up to the wall. It had thick metallic stripes that shimmered in the light. "That's much better. It's a pity we can't do the same with the outside of these houses. They're so boring."

"Why can't we?"

"Rikkard told me they created these weird bylaws years ago, and once something has been a part of the area's culture for thirty-five years or more, it becomes legal and difficult to change."

"Difficult but not impossible. You've got to give me something here. If we can't change the work problem, we could at least try to change where we live? Feel like we have some say in it?"

Alex climbed up the stepladder, holding a length of the wallpaper to the ceiling. "Could you discuss this at your meetings?"

"I could," I said, ignoring her sarcasm. I creased the bottom of the paper at the skirting board and cut. "I have to do something. I need to. I'm bored out of my brain and having some sort of project would be better than cleaning the house again. And it could benefit the community.

"What community? Nobody engages with us."

"I know. That's why having a project like this could help. Bring a sense of togetherness."

She nodded. "I agree with you, but they don't like change."

"Okay. So how do we do it?"

Alex looked at me. "Are you serious?"

I grinned. "I've been thinking of nothing else since my trip to Rovaniemi."

She climbed down the stepladder and placed the length of wallpaper onto the dining table. "Well, for any new act to be passed you'd need to suggest a proposal, with the backing of the residents, and take it to the board for approval."

"We could do this. Couldn't we?" I pasted the length of wallpaper with a thick grey paste that reminded me of my dad's porridge.

"I don't know what's possible with this place. It's full of dinosaurs."

"I know, but we've got to try. What have we got to lose?"

She pulled a face. She was right. Criticising Christmas Town and the people who ran it could make things difficult for everyone, especially Daniel and me.

Alex took the wallpaper off the table and climbed, taking care to find each step before resting her entire weight against the ladder. The two of us slid the paper into place and brushed the edges until the strip was glued to the wall. We stepped back to admire our handy work.

"Wow. That looks great. It changes the room instantly," said Alex.

"I know. Just imagine this wallpaper was on the outside of our houses. What a statement it would make."

"Yeh, I'm not sure stripy wallpaper would look right outside." Her face lit up when she laughed.

"I was thinking about what you said earlier. Preparation is key. We just need some people to help us prepare."

A suggestive smile came over Alex's face. "They won't like it. A woman suggesting change. But what fun it will be."

In the depths of my cold surroundings, I was warmed by a fire inside me. A fire I couldn't extinguish even if I wanted to, and I didn't want to. All I needed now were people who had the skills and the time. But that was the easy part. Christmas Town was full of them. Women! Women who had nothing to do.

Chapter 27

TV studio, 2009

Ms Grey introduces another break, which gives me time to look at my phone. As soon as I do, I regret it. Judging by the number of emails and text messages from the team, something has gone wrong.

The week before I left to be here was crazy. The Company had finally agreed the new Ice hotel, the latest stage of the development. We had been planning to build a hotel onto the complex for years but needed more money. We had built ten small ice igloos, but they could only accommodate two adults, so a larger property made sense. But even with the village income, we still needed more, which is why this interview was so important.

I find a quiet spot and phone Nic back. She explains how there is a dispute over the positioning of the ice spa. The builders have found an old pipeline that needs investigating before continuing with the dig, and the build might be delayed further.

"The plans have all gone in," said Nic. "We can't change them now."

"I agree. We've wasted enough time," I reply.

"We're so sorry to disturb you, but we thought the show would be over by now, and we know how much this means to you and it was your idea to add the spa to the ice huts and if we have to move them, I don't know where we will put them and—"

"Okay, Nic, take a breath. I appreciate you all trying to solve this, but can we just wait and see what Johan says? It might not be as bad as everyone is making out. You know what builders are like."

"But if this delays us, then we won't be able to open in October," said Katrina.

I smile, heartened by how much they care about this project. "We will open, but maybe the Spa won't. We still have an entire village for the guests to explore. All will be well. Put Katrina on."

I hear the phone swapping hands.

"I don't know how you can be so calm. Halfway across the world, telling everyone about your life story on television while the project you have dreamt of might be in trouble", said Katrina.

"I have to do this. There will be no project if I don't. Keep me posted but try not to worry. I will be home soon, and things will be clearer."

And I wasn't just talking about the ice spa. The director motions for me to come back to the sofa.

"I've got to go."

"One more thing. How do you feel it's all going?" asks Katrina.

"It's fine. I think I'm describing what people want to hear."

"Will you tell them everything?"

I pause. "I'll tell them what's necessary."

***

Emboldened, I sit opposite Ms Grey, who appears to view me differently. She looks at me directly when I sit down asking if I'm okay and do I need anything. Her questioning changes, too. She is looking forward to the next snippet of information I divulge, like a child playing pass the parcel, waiting for the next layer to be unwrapped.

"So, what happened during holiday times, especially Christmas? Was it fabulous to be in Christmas Town at Christmas time?"

I smile. It isn't her fault. It's a universal belief. A place dedicated to Christmas that makes and ships Christmas presents to children around the world must be magical at Christmas time. You can almost hear the carols sung by small choirs, see the elves distributing glasses of mulled wine, smell the mince pies and biscuits, everyone chatting and laughing. The most wonderful time of the year. What actually happens is very different from the elaborate scene I paint for Ms Grey. Holidays were not encouraged. Working eighteen-hour days was. Daniel, now a confirmed workaholic, wouldn't think about taking any time off even though he needed it. But at Christmas all employees were forced to take two weeks' leave outside of Christmas Town. So, Christmas Town was empty. Strange to comprehend that you would leave a place called Christmas Town at Christmas, but that's the way it was back then.

Alex was going to a couple's only retreat with Rikkard to Barbados. Toni was skiing in Canada, which was even colder than Lapland. Katrina was going to a Christmas wedding in Ireland and Nic was flying back home to France. Savannah stayed close to Christmas Town, cutting down on her 'carbs', which I didn't understand. She talked a lot about her 'carb footprint,' but then I never understand a lot of what Savannah said.

Daniel and I went home. Back to mum and dad. They insisted. Or rather, Mum insisted. I didn't care where we went as long as we could get out of Christmas Town. The work was crazy, and Daniel had been in the office every day, including weekends. We were like strangers, not a young couple in their first year of marriage.

London, December 1995

"What about a sandwich? A bag of crisps?" said Mum, delighted we were back home. "I have some of those new chocolate biscuits for you. Not sure you have these in Lapland."

"We're fine, mum. We had a massive lunch on the plane." I sat on the sofa next to Daniel, who stared at the football on the television. He hadn't seen a game since we'd left. Dad was in his armchair directly in front of the television, in the corner of the room.

"A plane meal is not substantial, and you've probably not had a ham sandwich since you left."

Whenever I talked about food or home stuff, mum was convinced I couldn't get it in Finland. I'd told her last week I was making stews, thinking she would be pleased that my cooking skills were progressing. She told me she would get some stock cubes when next in Tesco's, as we wouldn't have those in Lapland. When I told her about the drop in temperature and how the bed was freezing, she told me she had ordered an electric blanket. I couldn't get through to her that Finland sold a lot more warming products than the UK.

"A cup of tea, then? Daniel, you'd like a cup of tea? I'm certain you don't get a decent cup of tea in Lapland."

She was so exasperating, and I'd only been home an hour. "Mum! I've told you. You can get anything. It's not a third world country."

"I know. Don't shout at me." She walked back into the room just as someone scored a goal. Daniel and Dad shouted over the football commentary coming from the television. "Stop shouting! What is it with everyone shouting?"

"Mum, I've told you before." I lowered my voice and tried to remain calm. "You can get anything you want. It's just like home."

She frowned as she sat on one of the hard dining room chairs. "It's not exactly like home, is it? You've told me they don't have big shops there or a pub."

"Yes, that's odd," said Dad, averting his gaze from the television to join in the conversation for the first time. "What town doesn't have a pub?"

How many times do I have to explain? "It has bigger shops and pubs in the bigger towns and cities. We just live in a small area."

Dad shook his head, not happy with my answer. To be fair, I wasn't happy with my answer, either. It had been bothering me for months. Why was Christmas Town not expanding like the rest of the area? It couldn't be about money. Daniel was always telling me about how they were constantly reinvesting in the business. It didn't make sense.

"It's also one of the safest countries to live in, has one of the best education systems in the world and you get a really long maternity time." I sat back, pleased with myself. After my conversation with Daniel and the Home watch meeting, I knew I needed to look at Christmas Town differently, and it didn't hurt that I wouldn't lose face in front of my mother. I didn't need to tell her the place was weird, and that I may have made the biggest mistake of my life.

"That doesn't matter. You're not pregnant, are you?" She glanced down at my stomach, which I automatically pulled in and then sat more upright as mum always did. I closed my eyes so I couldn't roll them or at least be seen doing it.

"What Chrissie is trying to say," Daniel piped up, sensing my frustration, "is that we live in a beautiful, unspoilt area with clean air and streets, no crime and excellent food and drink. It's a fantastic place."

Mum and Dad gazed at Daniel. "Oh, we know. It's a wonderful place to live. You're very fortunate and hopefully our grandchildren—" Mum stared at my stomach again, "will be so lucky to be starting their life there."

I looked from Mum to Daniel. How did he do it? Daniel and his talisman.

"And you can stop rolling your eyes, young lady. You don't explain things as well as Daniel. That's why he's so successful. Isn't it, Robert? Though why I'm asking you is a mystery to me."

"So, Daniel," said Dad intervening, "tell us what's happening at work? Have you delivered any presents yet?" He laughed at his own joke.

Mum was still staring at my stomach.

"Mum, I'm not pregnant."

She sighed. "I assumed you weren't. You're far too skinny."

Chapter 28

We had five days of holiday left before flying back to Christmas Town. Five more days of Daniel and I being together, with no work getting in the way.

"What shall we do this morning?" I said as I stroked his bare chest under the duvet. We were still in bed at nine o'clock, the sun shining in from outside. An unusual Christmas Eve day compared to Lapland.

"Let's stay in bed all day." His eyes and hands roamed over my naked body.

"We can't do that," I whispered, feeling like an embarrassed teenager knowing my parents were downstairs.

"Why not?" His touch became more insistent.

"Because—" I jokingly pushed his arm away. "We can go out and actually do something, be with people."

He grabbed me as I tried to slide out of bed. "Come here." He kissed me and I forgot about being with other people. I forgot about my parents. Until there was a loud knock on the door, followed immediately by the door being opened. In swept my mother, carrying two mugs of tea.

"Thought you might like a drink to wake you up. You don't want to waste the day in bed."

My face felt hot. Caught red-handed by my mother, who was probably waiting outside the door for the most opportune moment to embarrass me.

"Thanks, Mary. Just what we needed. Something hot and wet," said

Daniel, looking me straight in the eyes. My face got hotter.

"Glad you appreciate it, Daniel." She didn't seem to catch the innuendo or, if she did, she ignored it. "What time are you going out?"

"About seven." Daniel and I were meeting the girls and their partners at the local pub before going to midnight mass.

"Your Dad was wondering if you wanted to go into town with him and get a coffee, although I will never understand why you have to go out to have a coffee when you can make a perfectly good one at home and save yourself money and the trouble."

This was our thing, mine and Dad's. We liked to go to our local cafe and get a coffee. I enjoyed having him to myself without mum criticising his every move, and he enjoyed the solitude and different scenery.

"Good idea. You go. I have work to do anyway," said Daniel. When he saw my face, he added, "Just a couple of hours, and then we will be together for the entire afternoon and evening. Something we've not done for a while." He kissed me on my forehead. He was right. Today would be a good day.

***

"Do you want chocolate on your cappuccino?" shouted Dad from the counter in the cafe. I sat in the corner at a table, covered with a red and white gingham tablecloth.

"Yes, please."

There were so many things to talk to Dad about, most of them to do with Daniel. We made small talk about the weather and neighbours, and then I told him about Daniel's job. Dad offered little in the way of guidance. Just said it was different for him, so I talked about how I was trying to find a job. Again, he didn't say much until I told him about my meeting with Donald.

"That's not right."

Thank you for agreeing with me. "But what can I do? I told Daniel, but he thinks it's all harmless. Truthfully, I think he's afraid of making waves and upsetting his boss."

"I can understand," he said.

There was something in his tone that made me react. "Can you?"

He sloshed the last of his coffee around the bottom of the mug, evading my eyes and the question. "You said Daniel works with important people. Could he tell them what's going on?"

"You mean the Board? I'm not sure they would discuss it. Donald is Father Christmas. He's the most important person there." *And I think they know anyway.*

Somebody dropped some cups on the floor, and we all turned to look at the waitress sweeping up the broken shards. Her cheeks flushed, embarrassed by the attention. That was how I felt with Donald, and I knew it would be easier if I could just sweep the whole thing up as if it never happened.

"Mum would have tutted if she was here. 'No need to make a scene'," I said in a made-up mum voice. I laughed, but Dad was silent.

"Chrissie, you shouldn't be so hard on your mum, you know."

I stopped laughing. *This is a surprise.*

"There's something I've never told you. Maybe now is right." He was fidgeting with his wedding ring, turning it round and round on his finger. "Before you were born, I worked for an engineering company. I was good at my job and ended up in management."

I didn't know.

"I invited my boss and some colleagues round for dinner one night, and your mum cooked. To be honest, I'd had too much to drink, so I didn't notice, but your mum—" He stopped, not taking his eyes off his ring which he turned round and round. "Well, the next day she told me my boss had touched her."

"Where?"

"In the kitchen."

I rolled my eyes. "No. I meant, where did he touch her?"

"She didn't say, just he had felt her up when she was tidying the kitchen." For the first time since he'd started talking, he looked at me. "I didn't believe her, Chrissie. I said she must have been mistaken and when she insisted, I said he was probably only joking around."

How many times do we hear that? "What happened?"

"Nothing. We carried on as normal until—" He was noticeably sweating, tiny drops stuck to his shiny scalp. "They invited us to the annual dinner dance, and your mum and I were at the boss's table. Your mum went to smoke a cigarette outside and — he forced her into an alley." He had tears in his eyes.

"And he—"

What?

"He— you know."

I don't know. "What are you saying, Dad?"

"He— he took advantage of her."

I couldn't make sense of what he was saying. "Dad— what did he do?"

"You know. He forced himself on her." He whispered this, looking around him.

The words went swimming around in my head. *Mum was raped? Mum?*

"Your mum wanted to make a big fuss and tell the police and I—"

What is he saying? He thinks something so terrible is making a fuss.

"Don't look at me like that. I believed her this time, but my boss was— difficult and I knew he'd make my life difficult, and I didn't know what to do for the best, so—" He sighed. "So, I left my job, and we moved." He looked at me, his eyes searching mine for some reassurance, for some agreement he had done the right thing. But he hadn't, and I couldn't give it.

I don't know what to say.

"Your mum seemed happy to move, so I thought I was doing the right thing, but it was hard to find another job. I didn't have any references, as I quit, and didn't serve any notice and I couldn't tell any future employers what had happened. I took whatever job I could find.

I think your mum blames me more for that than—" He couldn't finish the sentence.

I'd never heard Dad say so much in so short a time and ordinarily I would have been pleased, but now I wished he would shut up. All I could think about was Mum, and what this must have done to her. Now I understood the anger directed at Dad, the resentment she must have felt towards him. Until this moment, Dad had always been the injured party. She criticised and mocked and ridiculed him, and he said nothing and I never understood why. I defended him, told him he should have stood up to her when all those years ago he should have stood up for her.

I replayed memories in my head. Mum never seemed happy and now I knew why. We all need someone to be our person. The one who is there for you, who defends you, no matter what. The One. I always associated that phrase with falling in love, but 'the one' is more than that. They are your other half, sometimes your better half and definitely the one who will catch you or fall on their sword to protect you.

"Why did you never tell me?"

"Your mum made me promise. She said she never wanted to talk about it ever again."

"And so, you didn't." The waitress took the mugs from our table. I watched her wipe the table with the tea-stained cloth.

Cleaning. Another thing mum does all the time. Did she want to wipe herself clean? "Why are you telling me now?"

"What you said about Daniel's boss? I don't want Daniel to make the same mistake I did. I lost a part of your mum all those years ago and it's never been the same since."

"Have you spoken about it?"

He shook his head now, playing with his wedding ring again, turning it round and round.

"I think you should."

"It's been too long. I won't know what to say." It was sad seeing dad sitting there, like a lost little child.

"You have to try."

He nodded, staring at his hands in his lap. Being a grown up is hard, but behaving like one is harder.

***

When we arrived back home, I found mum cleaning the potatoes in the sink. I put my arms round her waist and hugged her. She continued to peel the potatoes.

"Chrissie, what's the matter?" I didn't answer and didn't let go. After a minute like this, neither of us saying anything she slowly turned. Then dad appeared in the doorway, shuffling his feet backwards and forwards, unsure what to do or say.

"He told you, didn't he?" she said when she saw him. "I told him not to." She turned away. She was her old self again.

"I'm so sorry, mum."

She kept her face turned to the sink. "It happened a long time ago."

I tried to imagine her as a young woman enduring such a terrible experience and keeping quiet about it. "Why didn't you say something?"

She sighed, a long heavy sigh. "I couldn't. I was ashamed."

"But you did nothing wrong."

"I must have, otherwise it wouldn't have happened."

After all this time, she thought it was her fault. I hugged her again, although she tried to resist. We were not used to showing affection to one another.

"But maybe if I had explained, you might not have run away. Or maybe I pushed you away?" she said quietly. She turned around after wiping her hands on a tea towel.

"You didn't push me away."

"If I hadn't been the way I am, we might have been closer." Her voice was uneven, rising and falling as she tried not to cry.

She was right. She behaved a certain way because of what happened to her, but the impact had been far greater than she could have imagined.

"Even if we had been the Waltons family, I would have moved to Lapland." I handed her a tissue. "I moved because of Daniel, not because of you."

Mum had always been strong-willed, uninterested in others' opinions, even cold, but now she looked vulnerable, unsure. I understood now. For mum, being at home was safe. At home, no one could take advantage of her. Dad protected her the only way he knew how which was to move and pretend it never happened. And that decision had so many ramifications. It broke the bond my parents made when they married, and I wasn't sure it would ever be mended.

Chapter 29

I wasn't sure about going out later that evening. My head was still reeling from Dad's conversation, and I was also nervous about seeing the girls again. Writing letters and sending cards had been great, but it wasn't the same as our regular meet ups and I was worried it wouldn't be the same.

Later that evening, Daniel and I walked into the Derby Arms. 'Last Christmas' floated out of the speakers, a sharp reminder of how different things were. The walls were decorated with festive garlands and tinsel and the room was illuminated with red and green blinking lights. All around us people were talking and laughing, having a good time.

The girls were all there, seated at one end with their partners at the other.

"You're looking well," said Lisa, standing up to hug me. "A little white maybe, but I suppose there's not much you can do about that." Lisa laughed. Her round face as familiar as it had once been.

After the hugs and general chit chat had subsided, there was silence, broken only by the merry chatter of drunken Christmas revellers.

"So, what's new?" I asked, desperate for it to be just us again.

"Not much," said Rebecca. "I've had a promotion at work. I'm now the accounts manager."

"Well done. You were always good with figures," I said.

Rebecca pulled a face. "It's not very glamorous and I have a dinosaur for a boss but it's okay."

"I'm still at ToneTech," said Nerys. She worked with computers and had always tried to educate us how amazing computer language was. "I have a couple of new school leavers that I manage now."

"Boss around, you mean," Paula said, and we all laughed. "I'm still working for my dad's company in recruitment, but I'm studying contract law at college one day a week so I can be more involved. Another string to my bow and all that."

"That's amazing," I said, pleased but envious at the same time. Not only did they all have jobs, but they were also thinking of their futures and planning where they would go next. I looked at Lisa. "And what about you?"

Lisa looked down at her drink, avoiding my eyes. She took a gulp of her snowball and sat back on the scratched wooden bench. "Let's not talk about work. It's dull. We want to hear what you've been up to. Far more exciting than our lives."

This isn't like you. What are you not saying? "No. Come on. What are you up to?"

Lisa's eyes sparkled like her dangly, diamanté earrings. "I'm going to do an apprenticeship."

"That's amazing. In what?"

She opened her mouth and a massive grin appeared. "Architecture."

We all exchanged excited glances, remembering her passion for architecture from years ago.

"And I start in January! It's what I always wanted to do but I didn't think I could." Her words stopped abruptly, and her gaze softened. "I'm sorry, Chrissie," she said softly, the light in her eyes now extinguished.

"What for?"

"You've been telling us how you're trying to find something to do and I'm going on about my dream career."

I hugged her. "Don't be silly. I'm really pleased for you. You never enjoyed doing data entry work. Now you get to do something which is more you." I turned to the others. "Thank you for the letters. It helped to feel less lonely."

As soon as I said it, I wished I hadn't. The girls looked visibly uncomfortable.

"It must be so pretty there. All that snow," said Nerys.

I might have slightly exaggerated what it was like in my letters, as I didn't want them worrying. It was a new country, a new adventure, but it wasn't easy and I felt guilty moaning about it. I'd told them how late Daniel came home and how early he left in the morning, but I wasn't sure they understood.

"It is beautiful but it's the temperature. Nobody wants to go outside the door when it's minus twenty degrees."

The girls all pulled a face. It wasn't their fault. It's hard to imagine temperatures like that until you experience it.

"So, any joy with the job hunting?" asked Lisa.

"I don't know why you're so keen to do that," said Paula. "I'd enjoy not working."

"Me too, " joined in Rebecca. "Always fancied being a kept woman with a sugar daddy."

You don't understand. "Yes, but in a new place, you need to meet people and a job helps."

Lisa looked at me. "Do you have a plan?"

"I made some suggestions at the last Home Watch meeting of how we could improve our homes, but now..." I paused. It sounded so ridiculous in my head.

"Go on," said Lisa encouragingly.

"I want to change the town too." The girls all raised their eyebrows at the same time. "To be honest it's not difficult, as anything you did would be an improvement."

"I thought you said the man who ran the meetings wasn't keen on you saying anything," said Paula.

"He isn't, but I want to do it anyway."

The girls all nodded their heads.

"Are you going to work for the council?" asked Rebecca.

"There is no council. There's the company made up of shareholders, then the Board who do their bidding. They are the ones I need approval from, but first I have to get support from the residents."

Nobody said anything, just nodded their heads once more. They were finding this hard to comprehend; a world where men made all the rules and you needed their approval.

Paula broke the silence. "But if anyone can do this, you can."

The rest of the girls agreed, shouting out their recommendations and what they would do if it was them, and I was grateful for their support, but this was something I couldn't include them in. "So, what are you doing for New Years Eve?" I asked, changing the subject and the mood.

"Big party in town," said Rebecca. "Everyone will be there."

The girls were eager to talk more about the venue and who would be wearing what.

"I found a dress. Last one in the shop," said Paula. "It's got a huge split and I'll have to starve myself as it's so tight."

Paula's voice was filled with excitement as she described the club where the party was being held and excitedly rattled off a description of all the people going. The banter evoked memories both pleasant and painful, memories that I was no longer part of. I felt invisible and excluded from their world. Lisa's hand slid over mine in a comforting gesture, as I fought back tears. A moment of solidarity between old friends, but things were different. We were different, living different lives.

We talked for hours, until the bartender announced last orders and it was time for us to go home. The evening ended with drunken declarations of love for one another and slurred promises of keeping in touch. We hugged and said our goodbyes, but something had shifted. Underneath the surface I could feel an awkwardness that hadn't been there before. I wanted to believe things were the same. But I knew they weren't.

***

A few days later, and it was time to head back to Christmas Town. The sun had set and the sky was now a deep shade of blue, as if in mourning for what had come to an end. I waved goodbye to my parents through the rear window of the taxi which took us to the airport. The taxi's upholstery was smooth and cool to the touch as I clutched onto the seat, struggling to hold back the tears welling in my eyes.

Daniel gave my hand an affectionate squeeze. Living in Lapland was tough, but he promised it would be better. The time we spent together this Christmas had reminded him to appreciate us again, and it reminded me that this was my life and it was time to take control.

Chapter 30

Lapland, January 1996

Every society with free speech has some sort of platform for people to speak and ask the questions that need to be asked. But where was the platform in Christmas Town? It felt secretive and we were deliberately kept in the dark. We needed a forum where we could talk openly, but for the Board to agree to any changes, I needed the backing of the residents. The only time I saw any of the neighbours was putting the bins out and you couldn't stop to chat. Far too cold. The Home Watch meetings was a better solution, but I wasn't sure Gerrard would like it. He kept saying the meetings were for the residents. Maybe we just needed a little help in finding our voice and, at this time, I didn't have any other options.

"Do come in, come in," boomed Gerrard, beckoning people into his living room with his long-outstretched arms. "Oh, it's you?" he said, recognising me once untangled from my scarf and snood.

I wasn't expecting a warm welcome, but a temperature slightly higher than outside would have been nice. "Hi Gerrard. I'd like to join the meeting, as I am a resident," I reminded him.

He stared, making me feel unsure of myself.

"I could take the minutes while I'm here."

His gaze went to the corner of the room where a stooped man, who must have been in his late seventies, was slowly sharpening one of the ten pencils placed on the table in front of him. Gerrard turned back to me. "Jansen has kindly volunteered to take the minutes—" He hesitated, looking once more in Jansen's direction who was still sharpening the same pencil. "But it wouldn't hurt if you also took the minutes, I suppose. I'm sure Jansen can loan you a pencil." And with that, he walked off.

I turned to the sound of friendly voices. I'd encouraged Nic, Alex, Katrina, and Savannah to join the meeting to help bolster opinions and ultimately be on my side, although with Savannah, I was never sure.

"Hi Chrissie. This is so exciting. Our first Home Watch Meeting. Not like you. You're an expert now. Thanks for encouraging us to come along. Did you save us some seats? Why have you got a pencil? Are we supposed to be making notes? You didn't say we had to take notes? I thought you said we could talk and discuss things and I didn't bring a pen." At her eventual pause, I jumped in.

"No, you don't need to write anything. Gerrard asked me if I'd take the minutes."

Alex raised her eyebrows.

"I offered. And yes, there are some seats here."

Nic and Katrina walked to where I was pointing.

"Good luck," said Savannah, winking at me.

What does that mean? I'm nervous enough as it is.

"Welcome everyone." Gerrards' voice boomed around the room, demanding everyone's attention. "It's 2pm exactly, so let's make a start. Item one on the agenda. Rubbish collection."

You could visibly see the room deflate as everyone sank into their chairs, probably wondering why they had bothered to come at all. The meeting continued like this for the next twenty minutes, and with the warmth in the room and the monotony of the meeting, it was a struggle to keep awake.

"Any questions? No. Let's move onto the next item on the agenda. Dates for the year ahead."

There was a shuffling of papers and a moving of bottoms on seats.

This was a more interesting point than the other seven items we'd already gone through, which focused mainly on the streetlights and people creating noise on a Sunday morning.

"I think everyone enjoyed the Kautokeino festival at Easter in Norway last year. We will be organising another trip this Easter."

There was a lot of chatting at this point, as everyone who had gone discussed how amazing it had been, and those who hadn't questioned if they should have.

Gerrard asked for quiet. "I know you're excited, but we have a lot of information still to share, so—"

The buzzing died down and he continued. "We have the Reindeer racing at Inari in June, always a popular event. Those of you who are going can either catch the local train or there is an option to share a minibus. I hope I don't have to remind you what happened last year."

There were some nods and low mumblings and a few people desperately trying not to laugh. I was itching to ask what happened, but I didn't want to risk it while Gerrard was talking.

"And we have the Midnight Sun Festival in July. Valma will be coordinating transport and accommodation for those who are interested. The last agenda item is any other business. Does anyone have anything?"

Now was the time for me to speak, but my mouth was dry. I had no saliva and couldn't swallow. The pencil I was squeezing fell from my clammy hands, making Gerrard look straight at me.

"Chrissie has something to say," shouted out Alex.

Thanks Alex.

"We think she should talk about it in the meeting, as we are residents and it affects all of us."

The more she talked, the further I sank into my seat.

Gerrard scowled. "Well?" he asked, looking as if he could see right through me.

Nic was waving her arms around, gesticulating for me to stand up or speak up.

I swallowed hard and tried to clear my throat, which at this point was so narrow only a small amount of air could get in or out. "Er, I was thinking— what I mean to say is, the residents, er—"

What are you doing? You sound like an idiot.

I don't know what to say.

You do know what to say.

I took a deep breath, trying not to look at Gerrard, who was busy blowing and huffing in the corner.

"Like all of you, I'm a resident here. Although our houses and streets are very modern and that's great—"

A few of the residents are nodding. Good.

"I think we can make them better."

Some annoyed faces. Not so good.

"I mean, improve what we have."

"And how do you think you can do that?" Gerrard's unmistakable voice rang out over the top of the heads of the other residents.

"Er, we make them more individual."

"I don't understand."

Take a deep breath. You can do this.

"We live in houses that look the same inside and out. All our streets are the same. But we could make them different, more individual."

Gerrard was quiet. No one said anything, so I continued.

"We could paint our houses with different colours. We could hang different styles of lights of assorted colours. We could brighten up the streets with more planting, and maybe troughs of plants at certain intervals or window boxes or—"

"Let me stop you there, Chrissie." Gerrard's voice was unusually quiet, which was unnerving. "Some residents, like myself, have lived here for a long time and from personal experience, I can tell you that your ideas will not work." I stayed silent, sad that Gerrard saw no merit in my suggestions. "This area is not an ideal place for growing plants and flowers, and you wouldn't even see the flowers with the amount of snow we have—"

That's unfair. I never even mentioned flowers.

"And the houses are the same for a principled reason. It means we are all the same. There is no hierarchy, no jealousy, no one has more or better than the other. This way we don't have the traditional problem that is seen in other places."

I understand, but we are only talking about some different coloured doors, not a complete housing development.

"It's not your fault. You're new."

I looked over at Alex and Savannah, who both shrugged their shoulders. Nic sat in silence. That spoke volumes.

"I agree."

I looked over to where the voice came from. It was the woman who kept staring at me at the last meeting, the beetle lady.

"I'm glad I have the support of the residents on this," said Gerrard, smiling.

"No," said the beetle lady.

"Sorry," said Gerrard, not understanding.

"I agree— with her." She broke this phrase up into two parts, pausing in between. It felt measured, almost robotic. I was so busy analysing her voice I didn't comprehend she was agreeing with me.

"Tanya, I don't understand. You have lived here for, what, ten years now? You have never said anything about this before?"

"I know. I have changed— my mind."

Brilliant! Someone else agrees with me.

"Our houses— are the same. Our streets— are the same. Our lives— are the same, but we are not— the same. It's time— for a change."

The other residents spoke up now. There were a few disgruntled voices expressing the need to respect traditional values. But most of the others seemed in agreement with whoever Tanya was, some so excited they began discussing door colours.

I stole a glance at Gerrard. He was watching the commotion in front of him like a headteacher who had lost control of his pupils.

"Please, can we all speak one at a time? Please."

The last word caught their attention, and the residents calmed down, waiting for Gerrard to speak again. He looked around the room, purposely avoiding me.

"This is obviously something people feel strongly about, so we must allow everyone to have their say. Tanya, do you agree with some ideas that Chrissie has mentioned?"

"Yes."

"Would you like to elaborate?"

"No."

"Anyone else?"

Unlike Tanya, Nic was happy to elaborate and frantically waved her arms around. Gerrard had no choice but to ask her.

"I agree with Chrissie. I've done some research into the type of plants and trees that would grow really well in this area, not flowers, so you don't have to worry about that. Also, if you were concerned about door or house colours, I've found a company that specialises in paint for this type of environment, and they could send us a colour palette so everyone's colours would complement one another."

I didn't realise you had gone to so much trouble.

There were some murmurings from the rest of the residents. Then Savannah stood up. "We could make Christmas Town more environmentally friendly, with living plants and eco-friendly paint as well as creating individuality."

I didn't think Savannah's green credentials would help, or that she would want to.

"I think we need to have a vote on this."

Gerrard looked sad. I never wanted him to feel this was an attack on him, but it was looking that way.

"Hands up in favour of implementing changes to the look of Christmas Town."

Bar two people, everyone else's hands went up. It was unanimous. Gerrard looked at me for the first time since this discussion started. "It seems you have an idea that is supported by most of the residents of Christmas Town." He didn't need to emphasise the word 'most'. I knew I didn't have his support.

"But now you must put together a proposal for the changes you are suggesting and present it to our CEO, Father Christmas. If he's happy he will submit to the company Board for approval. You will need help to put this together. I hope you have friends." He turned to the residents. "Thank you, everyone. The meeting is now adjourned. Next meeting is on Wednesday 27th February at 2pm."

Savannah and Nic walked over to congratulate me while everyone else made their way out of the door. I could see Tanya wrapping her scarf around her neck as she walked to the exit.

"Er, Tanya, excuse me," I shouted over the noise. She turned around and stared. "I just wanted to say thank you, and to ask you if you'd like to be part of the project to change Christmas Town?"

She cocked her head to one side and was silent as though she was contemplating something new before responding, "Yes. That would be— interesting." She swivelled on the spot and walked off.

Gerrard came closer. "I see you have made a new friend."

I frowned, unsure of what he meant this time.

"Your new alliance. You do know who she is?"

I shook my head.

"Tanya Pittman, the wife of Father Christmas. Good luck."

His wife? And she wants to help? Surely that's a good thing. Why then is Gerrard wishing me luck?

Chapter 31

If this proposal was to happen, the Company had to know I'd done the research and explored all cost implications. But how did I approach Father Christmas? I was just a housewife and a new resident of Christmas Town. I needed someone who knew Christmas Town, but my options were limited. Daniel refused to present it to Donald even though he worked for him, and Gerrard was not my biggest fan.

And then I had a lightbulb moment. Valma. She knew people and had lived here a long time. She could help. I arranged to see her when Gerrard wasn't around, as I knew he wouldn't approve of me using his wife to further our cause. Valma was delighted, although when she turned up on my doorstep, I got the impression she didn't get out much. She'd obviously just blow dried her hair, judging by the amount of hair spray that kept her front quiff bolt upright. Either that, or the icy weather had frozen it on the way over here.

"Is my makeup, okay? I don't normally wear it, but I thought I would today." She pushed her glasses up her nose, magnifying her smudged brown eyeshadow and thick black kohl-lined eyes.

I motioned for her to come in and made us some coffees.

"This is nice," she said, as she sat on the kitchen bar stool. "There are no opportunities to chat except for the Residents meetings."

"I agree and I'd love to know how you ended up in Lapland."

"All my friends were starting families, but it never happened to us. A friend of my father's told Gerrard about a Financial controller role. He applied and got it."

"Did you know that the Company was the establishment behind Christmas?"

"Oh, no, dear. They didn't divulge that until after we arrived."

So, things haven't changed.

"We knew a fresh start away from what people thought would help."

I frowned, not sure what she meant.

"That we weren't a family because we didn't have children." Grabbing a tissue from the middle of the table, she dabbed her eyes with it.

Poor Valma. It must have been hard. "You said you moved here because you wanted to." I tried to keep my tone reassuring.

She cleared her throat before answering, "Yes. A good choice in the circumstances."

You were happy you moved here? "What did you do?"

She explained how she wanted to work, but this wasn't an option. "But all that changed when Gerrard became Father Christmas. He suggested I become more involved in his job, and he was grateful for the help."

That's unexpected. Gerrard supporting a woman to work? I assumed he felt the same as the other men.

"Opening the post was my favourite job. They sorted the Christmas letters from other types of post at the sorting office in the Ring. Only the special letters were sent to the Centre, arriving in a large Santa sack. It was my job to sort them into age groups so the Company could understand the toys the children were asking for. I loved reading the children's letters. They were so unassuming and honest. I wished I could reply to them myself."

"Does Father Christmas do that?"

"Oh, no. He's far too busy. He has people who write the responses. You know, like your Daniel."

Daniel! I've seen him writing letters at home but assumed they were business letters for clients. Not exactly the high-powered task he led me to believe.

"The replies are quite generic. Understandable, I suppose, when you consider how many of them there are, but I suggested it would be more meaningful if someone responded to what they said."

That makes sense.

As we drank our coffees, she explained that the first quarter of the year, which begins just after Christmas, is the quietest. The second quarter is very busy with the toy making. The third quarter is crazy, fulfilling demands for each country's quota and organising the logistics. And finally, the fourth quarter. The most important time of the year. This is when distribution happens, shipping all products and checking delivery happens.

"How do you know the products arrive and are delivered to the right children?"

"They use a very sophisticated tracking device and satellite imagery to ensure— oh, dear. I probably shouldn't have told you that." She looked all flustered, her cheeks matching her lipstick.

This is just getting interesting. "It's okay. That side of the business doesn't interest me."

"Oh, no, dear. I've said too much." Valma looked around her as if she was a spy during a covert operation.

"Let's talk about Christmas Town. I've noticed in the very little time I've been here, that Christmas Town is very different to the Ring and to the places like Rovaniemi. Why do you think that is?"

She nodded, pushing her glasses back up her nose. "If Christmas Town was like Rovaniemi, then people would want to come here."

I frowned. "And?"

"It would change things."

"Like what?"

"The Company needs to keep this operation a secret. We can't have people knowing what we do here?"

This is what Daniel always says. "Would it be so bad if they did?"

"Yes."

"Why?"

"It wouldn't be a secret."

I was getting nowhere with these questions. "Okay, what about the fact the shops are rather dated and there is no pub or restaurant."

"There's a cafe at the Centre?"

"But that's only one option. And we know the workers at the Ring have a pub." I deliberately said workers, not women.

"Yes, but that area is modern and Christmas Town is more traditional."

"I agree. But don't you think they are conflicting ideas? The Company wants Christmas Town to be traditional, the woman at home looking after the houses, raising families. But the Ring is modern, advanced. It's as if the Ring is important, but Christmas Town isn't." I hoped she understood my inference substituting men for the Ring and women for Christmas Town.

She was staring at the floor, her glasses halfway down her nose. She pushed them back up and then asked, "What are you asking?"

Tred carefully. "I was wondering if we could change a few things. Nothing drastic. The things mentioned at the Home Watch meeting. The residents are keen to change the look of our houses and maybe some other things could change. The Ring is about self-improvement and changing with the times so we would only be imitating the Ring. It's a compliment, really."

Valma didn't speak.

"I know I must take this proposal to Father Christmas, but I don't know how to do this. Would you know?" *Please say yes. We need this. I need this.*

Valma was quiet. "I can't promise, but I will try. It's just Gerrard won't be happy and Donald Pittman is a very busy man."

Father Christmas himself! This could change things. This could change everything.

Chapter 32

TV studio, 2009

"We're going to take a quick break now, but please do stay tuned as we continue to talk to the wife of Father Christmas."

A bell rings, and Ms Grey rushes off to the toilet.

"Okay, take five," says the Director as he walks over to me. "Mrs Connor. You're doing really well. I was hoping it would be okay to extend your time on the program."

I smile. "Of course. I'm glad you're enjoying it."

"It's not me. It's the audience. Our ratings have increased since you've been on the air. Seems everyone loves the idea of a Mrs Christmas."

Do they? The mythical wife associated with the man in the red suit is often described as an elderly woman who bakes biscuits. The image we have of her is more akin to a grandmother, and yet I'm not a grandmother. And as for baking biscuits, there is a lot more food involved than that.

As I wait for Ms Grey, my mind wanders to Daniel. He wasn't supportive of me going on national television. He thought there was another way, rather than exposing the truth. He wanted to protect the company, but the business was losing money. We had to generate extra income. We had to move with the times. It was hard saying this to him.

He was tired. His skin pale and his eyes had lost their sparkle. I knew he worried about the truth getting out, but my worries about Christmas Town were real. He just didn't see it.

"Okay. So, Daniel is still working for Santa Claus, and you are not yet Mrs Christmas?"

I note the emphasis on the words still and yet. Ms Grey leans in and looks serious. Staring at me square on before glancing at the camera, she says, "Let's talk about you and Daniel? As Daniel was working in a highly pressurised environment, it must have been hard. What was your relationship like at that time?"

Our relationship? This will be difficult to talk about.

Lapland, February 1996

One evening, Daniel surprised me. We were going out. Out of Christmas Town to Rovaniemi. I was so excited to have Daniel all to myself. It would be like the old days when it was just about us. And it was the perfect opportunity to tell him my thoughts about Christmas Town.

Although Rovaniemi was always Christmassy, tonight felt special. Familiar carols and Christmas pop music took turns playing out to the streets on loudspeakers. The shops sparkled with coloured lights, white fairy lights hung above the shop front, yellow glowing lanterns lit up the doorway, neon pink reindeer signs and Christmas trees flashed from inside the shops. All the lights reflected onto the pavement like streaks of water colours across a canvas.

"This was a great idea," Daniel said, as we held hands walking up the main street. "You can work for the Company that makes Christmas and talk about it all year yet feel nothing. At least here I can see what Christmas looks like."

He was right. There was no evidence of Christmas in Christmas Town. No Christmas trees, as it was a crime to cut down a tree. No music, as it was noise pollution. Even fairy lights were banned, as they weren't energy efficient and created light pollution.

We shuffled into the restaurant, clad in multiple items of clothing, glad to be out of the cold. The room was warm and romantically lit with small glass holders with candles nestled inside on each table, and some grander light fittings in the shape of antlers on the walls. We sat in a cosy booth on one side of the restaurant with high-backed leather seats and brown fur blankets.

"Here's to us." Daniel raised his champagne glass, and we clinked glasses. "I love you Mrs Connor."

The intensity of his gaze made my stomach flip. Daniel could be annoying, inconsiderate and selfish, but when he looked at me, I knew he meant whatever he said.

"I love you too, Mr Connor, and I'm happy."

Daniel looked surprised but pleased. "Are you, really?"

"I know I have been moaning quite a lot recently."

"You haven't—" He saw my raised eyebrows. "It's only because it's been much harder on you than me."

"Thank you for saying that, although I don't think you're being truthful. You've always worked hard but this job—" I trailed off, unable to explain, and unwilling to ruin one of the first intimate nights we had had since moving here.

"I know," said Daniel, "but it will be worth it. We will have an amazing life, Chrissie. Right, let's look at the menu. I'm starving."

I don't know why he bothered looking at a menu when he always chose the same thing. We went through this ritual every time. He would look, discuss a few options, then end up ordering the steak. Although he seemed different tonight, and it wasn't that the little worry lines around his eyes had disappeared.

Daniel closed his menu. "I think I'll have the salmon. I fancy a change."

That is different. I didn't know yet if that was a good thing.

After a glorious meal with our stomachs stuffed and our coordination skewed, courtesy of too much wine, we wrapped ourselves up and stepped out into the hustle and bustle of the high street. We followed a group of revellers, who were also swaying as they walked, until we reached a stage that was being set up for a concert. The heaters above warmed our faces below, and the smell of cinnamon and orange wafted under our noses. Daniel bought two cups of gloggi, and we swallowed the sweet warm liquid, which heated our chests and further dulled our senses.

The area was thronged with people lifting equipment and chairs into place, while others looked on. The place was alive with sights and sounds and smells. People looked happy.

"This place is more like Christmas than Christmas Town."

Daniel nodded. "I know. It doesn't seem right somehow."

"But couldn't Christmas Town be more like here?"

"The Company like it the way it is."

"But what about the residents of Christmas Town? We are the ones who live here. Our houses and shops are all so boring, and there are all these rules."

"I suppose so. I don't know. Maybe you could discuss it at the next Home Watch meeting?" He looked pleased with his suggestion.

"I've already done that." *You look surprised.* "And I've spoken to some people." *You look annoyed.*

"Why?"

"I thought it would be helpful to ask opinions about Christmas Town, how it's changed or could improve."

He was silent for a while before asking, "Who have you spoken to?"

"Bert was helpful. He explained the history of the area. And Valma thought Gerrard might talk, but I'm not so sure."

"I don't know what Gerrard could add. He's retired and doesn't know what's going on now. He's out of the loop."

"Just a thought." *Touchy! Need to tred carefully with what I want to say next.* "If it's someone in the loop, Valma actually suggested going straight to Donald."

"No." His voice, firm and gruff, made me stop walking. I turned to look at him. The worry lines etched on Daniel's face were back and seemed to sink further in, leaving a larger crevice behind. "You can't speak to him."

"But why not?"

"He's not the right person." Daniel kept his head down.

"But why not? He's Father Christmas. Valma said he was the right person and she's going to ask him."

Daniel just snorted and carried on walking. I wrapped my coat around me more tightly, the warmth between us gone. This wasn't how I thought the evening, or the conversation would end. And it felt odd. *What are you not telling me? And why do I feel worried.*

Chapter 33

I didn't want to think about Daniel or our relationship. It was easier to ignore it, and working on the proposal to present to Donald helped distract me from wondering what was going to happen with Daniel and I.

The wives and I had produced a professional document, and Valma confirmed the meeting details, so all I had to do was tell Daniel. Easier said than done.

That evening, Daniel was sitting on the sofa watching the news. He was biting his fingernails, something I'd never seen him do before.

"I have a meeting with Donald at three o'clock on Tuesday," I said.

He wouldn't look at me, just kept staring at the television.

"I know."

"The wives helped me to write a proposal and Alex threw in some legal jargon, so it sounds more professional if that's what you're worried about."

"I'm not."

"And she researched all the bylaws, so we're not breaking any rules."

"I know," he said still staring at the television.

"And Toni found a local supplier through her old contacts who would give us the supplies at cost price, and I will organise the work-force, which is basically the wives who will do the work for free."

"Uh, huh."

"Daniel! What is the matter? I don't understand. We are doing it all properly. I won't embarrass you."

"Nothing is the matter."

"Then why are you being like this?"

He looked up, but then turned his attention back to the television. It reminded me of my dad.

"Just ignore me. I'm busy in work."

Busy in work? Or busy avoiding something?

I didn't know what was wrong, but it was too late now anyway.

***

The next day I was sitting in the foyer at the Ring. It was the closest I had ever been to seeing where Daniel worked. I pulled at my skirt and jacket and ran my fingers round the collar of my shirt. It felt like a noose that I couldn't loosen. There were slightly damp fingerprints on the top right-hand corner of the proposal where I had been holding it so tightly. I hoped Donald wouldn't notice. Not very professional. I rubbed the prints with my fingers. It made it worse.

Maybe I should have put it into one of those plastic wallets or a cardboard folder? Why didn't I think of that? Do I have time to get one?

Suddenly I heard bells ringing out to the tune of 'Once in Royal David's city' and the receptionist informed me Donald would see me now.

An interesting choice of song. Heralding the arrival of the king? Am I reading too much into this?

I walked up the white polished marble stairs and at the top, in an open plan area, was Daniel sat in an office space complete with desk and filing cabinets. It was smaller than I had imagined. Next to him was a grand room with large opaque windows and a conker-coloured mahogany door. He stood when he saw me and told me to wait. He looked flustered. I felt guilty. I knew turning up to his workplace to talk to his boss might be embarrassing, but I was only going to talk about lights and door colours. I wasn't discussing a Peace Treaty Agreement.

Daniel knocked gently on the door and went inside. His outline against the window looked like a shadow puppet against a screen. Daniel's shadow puppet stood still. A muffled voice became louder. Another shadow puppet stood up. It was small, smaller than Daniel, but with more bulk around the midriff. A Punch and Judy show followed.

Punch was not happy. There was finger pointing and arms being thrown around and shouts of 'That's not the way to do it!' I half expected Punch to get out a club and start beating Judy across the head. Or in this case, Daniel. Punch sat down and Daniel opened the door. He looked beaten up. I put my hand out towards him, but he moved away.

"You can go in now," said Daniel.

I'm not sure I want to.

I tiptoed to the door. My heart was beating so fast it felt like it would explode out of me at any moment. Donald's ominous shadow moved across the window and opened the door. His beaming smile spread from one side of his face to the other. He had lines that ran down from each corner of his mouth, like a ventriloquist dummy.

"Hello," he said, vigorously shaking my hand up and down. "You must be Mrs Connor. Do come in. I'm so delighted you're here."

This was not what I was expecting. He ushered me in, taking my coat and scarf, and hanging them on a pair of antlers attached to the wall. He followed my gaze.

"Not Rudolph's. I can assure you. Ho, ho, ho." He laughed out loud. Then he went to the thermostat to check the temperature. "Are you cold? I can turn it up if you like?"

I was amazed at his attentiveness. He was perfectly charming. He poured me a glass of wine, which I refused, as it was far too early in the day, and he asked how I was settling in. He told me how hard he had found it when he first moved here, but how happy he was now with his wonderful wife and three children. It was hard to comprehend that this was the same man who had been shouting at Daniel five minutes ago.

"So, Mrs Connor..." He sat on a padded red velvet seat shaped like a throne with gold embroidery lettering on the arms that said SANTA. It was very grand. "Would you like to sit on my lap?"

What? I wasn't sure I heard him right, but assumed he was joking, so I laughed and quickly sat on the only available seat I could see. It was a chaise longue, red velvet with gold embroidered piping, positioned next to his throne.

I perched on the edge. "Thank you so much for seeing me. I know you're a busy man."

"I am indeed, but never too busy for the lovely ladies of Christmas Town."

Why does every line you utter make me shiver?

Donald leant across and placed his hand on my knee.

I froze. *What are you doing?*

"So, what is it you want?" He squeezed my knee before leaning back into the white fur rug that trailed across the back of the throne. There was another one draped on the back of the chaise long.

"Thank you for seeing me." I kept my eyes on the floor. If I looked directly at him, I felt I might freeze like Mr Tumnus in Narnia. "I haven't been here long—"

"No, you haven't," said Donald, slurping his wine from a 'Santa is cool' mug.

"But I think the residents here at Christmas Town would like to be more involved?"

"Think or know?"

What? "I know the residents would like to be more involved, and I'd like to suggest some improvements."

"Improvements? I'd love to hear what you think we could improve on here." His tone had changed, and his voice was low and slow.

"Not here at the Ring." I laughed nervously. Donald's face was still as his eyes moved up and down my body. It was very disconcerting. I tried to move back, which was difficult on a chaise longue, as you look like you might lie down, which was definitely not the plan.

I looked around me, avoiding his gaze and searching for inspiration. His room was full of furniture. A chunky mahogany desk in the shape of a sleigh and two bookcases crammed with books ran from one end of the room to the other. My eyes ran down the spines, reading the labels. Most of them were self-help books or books about business. *'How to Win Friends & Influence People* and *Seven Habits of Highly Effective People*. "Have you read all these books?"

"I have. I believe it's very important to keep up with new ways of thinking, especially where business is concerned."

That's good. Maybe you'll be supportive of improving Christmas Town?

"I was at the Home Watch meeting recently and there was a discussion about the lights and not everyone is happy with—"

"The residents aren't happy?"

"It's just the lights and not all the residents obviously, but—"

"So, a few people are unhappy we have state-of-the-art lights." The way he said it made me sound stupid.

"Yes, they are amazing but—"

"And they cost a great deal of money, as we are committed to ensuring our residents have the best of everything."

Stop staring at my legs. "Yes, we know, so we have a proposition—"

"What kind of proposition?" His voice hovered over the words as his eyes hovered over my legs.

I feel sick. "Er, not a proposition, but a proposal."

"You know I'm married, right?" He winked before adding, "but that's never stopped me before."

Breakfast is on the way up. "I meant a business proposal."

The shortness in my tone made him sit up. "What is the problem, then?"

I took a deep breath. "We want to make it feel more personal."

"I like personal."

That's not what I meant. "What I mean is... is that it's very regimented in Christmas Town and there is no room for individuality."

He stood up. "More personal?" He walked over and sat next to me on the sofa.

"No, not personal." *I don't want to give him the wrong idea again.* "Individual is what I meant." I squashed myself up against the edge as far as I could go.

"I agree. It could be more personal." He put his hand on my leg, further up this time.

I closed my eyes. *Please stop. This is not what I meant.* Time stood still, and I didn't know what to do. Just then, there was a knock at the door. I looked up at the ceiling. *Thank you, God.*

Daniel's face appeared and I'd never been more pleased to see him. "I think Mrs Connor's time is up and you have your three thirty meeting," he said, looking directly at Donald.

Donald swiftly stood up. "Yes, of course." I saw him glare at Daniel before he turned to face me. "Mrs Connor, it's been a pleasure." He held his hand out to help me up, which was necessary getting out of the chaise but unwanted. His hands were clammy and made my skin felt itchy. "I wish we'd had more time. Maybe you could come back so we can discuss this in more detail?"

I didn't understand what he was saying. He was talking a foreign language, and I was just nodding, desperate to get out of there. I threw the proposal on his desk and ran out of the room, Daniel following behind me. I held it together until I got to the staircase.

"What's the matter?"

"Nothing. I'm fine." I lied.

"I knew this was a bad idea. Are you okay?"

"I'll be fine. You go." I tried to keep my voice as even as possible.

He hugged me. "We'll talk about it later. Forget about it now."

Forget about it? Are you kidding? The man who represents Christmas, the man adored by children all over the world, the man called Father Christmas, was actually a pervert. I would never forget this.

Chapter 34

I made bread when I got home. The kneading and pounding were therapeutic and better for my health than the bottle of wine I so desperately wanted to open. Not only was Donald a bully, but he was a predator. Happily feasting on vulnerable women. It made me feel sick. I couldn't understand how Daniel could work for and admire him the way he did. Did he know and ignore it? Or did he not know what he was? I hoped it was the latter but if it was, how did I tell him the truth?

I had baked my third loaf of the evening when Daniel arrived home earlier. He opened a beer from the fridge as he paced up and down the kitchen floor.

"I told you it wasn't a good idea. He's a tough boss, but good at his job." He sounded like a lawyer preparing the closing arguments for the defendant. "It's true he can lose his temper and make the office a living hell for everyone working there, but can you honestly say you have not felt the pressure to get the job done?"

I wouldn't know. I'm not allowed to know what it's like, remember?

"We are only human. Those of us with more demanding roles feel it more deeply, more keenly than those of us who can sit back and let things happen."

Are you talking about me?

"Donald is a driving force."

Yes, he likes to force himself on women.

"And isn't it natural to lose one's temper when pushed?"

My turn. "I would argue that although no one would question the work ethic of Donald, one would expect someone in the position he holds to speak to their employees as people of equal standing and to treat them thus. And to lose one's temper in front of work colleagues and behave unprofessionally is almost tantamount to… treason."

"Treason? What are you on about? "

Got carried away. Need to stop watching Law and Order. "What I mean is, it shouldn't be acceptable for him to demean his work colleagues in that way?"

"He was only shouting. When he gets stressed, he takes it out on those around him. It's just the pressure. He does it all the time."

Only shouting? What about the other stuff? "Someone should say something to him."

"Like who?"

"He must have a boss. He works for the Company."

"It's not that simple."

I cocked my head to one side, just like my grandma's dog, when she didn't understand what was going on.

"The role of Father Christmas. It's the Holy Grail. Everyone wants to be Father Christmas." Daniel pulled out a stool and sat down. "But you can't just put on a red suit, grow a white beard and be Father Christmas."

There were conditions and they were non negotiable.

- He must have lived in Christmas Town for five years
- He must be over thirty-five years of age
- He must have a minimum of 10 recommendations from the other departments
- He can serve two terms only and a term of office is five years

It seemed being chosen as Father Christmas was like being elected President, but without the campaigns or television appearances.

Daniel continued. "That person then officially becomes the C.O.C

."

I spat my beer out of my mouth. Some of it went down my nose, which made it fizz and bubble inside. "What?" I wiped my mouth and nose with a tissue.

"The C.O.C. The Chief of Christmas."

"Seriously! That is the funniest thing I've heard, and it really sums him up."

Daniel was looking at me as if I was talking in Finnish.

"Donald. The COC." I didn't sound out the letters.

"Oh, I get it. I hadn't even thought about it. Most companies use acronyms."

"Even that one." I was laughing hard now.

Daniel smiled. It had been a while since I'd seen his face looking anything but stressed, and I wondered if this job was worth it. Having met his boss, I was convinced it wasn't.

Opening the oven, I took out my last loaf. "So, what's your plan?"

"For what?"

"For the future? What's next after being the COC's whipping boy? I'm assuming you're not going to stay in this role forever."

Daniel brushed the hair that had fallen over his eyes to one side. "Donald has another three years of office before his term is up and I can't see the Board voting for him again."

Interesting? "Why won't the Board vote for him again?"

"He's good at the job, but it's the other stuff." He raised his eyebrows.

You know.

"It's not good for business."

Or for any woman in Christmas town.

"There are some good people on the Board."

"Like who?" I was enjoying this rare moment of relaxed conversation between us.

"There's Stefan. He's the Finance Officer of Christmas."

I spelt it out. "The FOOC."

"No. The FOC," said Daniel, not sounding it out. He laughed.

"It's good to see you laugh."

He looked at me. "I'm okay, Chrissie. And I do have a plan. After executive assistant is the FOC and then maybe the COC?"

I didn't laugh this time. Daniel had never mentioned this before. I knew he was ambitious, but this?

"At first, I didn't think it was possible, but I've seen how the company works. I understand their mission, and I know I could add value. My skills and knowledge are expanding all the time and yes, Donald is difficult, but he's taught me a great deal."

"We can be thankful for that, then." Whenever Daniel mentioned his name, the hairs on the back of my neck stood up like a dog. And how I would like to bite him.

Daniel grabbed my hand over the kitchen table, ignoring my sarcasm. He explained his trajectory and how we could have an amazing life in Christmas Town. He was asking my permission to pursue this dream he now had.

But this was problematic. How could Daniel carry on working for Donald? I was afraid of the impact this would have. And what did this mean for me? I had already agreed to leave my home, to follow him and his career. I knew I would have to take a back step in finding a job and it probably wouldn't be a career I wanted to pursue anyway, but still. This was about him chasing his dream, his goals. I stared into his eyes. Those beautiful hazel eyes always won me over, hypnotising me into agreeing with whatever he wanted to do.

"I've always believed in you, Daniel, and I knew you would change my life. But I didn't think it was going to be like this."

Having ambitious dreams requires support. He needed me to stand by him if he was to go for what he wanted. If in twenty years they did a play about our life, what role would I play? The stagehand organising the props or getting the actors ready for their big moment? Or the lighting engineer who creates mystery or suspense? Or would I be the carpenter? The person who builds the sets and makes the home the actor lives in. As I went through these thoughts, I realised I was imaging myself behind the scenes. Daniel was the star, the leading actor. I was the stagehand. Was that how I saw myself? Putting others and their needs first.

I was silent, thinking.

"I know this is a big decision to stay here in Lapland. All I'm asking is that you think about it."

He kissed my hands and glided out of the room. Lighter, happier. But this wasn't just about staying in Lapland and supporting him. If we were to stay, I needed a role too and not one that was chosen for me or convenient for everyone else. I might be the stagehand, but that would be my choice. And what Daniel failed to realise is that without all the people who make up the cast and crew there is no play, no film, no show, and it's the team who makes a star. Without them, he is nothing.

But what did I want? I knew I needed a project. I knew I could organise people. And I knew I could help change things. Not just for myself, but for everyone in Christmas Town. But changing the town was one thing, changing people's behaviour was a great deal harder. And where did I start with Donald?

Chapter 35

The following week, I arranged a night out with Alex, Nic, Savannah, Katrina, and Toni in Rovaniemi. There was a festival, where all the bars and pubs served new craft beers accompanied with Finish delicacies. We went to the Antlers Arms, where the music was easy listening and settled into the squashy sofas next to the fire.

"So, tell us about meeting Father Christmas?" said Savannah. "Is he jolly?"

"Did you sit on his lap and tell him what you wanted for Christmas?" joked Toni.

"He wanted me to."

"What?" they all said at the same time.

"I think we are going to need more drinks," said Toni, rushing to the bar. "Talk about something else for a minute."

Nobody spoke except Alex, who muttered something to herself about men and taking advantage. After what seemed an eternity, Toni returned placing a tray laden with pint glasses on the table.

"Continue," ordered Toni.

I told them the whole story, with every comment and innuendo. "But the worst part for me was how Daniel reacted when I told him, or rather how he didn't react."

"Don't tell me," said Alex, putting her glass down on the table. "He said he was just having a bit of fun."

The pub was filling up and becoming noisier, so the girls huddled closer.

Nic shook her head. "I don't know how many times I've had my bum groped and whenever you say anything, it's always batted away with 'Don't you know how to take a joke'."

"I don't bother saying anything. I just smile and move away as quickly as possible." Typical Katrina. She never made a fuss.

"I've not had a bum grope, but I've had a couple of boob rubs." We all automatically looked at Alex's huge cleavage, which was hard to miss. "I know what you're thinking. Yes, they are large, but these were deliberate boob gropes. Blokes who think they can put their hands on me in full view of other people and think it's funny."

"I had a full-on flash from some teenager out on his bike once," said Toni. "He rode past me, stopped up ahead, dropped his trousers and started stroking the snake. I didn't know whether to feel flattered or outraged."

Savannah waved her glass around to get our attention. "I wonder what men would do if we all dropped our knickers and started rubbing our clits."

Our mouths dropped open astounded that Savannah would even think about this, let alone say it, and then we all burst out laughing. I was enjoying this camaraderie, the closeness we now shared through our mutual situation. We were all wives of working husbands in a strange cult we weren't a part of, so we made our own. It felt comforting to belong.

"Any joy with the job hunting?" asked Katrina.

"I don't know why you're so keen to do that. I enjoy not working," said Savannah.

"I know I made some suggestions at the last Home Watch meeting how we could improve our homes, but now —" I paused. It sounded ridiculous in my head.

"Go on," said Katrina encouragingly.

"I want to change the town."

Alex smiled. "Our girl wants to change the world."

We'd had many conversations recently, and she knew my intentions better than me. But it was the first time I'd voiced this with the others. "I was thinking about what we could do to the town. Let's face it, it's not difficult as anything we did would be an improvement on what's there."

"I agree. But what can you do? You don't make the rules," said Toni.

I told them how the proposal for the Board about the house changes was ready, but I also wanted to get everyone's thoughts and ideas about the town, so if there was an opportunity at the meeting, I would have persuasive opinions not company propaganda.

"But I don't know how to do this. It's too cold to go canvassing opinions and the Home Watch meetings are too controlling. I want to know what people really think."

"I know, I know," said Nic, her arms flailing in the air. "What about writing on the Internet?" Seeing my confused face, she added, "You know, you write on a computer and then send it out into the universe for people to read on the World Wide Web. It's called blogging." She sighed at the lack of response from the rest of us. "Do you all not know what's going on in the world? It's the latest thing."

Daniel talked about technology, but he'd use lots of terminology and I would glaze over when he discussed the details.

"I'm not sure the company would allow that," said Toni, bringing me back down to earth again. "They like to control everything, so I can't see them agreeing to something that everyone in the World could see."

"Maybe not, but it's worth trying. They do love technology," said Nic.

"True but how many of the residents would have access to a laptop or computer, anyway? I mean, have any of you got one?"

The girls all raised their hands.

What! I'm the only one who doesn't? I felt foolish. If this was a trend the girls were supporting, I was behind the times. It made me wonder how many other residents had this device in their homes already. And if I wrote something on this blog thing, then I could get information to all the residents and find out what they really thought.

"The company is always saying how advanced they are," said Nic.

"Apart from the way they side-line half the population," said Alex.

They were right on both counts. The company was technologically advanced, but maybe the technology could work for the women, for once.

Chapter 36

"I'm going to write," I announced later that evening as Daniel and I ate dinner.

Daniel had been silent since he got home. I tried asking him about his day while I was cooking, but he didn't want to talk about it. Something was up, and I wasn't sure now was the time to tell him my plan. But I couldn't keep putting it off.

"Aren't you going to ask me what I'm writing?"

Daniel glanced down at his phone again, the continual beeping like the background music in a restaurant. "What are you writing?"

"I'm going to try this blogging thing and write something."

He still didn't look up. "Right."

"Yes, write." *Are you listening? To what I'm saying?*

"Right."

"What?"

"What?"

"Daniel, did you hear what I just said?"

He huffed and looked up. "Yes, you're writing or drawing something?"

It was my turn to huff. "I said, I'm going to try doing blogging and write something." Daniel didn't say anything. I folded my arms and stared at him. "I listen to you when you are talking about your work, and I ask you questions. Your lack of enthusiasm is disrespectful."

"My work is important." He buried his head in his phone again.

"This is important."

"Is it?"

I didn't know whether he meant the act of writing or me actually doing it. "No, I'm serious. I want to do this."

"Why?"

"Because I need a job. I need to do something. I thought you understood after our holiday back home."

"I get it, but what about your skiing lessons and your coffee mornings with the girls?"

Patronising. "I like my coffee mornings, but I don't want to just talk all day. And it wouldn't interfere with the skiing. Although I'm not getting any better."

"Maybe you should concentrate on the skiing and not start another hobby."

Hobby? Keep calm. Breathe. Continue.

"I think this could be more than a hobby. It could be a proper job."

He snorted. "You have a job. You write the minutes for the meetings."

"That's not a real job. I don't get paid."

"Will you be paid for writing?"

"Er, no." *Slight flaw in argument.*

"So you're going to do something else that you won't be paid for and spend less time at home doing the stuff you should be doing."

I can't believe you just said that.

"It doesn't matter anyway."

It does to me.

"And you're not a writer."

How would you know? My heart raced, and rage boiled up inside me. *I'll show you.* "I wrote a school newspaper." As the words left my mouth, I felt foolish.

"A school newspaper? I didn't know that."

"You don't know everything about me."

"Obviously." He paused. "I didn't know you wanted to be Rupert Murdoch."

You think you're so funny.

He put his phone down on the table. "And what will you write about?"

I paused just long enough for him to look up. "I thought I'd start with the history of Christmas Town, then canvass people's opinions and feelings on what we can do to change Christmas Town."

Daniel reacted like he'd just discovered a bugging device in our kitchen. "You can't do that," he whispered, looking around him.

I tried to keep my voice equal, but the more I spoke, the harder it was to stop the quiver in my throat. "I can."

"You can not." Every syllable was clear.

I didn't expect you to react like this. I was quiet, trying to think of what to say next.

"Have you found out if you can write this? Does the company know what you intend to do?"

I looked up at him. The surprise on my face obvious.

"You haven't asked, have you? I told you, Chrissie. The company has to vet everything, they must give their approval. It's the way it is."

His uneasiness worried me. *What is so bad in writing about Christmas Town?* "Okay, I'll ask someone."

"Who?"

"I don't know. You must know someone I could ask? You work there."

"I can't do that. I can't ask the Company for special treatment when I've just joined them."

Special treatment? Just joined them? I hate it when you talk like this. "You haven't just joined them. And it's not special treatment. It's asking if I can write a couple of articles about the place."

I got up from the table and stood behind him, putting my arms around his shoulders. "I know I haven't thought this all through, but I need to do something."

I kissed his neck hoping it might help my case. "If you could just get me a name of someone I could talk to at the company."

"I'll try but don't get your hopes up. I've got to get on with this." He shook me off.

The closeness I felt at Christmas had vanished, leaving me cold and confused. It was like Daniel turned into a different person when he was in Christmas Town, one I didn't know or more worryingly, even like.

Chapter 37

Not surprisingly, Daniel didn't get me a name. He said he didn't want to ask for preferential treatment for his wife and was too busy with his job. So, I asked Valma to help instead. She was delighted, keen for Christmas Town to communicate more and personally arranged a meeting with Sven Shields, the company's Public Relations executive.

I was nervous sitting in the company's waiting room. I hadn't dared to come back here since my meeting with Donald, but today he was away at a conference.

I looked around the room. On three sides, the white walls surrounding me were devoid of anything fun or colourful, which was disappointing considering this was the headquarters of the company who makes Christmas. It could have been any large corporation. The long corridors downstairs contained offices and men in white coats. Upstairs was smaller and more intimidating. The space was divided up into separate offices, all with black matching furniture and large imposing desks populated with screens, phones, and stationery.

A door opened, and a gentle voice called for me to enter. I walked into the room of Mr Shields. Valma, knowing how nervous I was, reassured me he was a good man who was happy to help.

I physically felt my mouth drop open. There was no mistaking Mr Shields was a good man. His face was good, his eyes were good, and from what I could see through his tightly fitting short-sleeved shirt, his body was good. I was slightly distracted by the smell of milk that's turned.

He shook my hand. “Hi, I’m Mr Shields. My friends call me Sven.” He smiled and a large row of perfect white teeth revealed themselves. Even his teeth were good.

Dazzled by his smile, I was a little slow in responding to his greeting. “Am I a friend?” *What did I just say?*

“Sure. Call me Sven.” He motioned for me to sit on the sofa as he sat back against the edge of his desk. I stared at the muscles in his arms, folded across his chest.

I wonder what it would be like to be held in your arms. Why am I imagining this?

“Now what can I do for you?” he said.

A lot of things. Perspiration rolled down my armpit to the side of my waist. *What is the matter with me? I’m acting like a dog on heat.*

I tried distracting myself by focusing on the patterned hard floor. “I’d like to write about Christmas Town, but my husband said I would need the company’s approval.”

“Your husband is correct. It’s Daniel, isn’t it?”

“Yes. He works for Donald Pittman.”

“Mrs Connor? Are you looking for something on the floor?”

I looked up into his dreamy green eyes that reminded me of hillsides and lush green landscapes and palm—

“Mrs Connor?”

“Huh! Er, no, er.” *You sound like an idiot. Say something sensible.* “I like the flooring.” *Pathetic.*

“Thank you. Nothing to do with me though.” He flashed his hypnotising smile again.

Get yourself together, Chrissie. Concentrate on why you are here.

“I wanted to talk to you about an idea I’d had to write about Christmas Town?” Looking into his eyes made me feel all dizzy, like I was being hypnotised. There was the smell again. *What is that?*

“Why do you want to write about Christmas Town, Mrs Connor?”

Be honest. “Because it would give me something to do.”

“Oh, are you not busy with home life, learning new skills?”

Maybe honesty is not the way. "Well, yes, but I want to do more." What I wanted to say was if women could work, then I wouldn't have to have this conversation.

"And what do you want to write about?" He uncrossed his arms and placed them behind him on the desk, which made his chest stand out more. My mouth salivated. He was like Svengali, making me focus on him rather than the answers I wanted to give.

Chrissie! Stop looking at him. It's a mind trick. I looked down at the floor again. It was safer.

"Just simple things. Everyday life here at Christmas Town."

"Like what?"

"What the residents are up to, concerns they might have or ideas to improve the place. I also thought I might do some personal pieces like a day in the life of our COC or what it's like to work at the Ring."

He sat up and folded his arms across his chest. "I'm not sure anyone would be interested in that."

Interesting reaction. I've touched on something. Need a different angle. "It's just for us, ladies. We want to know what our husbands are doing."

"I'm not sure it would be very interesting for you, ladies. That's why we have a full programme of events to keep you entertained instead."

Entertained? Is that what it was called?

"Oh, I know and it's all very helpful, but we feel we could sympathise more when our husbands come home late from work if we knew what they had to endure."

I watched his shoulders relax, as he resumed his perched position.

That's it. That's the angle.

"I see. And is there anything else you are thinking of?"

"Oh, just some recipes and maybe a few helpful housework tips. You know how us ladies like to bake and clean." *Let's keep the myth going.*

I couldn't believe I was saying all of this, but it seemed to work.

Sven stood up and extended his hand. "Thank you, Mrs Connor. Let me run this past the team and I'll get back to you. I hope you understand we must be very careful of what information is available to the public. Our ancestors worked hard to build this organisation and keep its workings a mystery to the world."

"Why is that?" I smile my biggest smile, so he's not suspicious.

"For the sheer pleasure and enjoyment of the children who benefit. The story of Father Christmas is legendary, and we wouldn't want anything to spoil that." He smiled his biggest smile, too. Touché Mr Shields. Spoken like a true PR man.

The smell returns, only this time it's sour or mouldy bananas. It's all very weird, and I'm grateful to leave the room.

Chapter 38

Daniel came home from work earlier than usual, keen to know what happened. I was making dinner in the kitchen.

"He said he'll be in touch once he's spoken to his team." I left out the weird smell and my bizarre attraction to Mr Shields. I didn't feel it would help the situation.

"Sven's a nice guy. Did he seem supportive?"

I know what you are asking. "He was nice, yes. He told me they'd discuss it," I replied.

"Whatever happens, I think you should be proud of how brave you were in going to ask for something that's never been done before."

I'm confused. You told me I needed to get approval.

"If they agree, what would you write first?"

I'm still confused. You're interested now?

I put the vegetables I was chopping to one side. "I don't know. Maybe an introduction to Christmas Town?"

"And then what?"

"Maybe some interviews with long term residents." I pause. *Say it.* "And maybe some more in-depth articles about what happens here in Christmas Town?" I watched his face. "Maybe about the Ring?"

His head shot up, and his eyes widened. "I didn't think you would write about work."

"What's the matter? Got a secret?" I laughed, but he didn't seem to see the funny side.

"I just ask that you don't embarrass me."

Embarrass you? And what or who are you afraid of?

Even though I had followed his instructions, he was still against me doing anything that might disrupt his workplace. 'This wasn't the way things were done,' he told me on a regular basis. You didn't ask and you certainly didn't question. Daniel and I couldn't agree, and we spent most of our time apart. I was beginning to wonder if any of this was worth it.

***

I decided they were likely to say no to my request, anyway, so I was very surprised when Sven phoned to say I could go ahead.

"Think of it as a personal diary. I'm sure you must have written one when you were a young girl with all your thoughts and secrets." His voice was deep and sexy and completely off putting. "You can write about Christmas Town and the recipes and tips, but on a personal computer, which we will provide, of course. Once I've approved what you've written, this can be sent to everyone in Christmas Town through email."

Writing on the computer is something Daniel does for work, and now I can do it too?

"So, everyone will see it?"

"Yes, if they have a computer. And if the company likes what you write, they may send it further afield to other towns."

Send it to other people? I could see it now. 'Life in Christmas Town' by Chrissie Connor. Me, a nobody, can now do something important. I'd be famous.

But what if the company doesn't like what I write? What if the residents don't like what I write? What if I can't write?

You're over-analysing. It's only a couple of articles about Christmas Town, not a Pulitzer-winning novel.

Eventually, the voices in my head subside, and I grasped the most important thing from this conversation. I had a job, although there was no mention of any payment for this writing.

***

All I knew of Daniel's work was what he told me, and the snippets the wives pieced together from each other. The main aim for writing this on-line diary, apart from giving me something to do, was to gather public opinion and suggest change. But this was an enormous opportunity with the company, and I wanted to build up their confidence in me and in myself. It had been a while since I'd written anything other than a shopping list, and I was desperate to make a good impression. I started small.

'Welcome to Christmas Town.'

But all the residents live here, so I'm not really welcoming them to Christmas Town.

'Christmas Town. The truth is out there.'

Too sci fi.

'Christmas Town.'

Short and to the point. It will do.

This is my first diary entry about Christmas Town, and I'm very excited to tell you all about Christmas Town. If, like me, you are new to Christmas Town, I'm sure you would like to know more about the place you're living in. Well, the first thing you will notice is how cold it is. The climate here is tough, and it's cold and dark for most of the year.

Not bad. They probably know it's cold, but I'm sure they will appreciate the use of the word 'climate'. Important to use trendy buzz words.

Lapland is an area, not a country.

Factual. Good.

Many people make that mistake. I did!

Good. Making it relatable.

We are in the Finnish part of Lapland, which is as big as Switzerland,

Holland and Belgium, all put together. That's big!

Interesting fact.

We are 8 km away from our neighbouring town Rovaniemi, which is often referred to as the capital city of Lapland, even though there is no actual capital city since Lapland is not a country. But you know that now, don't you?

I re-read the first draft. Writing this was harder than I thought. All it did was tell everyone what they already knew. I would not win any awards for hard-hitting journalism, but the company would be reassured I was no Kate Adie. The next one would be better.

***

The residents knew about what they could see, but what about what they couldn't?

I began. 'Christmas Town Centre. Is it the centre of everything?'

Witty and intriguing. I read somewhere starting with a question was a good way to hook the readers.

'Have you ever wanted to know what happens behind the scenes in the centre of Christmas Town? I have. And there is one person who has the inside scoop.'

I hadn't decided who the lucky person would be yet but this article was an enormous improvement on the first one, and I was enjoying it. I could feel the cogs in my brain turning again. And there was another bonus. As the articles were being sent to the residents of Christmas Town, my profile in the community snowballed.

Janne Neva, from across the road, waved at me now, even though I had lived opposite him, and seen him leave for work every day since we moved in.

Dorotea Korpi, from the next street over, called round with a Cloudberry jam she often made for the Home Watch meetings. "I normally charge, but this is a gift to welcome you to the town. Because you're new."

How lovely. It had only taken six months to acknowledge my existence. Working with these statistics, the whole town would soon know who I was in two years.

Alex was more positive when we were having our daily catch-up over a coffee.

"You're famous," said Alex.

"I'm not sure four hundred words about a small town no-one has heard of is the same as being famous."

"Probably not, but it's more exciting than hearing about the weekly rubbish debate about what can be recycled."

"Maybe I should write something about that?"

Alex grimaced. "Please don't or you will have to stop being my friend. By the way, I liked your latest entry and thought for the week. 'Being a little fish in a big pond isn't a bad thing. It means you have room to grow.'"

It was a deliberate tactic to introduce 'Thought for the week'. So far, the Company had happily sent out my snippets of information and I wanted to keep it that way—for now. But I wanted my next entry to focus on life in Christmas Town from a woman's perspective, and I knew needed to be careful.

In the five articles I'd written so far, I praised the technology used in Christmas Town, but in the latest one I slipped in a comment about individuality and asked for people's opinions. I wanted to know what the other residents thought, but I wasn't sure the company did, and this was risky. But maybe they would be okay about it? Maybe they weren't as bad as I suspected them to be? Maybe they would be open to suggestions to change Christmas Town? I realised there were a lot of maybes.

Chapter 39

TV studio, 2009

For the first time since the interview began, I notice the atmosphere in the studio has changed. Ms Grey looks bored, crossing and uncrossing her legs in 'the best possible taste' like Kenny Everett.

I'm not telling Ms Grey what she wants to hear. She wants me to talk about Rudolph and the gang grazing in snow-covered fields, houses made of candy cane sticks and the smell of hot chocolate billowing out of the chimneys. But Christmas Town was nothing like that, not then.

"Of course, it wasn't all work."

Ms Grey sits up like a meerkat. "That's good to hear. I assume, in a place associated with the greatest holiday of the year, you have plenty of parties and celebrations." Her eyes grow wide, her pupils dilate, willing me to give her what she needs.

"What is Christmas without a good party or two?"

Ms Grey breathes out, relieved.

"At least three times a year we hold the Elf Workers Ball. Everyone dresses up in costume and we play games like Pass the Christmas Parcel, although we use the reindeer to rip the paper off. They like to get involved in the fun. You have to watch Dancer though, as she likes to eat everything, including paper."

Ms Grey laughs.

Good. This is what she wants.

"And we have reindeer races, where each reindeer carries an elf on his back, and they fly to one warehouse about two kilometres away, then back to the start."

She likes that one.

"And we also have a 'build a snowman' competition. Four teams compete using whatever they want to build the tallest, fattest, skinniest, most lifelike snowman they can and Father Christmas judges. It gets very competitive, and there have been lots of arguments over the years."

As I said this, I made a note to myself to investigate the possibility of trialling some of these competitions and games with the guests. Although what I'd said about Dancer was true. You couldn't trust her not to eat whatever she found.

"And all the while you can smell spices and dried fruits coming from the kitchens, where they are making cinnamon biscuits and Christmas cake, roasting honeyed hams and turkey slices in the ovens and stirring hot chocolate and warmed wine in huge silver vats."

Ms Grey's stomach growls. Too much talk of food, and judging by the size of her, she didn't eat a lot.

"Yes, we have some great parties."

Some embellishment, but not all made up. Most people kept to themselves in Christmas Town, cocooned in their own homes, avoiding the weather and other humans. There were a few social events, but the first party I ever went to in Christmas Town was because of me.

Lapland, March 1996

When the online diary was first sent out to the resident's computer in-boxes, Christmas Town was divided. Half of the residents who had a computer welcomed change, whereas the other half didn't know what an on-line diary was and thought I should do my duty as a housewife, not ask questions or opinions on where they lived.

Daniel's reaction was confusing. He was delighted the company accepted my suggestion, but also guarded whenever I tried to ask his opinion or get him to read my work.

I took the next Home Watch meeting notes round to Gerrard's house. He allowed me to continue taking the minutes when he realised Jansen was not up to the job writing only three sentences at the last meeting, as he couldn't hear what everyone had said.

Gerrard's reaction was expected. He made it clear whose side he was on. "When I worked there, we adhered to the rules, and we wouldn't have changed anything. We were grateful we had such good accommodation."

"I thought it would be good for the residents to have a say in their community. Wouldn't you like to know what's going on now you're retired?"

His eyes flinched before he took a deep breath and inflated himself to full height. "No, I would not. It's worked very well for the last one hundred and fifty years." As he spoke, he seemed to shrink, as if the air was being expelled with each word spoken.

"But just because something has worked for a long time doesn't mean you can't try to improve it?"

"I will be in touch about the notes in due course. Good day, Mrs Connor. " And with that, he pushed me out the door and slammed it shut.

Thank goodness the reaction from my friends was different. Nicole announced she was having a drinks party in my honour, and inviting the neighbours. I was very excited, although it was more to do with not having a proper social evening since getting here.

"No one has had a party yet, and it's so difficult to meet up with this weather," she said on the phone. "And what better way than with the start of a new venture?

"It's only a personal blog." I thought it was a little extravagant to hold a party in my honour when I hadn't done anything, although I welcomed hearing people's thoughts first-hand.

"Stop putting yourself down, Chrissie. It's a big deal here in Christmas Town. Alain told me they never allow any kind of information sharing, which is a big deal, and add to the fact you're a woman and I think you'll see this is a special occasion and one worth celebrating. I must go now, but be at mine at seven pm sharp. Our star attraction needs to be there early, as everyone will want to talk to you. See you later."

I didn't hear her take a breath as she rattled through the justification of this party. The phone line made a low humming noise as I put the phone onto the receiver. She was right about one thing. We needed this. Christmas Town was beautiful and unusual, but it was isolated. The weather was a major factor, but it wasn't just the weather. I couldn't see a connection between the residents and the company, the workers, and the housewives. It was a giant jigsaw puzzle, and we were all separate pieces, housed in our individual homes with no reason or means to meet up. It was like we were deliberately kept away from one another, and a party could be the answer to make the pieces fit.

Chapter 40

Lapland, April 1996

At seven o'clock, we walked to Nicole's house, braving the minus fifteen-degree temperature. I looked up at Daniel through my frozen eyelashes. He hadn't said a word since he got home from work, seemingly far away in thought. The cold sat heavy on my chest, ominous, or was I more nervous than I realised? I took some deep breaths. Then the front door opened, the warm air a welcome release from the clutches of Jack Frost.

"Come in, come in. I'm Alain. Nicole's husband."

Nicole's husband was not I what I was expecting: dark-haired, with thick-rimmed glasses and so short even I towered over him. Nicole was so glamorous in comparison. They were an odd couple, like Tom Cruise and Nicole Kidman.

"Good to see you, Daniel."

The two men exchanged words as Alain ushered us into the hallway.

"Nicole is in the drawing room." His black round spectacles wrinkled up the bridge of his nose as he laughed at our bemused faces. "It's the living room, but she likes the word 'drawing room'. Makes it grander, apparently."

Daniel carried on talking to Alain, and I went to find Nicole.

She didn't disappoint. She had draped herself over the fireplace in a fabulous cocktail dress. I half-expected to see her smoking a cigarette from a long cigarette holder, just like Bette Davis.

"Darling, you're here. I love your dress. Very apt."

I was confused. It was a simple black and white dress.

"Black and white, like a newspaper."

I laughed. "It's a blog, not a newspaper."

"It's words on paper or a screen or something. It doesn't matter. It's the same thing. But what does matter is I need to show you off."

The men joined us just as Nicole finished her sentence.

"I need to tell you a joke," said Alain.

"Oh, please, don't Alain. You're not funny at the best of times," said Nicole, shaking her head.

"This is a good one." He sniggered, already laughing at his own joke. "What is black and white and red all over?"

Daniel and I shook our heads. Nicole rolled her eyes again.

"A newspaper! Get it. Black and white and 'read' all over. You think it's the colour, don't you? But it's not."

"It's a blog," I repeated. *This is going to be a tough evening.*

"Well done, Ronnie Corbett," said Nicole. "Now answer the door. The guests are arriving," said Nicole, smiling at me.

"Who's invited?" I asked as Nicole ushered me into the room.

"Everyone," she replied. "The whole town. Wouldn't be fair to single people out."

"Everyone?" *Will Donald be here?*

Nic took my hand, reading my face. "Don't worry. I didn't invite him. Now go mingle. You'll be great."

As I walked into the hallway, I saw Rikkard and Daniel talking together in the corner of the room. Alex stood to the side of them. I waved but she didn't notice. She seemed to be in a trance. I went over to her and asked who she had seen so far, but she was more interested in finding out how she could refill her empty glass. I changed the subject.

"What did you think of the last article," I said, "about suggesting changes to involve the women?"

"Great idea. Very good." She was still scanning the room as she said this, and her face lit up when she spied Alain holding a champagne bottle. "Just going to get a refill. Want one?"

Alex had said she was cutting down on her drinking, but that wasn't the case tonight. She seemed to be in a funny mood, one I couldn't help with. She made her way through the groups of people now nestled into their preferred positions, some standing, some sitting. There was one large group of people all standing around Nicole. She saw me and waved me over. She was doing a brilliant job of hosting and introducing as many people as she could, in a style combining Bridget Jones and a game show host.

"This is Ingrid. She is a mother of twins and is a wonderful painter."

"This is Terese. She has three grown-up children all away working and bakes the most exquisite macarons."

"Erikka enjoys reading crime novels and hiking in the Wild Taiga region."

She then turned to me and said, "And this is the fabulous Chrissie Connor. An undiscovered new talent who is writing Christmas Town's first online blog. She's a valuable member of the Home Watch meetings and makes amazing reindeer burgers."

I didn't recognise the person Nicole was describing. Ingrid, Terese and Erikka looked impressed.

"So, you're the famous writer," said Terese. "I must admit we were all a little sceptical when we heard the company would allow an unknown to write about here. You must know the right people." She stared at me, her eyes narrowing as she waited for my response.

What are you insinuating?

My mouth remained shut, so Nicole stepped in.

"Chrissie's husband is Donald's right-hand man. He has a very important job as the executive assistant to Father Christmas."

Terese breathed out a long 'Oh' and looked at the others, who nodded their heads in solidarity.

What does that mean? What do they think? That I only got to write this because of Daniel? But that's not true.

I couldn't get the words out. I should tell them it has been really difficult to be allowed to do this, but my mouth is dry. I just smile at Terese. A ridiculous half-hearted simper which basically communicated to Terese that she was right. Terese, Erikka, and Ingrid all turned to Nicole, the look of 'Next' etched on their faces. I wasn't even able to ask their opinion on women working in Christmas Town. I couldn't think of anything smart to say, so I stood silently listening to Nic continue her introductions and amusing anecdotes of how she now knew what a garlic press was.

Nic had really gone to town with this party. A couple of young men dressed in white shirts and black trousers were weaving in and out of the guests, topping up half full champagne flutes. There were two girls with identical hairstyles, carrying large platters of individual food. Prawns and beef wrapped up into delicate little packages and pastry cases filled with cheese and smoked salmon, you popped in your mouth in one go, very different from the parties I went to. Back home, party food was small bowls of crisps and nuts dotted around the room, balancing on the side of an armchair.

"Hey, why are you looking sad? It's a party for you." Daniel swayed next to me, both hands clutching a very full champagne glass. "Want one?"

"No." I really didn't. I thought a drink might make me brave, but the smell only made me feel sick. It was weird.

He swallowed the contents of his glass in one go before putting his arm around me. "Smile! You're the star of the show, aren't you?"

Every time he spoke, he sounded so patronising. I couldn't work out what was wrong with him and why he was so bothered. Was he jealous? No, he couldn't be. Everyone was pleased with him, although he hadn't spoken about work for a while. I presumed it was because we hardly saw one another. Whatever it was, he could at least be supportive tonight. I mean, I had moved two thousand miles for his career.

"Sure, you don't want one?" Daniel offered me a full glass and swallowed it in one go, when I declined.

"Think you'd better slow down, Daniel."

He leaned in close and rested his hand on my shoulder to balance himself. His breath stank of alcohol and his eyes were glassy. "I'll leave you to talk to the neighbours. That is what you're supposed to be doing, isn't it?"

He was drunk and on this night of all nights. But this party was for me, and I wasn't going to let him, or those other women spoil it.

Chapter 41

There were a few neighbours I recognised and some members of the Home Watch who never stopped to chat at the meetings but were happy to talk to me tonight. They were keen to be featured in the next online article. Gerrard and Valma weren't there.

"I think they had plans," Mia said when I caught up with her in the kitchen. I nodded, going along with but not believing the reason. Gerrard would never want to congratulate me.

Mia looked a lot slimmer than when I last saw her, having now had her healthy baby. She took out a photograph from her purse. "A boy. Adam. Very smiley."

"You look amazing. Motherhood obviously agrees with you."

"I wouldn't go that far, but I'm happy. And what about you? Any plans?" Mia examined my face.

I hated this question almost as much as I hated the question 'So what do you do?'

"Oh, gosh no. Not yet. We want to wait for a while." *Not strictly true. I want to wait.*

"I liked your last article about changing appearances. The houses could do with an update."

That's good. You like it. But you haven't mentioned changing the environment, just the houses.

"Very brave of you to speak up like that. What did the Company say about all of this?"

"They've been very supportive."

Mia raised an eyebrow.

“Honestly. They even supplied me with my own personal computer. It surprised me to begin with, but they, Mr Shields, really seemed to like the idea.”

“I am sceptical. I won’t lie. The company doesn’t usually listen, but maybe they’re changing with the times. I thought it was a great idea to introduce a bit of individuality to where we live. So simple in painting a door a different colour.”

You’re still only talking about the houses.

Maybe she doesn’t want to discuss this in a public place. “So, you’d be in favour of a makeover?”

“Yes, please. Could that extend to me too? I’d love a makeover.”

I laughed and leaned in closer with my next question. “What did you think of extending the improvement to all of Christmas Town? You know, involving the women?”

She looked at me blankly. This was not good. Mia hadn’t been at any of the Home Watch meetings since I took over the minutes. If she didn’t understand what I meant about change, I obviously didn’t make it clear.

“Hello,” said a voice. “My name is Reginald.”

A dapper gentleman dressed in a three-piece suit with emblems on his jacket interrupted us. He looked like he stepped out of a war film. “I hear you’re famous,” he said, with a loudness I imagined was because of a much-needed hearing aid.

I turned red. “Oh, no. Not at all.”

“But you’ve written a book.”

“Where did you hear that?”

“Nikita told me you were famous, as you’ve written a book.”

“I’m very sorry, but I don’t know who Nikita is and I’ve not written a book. I write an online diary or blog they are calling it now.”

“Bite a dog? I’m not sure that’s a good idea.”

“No, a blog. I’m writing a blog.”

“What on God’s earth is a blog? Sounds like a blob. Is it a blob?”

This is not going well, but at least you're talking about it.

"It's some words you write on a computer and then, with the help of technology, it's sent to lots of people to read on their device."

He stared at me. I think I lost him at 'computer'. "Are you writing a book?"

"No."

"Have you written a book?"

I shook my head.

"You're not famous then?"

"I'm afraid not."

"Well, why did she tell me you were?"

I didn't know what to say.

"Well, if you ever write a book, then I have some marvellous stories for you about the war. I could write a book, but my fingers don't work so well now."

"Oh, lovely. Thank you."

"Don't forget. When you are writing a book Reginald would like you to write about the war. And don't mess with that dog. It's never a good idea." He tried to march off, but kind of shuffled instead.

"I'm not sure he's read your article," said Mia, trying not to laugh, "but plenty of ideas if we ever go to war."

It felt like I was already at war. Canvassing opinions was proving harder than I imagined.

"What was all that about a dog?" asked a bemused Toni, who appeared by my side as Mia walked off.

"Apparently I'm writing a book."

"About a dog?"

"Not you as well." I swallowed the contents of my glass, which was now warm as I'd held it for so long in my clammy hand. I felt nauseous, yet I'd only had one drink. I also had no idea where Daniel was. I'd not seen him in ages.

"You look lovely," I said, changing the subject. "I don't think I've seen you in a skirt before."

"I do possess one or two." She straightened her skirt, looking very uncomfortable. "Let me introduce you to Brandon?"

We made our way over to where Brandon and Daniel were deep in conversation. His enormous frame almost dwarfed Daniel. I didn't know they knew each other.

"So, you're writing a newspaper?" Brandon glanced from me to Toni with a dead, straight face. "Only joking. I know you're writing a blog."

I breathed out, unaware I had been holding my breath.

"Good for you. Saying what you think and all that." Brandon's reaction surprised me, considering what he had done to Toni. "Are you going to dish the dirt on the top dogs?"

"So, you are writing about a dog!" laughed Toni.

"Hilarious," I said.

Daniel looked completely confused, but also very drunk.

"Toni?" asked Brandon. "Funny? She's never said a funny thing in her life. No. I think you'll find that I'm the funny man, not Toni. Isn't that right, darling?" He tried to kiss her on the cheek, but Toni stepped to the side, and he kissed the air instead.

I found that funny. Brandon didn't think so. He made an excuse and strode across the room, dragging Toni behind him.

"Oops. That didn't go down well," slurred Daniel.

"I don't think I like him."

"He's alright when you get to know him."

"I didn't know you knew him."

"I didn't until tonight. But I talk to people I don't know, and then I know them. That's how it works?"

You're so drunk. "Why do you always do this?"

"What?"

"Stand up for the man?"

"Same reason you always stand up for the woman? Another drink?" Daniel waved his empty champagne flute.

I shook my head. Daniel went off to find more champagne dissolving into the crowd of people now congregating in Nicole's living room.

Daniel had been drinking more and more recently. He liked a drink, but this was excessive. Something was bothering him.

"Chrissie! I haven't spoken to you all evening." Alex flung her arm around me and kissed me three times. Her enthusiasm as bubbly as the champagne she was quaffing.

Oh dear. Another one who's had too much.

"Come and meet some dear neighbours."

She introduced me to a variety of couples, who all knew I was writing the blog. I listened as they told me how long they had lived in Christmas Town. All of them had taken on the traditional roles of the women raising families with their husbands working at The Ring. Most of them were retired.

"Have any of your children stayed in Lapland?" I asked the large group of people now gathered around me.

There was silence. They looked at one another, some looked down, shuffling their feet.

Interesting! What have I touched on?

"Take a look around, Chrissie. Do you see any young people?" It was Terese again. Back for another insult. "Mine got away as soon as they could. Can't blame them, though. No prospects here."

"If you're a girl, anyway." This time, Erika piped up.

"You're both wrong."

We all turned to look at Jan. My neighbour. "There are no opportunities here because the town is not flourishing."

Exactly what I thought!

"The only people who come to work here are people who don't know what it's like."

Like Daniel.

"They are struggling to recruit, and I can't see it changing."

Daniel is always telling me the residents are happy with how it is, but that's not what I'm hearing. Are the people of Christmas Town ready for a change after all?

I overhear a conversation beside me.

"Those meetings have been going on for years and the formats always the same. Nothing ever changed."

Another younger woman nodded her head. "I thought when I came here all those years ago, our lives would be enriched with the beauty of this area, and we would grow as a community."

"But what they didn't tell us is how prescriptive everything is. Their rules. Company rules." This woman pushed her hair behind her neck to reveal a small flower tattoo.

"We knew nothing before we moved here." Alex's pitiful voice spoke. Her mood had turned, and the alcohol was no longer keeping her on a high. "I used to be a lawyer. Now I'm a nobody. Mrs Nobody."

The other women were silent. All distressed to see effervescent Alex in pain.

I put my arm around her bare shoulders. She was warm and her face flushed. "You could never be a nobody, Alex."

"But we do— feel like that."

I turned to see Tanya Pittman standing behind me. My first thought was Donald, but there was no sign of him. Tanya looked stunning. Her conker-coloured hair was shiny and swished every time she moved her head. I'd never seen her look so good. She was almost non-existent at the meetings.

"Alex is correct. We feel like— a nobody because— we have no purpose. For a community to thrive— everyone needs a purpose— men and women. Our situation is— dominated by working men— and their rules."

The other women echoed her views. Yes, we could work outside the area. But working outside of Christmas Town meant you were on the outside and how can a community grow if the residents don't feel they belong?

"Your blog— should help. We need to— tell the company— what we want. Our houses are— just the beginning."

I could write a mission statement. Daniel is always talking about that. I just need to work out what it is first.

This was what I needed to hear. Most of the residents who attended the Home Watch meetings were older and more accepting of the life here. And maybe that used to be okay? But Christmas Town was our town. We were young. We lived here and wanted it to thrive. We needed to change Christmas Town if it was to survive.

Chapter 42

I couldn't wait to tell Daniel. I was sure he'd be impressed with my idea of a manifesto about what the residents want. Surely the Company would be supportive of that? I searched through the house for him with no luck, but I found Alex. Or rather, heard her. She was holding onto a door, finding it difficult to stand upright but not finding it difficult to air her feelings, which she wanted everyone to hear.

"It's the way of the world, or this world anyway," Alex announced to the room, another ten decibels higher than her last comment. "Women were born to be subservient. We're compliant. Good breeding stock. Another drink, over here," she shouted to the waiter, raising her glass up in the air so he could see her. She needn't have worried, as he, along with everyone else in the room, could hear her.

"Alex, are you okay?"

"Of course," she declared, her voice too excited for me to believe. "Spit spot. Tickety boo."

"Let's get some air," I said, ignoring her refusal and pulling her through the partygoers to a small room at the back door which led into a conservatory. The door to the outside was slightly open, probably to cool down the guests. In the corner of the room was a chair loaded with coats, so I moved them and forced Alex to sit.

"Why are we in here?" she slurred. "I want to go back to the party."

"And you will. Just have a rest for a little while. Get ready for the next part of the evening."

"Okey, dokey." She went quiet and fell slightly forward.

I propped her up, so she ended up resting her head on my thigh. *Poor Alex. Things are obviously not good.*

I shivered. It was getting quite cold standing by the open door. As I went to push the door closed, I heard voices. Poking my head around I saw the outline of two men standing together, puffs of smoke escaping their mouths when they talked, their appearance blanketed by the cold fog that had descended during the party.

"So, how will it work?" I heard one man ask.

I didn't recognise the voice. The wind and their proximity not helping.

"Denis in IT has rigged up a website address that makes it look like it's real."

What are they talking about? I felt bad listening in, but only for a few seconds as, being the newly appointed mouthpiece for Christmas Town, it was important I knew what was going on.

"So, this online diary thing goes to the residents of Christmas Town?"

Was someone else writing an online diary?

"Yes," the voice answered.

The company didn't mention this. I thought I was an exclusive.

"Someone said they might send it out so other people could read it?" asked the other voice.

I heard a muffled snigger. "Nah. Not going to happen. They don't want anyone else knowing."

"And they don't change what she's written?"

"That's where it gets clever. Chrissie's diary entries were quite boring. Until the last one."

Me? This is my diary they are talking about.

"To begin with they weren't worried, but lately there have been some murmurings from Donald and the Board that she's stirring up the residents. They don't like it. They don't want anyone's opinions, especially not a housewife's. So now when an article is published, if they're not happy with what's been written, they rewrite it."

"Makes sense. I could never see the Board allowing this kind of information sharing, but I feel sorry for Chrissie."

"To be honest, she'll probably get bored after a couple of weeks and jack the whole thing in."

How dare they! They don't even know me.

"I hope she doesn't find out, for your sake, Daniel."

Daniel? What? My Daniel?

I felt someone had shot me with an arrow straight through the heart. It physically ached. Tears streamed down my face as I moved away from the door and their laughter. Alex moved her head, so I was now cradling it in between my legs. She made little sounds of snores and snatches of breathing interspersed with slurred affirmations of 'Love you.'

How could he do this?

I wiped my eyes with the sleeve of my dress. "Up you get, Alex! We need to get you home."

But really, it was me who needed to get home. I couldn't be here any longer. I felt sick.

Holding Alex up, I dragged her to the hall where, fortunately, Rikkard was coming out of the downstairs toilet. He shook his head. "The demon drink again. Thanks, Chrissie I'll take it from here."

I rushed to get my coat and boots from the cloakroom. I needed to get out of here. I couldn't breathe. The party was still in full swing, so no one would notice me leaving and no one looked like they would go home anytime soon. On my way to the door, frantically trying to get dressed in all the layers I had to put on, I saw Nicole chatting to Katrina in the kitchen.

"Darling, you're not going, are you?" said Nicole, when she saw me wrapping up in layers like a Christmas present.

"I've hardly spoken to you all night," said Katrina. "Are you okay? You look like you've been crying?"

That was all that was needed for the waterworks to start again. Katrina rushed to hug me. "What's the matter? Are you okay? Please don't cry."

"I'm okay," I said in between sobs. "I don't know what the matter is with me. I keep crying all the time." Not the real reason for my crying, but it was true I had been spending an inordinate amount of time lately with wet eyes.

"Period, probably? It usually is— or our husbands—"

The tears came again.

"Oh, dear. Is Daniel being an idiot?"

I shook my head, unable to say the words out loud. *Daniel lied.*

"I'm not on my period at the moment," I said.

The feeling of a brick weighing down on your womb is not something you forget. In fact, it had been quite a while since my last period.

"Or you're pregnant?" Nicole laughed.

I laughed too thinking how absurd that was. *Unlikely, with the amount of sex Daniel and I have had recently.*

And I had my period recently. Didn't I? I started doing calculations in my head. *When did I last have it? I think it was...before Valentine's Day. Oh god! Could I be pregnant?*

I stopped laughing.

Chapter 43

I couldn't speak to or even look at Daniel for the next few days. He was supposed to support me, be there for me. Weren't those the vows we made to each other when we got married? And then the other slightly bigger issue: I was pregnant. I knew Daniel would be pleased. He'd be ecstatic. It's what he'd always wanted, but I thought finding out I was pregnant with the man I loved would be romantic. Telling him over a candlelit dinner where he broke into tears and told me this was the most amazing moment of his life. And then going to the doctors for them to confirm what a peed-on stick told you the day before. Then there was the excitement of keeping it secret from all but your closest family and friends until twelve weeks, when I would announce to the world that I was indeed 'with child'.

What actually happened was, while annoyed and upset with 'said husband' for ruining my chances of a future career, a worthwhile community project and a life, I bought five different pregnancy tests, as you can never be sure they are accurate, and used all of them at home by myself as husband was working late, to find out I was definitely pregnant.

After three days, I still didn't know how I felt about it. My plan was to write and start a campaign to change Christmas Town, maybe start a movement to change people's views on women working here. And by people's, I meant men. Getting pregnant was not the plan.

I looked up at the clock. Nearly ten. Daniel had promised he'd be home soon, and that was at eight. Dinner and my appetite were ruined.

"Sorry babe," said Daniel when he eventually arrived home just before eleven, dropping his bag on the floor to hug me. "Work is crazy. It should calm down soon, and then I promise we will spend more time together." He paused and pushed me away after noticing I wasn't hugging him back. "That was lukewarm. You're not still annoyed, are you?" He went to the fridge and pulled out a beer. "I can't help working late. It's my job."

"Aren't you lucky you have a job? I thought I had one too, but I didn't. It was all a lie. And you knew all about it."

"What do you want me to do?"

I don't know.

"What?"

"I don't understand why."

"Why what? I didn't do anything."

"You went along with it. You lied to me."

"I didn't lie."

You've never lied before now.

"Chrissie, I know you're upset, but what could I do? I'm in an impossible situation." Daniel reached out for my hand, but I pulled away.

You should have stood up for me. "You should have stood up for me."

"They make the rules." He turned his back to me and picked up his beer bottle from the table. "I can't say anything. And even if I could, I'm too busy working."

"You said you supported me. You said I was brave and using my initiative."

"And you are, I do, but the company decided they want more input into the blogs you write." He swallowed the last of his beer. He'd finished it quickly.

"If I want to initiate change, I have to find out what people really think, and that isn't something the company will allow. I wanted people's opinions."

"You can still write them. Isn't that the point?"

"But I wanted them to read what I had written. I don't want to be Donald's puppet. Not like you." The moment the words left my mouth, I wanted to suck them back in again.

Daniel strode over to the fridge and took out a beer.

That's not going to help.

"You're only talking about some articles that some people might read. It's not going to make a difference."

I couldn't listen anymore. I ran upstairs and got under the duvet on our bed, my face hot tears streaming. I could hear him calling me downstairs, telling me not to be silly. But I wasn't being silly. I was hurt. How could I tell him he was going to be a father when he could do this? What father would do that? My father would never have done that. He always supported my dreams and told me to fight for what I believed in. I stopped. But Dad hadn't done that with mum. He hadn't supported up or stood up for her.

Was Daniel more like my dad than I'd realised? Had I married my dad?

I stayed under the duvet, lifting a corner of it so I could breathe and hear him when he came up the stairs to apologise, which I was sure he would do soon.

Silence.

When he comes upstairs and apologises, I will tell him about the baby.

I could hear the television go on downstairs.

If he comes upstairs in the next five minutes and apologises, I will tell him about the baby.

I wait five minutes. Nothing.

If he doesn't come upstairs soon and apologise, then I won't tell him and he'll be devastated, although he won't know, so I'm not sure that will be the case.

The television is still on. It sounds like the news.

Breaking news. Chrissie is pregnant and hasn't told Daniel. Chrissie said, 'Now he knows what it's like to be in the dark.'

I'm in the dark. Literally in the dark, under a duvet, waiting for my husband to come upstairs so I can tell him he's going to be a father.

It's ridiculous. No, I'm ridiculous because he's not coming, is he? He'd rather be downstairs listening to the news around the world than finding out our news. He'll be sorry.

Although at this moment, I wasn't sure he would be.

Chapter 44

I woke up at eight o'clock the next morning, still in my clothes from last night. Daniel wasn't next to me, but I could smell his aftershave in the air. I went downstairs. He wasn't in the kitchen, but there was a note.

'Gone to work. Will be back late'. No kisses. No 'love you'.

It's official. He doesn't love me anymore. And now we are going to have a baby and I will have to raise the baby as a single mother by myself.

I needed a distraction to take my mind off the three B's: blog, baby, and betrayal. Dusting and hoovering of the entire house had only taken me an hour. The vigour with which I attacked it sped up the process, but it meant I had more time to think, which was not good. Avoiding thinking, I opened a Finnish textbook and began practising some phrases needed to pass the language test.

"Mieheni on nimeltaan Daniel. My husband is called Daniel."

I could call him a few other names at the moment.

"Olen kotiaiti. I am a housewife."

And that is all I will ever be.

It was no good. It just made me think more about the blog. Or the blog that never was. I had to admit my imagination had got slightly out of control, dreaming of being the new Nora Ephron for my in-depth and riveting articles about gender bias and inequality in one of the biggest companies in Europe. Now I would be grateful if they let me write a dinner menu. And then there was the question of the baby. What was I to do?

I decided cleaning would be best and less problematic. As I began to tidy the pile of outer wear now snowballing in our coat cupboard, I heard a repetitive buzzing noise. It was coming from my handbag. I opened the bag and saw a light shining. I'd forgotten Daniel had given me a new phone they were testing for the Company. A Nokia 8110. I was used to moving around inside the house with our cordless phone, but with this phone you could use it outside. My memories of talking outside on a phone were from inside a phone box. Those red metal cuboid shapes, dotted sporadically along the roads, smelling of iron and urine. These beacons of joy, when needed, were as welcoming as hearing music from an ice-cream van on a hot summer's day.

It must be Daniel. I knew it. He is desperately trying to get in touch, to apologise and say how much he loves me.

"Hello? Daniel?" I shouted.

"Darling! How lovely to hear your voice."

Not Daniel.

"Robert!" Mum shrieked Dad's name so loud I nearly dropped it. "Chrissie is on the phone now."

"Mum? How do you know I have a new phone?"

"Daniel gave us your new number. It's amazing to think you are talking on a moving phone."

"It's a mobile phone."

"That's what I said. You sound very clear. This is a very good line, isn't it? Hang on a minute, your dad is going to listen in on the other phone."

"You've got another phone? When did that happen?"

I could visualise mum raising herself up. "It's cordless. Very upmarket. We got one with two handsets so your dad and I can speak to you at the same time."

What she meant was that dad would listen while she talked.

"How are you?"

I was quiet.

"What's the matter?" Mum's voice was concerned.

"Sorry! It's just hearing your voices."

"Oh, bless you. Did you hear that, Robert? She misses our voices. What time is it there?"

Not again. "I told you the last time. We are ahead by two hours."

"So that's ten o'clock your time, eight o'clock here."

"Yes."

"What's the weather like?"

"The same. Cold."

"What's the matter? Why are you so quiet?"

I can't tell them about the baby before I've told Daniel.

"It's nothing. Daniel and I were at a party on Saturday night and—"

"What was the party like? Are parties different in Lapland?"

"No. They're the same."

"How's Daniel?" Mum said, ignoring my tone.

I gulped down the air that was trapped in my throat, but it was no good. The tears came.

"What's the matter?"

"It's Daniel." And then it all came out. That he was working all the time, the fact he didn't have any time for me, the fact he had lied and, more importantly, he didn't care.

Mum was quiet and let me speak, unusually for her. "Is it exactly like that? I'm only saying because sometimes when we're sad we don't see the positives."

"It is. You don't know what it's like. I have no friends, no job and no husband." I blew my nose for the third time.

"Now you are exaggerating. You have a husband and Alex and Katrina are your friends, aren't they?"

"Yes, but they're not like my friends back home."

"And you said you were typing the notes of those meetings and starting a 'blob' or something?"

"A blog!"

"That's it. And Daniel is working hard because it's a new job and he has a lot to learn."

"I suppose so, but—"

"These things take time. It's still early days."

"That's not the only thing that's still early days." It was quiet on the other end of the line.

Maybe I shouldn't have said anything? Maybe she didn't hear me? "You still there?"

"Yes, I'm still here."

I was quiet now.

"Are you pregnant, Chrissie?"

"Yes," I whispered.

Then I heard sobbing down the line closely followed by, "Robert!" Mum screamed into my ear, forgetting to move the receiver away from her mouth. "Say something."

Dad cleared his throat. "That's wonderful news. Wonderful. What did Daniel say?"

"I— haven't told him."

"Why not?"

Because he lied to me.

Because I can't trust him.

Because he's a pig.

Because— I'm not sure I want a baby.

Saying it in my head sounded so much better than saying it out loud. "We argued."

Mum, having finally stopped crying, said, "That's no excuse. Your Dad and I are always arguing."

She was right about that.

***

Five minutes later I stepped out of the house to go and talk to Daniel. The morning fog had lifted, and there was a glowing pink tinge to the wispy clouds above me. Some light broke through, providing the daylight we so desperately needed and as it did so, shadows from the houses fell across my path. The conifer trees glistened, their morning coats dusted with icing sugar snow. It was beautiful. Maybe I was beginning to see what was in front of me more clearly.

Maybe a baby could be a good thing?

For whom?

Daniel will be happy.

What about me?

I felt guilty even thinking this. Women are supposed to want to have babies.

But I can't get a paid job anyway. I could still write. I will have loads of time when the baby is sleeping. They don't do much when they're little. And I can still try to change Christmas Town, at least with the houses.

After a brisk walk, I arrived at the Centre terminal where there were a couple of ski dogs parked. As I walked up to a waiting one, a ski dog pulled up and out got Katrina and Savannah, holding multiple shopping bags.

"Have you been shopping? Who knew there was so much to buy on a Tuesday?" I laughed, but stopped when Katrina tried to move the bags behind her.

"How are you, Chrissie? We were all a little worried about you."

Understandable, seeing as the last time I saw Katrina, I had been sobbing my eyes out. "I'm fine. What have you been buying?"

Savannah and Katrina were almost bursting, huge smiles on their faces. "I wasn't going to say anything until later but— I was buying for the baby," said Katrina.

"It's brilliant news," said Savannah.

My mouth dropped open. *Katrina told Savannah I'm pregnant.* "I can't believe you told Savannah?" I said, looking right at Katrina.

Katrina looked hurt. "I'm sorry Chrissie. I thought I would tell Savannah first. We're quite close, and I didn't think you would mind."

Mind? I only found out myself the other day. "When are you going to tell the other girls?" I couldn't contain the sarcasm.

Katrina said she wasn't sure yet, but maybe at our next coffee morning.

I couldn't believe what I was hearing. I didn't think Katrina would do this. "But it's not your news to tell."

"It is," said Katrina, looking confused.

Savannah put a protective arm around her friend. "It is Katrina's news. She is the one who is pregnant."

I couldn't say anything for a full thirty seconds while my brain tried to catch up.

Crap! They were talking about Katrina.

"I'm so sorry, Katrina. I thought you were talking about me." *Shit!* The words came tumbling out of my mouth like projectile vomit.

Savannah looked from me to Katrina. "You're pregnant too? That's wonderful news. Congratulations!" She hugged me as much as she could while wearing our twenty tog duvet coats.

Katrina wouldn't look at me, her eyes locked on the floor. "I would never say anything."

"I am truly sorry, Katrina." *I'm such an idiot.*

"I'm really pleased for you and Daniel," Katrina said with her eyes still downcast.

"We must run," said Savannah, pulling Katrina away from me like I had a disease they didn't want to catch.

I wasn't sure either of them would talk to me for a while and Daniel didn't even know.

Daniel! At this rate, most of Christmas Town will know before him.

Chapter 45

Waiting in the reception area at the Ring, browsing the magazines on the coffee table, I watched the receptionist writing things down and answering the telephone. Twenty minutes ago, he'd rung upstairs to tell Daniel I wanted to see him and was now irate offering non helpful comments like, 'He's a busy man' followed five minutes later with, 'Maybe an appointment would have been better?' And then, 'Are you sure you want to keep waiting?'

I looked at my watch. It was as if Daniel didn't want to know the news.

Why am I not a priority?

The longer I waited, the more irritated I became.

Why is he not coming? What is keeping him? Or should I say who? Maybe he isn't even in his office? Is he stalling until Daniel can get back to the office?

"Darling, there you are?" Daniel looked flushed as though he'd been running.

Why have you been running?

"What's the matter?" he asked.

"Where have you been?"

He looked puzzled. "Here. In work."

"But where have you been? I've been waiting ages."

"I was in a meeting, Chrissie."

"You could have made an excuse and ducked out."

"I would have if it had been an emergency, but it was a board meeting." Daniel looked around him and pulled me into an empty cubicle with chairs. "Look. Why are you here?"

"Am I not allowed to see you now? I thought women could still see their husbands at the Ring, even though they can't work here."

"Not this again." Daniel stood up. "All I'm saying is that it might have been better if you'd made an appointment for another day, or that we had agreed to meet for lunch and then you wouldn't have had to wait."

"I couldn't wait any longer."

"For what?"

"I'm pregnant," I said before I thought about how I might phrase it. *Has there ever been a more incredible scene since Gabriel told Mary she was up the duff?*

Daniel was silent for ten seconds, then pulled me into his arms. "My darling girl. That's wonderful."

His voice broke a little, and when I looked at him, he was crying. He wrapped his arms tightly around me and just held me. He hadn't done this in ages, and it felt nice.

"When did you find out?" Daniel tried to break the hug, but I carried on holding him, squeezing him tight to me. I needed to keep reminding him of how lovely a moment this was, and not let it be spoilt by what I would have to tell him next.

"Er, the other day."

He held my arms down and stepped back so he could look at me. He had this knack of making me tell him everything by staring into my eyes. *The old Jedi mind trick.* "When?"

"Saturday?" I could feel him flinch under his shirt. "But I didn't know for sure on Saturday. It was just a realisation that I could be, so I went to the pharmacy on Monday and got a test to check."

"You knew yesterday?"

Look down. Keep looking down. "Yes."

"Why didn't you tell me yesterday?"

It's your fault I didn't tell you. "You were late home, then we argued and then I was annoyed, so I didn't think it would be the right time."

He sighed but pulled me to him again, and we stood hugging for a few more moments.

Phew! It's all okay.

"This is great news, Chrissie. I can't wait to tell everyone. I mean, I won't say anything until your parents know, but then we can tell people. Can't we?"

Crap! I was silent.

"I'm so sorry, Chrissie. That was thoughtless of me. Of course, you want to wait until we know everything is okay with the pregnancy before we say anything. Don't you?"

I feel so guilty. He was staring at me now. *The force is strong in this one. I'll have to tell him*. "I've told my parents."

Daniel raised his eyebrows and ran his fingers through his hair, drawing attention to the hidden streaks of grey. He looked tired.

"But it was an accident." My mouth wouldn't close. "It's your fault though because you didn't get home until late, and we argued—"

"And you didn't think it was a good time to tell me, but you've told your parents."

The repetition of his words spelt out what I had done. I can't believe I didn't tell him what is arguably the most important news you tell your partner, along with 'I'm dying' or 'I'm divorcing you', because of a stupid diary.

He hugged me again. "Never mind. It's done now. Were they happy?"

I nodded, afraid to open my mouth.

"Are we going to wait until we tell anyone else? I just want to be clear about this, so I don't get into trouble."

He laughed. I didn't. He saw.

"What is it?"

"I might have told some others."

"Who? You don't know anyone else."

That's unkind. I know lots of people and haven't told them about the baby.

"It's a funny story actually— I was on my way to tell you when I bumped into Katrina and Savannah—"

"You told them too. So, everyone knows!" He pushed his hands into his trouser pockets, head down looking at the floor, like a small child in a mood.

"Not everyone. That's silly."

He was silent.

"What I mean is that, yes, I've told a few people, but they've promised not to say anything, and I promise not to tell anyone else, so it's all okay. It is okay, isn't it?"

"I suppose so."

I put my arms around him and waited for him to gradually uncurl, and hang his arms by his side until finally resting them on my hips. A wet fish could have hugged me better, but it would do for now.

"I have to get back to work." He pushed himself away. "We can talk about it later. The baby, I mean."

"What time do you think you'll be home?"

"Shouldn't be late. Meeting has been going well, so we should finish by six."

He leaned over and kissed me before turning away. It was the first time he'd ever kissed me on the cheek.

Chapter 46

The evening couldn't come soon enough. Everything was prepared. The dinner was cooking. I'd turned down the fluorescent lights in the dining room. It would have been perfect with a few candles dotted around the room, but it was against company rules. I took the cork out of a bottle of red wine to let it exhale or something Daniel told me I should do with red wine. I checked my watch.

Daniel was now late. I put on some music. This, as it turned out, was a good idea, and wasted lots of time. It took at least ten minutes to look for and retrieve my MP3 player—another new piece of technology we were trialing for the company—from behind the cushions on the sofa. Scrolling through the tracks was another ten minutes, then it took me fifteen minutes to work out how to play the music through the speakers. I checked my watch again to the sound of the Spice Girls telling me what they want, what they really, really want. Seven o'clock. He was now officially late, which although not unusual, was surprising considering how excited he'd been to talk about the baby.

Maybe he's still working?

He would have called.

Maybe he's had an accident?

The traffic from the Ring to here is all automated.

Maybe he's been kidnapped?

This is not Columbia.

Maybe he's with another woman?

There aren't any at the Ring. One bonus.

I phoned him. The constant ring tone droned on until a voice said, "Please leave a message." Voicemail. I looked at my watch again.

Maybe it's wrong? I checked the clock in the hall. *Not dodgy watch. Just dodgy husband. Where the hell is he?*

I didn't want to be cross. Not tonight. I went to get my book. Thank God for Amazon. They were a new company that could deliver books wherever you were in the world. Nic and Toni had been raving about them weeks ago, saying this was the future of deliveries and logistics and if only we could do this with all goods.

Half an hour of reading later, Daniel staggered in.

"Where have you been?"

I heard him drop his bag on the floor. "In work."

I walked to the hallway. "But you were going to be home at six. What happened?"

He took his outer layers off, struggling with the cashmere scarf, which he was inadvertently tightening rather than loosening around his neck.

That might come in handy later.

"It's not late. I'm early compared to normal." He kissed me. The smell of beer was pungent, cloying, like 'Poison' perfume.

"You had time to have a drink, though?"

"I only had a couple. I had to wet the baby's head."

I crossed my arms. "You do that after the baby is born."

He put his arms around me and squeezed. A boa constrictor squeeze, which rendered my arms useless and therefore impossible to push him away. "We're having a baby. We need to celebrate."

"You were celebrating? In the pub? Who were you with?"

"Just some of the guys."

"Did you tell them?"

"Of course, I told them. We could hardly celebrate if I didn't."

"I thought we weren't telling anyone?"

He stopped squeezing, his eyes struggling to focus. "You did."

"That was different."

"How is it different?"

"I only told people I knew."

He laughed, releasing his grip, and stepped away from me. "I only told people I knew."

"It's different and you know it."

"How? You told the people you wanted to, and you told them before you told me." His eyes narrowed together, creating crease lines above his nose.

This was not how the evening was supposed to go. We were going to have a nice dinner and talk about the baby, and he would tell me how amazing I was and would kiss me and maybe rub my feet as they were tired after all the walking I had done today. But no, we were arguing about who we had told.

I sat on the sofa and beckoned him to join me. "Let's start again." I still wasn't sure about the baby, but the thing that worried me more was Daniel and me. We were spending less and less time together and he always seemed stressed. "I don't want this."

He jerked his head up, a shocked look on his face. "The baby?"

"No. I don't want this." I gestured to the metaphorical space between us, which had been growing rapidly over the last year.

He cradled his head in his hands. "I'm sorry Chrissie. But it's work. I have to do it. There is so much pressure to get everything done." He paused, reluctant to finish his sentence. "I don't have a choice and I don't know what to do. What do I do?"

For the first time since we'd arrived in Lapland, he was acknowledging maybe this wasn't the great adventure he thought it would be. But I had some acknowledging of my own to do. I was married to a workaholic who now drank to cope with pressures at work. I was pregnant. I had no job. I could leave Daniel and go home. Plenty of women raise children by themselves. But for all his faults, I still loved Daniel too much to leave him. I wanted to be with him, but things had to change, or we wouldn't survive. The problem was I didn't know how to do this.

Chapter 47

TV studio, 2009

Ms Grey nibbles the end of her pencil. "How interesting. Parties with reindeers. I'm sure our viewers would love to see that." She looks towards the camera, relating to the audience at home. She is listening again and keen for more.

"But life can't always be about parties, can it?" Again, she glances at the camera. "What did you do in Lapland?"

She pauses after each word emphasising the 'you'. Ms Grey is searching for more than I have given her. She is looking for the truth. But does she and the audience watching really want the truth? People say this all the time. They want the truth. *Tell me if you're having an affair. What do you really want? Does my bum look big in this?* But if we are told the truth we often end up hurt or sad. The truth is... we don't know what to do with the truth.

I must decide how I'm going to tell the truth. Do I tell Ms Grey that during that period I was at my lowest point? That I felt trapped in a world which didn't acknowledge women in the workplace or what they could add? And then there was my marriage. Now that Daniel was in the inner circle, he saw how deep the rabbit hole went and, although he didn't approve, he didn't say anything, either. If I tell the truth to Ms Grey and the audience watching at home, will they be happy or sad?

"Chrissie? What did you do?"

Her question rouses me from my daydream. I think for a moment and then say, "I left Christmas Town."

Ms Grey shoots the camera a look that could have come straight from an Agatha Christie whodunit play.

"Only for a short time. I wanted to experience Lapland."

Ms Grey's face relaxes, and I continue.

Lapland, Summer 1996

Winter had been a challenge for many reasons, but the summer months were just as hard. There is nothing in the Arctic circle to block the sun, so you have twenty-four hours of daylight. It was like stepping into a parallel universe where the laws of nature had been suspended. The locals made the most of the extra daylight hours by travelling or going on holiday. We'd been told by the other residents that it was like one big party that never ended, and the girls and I were ready for something different and the chance to escape for a little while.

"Let's book the Kylma Hotel in Rovaniemi," said Nicole, as we perched on chairs in the upstairs bedroom she had turned into a study. "Much nicer than the boring Inn." She pulled a face and we laughed.

The Inn was the Company hotel where they put guests as they didn't allow visitors to stay, ensuring Christmas Town remained a secret.

"Mari, my concierge friend, will sort us out."

Nicole had embraced the new technology of email and on-line shopping and turned her passion into a business. She helped the residents organise trips and excursions, could get her hands on anything, and had an enviable contacts list.

"Thank you for doing this, Nic," said Alex. She was still struggling but wasn't willing to talk about it. We knew the break would do us all some good.

"Not a problem. I've got tickets for the Midnight Sun Festival in Rovaniemi but what else? Nothing too strenuous," she said looking at my stomach. "Stand up paddling? Swim the arctic circle?" She typed as she talked, her red manicured nails tapping at the laptop she carried everywhere along with the latest Nokia phone.

"Better not," I said, "unless you want this one to arrive early."

She turned her laptop so we could get a better view over her shoulder. "What about going here?"

"Perfect," we shouted out, knowing that escaping Christmas Town for a week with girlfriends was just what we needed.

***

When I told Daniel about my holiday plans, his grey face worried me. Donald was still making life difficult for him, and my questioning everything to do with the Christmas Town was not helping, as was the lack of sleep and drinking too much. But more worrying, was the feeling Daniel would explode at any moment, and that we hadn't touched each other in months, not even a hug. I tried to ignore it all, pushing the worries down, burying them under the weight of the baby even though I knew they would both inevitably come out.

"The girls and I are going to go away for a few days. Maybe even a week?" I said, searching his eyes for some connection.

"That's nice." He forked his food into his mouth, staring at his laptop the whole time.

"Are you listening? Daniel?"

He looked up, a flash of recognition that he hadn't been.

"Sorry, Chrissie. Got to get this done for tomorrow." He closed his laptop. "What did you say?"

"I'm going away for a few days, with the girls."

"That's great. Where are you going?"

"Rovaniemi, for the Midnight Sun Festival."

"What a great idea."

You seem genuinely delighted I'm going away.

"It's good timing. I'm going to be so busy over the next few weeks."

How is that any different to normal?

"Will you stay at the Inn?" Daniel smiled, delighted with his suggestion.

Definitely not. "We have other plans. But I was wondering if you might be able to come join me for the weekend?"

The look on his face told me everything.

"I have work. You know how it is."

I do. I always know how it is.

He reached across the table, taking my hands in his. "I'm sorry, Chrissie, but make the most of it. There will be so much for you to see and do. You'll have a lovely time, and I can always do it next year."

I won't hold my breath.

***

We ignored Daniel's advice to stay at the Inn and went straight to Rovaniemi. There was so much more to do, and in the Summer, it felt like a summer holiday resort. Nicole had suggested staying near the beach, only a five-minute drive away from downtown Rovaniemi. It was actually a beach next to a river, not a traditional view of a beach, but then everything was different here. The water was cool, but the air temperature was hot enough to entice us to get into the water and swim. And we weren't the only ones. We were all speechless for about a minute when, from our sunbathing spot on the wide sandy beach, we saw two reindeer swimming in the river.

"I've heard of swimming with dolphins, but reindeers?" said Alex, pushing her sunglasses up her nose to get a better look.

Toni and Nic went to get ice cream while Alex and I lay back on the beach towel, soaking up the sun's rays. I'd missed the heat and felt like I was finally beginning to thaw out after the months of freezing weather. We were both silent for a while, listening to the intermittent voices scattered between the sound of the water dragging over the pebbles.

"So. How are you?" I asked. I'd been wanting to check in with Alex for a while.

"In a conscious effort to be sober, after what happened at the party, I'm channeling all my energy into my interior design work. Changing the inside of people's houses might help change how I feel on the inside too." She gave my hand a reassuring squeeze. "Don't worry about me. That night was just a low moment. At least we can keep each other company." Alex smiled and glanced towards my stomach. "What about you?"

"I'm okay but Daniel really needs a break. I hoped he might come here for the weekend, but—" I trailed off, feeling emotional and not wanting to make a scene.

"He loves you."

I shrugged my shoulders. "I've asked him to take some time off, but he always says he's too busy or something has come up or he will when it gets quieter, but it never does."

"I know. It's not easy being married to these men in this environment."

She was right. It was exhausting. She reached out for my hand and squeezed it.

Just then Toni and Nic came back, with ice cream dripping down the side of the cones onto their fingers. "You two, okay?"

"We're happy we're on holiday," I said.

"Understood," she replied as she handed out the ice creams. "I'm looking forward to tonight, although it seems so strange saying 'tonight' when there isn't any night."

***

Later that evening, we gathered with the rest of the crowds in the centre of Rovaniemi. Some people were wearing colourful traditional Finnish costumes to watch the procession of dancers and musicians, illuminated by the golden glow of the midnight sun. The folk bands struck up lively tunes and beckoned for us to join in the dancing. The rhythm was infectious and soon we were all showing off our best moves—even Toni who rarely did anything spontaneously.

When the dancing subsided, we followed the array of smells coming from the main square. Long trestle tables laden with freshly cooked salmon, reindeer meat and cinnamon buns were surrounded by a cheerful group of people. They laughed, talked, and shared stories, both traditional and familiar. We took a seat at one of the tables, feeling like we were part of something special.

As the night wore on, we moved to the huge roaring bonfires to eat sausages and drink cider for extra warmth. There was a group of men and women singing what sounded like traditional folk songs so the girls and I sat and listened. As I looked round at all the people with their relaxed, happy faces enjoying the night, I felt a tremendous feeling of excitement and pride in belonging to this rich cultural heritage, and it clarified what I knew was missing from Christmas Town.

After a couple of days enjoying all the free concerts and entertainment, we headed to the National Forest at Korkalovaara. This beautiful piece of paradise was where we hiked and picked cloudberries that looked like orange blackberries, listened to the sounds of the Arctic birds, and tried to spot all the creatures living in the woods. It was magical and the week flew by. We all agreed it helped to see another part of Lapland so different to Christmas Town, and although the others were content for now, I was more determined than ever to do something to make our town magical.

Chapter 48

After the party, I stopped writing the blog. There didn't seem to be any point if no one could read what I'd actually written, but if they thought that was going to deter me, they were wrong. I knew getting everyone together to share information would help build our community, so I started hosting get-togethers at people's homes. It was a huge success, and all the women enjoyed having someone to talk to during the long nights.

We talked about everything from current events to family worries. We made decisions on decorating our houses with eco-friendly paints and how salmon walls wouldn't quite match lilac doors. We also agreed to do most of the work ourselves, which saved the Company money and kept us busy and eager to do more.

The Board, surprisingly, had agreed to most of the outside changes we requested to the houses. I thought Donald might interfere as a way of getting back at me for not doing what he made clear he wanted us to be doing. At one point I found myself actually thinking I may have imagined his innuendos and wondered if I'd made a mistake. Maybe he was just being friendly? Then I remembered the look on his face and Daniel's. I decided it was better not to think about Donald and what he wanted and to concentrate on what I wanted. I still thought we could change other aspects of the town with regards women working, but the Board would never discuss how using women could create a better environment for everyone. Not yet anyway.

The next arranged get together was at Toni's house. A few of us were seated around a large wooden table with a bowl of fresh fruit in the centre, the chairs spaced evenly around it. Nicole and Toni were typing furiously on their laptops, responding to emails, and answering queries on deliveries of materials and paint.

"Tonight is going well," I said. "We have at least ten residents from every block, and they're really pleased with the changes made so far." We had made a start on the rendered walls, painting over the dull, smoky ash colour with a more uplifting tangerine, aqua or cerise. The eye-catching colours, too striking for a sunny environment, perfectly balanced the dark skies of Christmas Town and cut through the fog when the visibility was poor.

"You've organised us all so well. Thanks for looking after us." Alex kissed me on the cheek.

I knew she was talking about more than the house changes. Being able to use her creative side gave Alex an outlet to save her from insanity and alcohol. It did the same for all of us. But I was still curious. Curious about why Christmas Town was so old-fashioned and why it hadn't changed with the times? What were they scared of?

"And what about the other thing bothering you?" said Alex.

I smiled. Alex always seemed to know what I was thinking. Nicole and Toni looked up from their laptops.

Katrina walked into the room and sat down at the table. "You lot look secretive. What's going on?"

"Chrissie is about to tell us," said Toni, closing the lid of her laptop.

"It's nothing," I said.

"It's never nothing with you, Chrissie," said Katrina.

I sighed. "It still bothers me. Why we're not treated the same as the men? I know we've made some headway with the house changes, but I want more."

"I thought it was unlikely they would agree to the house changes, but miraculously it happened and that was all because of you, so I suppose you are the one to start the revolution or whatever." Nicole laughed. "But what else can we do?"

"I want to speak to someone within the Company or one of the members of the Board, yet that seems highly unlikely. Daniel won't help and I don't want another meeting with Donald. I need someone who knows what happens at the Ring, knows the history, someone I can trust."

"Why don't you speak to Gerrard?" suggested Katrina.

I pulled a face.

"I know he's not your favourite member of the community, but he has led an interesting life."

She had a point. He used to be Father Christmas. He would have some stories. The only problem was he hated me and he didn't trust me.

"Gerrard was once the most important person in Christmas Town. It must be difficult for him now."

"I just want answers and to ask questions," I said.

"I know, so why don't you get to know him, listen to him."

"Chrissie? Can I— speak to you?" The familiar voice pattern of Donald's wife, Tanya, interrupted our conversation. "The changes need— to be right— if we are— to succeed— with the next stage."

I wasn't sure what she meant. "Next stage?"

She leaned in close so only I could hear. "I think— you and I— want the same?"

I was now confused and slightly concerned with the whispering and leaning. *What do I want? Is this that swinging trend I'd heard about, the keys in the bowl scenario? Where did I leave my keys?*

"Change in— Christmas town. Real change."

I breathed out, not realising I'd been holding it in.

"I'll organise— a dinner party. Please come. We have much— to discuss."

I nodded as she walked off, leaving me elated that she felt the same way I did and wanted me to go to her dinner party.

A dinner party! I hadn't been to dinner party in ages. And there would be other people, people who might feel the way Tanya and I do and—

I paused while my brain caught up with what I'd just agreed to. *Donald will be there. Father Christmas.*

Chapter 49

A week later there was a good turnout for the Home Watch meeting, and lots more debate and interaction than normal. I hoped this was because of the regular get togethers.

Gerrard stood at the front of the room, wearing his bright blue trousers. He rocked back and forth on his feet as he tugged repeatedly on his red braces. The clashing colours, combined with his towering height, made him seem larger than life.

I stayed silent throughout the meeting, convinced Gerrard had his eyes fixed on me, willing me to interrupt but I resisted all attempts and felt very pleased with myself when we got to the end of the meeting.

"Are there any questions?"

This was it. My moment to keep quiet. I sat on my hands and smiled to myself, pleased I could keep my mouth closed.

"Chrissie, do you have anything to say?" Gerrard was looking right at me.

Why is he making this so much harder than it needs to be?

"You looked like you wanted to say something."

I shook my head dementedly, my lips sandwiched tightly together. *I will not say anything. I will not say anything.*

"Well, if you really don't have anything to say," he said to me, before addressing the room, "then let's finish this meeting and I look forward to seeing all of you next month."

The others got up to leave as I inched my way over to Gerrard. "Hi, Gerrard. Can I just say—"

"Oh, so you do have something to say. Why is your face so red?"

Holding your breath will do that. "I wanted to say I enjoyed the meeting."

He glared like a teacher studying an unconvincing student, his lips pursed together as his eyes squinted in disbelief.

"Thank you."

You don't believe me. "No, I mean it. It was very informative, and I think the point you made was valid, about people wanting to lie in on a Sunday morning and not listen to grating spades, clearing snow."

"Thank you, Chrissie." His eyes sparkled, crisscrossed with tiny blood capillaries, tinged with yellow, looked like they were smiling, and it made me happy. He must have been a great Father Christmas.

"I was wondering what life must have been like for you when you were Father Christmas?"

The sparkle in his eyes disappeared. "Why?"

"I'm interested. I know how hard the job is. Daniel tells me a little of what it's like for Donald and—"

He huffed. "Does he now?"

I've said the wrong thing. Maybe Daniel's not supposed to talk about work to his wife?

"What I mean is— Donald works very hard and—"

He huffed again, but louder this time.

Ah, this is to do with Donald, not Daniel.

"I wondered if you'd tell me what life was like when you were Santa Claus."

There was a long pause. Not a good sign.

"Is this for your— online diary?"

"No. I don't write it anymore. This is just for me. Your story is important. I think the people in this town should know how hard you've worked for the children around the world." I glanced down at my expanding stomach. "When my kid is old enough, I'd like to share your story with them."

"I didn't do the job for that."

He looked over at Valma. She smiled back at him. *Is it a sign? Has she spoken to him?*

"Okay. We can talk. I hope you're serious about this, Chrissie. I don't want to be ridiculed and I don't want the Company to look bad."

"I promise. That's not what I want to do."

***

Two days later we were sitting in his study, me on a small black leather chair, Gerrard behind his desk. The wall behind him was decorated with framed photographs from his time as Father Christmas: a family photo with the elves, a closeup of him and Rudolph touching noses, and a pack of men dressed in suits standing around Gerrard wearing his traditional red suit and holding onto his braces.

"So," I said, "What was it like being Father Christmas?"

Gerrard leaned back in his chair and closed his eyes. "To bring joy and happiness to so many children was the best job in the world. It wasn't hard to stay in character. I believed I was Father Christmas and so did the children. I knew what my duty was."

Gerard went on to explain how he learnt many magic tricks, and excelled at finding or making the special or unusual gift some children had asked for. "Nothing was too much trouble. That was the job."

Gerrard's face lit up when he spoke of the places he'd visited and all the children he made happy with his deliveries. There was no drama, only tales of good deeds and contentment. Gerrard had been a Father Christmas who took his job seriously.

"What did you miss most when you were no longer Santa Claus?" I asked, enjoying this relaxed and happy Gerrard.

Without hesitation he said, "The magic." And then his face changed. "Of course, being Father Christmas is a serious business, and the appointment of a new Santa Claus even more so." He pulled down on his red braces, almost to finish one thought before beginning another.

"When I was first nominated and then chosen as the new F. C," Gerrard paused and puffed out his chest, looking like a Sergeant Major telling his squadron the purpose of the mission, "the board included Donald. He was silent during meetings. Never said anything for the first few years. But then he started to have side bars with individual board members."

"I don't understand."

For the first time since he began talking, Gerrard looked uncomfortable. He looked around as if he was being watched. "Can I trust you? Valma says I should trust you and she is always right."

"Okay." I pulled the imaginary zip over my mouth.

Gerrard rolled his eyes. "It was odd. Donald would single you out and talk about something mundane and then he would ask you something more direct, but he wasn't asking. He was telling you what to think. It was odd." Gerrard looked at my confused face. "One time I remember he talked to James, the Company lawyer. When James was on his own, I asked him what he said. He told me he thought Donald was right about a debate we'd had about women working for the Company."

I raised an eyebrow. "And what was odd about that?"

"To begin with, James had been a supporter of employing women, but then he changed his mind. I couldn't understand it. But I realised it was Donald. He had a way of alienating you and making you agree with him, boxing you into a corner to get you to accept whatever rubbish he was selling, and he was doing this with all the board members."

"Sounds more like bullying to me. Did it work on you?"

"Really Chrissie?"

I shrugged my shoulders.

Gerrard looked around him like he was carrying out a covert operation. "I found out too late what he had been doing." He took a breath and continued. "A lot of the board members were retirement age and afraid to say anything in case they jeopardised their pension. When it came to re-election, Donald swung the vote and became the next Father Christmas. They packed me off with a bonus and the promise of a return to the Company, but it never happened. Mainly because I asked too many questions."

I smiled.

"Yes, like you. That's the problem with this place. Asking questions gets you into trouble and I have grown accustomed to accepting the 'status quo'. I thought if I went along with it, I could be more effective later."

"So, what happened next?"

"He fired most of the original board and the new crop were all hand selected by him. Goodness knows what he's promised them or paid them. Donald controls them and how they vote. He has a board who agrees with everything he says."

"But what does it matter? The job is still the same. Getting presents made and delivered to children for Christmas day."

"You would think so. But—"

I was silent. This was the first time I'd heard something concrete about Donald and his business practices.

"He's quite open about his resistance to working with women and will discuss openly his views on immigrants and how they are not to be trusted, but it's more than that."

"Like what?"

"The usual suspects. Money and power. If he controls the Board, he controls all the decisions. And if he controls the decisions, he controls the money. I wouldn't be surprised if he is stealing money from the company."

"But if this is true, surely we can get rid of him." I was smiling now. Finally, there was a glimmer of hope.

"It's finding the proof which is difficult. Everyone covers up for him."

We were both quiet, contemplating.

"Tanya has invited me to a dinner party," I said.

Gerrard's bushy grey eyebrows crept towards the middle of his face.

"I know you don't trust her, but I think she might help us. She talks a lot about change."

Gerrard stood up and began pacing around the room. "She's been married to him for ten years and said nothing. Why would she want to change things now?" He was quiet, pulling his braces back and forth. He seemed anxious. "There's something you need to know. About Donald."

"I know about his wandering hands."

Gerrard looked up in surprise, letting go of his braces, his hands flopping down by his side. "It's more than wandering hands. There have been women who found themselves in a— situation with him. Some by choice. The power of Father Christmas is quite an attraction for some." He paused. "Others have been— unlucky."

I tutted. "Unlucky? I don't think that's the word I'd use."

"No, you're right. I apologise. But they seem to be in the wrong place at the wrong time."

"You're missing the point. No-one should feel they are in the wrong place. If this is how he behaves, he shouldn't be Father Christmas. He shouldn't be anything." I was irate now. He had been behaving like this for a long time and no one had stopped him.

Gerrard was quiet, staring at the photos on his desk. "You're right. Being Father Christmas was an honour. It wasn't about the money or the status. It was about the red suit and the children, an expectation that you served the public. Donald sees it the other way round. Everyone is here to serve him."

Gerrard was surprising. I could see how much the role of Father Christmas meant to him, and yet he had confided in me. But was he ready to bring about change in Christmas Town?

"I think everyone has had enough, especially the women," I said.

"You've given me a great deal to think about. I can't believe I told you as much as I did."

Nor me and I have an idea. "Will you help me?"

"How?"

"I need to talk to the Board, but when Donald isn't there."

"I'm not sure, Chrissie. I know I said— "

"I thought I could start with explaining the renovation work."

"And?" Gerrard's eyes twinkled in the light.

You're perceptive. "I want to explain what it's like living here in Christmas Town and suggest some ideas to change it. That's all."

Gerrard silently paced up and down the red and white patterned carpet.

"We need to bring the magic back."

Gerrard turned to face me. "Okay. I'll see what I can do."

The thought of doing this made my stomach turn. But the hope Christmas Town could change for the better was the only Christmas wish I wanted. And where else should wishes come true than in Christmas Town?

Chapter 50

True to his word, Gerrard set about making plans to speak to the Board while I tried to find out when Donald would be away. I got my opportunity the next night when Daniel was working in the study at home. Surrounded by papers, I grabbed the edge of some and pulled them towards me.

"Don't get them out of order," he said, shuffling them back towards himself.

"I was just looking."

"Those are board papers. They're important. You don't understand."

His voice was angry. His face strained. This interjection happened daily, and though I became used to it, it still upset me he could speak to me like this. It was obvious working for Donald was not good for Daniel or our relationship. But I wasn't sure Daniel saw that or wanted to see it.

"Sorry. It's just I've got loads of work to do for this board meeting on Thursday and Donald is being particularly difficult, as he won't be there."

My face lit up at those words. Daniel mistakenly took my delight for interest in his work. He picked up a manuscript thicker than the Bible, bound with a black plastic spiral spine.

"This section is about compliance matters, and this section here is a strategy plan for expansion that I worked on with others in my team. It's all quite exciting—"

After five minutes of Daniel explaining the intricacies of board meetings, I wished I hadn't asked. I now knew why they called them 'board' papers. But Daniel's mood had lightened, so I thought I would tell him what Gerrard was organising.

His forehead creased like a concertina blind and his eyes darkened. "I don't like this, Chrissie. Why do you have to go too?"

Keep calm. Smile. "I'll be able to explain in more detail the renovations carried out so far. And as this has been my idea all along, I want to see it through." *I wish you'd be more supportive.*

"Maybe you should wait until Donald is back from America." Daniel scratched behind his ear, making it bleed. "He will think you're doing it behind his back."

He'd be right.

"And he'll be so mad. My life will be even more of a misery."

I didn't want to make things worse for Daniel, but he was thinking about himself, and I was thinking about the whole community or at least half of them. I had to continue.

"I promise I won't embarrass you."

Daniel was not happy, but I wasn't backing down, not this time.

***

At the meeting on Thursday, Gerrard and I took our seats at the oval mahogany table, the light from the giant glass windows cascading onto it. It was so shiny you saw your reflection staring back at you, like a mirror. The twelve men around the table, except for one, were a similar age to Gerrard. I was the only woman in the room.

The Board were more than happy to see Gerrard, as the chair of the Home Watch society and an ex-Father Christmas. Gerrard introduced me as his assistant who wrote the meeting minutes, and no-one questioned it.

"And finally, we come to item four— Christmas Town: suggestions for improvements." The chairman had a lovely, deep voice. A voice for radio. "Gerrard. I understand you're going to talk us through a few ideas you've had about improvements?"

Gerrard cleared his throat, playing with his braces as he did so. "That's right."

"I must admit I'm a little surprised, as you have always said how you couldn't improve on Christmas Town," said the chairman.

Interesting!

"I have indeed said this, but times have changed, and we need to look again."

"How so?" asked one of the oldest men of the group. He sat at the end of the table, a walking stick in his left hand.

Gerrard cleared his throat. "We have always embraced technology and used it to make the Company and Christmas Town better."

There were nods and encouraging noises from the rest of the board.

"We pride ourselves on being forward thinking, of being innovative, on trying to be at the forefront of change and development. But do we apply this to everything? Are we using all our assets?"

The youngest man at the table spoke. "But Gerrard, we hire the best men for the job, and spend a great deal of time on training and ensuring our task force is the best it can be. Isn't that right, gentlemen?"

There were more cries of encouragement, and the members become more animated with their gestures.

"I didn't think Christmas Town could be improved either," continued Gerrard, "but listen to Chrissie and then decide."

The board members looked uncomfortable, looking at each other for reassurance. I felt the blood drain from my head and my hands wouldn't stop shaking. I stood up, not meeting anyone's eyes. "Thank you for allowing me to talk to you today."

Gerrard had stressed the importance of eye contact to make me real, more relatable. I looked at the men around the room. Judging by their faces, they 'really' weren't happy. Then I froze. I couldn't remember what to say next. Gerrard and I had rehearsed exactly what I would say and now I couldn't remember.

Come on Chrissie, pull yourself together. You can do this.

I can't.

You can.

I looked over at Gerrard.

"You were going to tell us about what's been happening in Christmas Town recently?" Gerrard gently prompted.

Relief flowed through me as the words flooded back like a tsunami. "That's right. I moved here over a year ago now. No one can deny that the Ring and the technology make our lives easier."

Lots of head nodding. Good.

"But everything can be improved upon."

No head nodding. Bad.

"I know it's only a little thing to you important gentlemen, but we have made changes to the outside decor of our houses and installed different styles of lights. Now you might think that there was no need to do that or that you don't see what difference it made, but if you talk to your wives and the women of this community, you will understand the enormous impact it has had on how we view our houses. What before was just a box like every other house in the street now has its own identity with its own-coloured front door, plants in window boxes and a more welcoming feel."

They're not saying anything. Is that good or bad?

"Everyone agrees our streets and houses are now more appealing and we look after them more."

Remind them we will still be cleaning.

I continued to explain how the work was done as Gerrard handed out the papers with numbers on to illustrate how cost effective it had been.

"I don't really see what this has to do with business." The old man with the walking stick was agitated, constantly tapping the stick on the floor next to him.

"No man thought we had to change the houses or the feel of the neighbourhood," I said. "The women thought differently."

"That's because the women are at home and the men are going to work, so their priorities are different. I don't see how this is helping," said the old man.

This was not going well, but I knew I would only have one shot. I looked at Gerrard who nodded encouragingly.

"I've been doing some research into how businesses develop and thrive. All the decisions you make about the business are made here in this room after, I'm sure, many discussions and reports from managers on the shop floor and in the other offices. But how many of those people are women?"

There was silence and a lot of side to side 'Action Man' eye movement.

"There aren't any in this boardroom or on the shop floor. You have no women engineers, no women managers, no women workers."

There were a lot of muttering and grumblings. Whether it was the suggestion or that a woman had suggested it, I wasn't sure.

"We don't need women at work. We need them at home," the old man shouted out, his face puce.

I wanted to finish what I needed to say, but they shouted louder.

"But who are your consumers?" Gerrard's booming voice filled the room. "Who are your clients? You are in a business which provides toys to children. Who knows the children best?"

The room quietened and I found my voice. "Women still undertake most of the childcare in the world. Having women in a business ensures the workforce is a representation of its clients and its consumers. Women are good for business. They bring a different perspective. They are good at multi-tasking, and they pay attention. Some of them are also extremely talented at what they do. And there is raw and unused talent out there. Now imagine what the Company could achieve if it used all the talent available."

I stared at Gerrard, afraid to look at the faces of these other men.

"You have raised a very interesting discussion point," the chair said calmly, quietening the more aggressive voices around the table, "but we need to discuss this further and Donald needs to be here. Did he know this was on the agenda today?"

"Donald has always known about this point." Gerrard paused, looking at all the men in turn who knew he was right. "But no, he didn't know about today and I agree he needs to be here."

Gerrard as honest as ever.

Gerrard signalled to me it was time to leave, so we left and walked down to reception. I was still shaking. I couldn't believe what I had just done.

"Well done, Chrissie. You were calm and very clear."

"I must admit I'm surprised."

Gerrard looked over, a confused expression on his face.

"About what you said? I always thought you were against women working at the Ring."

"I never thought that," he said quickly, "but Valma and I have been talking recently, and she reminded me of some things I used to believe in."

"Well, I believe in you," I said, hugging him. "Who'd have thought I believed in Father Christmas after all?"

"We mustn't get too carried away," said Gerrard blushing. "Donald is back on Tuesday, and it will need to be discussed with him. I hope the others see the bigger picture."

Gerard was right, but we didn't need all the members to agree, and it was obvious some of them never would. But just a few members to champion our quest might be all that was needed. I was on such a high I thought I would never come down.

***

But I did come down. Three days later, Daniel came home from work just after ten o'clock, going straight to the fridge for a beer. While I heated his dinner in the microwave, he told me how Donald talked about my 'interference,' as it was from then on called, and had done a little interference of his own.

"I knew it was a bad idea, Chrissie," said Daniel. "The whole thing has blown up in my face."

"What happened?"

He swigged his beer before answering. "Donald asked the board members what they thought about your suggestion. They thought you were a very accomplished speaker and very passionate."

"That's great! I—"

"Hold on. They agreed to discuss renovations to the shop fronts in Christmas Town, but when the suggestion of allowing women in the Company came up, no-one said anything. Nothing at all, not even the chair who I know investigated the company's recruitment and hiring policy. You've made this ten times worse now."

I sat there openmouthed, not able to speak. *My fault? Wanting to improve is my fault?*

"Donald openly laughed at Gerrard for wasting his time. I tried to talk to some of the board members. Their answers were all the same. 'Don't think it's a good idea. Something for the future, but not now. Donald is right.' And I knew Donald would gloat, but..." He took another swig, finishing the bottle.

"But what?"

"He asked how you would take the news."

Me? Donald is only ever concerned about himself.

"I told him you'd be disappointed, obviously. That you'd done a lot of research." He paused momentarily, looking up at me.

"Go on."

"He said it was a shame you didn't share your opinion with him."

I bet he did. I can only imagine what he would have liked to share with me.

"And then he asked how you would feel losing the support of the board? And he kept on repeating, how would you handle losing and it must be hard to be a loser."

Who does he think he is? I felt a rush of blood and my face grew warm.

Daniel pushed his plate away, untouched. "Now they're all avoiding me, probably on the orders of Donald. You can't win. He's made it perfectly clear that everyone must do what he wants, including you."

I know what Donald wants but I'm not playing.

We sat in silence at the table. I thought it would scare me when Daniel said this, but the opposite happened. His reaction made me more convinced than ever this was worth pursuing. He was a bully, using tactics to intimidate us, the weaker sex as he saw us. But we weren't the weaker sex, and I wouldn't let Donald dictate what we could and couldn't do. This was our town, not his.

Chapter 51

Lapland, October 1996

It was a minor victory. We had approval for the shops in Christmas Town, but nothing else. I wanted to continue to fight but it was a step too far for most of the residents to upset the way it had always been. The shop renovations and decorating the nursery kept me busy, and Daniel kept reassuring me Donald had improved but at what exactly, he didn't say.

Things happened slowly in Christmas Town, as I discovered the longer I lived there. When Tanya said she would do a dinner party, I assumed it would be soon, but months later, we finally stood inside the glass vestibule of Donald's and Tanya's house waiting to go inside. I pulled my dress down as it kept rising over my huge baby stomach.

"You look lovely. Stop fidgeting," said Daniel. He held Donald's favourite bottle of red wine in his hand. "You'll see a different side to Donald tonight."

I've already seen a different side to him. I don't need to see any more.

I really didn't want to be here tonight. Three months ago, I would have jumped at the chance to have a showdown with Donald but now I was tired and fed up with being pregnant.

Tanya greeted us at the door. "Come in. I'm glad—you could make it."

Tanya ushered us into the main living room, which looked like someone had thrown boxes of Christmas decorations into the air and they remained where they fell. The cream walls were dotted with large, red satin swags and tails that framed pictures and family portraits. When I looked more closely, I realised each one of them was a photo of Donald in different poses flanked by a VIP: arm around Bill Clinton, shaking hands with John Major, back-to-back with Tom Cruise, air guitaring with Bruce Springsteen, even kneeling in front of the Pope. It was impressive.

"He gets around," said Tanya, reading my mind. "A drink?"

I nodded, looking for Daniel, but he had already wandered off. Standing by myself at the edge of the room, I looked at the rest of the guests. Most of them were male, work colleagues, standing in small circles while the few female guests all stood together in a separate circle. The wives, no doubt.

The noisiest and largest group of men surrounded Donald, all trying to attract his attention. They reminded me of schoolboys, all desperate to be picked to be on the same side as Donald for a game of football. And there in the huddle stood Daniel. He was one of these men. I watched them laughing at something Donald said, looking for signs of approval, changing their opinions or apologising if the reaction went the wrong way.

"Like chicks flocking round the mother bird desperate for a worm," I said out loud only to myself.

"Robin, magpie or vulture?"

I turned around to see Tanya holding my drink. "Sorry?"

"Don't apologise. You are correct. My question is—which bird?"

She continued seeing my confusion. "A traditionalist, a thief or a—bloated parasite."

I laughed at the image of Donald in a vulture costume. "I actually visualised him as all three."

It was Tanya's turn to laugh. "You could—be right. I must mingle—but would like—to talk later."

I made my way over to the group of wives and did my duty as a good wife in making small talk, discussing recipes and children. Being pregnant was quite useful, and the other wives enjoyed treating me to their advice.

"Hello, Chrissie."

The hairs on the back of my neck stood up as Donald spoke from behind me. "How lovely to see you again." His way of 'seeing me' made me feel I was naked.

"Still stirring things up? I think you like to live dangerously."

With each sentence, he moved closer to me, his breath pungent. I backed away, but like an inchworm, he moved closer.

"No, not at all." My skin felt itchy.

"What's your next move?"

Moving away from you.

Over the last few months, I had put Donald out of my mind, but being here now, trying not to breathe in the stale smell of wine and cigarettes on his breath, made me remember why I was so desperate to expose him.

"Nothing. I'm not important like you."

His nostrils flared as he sucked in his breath. He knew I was being sarcastic.

Careful Chrissie. "But, I'd love to know what it's like to be Father Christmas?"

"I see. Do you mean what it's like to be known as Father Christmas or what being Father Christmas physically entails?"

"The latter." *I know you'll be happy to talk about yourself.*

"Are you sure?"

I looked blankly at him.

"Are you sure you would like to know what it's like to be Father Christmas?" The tone of his questioning changed.

Come on, Chrissie. Don't let him intimidate you. I calmed my breathing. "Yes, I would."

He paused but kept looking at me, his eyes still scanning up and down my body, making me feel sick. "Would you like to know that I rarely sleep due to work pressure?"

That explains the eye bags.

"Would you like to know I have very few friends because of this job?"

Maybe your personality at fault here, not the job.

"Because that's what it's like being Father Christmas. It's very lonely." As he said the last sentence, he reached out his hand and pushed some of my hair away from my eyes. He couldn't have been more obvious.

I moved away from him, looking round to see if anyone else was watching, but they all seemed deep in conversation. I couldn't see Daniel anywhere either.

"Why don't you describe an ordinary day in the office?" *That should distract him for a while.*

He squeezed his lips together, pretending to smile. "First, I get here around five o'clock in the morning. Then I read the millions of letters and now emails I receive."

"I thought you had people to do that for you?" I thought of Daniel wading through the correspondence that Father Christmas received every day.

"I do, but they don't always deal with it correctly." He raised his lips in a smirk.

Daniel isn't doing his job properly?

"And then I have to deal with incompetent managers and useless engineers who don't know how to do their job."

The last words were each said louder than the one before, and a few of the guests turned to see. I noticed that most of them quickly dropped their gaze when they saw it was Donald except for Tanya, who continued to stare. I felt trapped in the middle of a wasp's nest, being stung left and right, with no sign of escape. My armpits were sweating and I felt very uncomfortable.

"So, you see, it's a tough job, and that's why I need the right people around me. People who can ease the tension."

His voice was low, ensuring no one heard what he said except for me.

He put his hand on my waist, and I froze.

"You seem like a bright young thing. I would encourage you to come and speak to me at my office next week. Maybe we could work out a position for you."

I do not want to be in any position with you. And I'm pregnant for god's sake. What is wrong with you?

"Another drink?"

"No, thank you," I said, holding it together just long enough to walk to the bathroom. I splashed my face with cold water and tried to calm my breathing.

That man is disgusting. How has he got away with it for so long?

Taking a deep breath, I opened the bathroom door to see Tanya waiting.

"We need to talk—about Donald."

It appears I'm not the only one.

She took me into a small room off the kitchen, tastefully decorated with Nordic furnishings and soft throws. "My escape room," she said, as she motioned for me to sit in a comfy leather armchair. I could understand why she would need one.

Over the next half an hour, she told how she met Donald at Harvard University. Tanya worked her way up in marketing while Donald went down the business route. All was good to begin, but his roving eye became apparent when he stopped coming home, claiming he worked all night.

"There were signs. I looked away."

The move to Lapland was a fresh start, and since there weren't any women working at the Ring, she felt safe. Until the trips abroad, all supposed business meetings found her once again doubting his commitment to her.

"Meal receipts. Lipstick marks. Perfume smells. The usual."

She didn't stay quiet this time, but Donald refused to admit anything and implied it was all in her head.

"Mind games followed. He was good. I suffered."

Listening to Tanya describe Donald worried me. I was suddenly scared for Daniel. If Donald could bully his wife and twist events, he could do it to his assistant. And the affairs?

Daniel wasn't like that. He wouldn't do that.

But that's what Tanya thought initially.

"The job—changed Donald. Mind games—are his favourite. At work—or at home. He's the same. You don't want—it to happen—to Daniel."

I didn't know what to say. I wanted to reassure her that Daniel was not like Donald, but I couldn't. Daniel had changed and although I questioned whether he had the time to have an affair I didn't want to be complacent. Relationships are built on trust and open communication but there was very little communicating going on with Daniel and me.

"It's time. For a change. In my marriage—and this community. I like you. I think— you are brave. You could change— this town."

"But how? I tried at the board meeting but none of them want to hear, and the residents have given up."

"It's hard. This town—is slow—to change. But ask the questions. Start with why? It's all about—heads and hearts. What is close—to you?

I was more confused than ever. She seemed to be talking in code.

Just then, we heard a clock chiming. Time to sit down for dinner.

I stood up. "Thank you for confiding in me. I need to talk to Daniel."

"Of course. Don't mention me. Not yet. I need time."

***

As I walked to the dining room, I saw Daniel staggering out of the kitchen.

Drunk already? "Daniel, I need to talk to you."

"Chrissie," he slurred, elongating the 'e' on the end as he hugged me, crushing my face in his chest.

"Daniel!"

"I love you, Chrissieeeee."

I hate it when you're like this. "Daniel. We need to talk."

He pushed me away by my shoulders. "Not this again. Can't we just have a nice evening?" It was then he noticed everyone sitting down. "Look. We need to go in." He zigzagged a few paces and almost fell into the dining room, leaving me bewildered and annoyed.

The long dining room table stood centre stage. It was adorned with a red tablecloth hidden under paper snowflakes and plastic icicles. I breathed a sigh of relief when I found my name on one of the reindeer shaped place cards at the opposite end to Donald. At least I wouldn't have to worry about him groping my leg under the table. Then I saw Daniel sit, or rather slump down, next to Donald. There would be no chance to talk to him until after dinner.

I sat in between a husband and wife who had similar names. Small talk ensued while we ate the first course; sautéed reindeer balls, a delicacy, I was informed by the wife. I told her my stomach felt delicate, whereupon her husband leant over and stabbed the ball with his fork.

After we had finished our main course of 'Rudolph en croute', there was a clinking noise of a spoon on a glass and we turned to see Donald stood, glass in hand. He put the spoon down and waited for everyone to be quiet.

"Thank you for joining me here tonight." I looked at Tanya sitting on Donald's left-hand side. She smiled, seemingly happy to be there.

How deceiving appearances can be.

"This evening is not just a celebration of friends and life. I have a formal announcement to make and wanted you all to hear."

You're leaving. You've realised what a disgusting person you are and have booked into rehab.

"I couldn't have got by this last year without someone special."

I waited for him to look at Tanya, but he was staring at Daniel.

"He's had a difficult time of it, what with starting a new job in a unique environment. But he's remained positive, dealt with problems calmly and efficiently and has shown me daily the potential he has to go all the way in this industry."

Daniel looks flustered. Did he know this was happening? I tried to catch his eye but failed.

"And I've decided, with the board's approval, of course..." He winked at some members sitting across from him who looked as flustered as Daniel, "that I would like Daniel to be the next Finance Officer of Christmas. Here's to the new FOC!"

What the FOC!

"What do you say, Daniel?"

Don't say anything.

Daniel raised himself up, using the table to steady him. I raised myself up in my seat, desperate for Daniel to see me.

Donald is manipulating you.

I waved my hand, sure this would catch his eye. When that didn't work, I coughed. Nothing. Daniel just stared at the table. Then he looked up and cleared his throat.

"This is an amazing opportunity and one that requires some thought."

I let go of the breath I'd been holding in. *Thank goodness. I was afraid with all the drink, you may have been stupid enough to have said yes.*

"So, I've thought about it— and the answer's yes."

What the FOC!

***

After the announcement, the only thing that moved was the food churning in my stomach and thoughts in my head, each one worse than the one before. *How can Daniel continue to work for this creep, and now, with a promotion to make him more of a loyal dog than he already is.* My limbs frozen in time, like the volcano victims at Pompeii. Nobody could physically move as we had another two courses to eat, and each course became a test, trying to catch Daniel's attention while holding a conversation with Harold and Helga Bernt about the North wind and the state of the transport system. When the last course, chocolate mousse in the shape of a moose, was over, I finally removed myself from the table and found Daniel in the middle of a group of men who were all congratulating him.

"Helloooo darling!" He swayed out of the circle and bent to kiss me.

I pulled him to one side. He didn't say anything, just stared; his eyes glassy, pupils dilated.

"You can't work for him. He's—he's—" I couldn't think of one word to describe him, I could think of hundreds and didn't know which one to choose. "You just can't."

"I knew you'd be like this."

"But he's a—leech." I'd finally said it out loud.

"Don't be silly. He's just tactile."

I can't believe what I'm hearing. Are you so under his spell you don't know what kind of man he is? Or don't want to know?

"Sometimes he's a little inappropriate."

"Inappropriate? I'm not sure that's the right word."

"You're worrying over nothing, Chrissie. Just have a drink and enjoy yourself."

"He's bad news, Daniel, and he's hiding something. I'm telling you—"

"I'm telling you, Chrissie. This is disrispect, disrispict, dispect." He couldn't get the word out. "You don't know what you're talking about."

This was troubling, like a tiny dinghy bobbing in the ocean, I was alone and out of my depth. But not for long. Donald swooped in, laying a hand around my swollen waist in full view of Daniel.

"Here's my favourite couple. What do you think, Chrissie? Your husband is moving up in the world."

It wasn't the only thing that was moving up. Donald's hand wandered up from my waist to under my breast as my chocolate mousse made its way up my stomach. I couldn't say or do anything. Afraid to move, afraid to react.

Daniel. Do something!

"That's the thing with this business. We're like one big family. We do things for each other. Help each other out. Have each other's backs."

He continued to stroke mine up and down. I felt nauseous, then a cramp, deep in the pit of my stomach.

"You have a bright wife here, Daniel. And there could be a place for her at the Ring. We've never done it before, but maybe she could work there, under my wing, so to speak."

Visions of the vulture flashed before me. My stomach cramped again. *I'm going to be sick.*

"You'll need to drop this woman working thing and concentrate on the business at hand." His hand caressed my backside as he looked at Daniel square on.

"If you'll excuse me, I don't feel very well."

I raced to the toilet and promptly threw up my chocolate mousse. Tanya was waiting for me when I came out.

"You don't—look well. Maybe tonight—was a bad idea. Go home. But warn Daniel—before it's too late."

"I think it might be too late, anyway."

And with that, my waters broke.

Chapter 52

TV studio, 2009

Ms Grey looks shocked, and the studio is silent. I argue with myself for all of ten seconds and then come back to reality. It was time for the truth to come out. It should have happened years before.

I lean close to Ms Grey, her eyes covered with a shiny film. "Is everything okay?"

She rouses herself and looks at me. This time she doesn't try to look at the camera. "That must have been a very difficult time for you. For all of you. It sounds like you were living in the 1950s with its sexism and misogyny."

"I know and nobody expects anywhere to be like that, not in this modern era," I reply. "And yet in some places it still goes on and what do we do about it?"

Ms Grey nods. "I suppose that's the point. We have a duty to highlight these issues, to speak up for all the people who live in places like Christmas Town."

"It's not like that now," I say quickly. I don't want her to think we would still be putting up with that behaviour. But then I remember. We did, and for a long time. "I must admit I'm ashamed of what I did next?"

Ms Grey pats my hand which is resting on the suede sofa and softly says, "Take your time. What did you do?"

I take a deep breath, remembering this is for the business and welfare of the people back home. "Nothing. We all turned a blind eye."

Lapland, June 1999

After Sami was born, my life revolved around her. Trying to change Christmas Town and the rules that governed us was not top of my agenda when I had family life to deal with, but truth was, it was too difficult. It felt like no one wanted any change, apart from myself and a few friends. Although the neighbours had been excited over the prospect to begin with, without my involvement, they lost interest. We all carried on as we had, not doing anything and not admitting that things were very wrong in Christmas Town.

Time disappeared. I know people say this all the time, but it did. One minute I was feeding my baby and the next she was running around as fast as she could loving life and wanting to experience everything. I had put her first for years, but her thirst for new things and watching her grow made me think more about the future and what opportunities were available to her. While watching her playing with her toys and trying to put a square block through a round hole, I started thinking about Christmas Town again and wondering if change was still a possibility.

Daniel was engrossed in his new job and new status and felt relieved I had something else to occupy my time apart from, as he put it, making trouble for him. He never mentioned the dinner party after Sami was born, and whenever I tried to, he would change the conversation. The only thing he would admit was that Donald was a tough boss with high expectations. He never said anything else about Donald and his unacceptable behaviour, and he never again asked for my opinion on what he should do. With the promotion, Donald had secured Daniel's obedience and my silence.

We no longer had dinner together. The sleepless nights ruined any routine we had, and I couldn't stay awake late enough to eat with him.

Our conversations became transactional; what time Daniel would be home from work, the days he would be away, what jobs needed doing around the house and what to do about the funny smell coming from the downstairs toilet. The only thing Daniel and I could talk about properly was Sami and, even then it was like a business transaction, explaining what had been achieved that day.

Daniel missed all of Sami's firsts: the smile, laugh, roll over, crawl, walk and talk. He also missed it the second time, the third and the fourth. He was never home before Sami went to bed and gone in the morning before she woke. We were strangers, drifting in and out of the house, crossing paths. Never together long enough. Our relationship had once been like a sea where the tide pulled one of us in one direction but then pushed us back together, but recently it felt more like a calm, flat pond, no ripples—no movement, and we were slowly drifting apart to opposite sides.

***

Over time, my friends became my family. Alex was my sister, my partner in crime. We did things together and egged each other on. Nic was the mother. Positive and upbeat, organising everyone and making things happen. Toni was the father, supportive and loving but always told us the hard truth. And then there were the grandparents. Gerrard with his stern but caring ways and Valma with her smiles and sensible advice.

"Be careful with Ukki", I shouted down the garden. Gerrard was on all fours, with Sami desperately trying to hold on to his back like a sloth. Gerrard and Valma were at our house more than their own. "Grandpa's an old man."

"Ukki a dog," shouted Sami, so pleased she could now say sentences.

"I'm neither!" Gerrard stood up and consoled Sami by telling her he would play with her properly after a cup of coffee.

Valma laughed as she finished folding Sami's clothes that had been on the airer.

"You're so good with her," I said, as he took off his coat and boots.

"I love children. Always have. I don't think there is a better job in the whole world than to be a father and grandfather."

"Even better than being Father Christmas?" I said.

He placed his fingers behind his red braces and pulled on them, a habit he'd picked up from his days as Father Christmas. "Yes, even better. A father is real. Father Christmas was a job. A job I loved, but still a job. Excellent coffee. You've improved." Gerrard swilled the end of his coffee round in his cup.

"I had a wonderful teacher." Coffee was an art in Finland, as I found out when Gerrard first came round and disparaged my coffeemaking.

"How's Daniel?" Valma asked as she tidied up Sami's toys that were sprawled across the floor.

"Busy." I'd had this conversation many times with all my family members.

"Daniel needs to spend more time with his family and you," said Gerrard. "He's a lucky man. But then I suppose it was easier for me. I didn't have the demands put on me by a family." He looked at Valma. They exchanged glances and smiled at one another.

"And you didn't have to work for Donald!" I said.

Gerrard pulled on his braces and sighed. "That man. He's a disgrace to the name Santa Claus."

"Well, they voted him in again for another term, so he must be doing something right?"

"Exactly. But what is the something?" He paused, wrestling with an idea like a worm under his forehead. "I've looked the other way for too long and Donald is bad for the business. I'm convinced of that."

I put my coffee cup down. "But what can we do?"

Gerrard got up, placed his thumbs through his braces and began pacing up and down the kitchen. "I don't know but I think Donald is acting outside of his Father Christmas duties. I spoke to two board members recently who hinted the business was not what it was, even though Donald convinces everyone the figures are better than ever, but neither of them will go on record with this. I've spent too long ignoring this."

I understood. I'd ignored it too. "So have I but I don't want to anymore. I'm worried if I don't do something soon, I will lose it all, including my sanity."

Gerrard looked sad, his salty white eyebrows and thin lips turned downward. He said nothing as he took my hands in his, squeezing them gently. We sat quietly for a moment, the only sound coming from Sami making plane noises as she ran around the garden. Finally, he spoke. "I'm so sorry to hear that Chrissie but not surprised. This job sucks all the life out of you and Donald...I won't waste my breath. If you want my opinion—"

I nodded.

"You know how much we love you, Chrissie. But your priority is your marriage not Donald and Christmas Town. You deserve to be happy." He let go of my hands and gave me an encouraging smile.

"Maybe you start with some time away. Just the two of you. I'll babysit," said Valma.

"I don't know if that's enough."

"It won't be, but you'll have time to talk. And then maybe we look at Donald and start asking some difficult questions."

They were right. Daniel had changed, and I didn't know how to reach him. If I could get Daniel away from Donald and out of Christmas Town just for a while, we might have a chance.

***

"We're going to Kuusamo," I told Daniel, later that day. "It's two and a half hours away and I've booked a hotel."

"When?" He dumped his work bag on the floor.

"Friday night. Just for one night," I added when I saw his disgruntled expression. "Nicole has organised it all, and Gerrard and Valma are looking after Sami."

"But I have work to do. You can't just organise something like this without asking me first." Daniel's face was the tired, grumpy one I was used to.

"I just want to take my husband away. You need a break. We both do." *Please listen to me.*

"I don't have time." He scrolled through his phone, hiding from the conversation.

Try again. "You're always saying all you do is work, so I thought—"

"That's the problem. You're always thinking and making my life difficult. I'm going to do some work."

He stormed off.

Why is work all you think about? I have to make you realise before it's too late. I knocked on the study door. "Can I come in?"

Daniel sat, his body slumped in front of his computer. He looked like the Greek God Atlas holding the heavens and all its problems on his shoulders. He sighed, then began to cry.

"I'm sorry, Daniel. I should have asked you. I—"

"No, I'm sorry. This is all my fault."

What?

"I never should have made us come here.

What?

It's not what I thought it was going to be.

What?

"This place. This job. This place is the job. The job is this place. The two are so entwined, I can't see any of the good stuff."

I turned his chair around to face me. "You see us, don't you?"

He looked at me, the spread of lines around his eyes like a child's drawing of a sun.

"Yes, but I don't spend enough time with you or Sami. I'm missing it all." He grabbed my hands tightly, as if afraid he would fall.

Finally! "You work hard to provide a good life for me and Sami, and we love you for that. But... there is more to life."

"It's the job, it's—"

"Donald."

He nodded. "The environment is toxic. He's toxic. I don't know what to do."

"About Donald or the job?"

Daniel shrugged his shoulders, staring at our hands. "Both."

"I've spoken to Gerrard about Donald."

Daniel was silent.

"Don't you want to know what he said?"

"I know what he said."

I was silent.

"That Donald is a corrupt COC. That the Board is made up of yes men."

"He didn't say that, exactly," I said, looking down.

Daniel stared at me, one eyebrow raised. He knew.

"He said Donald fired most of his board, then handpicked his new board. He makes some strange decisions, and if you don't agree with him, he gets rid of you."

"That's what I said. The board is made of yes men and I'm one of them." He buried his face in his hands. "I'm a prisoner of my own making."

"No. He makes you a prisoner. He makes you doubt your own judgement, your own thinking. He's clever."

"But I can't do anything about it. Gerrard tried and got fired."

"No, he didn't."

Daniel looked up. "That's what Donald said."

"Donald wants everyone to be afraid. He threatened the board with losing their pensions if they didn't vote in him, and Gerrard was forced to retire and say nothing. He left quietly as he didn't feel he could do anything about it."

"You see. The only solution is to leave this place."

"Gerrard realises now what he did was wrong. He should have stood up to him. He should have revealed Donald for what and who he is."

"But what can I do?"

The question I have been waiting for you to ask since we arrived here in Christmas Town. "You need to figure out what you want."

I held him close as he sobbed into my chest. Daniel never cried, even when he talked about his parents, and he didn't deserve this. He really needed a break before he broke.

Chapter 53

On Friday evening, Daniel burst through the door earlier than I expected. I thought he would be late, finding an excuse to carry on working, but here he was, excited, raring to go. He wrapped me in his arms and kissed me, igniting the switch that hadn't been turned on for a long time. We were like strangers, but I still wanted him, still wanted to be with him. My only concern was the state of my lingerie collection, which now consisted of nursing bras and grey high waisted pants. I'd just have to make sure the lights weren't on.

As we drove, listening to classics from the 80s on the radio, I looked across at Daniel. His worry lines had disappeared, and he looked years younger. The Daniel before we moved here.

We pulled into the lodge, fairy lights lighting the path to the hotel entrance. It was nestled into the wood and looked like a face with a full head of thick snow hair, white bushy eyebrows, windows, and a red mouthed curved doorway.

An hour later, we were lying on the fur rug in front of the fire sipping champagne, feeling very decadent and not the normal Friday evening we were used to. The heat from the burning log fire was beautiful.

"Why don't we do this in our house?" said Daniel.

I was lying on my front across Daniels's lap as he stroked my bare back. "It's not quite the same lying on a heated floor."

Daniel was gazing at the fire, hypnotised by the dancing flames. "Why don't we have a fire in our house?"

"Because we have underfloor heating and we're not allowed to have log fires."

Daniel stopped stroking. "Who said?"

"The company. It's a fire hazard and bad for the environment." I was repeating what I'd heard in a Home Watch meeting.

"They have a lot of rules."

I've never heard you say anything negative about the company. Maybe you're ready to admit things weren't right? "It's also why we can't have bonfires, or fairy lights or—"

"Any fun."

I turned over. "Exactly."

"They could do more to make the area more—" he paused, looking for the right word.

"Christmassy?" I offered.

"Is that even a word?"

"We live in an amazing place which is devoid of anything to do with Christmas, but that is what the company is selling."

"It's been like this for years." Daniel's voice was flat, drained.

"We could change it."

"We can't."

I pushed his hair away from his eyes. "We could try."

He was silent. His breath moving in steady rises and falls. "Should we move back home? Back to England?"

What? There have been so many times I would have jumped at this, but now? "I can't believe I'm saying this, but I don't think so. Your workplace is toxic, and something has to change, but running away is not the answer. Donald is what makes the place toxic. If he wasn't there, we could make changes."

Daniel buried his face in his hands, the crown of his head all grey, the job aging him faster than it should. "He's probably at the office now, hiding all his dodgy deals. I was so stupid to think I could work for a man like Donald."

Like an addict, Daniel had taken his first step in admitting there was a problem. Only eleven more steps to go.

After a rare and enjoyable breakfast together the next morning, Daniel and I went for a walk which crossed an adventure park. We saw ski areas for beginners with wide, tree-lined slopes. A rope tow dragged skiers up the slope to the base of the main lift, which climbed high into the sky. There was another ski park for more advanced skiers with small jumps and zig zag slalom courses. Another part of the ski area had trails marked with flags for alpine touring, perfect ski runs through trees and open snowfields that connected between glacier-capped mountains. People on kick sleds and fat bikes moved around us, and we saw a large ice-covered lake where people sat on their stools, fishing through holes punched into the ice.

At first, I laughed, then my mind whirred. Christmas Town had all the same ingredients. Snow, space, slopes. I could visualise the visitor centre by the entrance of A Block in Christmas Town. The new out-buildings and animal enclosures would need to go at the far end of Block D, where it was flatter and Father Christmas's house could be built by the river. But we could have some ice fishing and alpine touring areas, and bring in some fat bikes for the visitors to rent.

Daniel was staring at me. "Where are you? You're lost in thought."

I wanted to tell Daniel what I had been talking about with the girls but still wasn't sure if he would get it. *But would there ever be a right time?*

"I've been thinking about Christmas Town. I know we've improved the general area and given the place a little character, but we want to do more."

Daniel was silent, but he appeared to be listening and wasn't looking at his phone. I realised he hadn't looked at his phone since we arrived.

"We need to make Christmas Town an attraction. A holiday hot spot. Or rather a cold spot. A tourist destination for families with Christmas and snow activities all in one magical wintery setting. For children and adults who want to spend time together in a stunning winter landscape, where Father Christmas lives."

Daniel was visibly confused. "But Christmas Town is just an ordinary town?"

"I know." I hardly stopped for breath. "We need to change it. It could be a better Christmas Town with a real-life Father Christmas house, a workshop, a post office, shops and animal enclosures. We could offer reindeer walks and husky rides. Maybe they could feed the reindeer too? There could be a Mrs Santa Claus who bakes cookies and biscuits and makes lunch for Father Christmas and elves wrapping presents and sorting Christmas cards. And we could arrange visits to see the real Father Christmas working in his workshop."

Daniel stopped walking and dropped my hand at the same time. "No. That's a step too far. You wouldn't want any child meeting Donald?"

"I don't mean Donald."

Daniel's brow furrowed. "But he's Father Christmas?"

"No. He's the COC, remember. We would have a proper Father Christmas, like they do in the department stores, but one that looks real. Is real."

"You're suggesting we turn Christmas Town into a tourist attraction, build all these different areas with Christmas activities and invite people to come visit?"

"Yes." My heart was racing, exhilarated by the prospect of a new town and a new project.

"But Christmas Town is where we live. Where our houses are. I'm not sure the residents would be happy with that."

You have a point. The building work would be intrusive and noisy. "Okay. That's fair, but we haven't spoken to them yet and they were all happy with all the street and house changes we've done so far."

"Yes, but this is different. You want to turn a town into a tourist destination." He repeated my words but with an air of incredulity. "And there are a couple of things you're overlooking, Chrissie. First, we don't let anyone visit. The place is top secret. We don't exist."

And what a stupid rule that is. "We do exist, and it's about time we let the world know we are here."

"And how would you do that?"

Ha! Something I do know the answer to. "Advertise. Nic and I have discussed this. We need to design one of those website things that would act as our hub of information for visitors, providing updates on weather conditions, events and activities taking place each month during the winter months. Local newspapers and radio can help spread the word about what we are doing and in time we can expand."

Daniel did not look as happy as I thought he would. "So how do we still keep the Ring a secret?"

You're missing the point. "It shouldn't be a secret. If we were more transparent, it would generate more interest in the business model, and you could attract more highly qualified people."

"And who's going to pay for it?"

Crap! Forgot about how we would pay for it. "The financial side of this hasn't been worked out yet but we are looking for opportunities." *I sound desperate.*

"I don't know, Chrissie. There is so much you still don't know, and it feels too...ambitious."

You don't believe we can do this, that I can do this. "I know there are obstacles but on the positive side, we do have a workforce."

Daniel screwed up his face, unsure, and then I saw the light flicker on behind his eyes. "Women!"

I nodded. "Donald will hate the idea."

Daniel laughed. "He sure will. Okay, so how do you build a new town when Donald will be against the idea, and he will get the Board to side with him?"

"We need to get rid of Donald."

"And how will you do that?" Daniel asked.

"I don't know," I said. "But we have to find a way."

"Wouldn't it be easier to let him finish this term of office and wait for a new COC to come in?" Daniel was quiet, contemplating, my words weighing heavily on him. He was still reticent to go up against Donald.

"No. We have to do this now. The longer he stays in power, the longer it will take to clean up his mess. His legacy will have a detrimental effect on this town and the business. Maybe not right this minute, but it will have consequences."

I know I would have agreed with Daniel a few years ago, but I could see more clearly now. I was stronger. I was burning to put plans in place and make a real difference before it was too late.

Chapter 54

The weekend away with Daniel had been perfect. It had given us time to talk. Although he wasn't a hundred percent behind my vision for Christmas Town, he could see it was a massive opportunity to change things. He was less certain of getting rid of Donald. One thing we both agreed on was our relationship needed work, so we began talking more, sharing jokes, watching the latest sitcom together, anything to help us to reconnect. The new Christmas Town was not discussed. It was my baby, and like all good mothers, I would do anything to protect it.

A few days later, Valma and Gerard popped round to see how the weekend had gone.

"That is good news," said Valma. She was sat behind Sami plaiting her hair into braids. "A fresh start is what you needed."

"I'm pleased you feel that way as there is something else, I need?"

Valma saw me catch Gerrard's eye. "Come on Sami. Let's go and play. We don't want to listen to boring conversations, do we?" Valma winked at me as they left the room.

"What is it? More babysitting? Though I cannot fathom out why you need to meet up with your friends so often."

"No, not that." I felt my cheeks warm. He had been very good, especially recently. "We've been talking, Alex, Nic, and myself and we have this idea but..."

Gerrard began pacing around the room. It helped him to think more clearly. "Go on," he said.

"We want to make Christmas town a tourist destination."

Gerrard frowned, his white, bushy eyebrows meeting in the middle of his face. "I don't understand. How would that work? And how does that help us with Donald?"

"This is just an initial idea and there are issues, but I've invited the girls round so we can try to explain what we are thinking."

Just then the doorbell rang. I opened the door to Alex who almost ran into the kitchen. She stopped when she saw Gerrard.

"Hi Gerrard. How are you?" She didn't let him answer so desperate to let out what she had been holding in.

"I found something," she proclaimed before stopping and staring up at the ceiling.

"What are you looking at?" I asked.

She began waving her arms up at each of the corners of the room. "Are they listening in? Can they see us?" she whispered.

I shook my head. "No one is spying on us. This isn't *Mission Impossible*."

"I wouldn't put it past them."

Alex had started calling the company 'they' and, as far as she was concerned, 'they' were not to be trusted. She scattered the folders she had been holding under her arm across the kitchen table.

"I think we need to make new laws for Christmas Town. Having gone through the Company's policies, all very accessible with technology now, what I found out is they don't have an Equal Rights policy, which is not ethical, and we need to use Everyman's Right Law."

She explained how this well-established law in Lapland gave everyone the freedom to travel and camp across most of the land, regardless of who owned it.

"This should convince the Board we need more freedom and transparency in Christmas Town, not less, and that anyone is allowed to visit and stay at Christmas Town. And that would help with the next stage."

The doorbell rang again. Alex looked towards the front door and then flung her body onto the table, covering up all the documents.

"I knew it. They're watching us," she said, staring up at the ceiling again.

"Don't be silly. It's Nicole."

Nic walked in with a selection of folders in one hand and a bottle of Cloudberry cordial in the other. With Alex working on the legal requirements, Nic was helping me put together a visual plan to combine Christmas Town with the new tourist area.

"Hi Gerrard. So lovely to see you. How's Valma? Where is she? Is Sami here? Are you staying for lunch too? How lovely. We have lots to talk about and lots to show you."

As she took a breath, I jumped in. "Nic and I have drawn up an area which could possibly be the visitor centre, with the animals housed towards the river..."

"Animals? I'm not sure we can have animals here in Christmas Town?" Gerrard looked genuinely concerned. And if he was concerned, what hope did we have?

"I was unsure about this too, Chrissie," said Nic.

Not Nic too. This is not going well.

"The building work would be difficult, there would have to be compromises and the residents might not be fully supportive of a plan which would affect their day to day living. But I think I have come up with an alternative." Nic was beaming.

Gerard and I looked at each other confused.

She continued. "I think it would be easier to start again. To build a new town which could house all the areas we wanted, without causing noise and disruption for the residents. And to have the two areas separate would make life much simpler with our own privacy and the issue at the Ring."

Nicole put her folders on the draining board and unrolled a large scroll of paper and some photographs. "When I was going through the arial photographs to look at the typography of the land, I found a piece of unused land about seven kilometres away in between Christmas Town and Rovaniemi."

She then explained how the land had been left over from World War Two when the Germans had built an airfield and barracks there. It had been up for sale ten years ago, but no one had been interested, so now it was just wasteland.

"It's an odd, shaped piece of land, but cars and sleighs could move easily through it. It's not workable for farming, but has an arable area, which is perfect for reindeer and huskies."

We examined the photographs more closely. The shape was irregular. In fact, from above it looked like a reindeer. There were a few outhouse buildings and barns on the land which, although neglected, would still be standing for the next fifty years with little maintenance, as the owner had assured Nicole.

"It's an extensive project, Chrissie, but I think this could be the new Christmas Town. A place where people could come and visit and do all the Christmas activities they wanted to and see Father Christmas. I can't believe it hasn't been done before now quite frankly. People would come from miles away for this."

As with everything, there was a cost implication. Frederick was helping put together some numbers for the cost, and Nic asked him to look at similar tourist attractions around the world. They decided people would spend a lot of money for a unique experience.

"And it doesn't come more unique than seeing Father Christmas up close and personal," Nic said.

"We don't want to see Donald up close and personal," said Gerrard.

"That's the beauty of this idea. We won't be anywhere near him," continued Nicole. "No one wants to see a man like Donald who is, after all, just a man in a suit. They want to see the man in the 'red suit'. They want to see him sitting in a sleigh being pulled by reindeer with elves surrounding him. A nice jolly man who likes children and animals. A real Father Christmas, and that is definitely not Donald."

I knew Gerrard was thinking as he pulled down on his braces, mulling the idea over in his head. Was he imagining himself being Father Christmas? I know I was.

It's a brilliant idea, but there will be a lot to do, and it will be a more expensive option. And then there would be planning constraints.

The doorbell halted my thoughts. I wasn't expecting anyone else. Alex, seeing my face, launched herself at the table again.

"Stop. You don't need to do that, although it would impress Tom Cruise. It's possibly Katrina or Savannah."

"Did you invite them too?"

"No. I did invite Toni but she's helping Brandon with something, and I don't think we are ready to involve the others just yet." I pressed the video control button and found myself staring at Tanya.

"What's she doing here?" hissed Nic, snatching the scroll and rolling it back up.

"I don't know. What shall I do?" Tanya was the last person I expected.

"You can't leave her standing on the doorstep. And it might be interesting," said Alex, who delighted in knowing people's business.

As Nic and Alex put everything away, I walked to the door, wondering why she was here. After Daniel became the FOC, I hardly saw her. The occasional social and Home Watch meeting where we made small talk, but nothing like the night of the dinner party. She had not tried to be in my company, and I didn't know what had changed. She had been so believable that night, but I realised Gerrard had been right about her all along.

"Hello Tanya. What a nice surprise?" I said as Tanya pushed past me, the scent of lilies and lemons filling the hall.

"Is it?" she asked. She didn't look happy and suddenly I wondered if Alex was right about 'them' listening in. Maybe 'they' had sent Tanya to let me know 'they' were on to me.

On seeing Alex, Nic and Gerrard in the kitchen, Tanya said, "I'm interrupting?"

"We're going to have lunch," said Alex, watching her closely.

Tanya looked confused.

"Would you like to join us?" I asked, hoping she wouldn't say yes.

"No."

We made conversation around the table, all unsure and nervous as to why Tanya was here.

"I'm divorcing him," said Tanya when the small talk had run out.

We all looked at one another. This was not what I thought she'd say. *And I still don't understand the significance of you telling us.*

"I'm sorry to hear that, but why are you telling us?"

"He doesn't know. I want— to help. Change this place— for the better— before I leave."

"But if you're leaving him, then you'll be less interested in helping, not more," said Alex, who basically said what everyone was thinking.

"Divorce is difficult. Makes you realise— things you— should have done. Donald will be— angry."

"Of course, he will," said Gerrard. "He doesn't have a great track record in the trust department, but I still don't see how this will benefit us. In fact, it's more likely to make him behave worse than he already does, if that's even possible."

"He will— hide things."

"What things?"

"Assets. Money. Evidence."

"Evidence? Of what?" said Alex, her legal nose smelling something.

"Accounts."

"But that's your personal business. I don't see how this will help us change things around here," I said.

"Not personal— business accounts."

Tanya explained how Donald, one drunken night, admitted to her he was transferring money from the business into his own personal account, boasting at how no-one knew and how stupid everyone was. She had known for a while, but wasn't sure if she could trust me as Daniel was the Financial Officer, and would surely have seen some of these transactions himself.

"But Daniel has never said anything about this," I said, embarrassed in front of my friends and very worried he might be involved in this too.

Tanya shrugged "He dupes everyone. Including... your husband."

"If we can prove it, how do we get rid of him?" asked Nic.

"We would need evidence and it has to be attained legally," explained Alex looking directly at me.

"How would we do that? Donald is as slippery as a baby in a bath," said Gerrard.

"I have passwords. They should help," said Tanya.

The room fell silent as we all looked at each other in surprise. Tanya had been married to Donald for a long time, so having this kind of information was remarkable. Even more remarkable was the fact that she trusted us enough to share it. I wanted to kiss her right there for making my life a hell of a lot easier.

"It seems— you are pleased? I won't ask. I don't want— to know."

She left as quickly as she had arrived, but you still felt the weight of her words lingering in the air. With this information we could remove Donald from his post once and for all. But Tanya had been married to Donald for a long time. I didn't know if we could trust her.

We all looked at each other, waiting for someone to speak.

"We need a plan to get into his office," Alex said, her face serious and focused. "We need to know Donald's every move, his patterns and habits, and when he is likely to be away from his desk."

"Away from the Ring would be better. It would give us more time," I said, imagining myself dressed in black, abseiling down the glass windows of the Ring.

"Yes, exactly," enthused Alex. "Then we need to find out what accounts he uses, apply the passwords, and extract the evidence of his theft or any other evidence of wrongdoing. We can use this to prove Donald's guilt and show the board he must go."

I think it would be easier to abseil.

We nodded in agreement, the feeling of elation vanished, now realising the huge undertaking we had agreed to. And such a huge task meant we had to involve more people.

Chapter 55

The problem was I couldn't trust all the people I knew to join us, while also keeping quiet about the whole thing. It required a certain mindset, a certain thinking about where this journey could lead and how to best achieve it. Many of the wives had been residents for a long time and would find themselves torn between wanting to help but also being loyal to their husbands and the Company. I suspected they'd been slightly brainwashed over time about how amazing this place was.

Toni, Savannah and Katrina were different. They had seen the developments so far and been part of our conversations about change. I was confident they would help once they heard everything but who else? What I needed was a workforce of likeminded women who had no attachments to Christmas Town. It didn't take me long to figure it out.

Many phone conversations and emails later resulted in Lisa, Bec, Nerys and Paula swearing their allegiance to the cause and organising flights to Lapland. They weren't a part of my life here, but were determined to help me create a better one.

The following week I invited Savannah, Toni and Katrina over to my house. They thought they were coming over for a catch-up, but soon realised there was more to it when they saw the plans laid out on the kitchen table next to the nibbles and wine glasses.

"These are all just preliminary drawings. It makes visualising easier," said Nic, spreading the plans out so everyone could see.

I talked about what the future could look like, using the initial plans for the new Christmas Town, drawn at various stages alongside a timescale for implementation.

The women took their time studying the drawings, asking questions, raising problems and issues. They listened to answers, accepted there were no answers to some questions at the moment, and agreed this would be difficult. Being a fly on the wall of this kitchen would have been a great learning experience for the men of this town, especially the Board. I wasn't sure they had ever had such an in-depth and relevant discussion.

Savannah was, not unsurprisingly, shocked by the idea. "But Chrissie, that's not how it's done here in Christmas Town. This sounds like a mutiny." Savannah finished breastfeeding child number four and expertly fastened her top. "What will our husbands all think? They won't be pleased."

"Don't tell them," I said straight-faced.

"I'm not sure I can do that. I never keep secrets from Beau," Savannah whispered, looking around her.

"You'll have to, Savannah."

All of us turned to look at Katrina seated at the head of the table.

"I have two girls now and I'm happy here in Christmas Town, but I do think about the future. There are no opportunities for them here. They will have to emigrate because they will have no other choice."

Well said, Katrina.

"She's right."

Our heads all turned to Toni at the other end of the table, like spectators at a tennis match.

"I've stayed quiet for too long and where has it got me? An unpaid job without a title and a husband who takes all the credit. I know I could have done the job better than Brandon. I am almost doing his job for him. Every decision is run by me now, and still his colleagues haven't worked it out."

About time you said it, Toni.

Nic and Alex added their own opinions, commenting on the wealth of talent that was available here in Christmas Town but not being utilised. We didn't divulge what Tanya had said. There was too much distrust of her and her husband, and we didn't know what we would find out.

"We are living in a community designed by men, run by men, and decided upon by men," I said. "But building a community needs everyone to be involved, and that includes the women. Not just for the cooking and cleaning, but for the big decisions that affect all of us. Don't you want to be a part of a community that values what women can add and be part of a change to make it happen?"

I tried to sum up the discussion and find a way to move forward but Savannah still had a worried look on her face as she moved her baby across in the sling to her other side.

"What is it, Savannah?"

"I don't understand how building a new town can help get Toni a job? Or make more opportunities for our girls? Why can't we just ask the company to change their rules and employ more women?"

Alex stood up and looked at each of us like a defence lawyer looking at its jury. "First, you need to understand that this company has been in place for a long time, and the men who run it don't feel it needs changing."

Savannah fiddled with the sling again, visibly uncomfortable with the conversation.

"We need to get the balance right. No one industry or town can improve without the involvement of its entire community." Alex raised her forefinger in the air as she said the word 'one'. "Just because something has been operating a certain way for a long time does not mean that it is still working or working for all its residents. Determining what people want, what all people want, listening to everyone's views, asking questions, challenging traditions and customs can and should be a good thing."

Well said, Alex. My turn. "Our men believe they have all the answers, and we need to show them they haven't thought of everything," I said.

"There is always more to do to bring about change, a change that benefits everyone. Savannah?" My voice forced her to look up from her downward fixed gaze. "We love our men, but they are following orders from a man who doesn't operate in the best interests of this company or Christmas Town. I implore you not to say anything, but we hope to prove that Donald has been lying about the financial position of the company, and the impact this will ultimately have on our lives and the future of our town." I paused. "But we need to find this proof and come up with a plan for the longevity of the company, then the Board and the company will have to listen."

Toni, Katrina and Savannah huddled together and started whispering. There was some nodding and shaking of heads, then Toni said, "We want to help. I know you might not trust me because of the work I do for Brandon, but—"

"We do trust you. It's just we weren't sure if you would think we were being ridiculous and to be honest, we're still not sure we're not." I looked over at Nic and Alex who were nodding. "It feels like a long shot, but we've had help from Tanya."

Toni rolled her eyes. Katrina and Savannah were silent.

"I know what you're thinking, but she is getting divorced, and she has passwords."

"Go on," said Toni, her voice encouraging.

Alex and I explained the plan. Unaware we now had the passwords, courtesy of Tanya, Donald continued to act as he always had. All we needed was time and someone to help us find what we were looking for. Daniel wanted to help, but it was too risky with him still working for Donald at the Ring. The obvious answer was Gerrard. Although not technologically savvy, he knew about the finance set up, and could help us decipher some of the paperwork and accounts found online. This was part one. Part two involved getting into Donald's office, not a straightforward task, but necessary as the accounts showed anomalies, and there were missing documents in the paper trail.

The women were silent, and I was wondering if we had done the right thing by telling them.

"This is unbelievable," exclaimed Toni.

Crap! I thought Toni would understand. There's no hope for the others.

"It's the most unbelievable thing I've heard in a long time. I'm in."

It took me a while to realise she had agreed and, when I did, the euphoria exploded. We danced around the kitchen table holding hands. Our decision united us, and that night, the plan for 'Operation Christmas Town' began.

Chapter 56

A few days later, reinforcement arrived in the shape of Lisa, Rebecca, Nerys and Paula. They were staying at a hotel in Rovaniemi keeping a low profile until it was time to act. I hadn't told Daniel anything, although I suspected he knew something was afoot. He thought it was too risky to involve outsiders with whatever we had planned, but I knew it was the right call. It was also perfect timing, as he and Donald would be away for a few days on business.

The plan was for Gerrard to drive to the Ring and negotiate his way into the building one night, when there would be a skeleton staff. He knew most of the security guards and receptionists by their first names, so he figured it would be easy to get in and not raise suspicion. He would then go to a disused area which housed a dumbwaiter, accessed from outside the building. This contraption was used years ago to bring women and bottles of whiskey up to the top floor and the COC's office, hidden from the rest of the staff. This secret lift could house a smallish person, so, one at a time, we made our way to Donald's office. Gerard stayed by the lift and waited for the signal to get us down again.

Katrina, Nic and Savannah went to meet Lisa and Paula, pretending we were having a night out so we could cover one another if needed. Meanwhile Toni, Alex, Rebecca, Nerys and I stood in the dark in Donald's office afraid to move, not knowing where to start.

Donald's office was foreign in the blackness, a place none of us, apart from me, had ever been before. The faint hum of the electricity seemed menacing, like a warning. But despite the fear, there was a sense of camaraderie. We each switched on our torches and moved in different directions, searching for anything that might reveal the truth.

I moved silently towards Donald's desk, Rebecca and Alex went to the filing cabinets, while Nerys and Toni sat at the computer. Using Tanya's passwords, Nerys began searching through Donalds accounts as Toni looked for clues as to what Donald was hiding.

"That's strange," said Toni looking over Nerys's shoulder, their faces illuminated by the light from the screen. We all looked up from what we were doing. "It looks like the company has a Swiss bank account. Nerys, can you bring up any more information like when and who set up the account?"

As Toni read the information on the screen, her face changed from confusion to anger to elation. "Now we have something," she said.

The rest of us rummaged through papers, through files, through drawers. Nothing. Nothing of any consequence. At the back of Donald's desk my hands brushed against something soft. I pulled it out to discover a pair of ladies' pants. "That man is disgusting," I said, holding the underwear aloft for all to see.

There was nothing important in his desk. As I sat back, disappointed and concerned that tonight might not be the big event I'd hoped it would, I noticed something. Where the bookshelves finished was an outline. I hadn't noticed it before, but the moonlight illuminated a door shaped shadow. I went towards it and pressed, eager to see if it was my overactive imagination, and almost fell as my weight tumbled through the opening into a tiny dark room. Cardboard boxes were strewn across the floor, sets of folders tucked away inside straining to be released. If Donald had something to hide, this is where he would hide it.

"I think I've found Santa's secret cave," I whispered.

The girls immediately stopped what they were doing, and, with military precision, we hunted through the boxes together as quickly as possible. It didn't take long before we were all asking each other questions about pieces of random papers hidden between legitimate documents. There were loan agreements, results of shareholders votes along with scribbled non-disclosure agreements, all in Donald's dodgy handwriting and hundreds of receipts for expensive items that were never seen at the company.

"He must have all this stuff at his house," said an enraged Toni.

Then Alex signalled for us all to stop. We all crept closer and huddled round as Alex and Toni flipped through some pages, eyes widening as they read. Toni's voice was barely audible. "Girls, this is the company manifesto."

"What's a manifesto?" Lisa asked excitedly.

"It sets out the company's key priorities and values to promote trust between a business and its clients," said Alex.

Lisa's face fell. "I thought it would be more important."

"It was very well hidden, so it must be something. But we need to show it to Gerrard. See what he thinks," said Alex.

One by one, we made our way down in the dumbwaiter relieved to be out of the darkness, but nervous about what, if anything, the documents might reveal.

Just after ten, we arrived in Rovaniemi at an apartment Nic had rented for the night. When we saw the others, we couldn't stop smiling. Gerrard was not quite so exhilarated.

"I'm too old for this." He straightened and stood with his hands behind his back. "All this cloak and dagger stuff takes its toll. I shall be glad when it's over." He glanced at me and immediately said, "Don't worry. I'm fine. And this is, I hope, for the good of the company."

"It will all be worth it," said Toni, "especially when Chrissie explains what we found."

Nic, Lisa, Paula, Katrina and Savannah were silent, waiting anxiously, willing us to put them out of their misery, as we put the files down on the table.

"We finally have proof Donald has stolen company money," said Toni.

"And we made copies of Donald's emails and account statements," said Rebecca.

"And we found the 'Santa Clause'," chipped in an excited Alex.

"What? Another Father Christmas?" Katrina frowned.

"No. The 'Santa Clause'", said Alex, "was a paragraph written into the employment contracts when the company was first set up. The contract was used to define the employees' rights, duties, and privileges."

"And this clause was written into the contracts of all COC's," explained Gerrard, "including mine. But here's the interesting part. When I compared my contract to Donald's, it seems this clause is missing in his contract."

"What does the clause say?" asked Nic.

"If a COC acts 'ultra vires', outside of their specific duties and not abiding by the values and ethics of the company, the board can vote to remove them."

"But if the clause is not in Donald's contract, how would it work?" asked Katrina.

"And even if you could prove this, the Board will never vote against him anyway," said Savannah.

"Exactly!" Toni looked like the Cheshire Cat from Alice's adventures.

"This is hopeless," said Savannah, openly annoyed with our reactions.

Gerrard took pity. "The clause states that if anyone on the Board feels they are being influenced by the COC to the detriment of the Company, then they can demand the 'Santa Clause' is activated. This clause is included in the Christmas Company Manifesto which we found hidden in Donald's secret room. Donald doctored his contract, then hid all the manifestos so no one would see."

"But you still have the same people voting, and you said they would never vote against Donald. I don't get it. Is it all the wine we've drunk tonight?" asked Paula looking at her empty wine glass.

Gerrard continued. "The 'Santa Clause' states that a group of men, good and true, are brought in to vote on whether to remove the COC."

"More men? I'm not sure this place needs more men," said Katrina.

"I agree," said Toni, "but this is Ex board members and retired Santas who will vote. Not the Board as it is now."

"You mean like you?" said Lisa, looking at Gerrard.

"Yes, and another eleven, just like me."

Men like Gerrard. Good men. Genuine Father Christmases. Men who would know what to do. I did some calculations in my head. "Slight problem. Will we find another eleven like you? I mean, they'll be quite old, won't they?"

Gerrard stopped smiling, clearly unimpressed with my comment. "Not every Father Christmas or board member is of the more mature variety. And don't forget, with maturity comes experience."

"I know. I'm just thinking this through. There's a lot to do."

And we weren't leaving the apartment until we had a plan in place. Now experts with the IT, Katrina and Nic, with the help of Nerys, insisted they trawl the internet, to track down the ex-board members. Savannah, Lisa, and Paula agreed to sift through the paperwork, organising it into categories and Rebecca would look at the accounts and bank statements. Alex focused on the contracts and the legalities and Toni oversaw logistics where she had to deliver.

Gerrard and I worked on the facts and figures, what was happening to the company, and the proposal of how we could make the company money by planning and building the new Christmas Town. The Santa Clause was essential to the success of the plan. We could only guess how Donald controlled the Board, and he would never resign being too proud and arrogant. We had to force him out and the Santa Clause gave us the leverage. But we had to be careful. We couldn't risk Donald finding out what we were up to. The stakes were high, and if anyone discovered our plan, there was a danger it wouldn't happen.

***

A few days later, with Sami tucked up in bed, Daniel and I were enjoying a peaceful evening meal together. Every day was more unbearable working for Donald. He tried to pretend as if nothing had changed, but after the business trip Donald was different with him, not as trusting, sensing Daniel's uneasiness, and he made sure Daniel knew it.

"I thought if I could find something, proof that Donald's hiding something, then I could get rid of him," said Daniel, placing his knife and fork together on the side of his plate.

I want to tell you what we know. "And did you?"

"No. I scrutinised the recent board papers before the meeting and tried to question discrepancies in the figures with some of the other members, but I think he has spies in the team."

I feel so guilty.

"He came out of his office, shouting to the whole of the top floor, 'I think Daniel needs to go back to school. His figures don't add up. Or is it my figures that don't add up, Daniel? Which is it?"

I reached out for his hand across the kitchen table. He squeezed it and smiled at me. There was no doubt this was affecting Daniel's health. He looked tired, and his skin was sallow and puckered. How could this happen to my effervescent Daniel? Was any job worth this?

After dinner, we wrapped up and went and sat outside on the porch. Snuggled up, under a blanket on the swing seat, we watched the waves of green in the sky overhead. The auroral displays took my breath away every time we saw them. As we gazed at the sky, Daniel spoke about Donald's latest attack, calling him 'a loser' and saying whatever he had planned would not work, just like him. He had tried, without success, to convince the other board members that Donald needed to go. Some of them knew it was the right thing but were scared to go against Donald. The rest seemed to be under his spell, willing to do whatever he said.

"I'm so sorry, Daniel."

"I think he will fire me which might be good thing. I don't want to do this anymore."

There was a quizzical look on his face, his eyes searching mine.

"We have a plan. I can't tell you everything, but we think it will work."

"We?" he asked.

My face lit up, warmed by the expectation of what we were attempting. "Just a few of Santa's helpers."

Daniel's face turned gloomy. "I hope it isn't Santa's helpers. If I had to rely on the Board, I'd be worried."

"It's not what you think. Toni has organised a delivery."

What he didn't know was that the delivery was the twelve ex-employees. The girls had found more than we needed, which was just as well, as some of them, despite what Gerrard said, were quite infirm. Toni then arranged transport, created shipping slips, and ordered storage containers to ensure our goods, the ex-board members, were received and stored safely until we were ready. She then falsely requested a visit from a religious sect who were keen to see some of the setup of the Company in return for a healthy donation. Katrina, Nerys and Nic created a fake website with details, including their assets, which made it easier for greedy Donald to agree to. She had named them The Apostles and Toni wrote this on the shipping dockets.

The process was seamless and efficient. Since the operation began, Toni had been amazing. She took charge without realising. Every decision and idea oozed confidence and knowledge. She had a good hold on the reins. I didn't tell Daniel any of the details. He needed to be in the dark to help with the scene created when they arrived.

"Didn't Brandon question it?"

"She told him the delivery would bring in funding and was a good investment—which it is, if this plan works. Look at the sky."

The colours changed from shades of green to blues and purples. This was unusual. We never saw this colour palette very often. Maybe it was a sign? Waiting for this moment had been excruciating. Disguising what we were attempting to do from the outside world, we had to remind ourselves why we were doing this, and find encouragement from wherever we could.

"We need your help."

He sat up, a small glint of anticipation lit up his face. "What do you need me to do?"

"We need you to organise an emergency board meeting. If we get the delivery onto the premises for the meeting before Donald realises, we'll be fine. And if we can do this quickly, Donald will have less time to jeopardise it."

Daniel was mute, staring hypnotically at the sky.

"You said Donald never looks at the manifest, which will have their names on. It was the only thing that could prevent access."

He still didn't say anything.

"We've arranged everything. We just have to see it through."

He mumbled something inaudible.

"Daniel, it will be okay. We have to do this. For Sami. For everyone."

"You're right, I know you're right. I'll sort it. Don't worry." He stopped staring at the sky, which now resembled a distorted picture on a television screen of blurred bent lights and looked at me. "You've changed." His tone was soft. It wasn't a criticism. "You're strong and brave and determined. Maybe it was always there, but I'm only just seeing it. I'm sorry it's taken me so long to see you clearly."

I put my head on his shoulder. I didn't need to say anything. He was right. I was stronger and braver. Maybe it was having a focus or a project? Maybe it was more belief in myself? Whatever it was, I knew I had changed. I felt it. And there was no turning back.

Chapter 57

Lapland, November 1999

D-Day had arrived. A fitting title, we thought. Per my request, Daniel called an emergency meeting and Donald was livid. His attempts to humiliate and taunt Daniel had not resulted in Daniel resigning, as he'd hoped. He tried to fire him but Daniel knew Donald couldn't do this without a valid reason for dismissal. What could Donald say? He had no carrot to wave over Daniel's head or stick to beat him with, which incensed Donald further. Daniel agreed to leave, but not until after the meeting. He didn't want to miss whatever it was we were going to do.

At midday, a minibus carrying twelve men in dark overcoats and hats slowly made its way down the long path from the town to the entrance gate of the Ring. Toni, Paula, Lisa and I were also onboard. The plan was for Lisa and Paula, unknown to security and personal at the Ring, to pretend they were escorting this religious sect into the building for a tour. Once in, Toni and I could direct everyone where to go and wait until it was time.

I stared out of the window of the bus to calm my nerves, but the glass was fogged up with our warm, nervous breath. Nobody spoke. Silence, except for the windscreen wipers squeaking across the front window, frantically trying to clear the large clumps of snow obscuring the driver's vision. It felt a much longer journey than normal.

Paula and Lisa sat up front while the rest of our passengers spread out, disguising their identity as much as they could. The weather helped. No one would see much if they glanced at the minibus coming down the drive. The main problem we faced was anyone looking too closely inside.

When we reached the security point, Paula, and Lisa, shrouded in layers of coats, scarves and gloves got off the bus, manifest in hand, leaving the door slightly open so Toni and I could hear the conversation.

Paula handed the guards the manifest. "The company thought having some women around would help make the visit more enjoyable for the men." She then nudged one guard and winked at the other. "You know what I mean."

The guard laughed. So far, so good. Unfortunately, the other guard was more diligent, and looked at the manifest closely. He wanted to check the number of passengers and asked to see inside the bus. Lisa nodded. She looked tense.

The guard stepped onto the minibus, looked, and counted us all and then got off. By sheer luck he was a new guard, and more interested in the number of people than who they were. He stamped the manifest and counted out sixteen passes. We were in the clear, for now.

Lisa and Paula climbed back onto the minibus, passes in hand, and relieved smiles on their faces. "That was close," Lisa said, brushing the snow off her hood onto the floor.

"I knew it would be fine. You worry too much," said Paula, trying to reassure us although she looked quite frazzled herself.

As we drove past the gate, I turned to look behind me. Gerrard sat at the rear, neck sunk into a large polo neck and big black coat, his head covered in a cap. I waved. He shooed me away with his hand, but not before smiling. He was enjoying this, even though he'd never admit it.

As we approached the main building entrance, Toni stood up and turned to face the Apostles. "Remember, we need to keep a low profile here until we get past the front desk. Do not to talk to anyone, including each other. We can't risk anyone recognising any of you. And thank you gentlemen for being here. It means a great deal to many people."

As Lisa, Paula and I clasped hands in a show of solidarity, Toni took a deep steadying breath and stepped off the bus. I watched as she marched determinedly towards the building entrance.

One by one, the Apostles filed out of the bus, their heads bowed, hands clasped together in prayer-like poses. It was like watching a procession of religious monks. I handed out the passes in turn, feeling my own heartbeat faster each time.

When Toni emerged from the building, she was grinning from ear to ear. "That was easier than I thought."

"It's not over yet," I reminded her. "And where is Donald?" It was the one thing that had been bothering me on the journey here. If he knew who was visiting today, the plan would be ruined.

"In his office," said Toni, still grinning. "He's so arrogant he wouldn't dream of coming downstairs and introducing himself. We must go to him, and only when he's ready. It will play straight into our hands."

Once we were inside the building, a receptionist escorted us into one of the nicer waiting rooms, which had a splendid view of Christmas Town. The Apostles kept their heads covered and eyes down.

As the receptionist turned to leave, he looked back, puzzled. He walked up to me and Toni.

"Excuse me. This is strange."

Crap! *He's recognised us*. Like playing hide and seek, I held my breath trying not to get caught.

I nodded, hoping he would take my silence for a greater understanding of the situation. He leaned in closer, out of earshot of the apostles.

"Are they like one of those cults that don't speak?"

I looked up at the ceiling. *Thank you, God.* "Yes. They're very religious," I whispered.

The receptionist, happy with this explanation, left, closing the door behind him.

Then, like a sped-up version of a Full Monty male strip show, the

Apostles flung off their outer garments to reveal what they were hiding underneath. Every one of them was wearing a complete Santa suit. Pillar box red jackets trimmed with white fur, adorned with large gold buttons down the middle. Thick, black belts held back their ageing stomachs. Shiny black rubber boots completed the look. It had been Toni's idea: a uniform to show solidarity and remind everyone what this company was about.

"Gather round everyone." Gerrard waited for all the Apostles to settle down before continuing his speech. "We've all seen the paperwork outlining what Donald has done and the financial state of this Company. We must now do our duty. The future of Father Christmas is in our hands."

I glanced at my watch. It was time. "Ready?"

Gerrard nodded, and the Apostles fell into formation, resembling a train of reindeer pulling a sleigh through the sky. It was a fantastical sight, and a beautiful scene.

As the door opened, out poured the troupe, marching in pairs down the corridor, a sea of red. Everyone they passed was so astonished, no one said anything. With Gerrard leading the way, everyone moved to the side to let them through, like Moses parting the waves. They continued up the stairs and into the boardroom.

And then we flowed into the not-so-pleasant sound of Donald's voice shouting at forty decibels above his normal volume. "What the hell is going on?"

Toni, Lisa, Paula and I raced up the stairs behind them, not wanting to miss any of this. And it seemed we weren't the only ones. Word quickly spread through the building that something was going on, and now there must have been thirty people all craning their necks to get a good view of the boardroom.

"Get back to work! What are you looking at?" shouted Donald, his face red, a large vein pulsing in the middle of his forehead. "And you lot can leave right now," he said, thrusting his arm out at the Santas. "This is a private meeting."

Gerrard's voice boomed out. "No, Donald. We are not leaving. We have a right to be here."

At first Donald laughed. "I might have known you'd be involved. Well, whatever you are up to, it's not going to work. Security will throw you all out."

"They won't," said Daniel, appearing beside Gerrard.

Donald just shook his head. "You're an idiot, Daniel. Getting involved with this lot. You had a cushy number here, but now you'll be lucky if you ever get a management role again. You all need to leave."

"We are not going anywhere until we vote," said Gerard, his calm voice jovial, enjoying the moment.

"Vote for what?"

"To get rid of you," I said. I surprised myself with the seriousness in my tone.

He glanced down at me. "Good luck with that. This is my Board. This is my company. Now get out." Donald's face matched the Santa suits.

Just then, the security guards appeared. Gerrard put his hand in the air, his palm facing the security guards and spoke. "Before you lay one hand on us, you should know we have the authority for an extraordinary meeting."

"What authority?" said Donald spitting the words out.

"The Santa Clause."

His face turned as white as his beard. Like a guilty man at a hearing, knowing what was coming next and that he would have to answer for his wrongdoings.

Gerrard continued, "We are here to vote to on whether Donald Pittman should continue in his position as Chief of Christmas. Restrain that man!" Gerrard said to the security men, now clearly delighted they could physically apply force to a man who made their lives hell too.

I flew around the table, handing out the file of evidence to the board members. There was a great deal of talk and paper shuffling and cries of protest from some board members, but Gerrard persisted, determined to be heard.

"It's all there in the documents. If any board member believes the Board is compromised, the 'Santa Clause' is activated, and twelve ex-board members are brought in to vote in their place. We have evidence of Donald's illegal business dealings, and proof he has been stealing from the company. Now it is up to you."

A gasp emanated from the audience now gathered outside the room. It seemed most people watching were keen for battle to commence, like spectators at a boxing match.

After five minutes of Donald shouting and trying to persuade the other board members that we were crazy, Gerrard ran a Christmas bell. "I have one question. Does anyone on the Board feel they have been influenced by the COC to the detriment of the company?"

Although we had the proof, we still needed one board member to activate the clause. Most of the board members kept their eyes down, either afraid to look at Donald or afraid of what they had done.

The chairman rose from his seat and looked around the table. "There are no excuses. I am fully aware of the choices I made, and am deeply ashamed I played a part in these illicit actions. I will cooperate fully with any proceedings that follow, and will activate the Santa Clause myself." He shook his head and addressed the Apostles. "Gentlemen. Please take your seats."

One by one, the board members left the room as the Apostles each took a seat at the table.

"Not you, Donald. You need to stay and see what happens." A satisfied smile spread over Gerrard's face.

What happened next happened quickly. A secretary came in to take the minutes and ensure the clause was followed appropriately. The rest of us left and stood outside like Catholics at the Vatican, nervously waiting to see the colour of smoke billowing out of the chimney. I forced my way out of the crowd, unable to breathe.

"You, okay?" said Nic, grabbing my elbow so I didn't fall.

"I will be." We clasped hands and waited.

It was an agonising wait. Fifteen minutes later, the door opened. There stood Donald. He walked one way and then the other, disorientated, like a bee smoked in his hive, uncertain where to go. Amazingly, he caught my face in the crowd and glared. His sneer recognisable, but not terrifying. His power evaporated.

The next person out of the door was Daniel. His face free from worry lines, as if he'd had Botox. He stood there, jacket undone, searching the crowd. His eyes lit up when he saw me, and he beckoned for me to come forward.

"It's done. Donald is out." He stepped towards me and pulled my body into his.

It was the longest hug I could remember, and it felt like that old cliché, but time stood still. All I could hear was his heart beating. All I could feel was the warmth from his body. All I could taste was the salt from his tears. I sank into his arms, relief washing over me. After four years, all the worries and difficulties, the secrets and problems, it was finally over. Without Donald, there was now time and space for us and our relationship.

"Is Gerrard okay?"

"Come and see for yourself." Daniel and I pushed our way through the crowds of employees congregating around the boardroom.

At first, I couldn't see Gerrard. He was in the middle of the room, surrounded by a mass of people in either a black or red suit. People were pumping his hand up and down, slapping him on the back, talking to him or trying to talk to him. It was noisy and hard to hear what anyone was saying.

Daniel cleared a path with his long arms and Gerrard looked up. "I hate to break up this happy sight, but we have the important job of the inauguration to carry out."

I looked at Daniel, puzzled.

He smiled back. "You'll see."

Daniel and Gerrard made a space in the middle of the room and asked everyone to be quiet.

I wound my fingers around Daniel's. One of the Apostles held a red and gold velvet stole up in the air and placed it around Gerrard's neck. He opened a large bound book, worn around the edges and embroidered with gold thread, and placed it on a lectern in front of Gerrard. One of the other Apostles offered Gerrard a small box wrapped in gold paper and tied with a red bow.

"We, the Board of Christmas, offer you this gift to symbolise the tradition of giving gifts. From now on you will be the giver of gifts, the symbol of Christmas and the head of our company. Please open the gift."

Gerrard's hands were shaking as he unwrapped the present. Inside was a solid mahogany box which contained a thick gold banded signet ring. He looked over at me as he held onto the ring.

The Apostle then indicated for Gerrard to place his hand on the book sitting on the lectern.

"Do you wish to do your duty and to carry out your role as Father Christmas to the best of your ability, acting within the Company's code of conduct at all times?"

"I wish."

"Do you wish to abide by the long-held tradition of delivering presents to the children of the world?"

"I wish." Gerrard's voice faltered a little. He had tears in his eyes and was trying to contain his emotion. It was hard to look at him without welling up.

"Then I ask you, Gerrard Gunher, to take the Father Christmas oath."

Gerrard took a deep breath. "I do solemnly wish that I will faithfully execute the office of Father Christmas and, to the best of my ability, preserve, protect and defend the covenant of Christmas."

The room erupted with a large swell of voices and cheers. Gerrard whispered something in the ear of the Apostle, then they looked over at me.

"Chrissie? Can you come over here please?" Gerrard looked very serious.

As I stood next to him, he bent down and asked me if I was ready.

"Ready for what?" *What is going on?*

"To make a difference." He stared at me. "My position is only short term while the new Board is recruited, and I imagine Daniel will be made COC when the time is right. But we decided in the board room that there needs to be another change if Christmas Town is to be better and do better."

I'm confused. What are you suggesting?

"Will you marry me?"

What?

"I know it's sudden, but we think it's necessary."

We? Has Valma agreed to this?

"The business will need a safe pair of hands."

We have been spending a lot of time together. Have I have given you the wrong idea?

"And I won't be doing this job for long."

Are you not well? Are you confused?

He stared at me. "So? Will you be my work wife? We need a Mrs Christmas, and you are perfect."

I breathed out long and slow, relieved Gerrard was not having a mental breakdown and that this was not another weird bylaw in Lapland. Then my brain processed what he had just asked me.

I turned to face Daniel. This was a huge undertaking and wouldn't be without problems, but it was also a way to change things. All the things the girls and I had talked about, the new town, a better life for all the community, jobs for women, a more equal society.

"It's up to you, Chrissie? You deserve it but only if you want it."

Yes, I wanted it, but it was more than that now, more than me. This was about everyone who lived and worked here, and I wanted to see this through.

I nodded. My legs unable to move, Daniel took my hands and positioned me in front of Gerrard. As this had never been done before, there wasn't another ring and stole, so Gerrard took his off and gave it to the Apostle to go through the same inauguration with me.

"Do you wish to do your duty and to carry out your role as Mrs Christmas to the best of your ability, acting within the Company's code of conduct at all times?"

"I wish," I replied, twisting the large golden ring round and round on my finger.

"And will you recite the oath?" He passed me a piece of paper with the words written on it.

"I do solemnly wish that I will faithfully execute the office of Father— Mrs Christmas and will, to the best of my ability, preserve, protect and defend the covenant of Christmas."

The room was loud again with clapping and cheering. After lots of handshakes and hugs, Daniel appeared. "You did it, Chrissie. You are now officially Mrs Christmas."

I had been Chrissie Wall, then Chrissie Connor and now Mrs Christmas or Mrs Claus. So many names I didn't know what to call myself. But I realised something. I no longer felt like Mrs Nobody.

Chapter 58

TV studio, 2009

A snuffling noise disturbs the replay in my head. I look at Ms Grey, who is struggling to locate her handkerchief. I pass her my red cotton handkerchief with the COC embroidered in the top right-hand corner.

"How lovely," she says, noticing the logo.

"Yes, we have our own merchandise now, but this one is more sentimental." I look down, not wanting to catch Ms Grey's eyes. Daniel gave it to me for safekeeping.

Ms Grey dabs her eyes, her voice a little uneven as she addresses the camera. "It's certainly time for a break now. But when we return, we will be looking at the plight of the common woodlouse, and the woman who is determined to save them and a man who, through Facebook, discovered he was related to Christopher Columbus." Her face lights up through her terrific acting skills and the hundred-watt bulbs in the studio. "All of this after our extended live interview with Chrissie Christmas."

"And cut," shouts the producer. The camera crew, lighting crew, makeup artists and production team all bustle around, checking the studio and presenters.

"This is terrific, Chrissie," says the controller, looking from his mountain of notes to me and back to his notes. "We need to wrap it up now, though. Time moves on."

So true. I nod. *But what else do I want to say?* I have told the story of a town like no other in Lapland. I haven't divulged everything, as some of the magic must remain for the sake of the children. But explaining the 'Santa Clause' felt right. Highlighting it would help ensure we learn from our past.

The lights dim, the camera rolls again. The last act of the play starts. I look at Ms Grey. She stops staring at the camera. It feels like it's just her and me having a chat over a cup of coffee.

"It's amazing what a group of people can do. The change they can create. Women who had all these skills but were excluded, and people over the age of fifty with all their experience, who became invisible." It's my turn to look at the camera now. "If there is anyone listening to this who wants to change something, something they think they can't, then please take strength from me. I was once like you."

Lapland, February 2000

After the extraordinary meeting, a new board was put in place. The company was in a worse financial position than Gerrard and Daniel feared. Donald had wasted the company's money by buying inferior quality tools and equipment, and firing some of the most capable employees. All to cover up his poor investments and loans to fund his lavish lifestyle and many affairs.

Gerard had agreed to run the Board for a year until a new Father Christmas was appointed, and Daniel would remain as Deputy. Daniel was surprised Gerrard was happy for him to stay, but Gerrard had experience of Donald and knew what he could do to a man and how you could change. Gerrard hoped, with time, Daniel would be ready for the role of Father Christmas.

"I have to trust my board, so will need new members," Gerrard said to me that night of the inauguration. He'd tried to persuade me to join, but I knew Toni and Alex would be a better choice. Even Brandon had been supportive. In fact, he actively encouraged it, relieved I believe he could now stop pretending and do something he was actually good at. Which, as it turned out, was cooking. He eventually set up a restaurant and looked happy for the first time in years.

I had been mulling over my role for weeks. I was officially Mrs Christmas, or Mrs Claus. I wasn't sure what my title should be, but it didn't matter. I had a role, a purpose, and now I wanted to put plans into action.

"I've been thinking—"

"Oh, no. What have I done now?" Daniel was in his study, working from home. A recent idea he and Gerrard had implemented, so he could spend more time with me and Sami.

"Nothing yet, but—"

"I know that voice."

I punched him gently on the shoulder. He swivelled around in his chair to face me.

"Remember when we discussed building a Christmas Town people could visit? But how do we keep what we do here secret?"

"Go on. I'm listening." He pulled me into his lap.

"The girls and I have found a piece of land we could use halfway between Christmas Town and Rovaniemi, and I think we could build Christmas village there. Home to the real Father Christmas, packed with activities for visitors to do."

"Okay. Go on."

"We would use the land for the animals and have feeding times when visitors watch and feed them and even make their feed. And maybe be a reindeer warden for the day? And then we would have other barns made up of different activities, like biscuit decorating with gingerbread biscuits in the shape of Christmas trees or stars and reindeer. We would have a toy wrapping activity with elves and maybe some Christmas stories with Mrs Christmas? In another barn there would be food and drink, and, again, theme it so, for instance, Santa sandwiches or Elves Eggnog, Father Christmas Pudding or Christmas Cookies."

"It would require a lot of money and—"

"Yes, but when you entertain people, they are happy and spend money. More money for the company means more work for the community and a better economy. We could start small and see what interest there is? And you never know—"

"Interest?" Daniel shouted, jumping up, forcing me off his lap. He walked out of the study and paced up and down the hall, muttering to himself. "Christmas Town has always been a philanthropic interest, but if we make it a business interest, an investment opportunity..." He came back into the study and started making notes.

"But not only that. Christmas is for children, all children. With the business as it stands, we have never factored in the children whose parents can't afford presents. It's always been for those who could. We are a philanthropic business and should subsidise people of different incomes. But we have forgotten."

Daniel looked up. "I agree with everything you are saying, but the company is not in good shape because of Donald. How can we do this as well? If the new town is successful and people want to visit, then we can think of helping more, but it will take time." Daniel squeezed my hand, believing the conversation was over. It wasn't.

"But we could make this work financially. I know the new town will be successful. And then we will want our visitors to stay as long as possible, so, what we need is somewhere they can stay?" I raced on before he had time to interrupt. "A hotel. A Christmas Hotel complete with sleigh taxi rides, elf doormen, themed bedrooms, and reindeer in the hotel grounds. Nic has researched the surrounding area and found the land, Lisa has drawn some preliminary sketches, Alex is looking at the sale contract and Toni is looking at how we can buy it."

Daniel was quiet, playing with the pen in his hand. "I've told you I agree in principle. And the new town is a great idea, but a hotel? I think it's too soon to start thinking that big."

I've been thinking about this for years. I can visualise the land, the hotel, and the hotel's monogrammed towels: fawn brown, with a reindeer face and gold initials.

"Don't be sad," he said looking at me. "It's something for the future, just not yet. But the Christmas Town idea. Genius. Let's get a meeting set up soon. We will need to sell this to the board. It's a big decision."

"I know, but now we have a board that is more likely to listen to new ventures, and we have Alex and Toni."

He paused writing and turned to me. "And our magic ingredient?"

I frowned, puzzled. What actual magic did we have?

"We have you. You could sell this to the board."

He was right. No one knew more about this vision than me.

He wrapped his arms so tightly around me I could hear his racing heartbeat as he cocooned me in his chest. "Have I ever told you how much you mean to me? I could never have done this without you. I would not be in the position I am without you. And you, amazing you, are about to change the way the Company does business."

"They haven't said yes yet."

"They will. It's a brilliant idea. You are brilliant. You came to this tiny town, not knowing anyone and built relationships, built a community just with small actions and wanting to make something better for everyone. You're so much more than just my wife and I'm sorry I'm only just telling you."

It's funny hearing this now. I always wanted your approval, but I found out what I was capable of. I just had to believe in myself.

Chapter 59

TV studio, 2009

Everyone was silent: the audience, crew and assistants. All eyes on me. Ms Grey's the most intent.

"And did it work?"

I smiled. "The board voted unanimously."

Change was necessary if the business was to survive, and they recognised how excluding half the community had cost them more than revenue. They needed to rebuild their reputation and make people trust and believe again. Believe in the magic of Christmas, in Father Christmas, in each other.

I looked around the room. "Isn't that what Christmas should be about?"

The crew were all nodding, and I heard some sniffs coming from the darkness at the back.

"And not just at Christmas time. We should be like this all the time. All believing, all excited about what will happen next."

For us it was liberating. Women and men, old and young, were all needed to help make this idea a reality. Toni became indispensable to the Company. She maintained her focus and directness in her speech, but she'd softened and was more considered. No longer hiding behind her husband, imprisoned with how others thought she should act, she could be herself. She was making the decisions, and it suited her.

Alex was another one who changed in her new role. She had been busy since the Emergency Board meeting, going through the new contracts to replace the ones Donald had doctored, and leading on the conveyancing sale of the land. She was busy. She had a purpose. She was happy.

This decision changed everyone, even Lisa and Rebecca. They decided to move to Christmas Town to help us with our vision, certain they could have a better life with this new venture: Lisa with the chance of designing a hotel and Rebecca with all the new accounts the business would bring in.

Daniel had been right. Investment was key. With plans for the new village and armed with facts and figures, Gerrard, Daniel, Toni and Alex met with investors and government officials. It was a tremendous ordeal, but they secured funding for the development of the new land. All of this, while running the business of developing and manufacturing toys to ensure Christmas still happened.

I uncross my legs and look at Ms Grey. She looks confused, almost panicked.

Surely, you have heard enough?

She keeps looking down at her notes, as if she wants to keep the conversation going. "But Chrissie, what about you? What did you do next?"

Just a little more. The curtain call. I clear my throat. "What didn't I do?"

Ms Grey laughs and clutches my hand. "Tell us."

"First, Valma and I developed the role of Father Christmas. Our favourite part was reading all the letters the children wrote, and we wrote detailed and comprehensive replies to every letter received. This helped us engage with the children and our consumers, the parents, and helped with the manufacturing of presents, reminding us of what Christmas was about. Then I managed the new Christmas Land project with Toni, Alex and Lisa. Nic, Rebecca and Katrina worked on marketing the place and Savannah, well, Savannah was surprising.

"After the initial meeting, when we discussed how Christmas Town needed to change, Savannah offered to look after the children of the women wanting to work. She ran it from her home to begin with, but then it became so popular she used one of the conference suites at the Centre. It was an enormous hit for those working at the Ring, as the workers could drop their children off on the way to work and pick them up at the end of the day. The first creche in Christmas Town. It was quite an achievement."

"It all sounds remarkable."

"It was. I remember about a year after Santa Gate, as we affectionally called it, looking at the new Christmas Land we had created. We had an official site meeting to decide if we could open Christmas Land to the public in six weeks. It wasn't quite ready, but for the first time it looked like a proper destination, a little corner of the world dedicated to Father Christmas, like standing in the middle of a winter snow globe."

Lapland, October 2000

We had worked hard to create this small village; snow-covered buildings made of timber and straw, with twinkly diamond snow roofs. There was a post office, bakery, workshop, farmhouse, cafe and gift shop as well as the main house for Father Christmas. We even created a stone quilted patchwork path for visitors to follow around the village. This path was dotted with activities, from making biscuits in Mrs Claus' kitchen to hand-picking fruit at the farm or making a toy in the workshop. Each child could choose their own path around Christmas Land and create their own unique experience.

"It's beautiful," said Katrina, her tears freezing on her face like a Pierrot clown.

"I think it's amazing what we've achieved, especially in such a short time, and with all the problems we had to begin with and then battling against the weather to get it done. I think it's amazing. I think we are amazing." Nic never had a problem getting her words out, even in the bitter cold.

"I agree," said Alex. "I think the buildings in particular look spectacular." Under Alex's supervision, we had been meticulous in putting together each building, making sure it was given its childlike charm, painting it in vibrant hues of red and white and adding candy canes and tiny wreaths on the doors. Each building was stocked with presents and decorations.

"We still have more to do," I said. "Icicle lights will be hung on all the buildings, and we have to build the snowmen." I decided the village needed its own set of purpose-built snowmen guards in every corner of the village to protect this winter wonderland we had built. "But what are we missing?"

"You know what this place needs?" said Toni. The rest of us looked blank, feeling the cold get to our heads. "Music. Can't you hear holiday music ringing out from the loudspeakers and maybe some bells." We all smiled, nodding our approval.

"I know. I know," said Rebecca, her arm raised like a child desperate to tell you the answer. "Smells."

Our smiles turned to frowns unsure what Rebecca was envisioning.

"Let's face it. There are no smells here, except for maybe animal ones from the reindeer and huskies. Look at Father Christmas's house. Now can you visualise a hint of woodsmoke coming from the chimney. And then the streets with a wafting aroma of cinnamon and gingerbread from the bakery, pine and peppermint from the gift shop and cocoa and nutmeg from the cafe. Heaven!" Rebecca closed her eyes as she breathed in the make-believe smells.

She was right. I made another list and prayed it could be completed in time.

"All this talk of smells has made me hungry," said Gerrard, his large stomach growling. "Shall I call this meeting to a close and we can go to the pub?"

Gerrard had never wanted to retire, but after twelve months of being in the boardroom, it was losing its appeal. There was a much more important role for him in Christmas Land. Father Christmas. Not a COC or a figurehead, but a real-life Father Christmas. He already had the authentic white beard and wobbly stomach, and he loved children. He was perfect.

***

Ten minutes later, we were sitting in the pub, glad to be in the warm; another change that happened after the Santa Clause. The Ring and all its amenities were open to everyone, and the pub had had a makeover. Fur rugs on seats, cinnamon candles on each table and caricatures of each of Rudolph's reindeer now hung proudly in the alcoves next to the wooden antler hooks for coats, scarves, and gloves. Alex had overseen the renovations. A woman's touch softened the place, made it more functional.

"Here we go," said Toni, placing nine enamelled mugs on the wooden sleigh table. The scent of mulled fruit rose from the centre of each mug. We each took a mug, looking for our favourite on the tray. I cuddled the mug in my hands, covering the face of Cupid. Alex grabbed Prancer and Nic picked up Blitzen.

"A toast! Here's to the next stage of Christmas Land," she said, holding her mug with Comet on up in the air.

She was now the deputy COC. And how we loved calling her that.

"Is this not getting boring?" Toni asked when we presented her with her own enamelled mug, beautifully illustrated with a penis and the words 'Deputy COC' underneath.

"No!" we all sang out, happy to see how delighted she actually was.

"I have some news," said Alex, drumming her fingernails on the table.

"I'm pregnant."

Crap!

Everyone was silent, hesitating whether she viewed this as a good thing. "It's good news."

Seeing our unconvinced faces, she continued, "I'm super busy with work, have no idea how I'm going to manage, but Rikkard has agreed to help with the childcare, and we are both thrilled."

I didn't think this place could change anymore, and here was a male offering to do some childcare. What next? Offering to do the housework?

"Has anyone heard from Tanya?" Savannah asked.

"She's settled back in Texas and is retraining as a counsellor. She feels her life experiences should help." I often spoke to Tanya, forever grateful for her help. I also admired her bravery in leaving Donald and the security he could offer in favour of an unknown but freer and happier life.

"Here's to Tanya." Alex raised her mug, and we all joined in.

"She's also been a darling and helped me to build more contacts in the US," said Nic, who was busy putting together a proposal for tourist experience packages at the new hotel.

Deciding on a new name for the hotel had been difficult. Initial ideas included 'Santa's Shack' and 'Santy Shanty' but with the help of a competition, the children of Christmas Town chose the name Rudolph.

"A three, five, or seven-night stay at the Rudolph Hotel would include all meals, a choice of two activities per day, things like biscuit decorating or husky rides—" Nic sounded like an advertisement, "culminating in a meeting with Father Christmas and a choice of gift. Obviously, I will choose a range of gifts, depending on the age of the child."

"Well, we know you love shopping," I said.

Laughter rang round the table.

"I was also thinking," said Nicole not pausing for breath, "As well as our charity scheme for disadvantaged families, I thought we could offer different levels of luxury, with a pricing strategy for each level to make it affordable for all families. So, for example, Band 1 could be biscuit making and feeding the reindeers and ten minutes with Father

Christmas, whereas Band 4 could be quad biking and training the huskies and ten minutes at Father Christmas's house. What do you think?" She looked directly at me.

"I think you will end up running the place one day."

Nic pulled a face. "No, thank you. I'm quite happy with what I'm doing. It's like going shopping every day but with other people's money."

"Talking of shopping, I have an announcement," said Savannah.

Nic cocked her face to one side like a Labrador. "I thought you were doing the childcare thing?"

"Yes, I'm still doing that, but I've just bought a shop front in Christmas Town."

"What are you selling? Children?" joked Alex.

Savannah ignored her. Although they got on well enough, they never understood one another, preferring to hide behind humour and gentle banter.

"Anything I can crochet or knit. Scarves, hats, gloves, and throws for the bed and sofas. All the products are one hundred percent natural and biodegradable. Everything has to be organic."

It was the latest trend, and Savannah was its biggest advocate. She was determined to be 'organic' in everything she did.

"I think we should make all the shops more organic, and I have meeting with Daniel next week to discuss it."

"Good for you," I said. "It looks like you might be a working girl after all."

We both smiled, remembering her initial reaction to such an idea.

"And what's next for you, Chrissie?" Katrina asked.

"I don't know. I suppose I'll help support Daniel. He's going to be very busy." When Gerrard informed the board of his resignation, Daniel was chosen as the next COC.

Alex glared. "Now you listen to me, Mrs Christmas. You have done enough supporting, and although Daniel will appreciate your help, you are not just a wife. You are an entrepreneur. You changed a town. We have opportunities now. Being sat here in this pub is because of you."

"Okay, okay," I said, my face warm from the drink and the flattery.

"Never doubt you are the main reason that this was ever a possibility. We believe in you."

As I looked around at all we had achieved, I was finally believing in me too, and it was an amazing feeling.

Chapter 60

TV studio, 2009

I pause and look around. Everyone is waiting for me to finish. I have told everyone the story of Christmas Town. The town that didn't acknowledge women and what they were capable of. The story of Father Christmas. The worst Santa in the history of Santa's. But—

I haven't told the whole story.

Lapland, 2007

After six years of sorting out the mess Donald had made, rebuilding reputations, and growing a new village, Daniel stepped down as COC to undertake cancer treatment. He'd had some symptoms but didn't say anything, wanting to concentrate on the project. But eventually he realised he couldn't carry on. He was tired, and Daniel's treatment took us out of Christmas Town for long periods of time. He'd insisted it wasn't necessary for me to go with him and was fine on his own, but caved in after five minutes of silence from me.

With Daniel's resignation, Toni became the new COC, and everyone was delighted. At her inauguration, Daniel announced it was right we finally had a female Father Christmas. There was much debate about changing the name, but in the end, keeping it felt right. The myth of Father Christmas is nearly as old as Mother Nature, and we wouldn't want to mess with her.

The hospital appointments were arduous and draining for both of us. I tried to keep him entertained, but it was difficult. The notebook had been Daniel's idea. It was his way of making things better. And it helped. We were often at the hospital for hours, and I would sit by Daniel while he had his chemotherapy treatment and write down what we could remember. It made us ask questions. Why did we do that? What happened afterwards? Who said what to whom? We both tried to prove to the other our memory of the event was the real version. We reminisced, we argued, we laughed, we cried.

My role now was to care for Daniel, keeping him rested and worry free. But the girls knew I wanted to be kept up to date with the project. From then on meetings took place in the sauna so I could be near Daniel, but he couldn't hear anything about work.

"Visits to Christmas Land are down for the first time since we opened," Nic said.

A moment of silence passed in the sauna, interrupted only by the occasional crackle from the stones when Katrina poured water on them.

"Nic's right," said Toni. "We've invested in some different marketing strategies, but it's proving difficult. We don't have enough money so work on the hotel will have to stop."

The aroma of eucalyptus and rosemary permeated the air. I breathed deeper, trying to suppress the anger rising up. "But I thought the business was doing well?"

"Yes, but we have competition now," said Toni. "All these other companies have set up using our business model, and there seem to be more every day."

"But we are the original Christmas company, the real one. We have the real Father Christmas not the pretend one," I said, fired up by more than the heat of the sauna seeping into my pores.

"I know but we can't reveal that." Toni sounded despondent.

I rolled my eyes.

"You don't agree," said Savannah.

"You know I don't."

"Neither do I," piped up Lisa. "I think being more open might help."

Savannah glared at Lisa. I could see how the hotel project would affect Lisa more than the others, but she hadn't been a resident as long as the rest of us and, judging by Savannah's reaction, she shouldn't be saying anything. We were all quiet, contemplating, listless.

Toni spoke up again. "We need to come up with a new strategy," she said, her voice strong and determined.

I closed my eyes, wiping the warm perspiration dripping down my face, trying to think of something we hadn't done before, something that would give us an edge. We had to promote the holidays, and the hotel was the key to our success. No other company had a hotel. But to build it, we needed money, and that meant revenue in Christmas Land needed to increase. But what else could we do?

I looked at the girls, perched on the two tired wooden benches, red faces and white bodies covered in sweat like Amazonian scarlet macaws in a downpour. We had worked so hard to make this make-believe world more of a reality for us. To build a community and to connect with one another. It was a great story.

It is a great story. It has all the ingredients of a great story: a villain, a hero, the quest. People would love to hear our story.

The ideas started to flow. And then I had it. A plan: a daring and ambitious one, but one that might just be enough to save us.

"What are you thinking?" Lisa said, a hopeful smile on her face.

Toni did not look so pleased. "Please tell me it's not going to involve me wearing a red suit and white beard?"

"We need to tell our story."

"Are you going to write another blog?" said Nic. "I didn't think you were going to do that anymore as it didn't exactly work last time?"

"Shush. Let her speak," said Alex.

"Not a blog. Bigger than that."

"A book?" said Katrina.

"Nope. A television interview."

I heard a groan coming from Toni. It would be a gamble. Everyone in Christmas Town knew what Donald had done, but the rest of the world didn't. That was the story. There was no place for Donald or people like him. We had to do the right thing, and that meant sharing the whole story. And what better way than a television program?

***

We came up with a plan and on one of Daniel's good days, I told him what we were proposing. Daniel slept most of the time now. We'd converted the downstairs lounge as he couldn't go up the stairs anymore. In his more lucid moments, I would talk to him about Christmas Town, desperate to keep him engaged, keep him awake, keep him alive.

It was hard to look at him, his body so frail. He agreed with Toni and thought telling the world about Donald would harm the business.

"It won't change the past," he said slowly, his mouth dry, his voice hoarse, "but I've realised that you, Mrs Christmas, always make the right decisions. And you make everything right."

As he squeezed my hand, my tears fell like snowflakes, silently, onto his gaunt face.

TV studio, 2009

I feel the tears fall again. Ms Grey is now holding both of my hands in hers.

"I'm sorry for your loss," she says quietly in my ear.

I nod and wipe my eyes. "The Company made mistakes. It was about greed and power, but that's changed, and I wanted to tell you our story for two reasons. One is we need the help of the public. I need them to share this story, to remind large organisations they are a community of people and have a duty to care for all the people who work there.

And second, we need your audience to come and visit Christmas Land, to support all the people who made this a reality. We are building a brand-new hotel with a spa, and we want you to see for yourselves how magical the place is, and spend time there with the people you love."

But there is a third reason. This is also telling my story, and how I changed following someone else's dream. I always thought supporting someone else who had 'the big job' meant my role was inconsequential. I was never the star. I was in the background, a nobody. But I changed the way things were done in Christmas Town. Women and men. Young and old. And now everybody was important.

I must say this too. I turn to the camera with the flashing red light. "I say this to all those people out there who think they are nobodies. The people behind the people who get the credit. The people who work long hours and days and no one seems to notice. The people who do the menial jobs that have to be done. There are hundreds, thousands of us trying to make our lives, and the lives of those around us, better. We could be the dustbin workers, the window cleaners, the van drivers. We could be the nurses, the teachers, the hospital porters. We could be the partner, the carer, the mother, the son, the grandparent. We're not famous or important, but we are important to someone. People rely on us to do our job so they can do theirs. Every one of us is important. And if we are brave enough, sometimes we can help change people's lives and change our own lives too."

Ms Grey shuffles her notes and legs at the same time before fixing her eyes on me. "Mrs Christmas, it has been an honour, and never again will I think of Mr Grey in the same way." Then she fixes her stare on camera number one. "Mr Grey! Thank you for all you do for me so I can do this job. I do appreciate you and I'm sorry I haven't said it before now."

A dramatic pause follows, before she regains her composure and finishes the interview. "Well! It has been a most extraordinary interview. You should write a book about all of this."

Daniel had already suggested this, but for now, I needed to concentrate on the future of the hotel. But maybe something for the future.

Chapter 61

"So how did I do?" My first Skype call after the interview was with mum. She insisted on a virtual call, stressing 'cameras do lie' and wanting to check, even though she would have just seen me on the television.

"I'm so proud of you," she says, desperate to get the words out. "You talked so eloquently, and Ms Grey was impressed. I should know, I've seen her do a lot of interviews. She normally has one eye on the camera and one on the guest, but she kept both eyes on you."

You can always count on mum to say how it is.

"Dad!" she shouts, still forgetting I can hear her as well as see her. "Chrissie is on the phone."

I couldn't see all of dad, just his ear, as he speaks into the computer as he would a phone. Technology was still too difficult for my parents.

"So proud, Chrissie. Daniel would be too. I'll leave you with your mum. She's better at talking than me."

Some things never change.

Mum moves into the screen shot. She's been practising. "I liked your outfit too. I've not seen you in the traditional costume for a while. Have you thought about maybe changing the colour for something a little softer? That colour can be harsh on an older woman's skin."

I roll my eyes in plain sight.

"I was just saying."

"Look, mum, why don't you save all this for when I see you?"

"But we won't be coming over for a couple of months, and I really want to go through some things you shared."

"I'm coming to you. I might stay for a few days."

"But I thought you had to get straight back because of the hotel."

"I changed my mind." *I've been doing a lot of that recently.* "They can survive without me for a few days."

The truth was everyone in Christmas Town wanted me to have a break. After Daniel died, I was the one who insisted on burying myself in work, in the hotel build, in the hotel's promotion. I worked all hours, spent late nights going over figures and invoices, waking early to receive deliveries. But the work saved me, too, and gave me a future.

Nic sounds relieved when I phone and update her with my plans.

"I'm glad. You should spend some time with your parents. We're fine here. And as for the earlier problems, Lisa sorted the elves' costumes, and she got a discount for the inconvenience. Frederik worked a miracle and not only fixed the broken sleds but has made his own and said we can have them at cost. He's such a craftsman, they're bound to be better than the ones we currently use, and I spoke to Krystoff, and he said he will talk to you about altering the guests' program to include the picking up of poo. He seems to think it's a good idea, and we will have lots of takers. Personally, I can think of nothing worse."

"Is that everything?"

"No."

What now?

"Building work on the spa can resume."

"Brilliant! They sorted out the pipework then?"

"It's better than that. We can afford to get it fixed properly and quickly. Katrina has been inundated with emails and phone calls for future bookings for the hotel since the interview. It seems everyone would love to stay at the Rudolph Hotel. Your plan worked... again!"

I look up to the heavens, to Daniel. I've not jeopardised the hotel and future of Christmas Town, after all.

"You stay for as long as you like," Nic says. "We can manage without you, although we prefer it when you're here. It seems to go more smoothly when you are."

I'm not sure that's true. There are always problems. "Thanks Nic. I'll let you know when I'm on my way home."

Home. Saying the word is hard, but it's still where my heart is.

***

"It's you again," says the familiar voice of the taxi driver who dropped me off that morning. "Where to, love?"

"Leatherhead, please. By junction 9 on the M25."

He's quiet for exactly sixty seconds, just enough time to get out of the car park. "Can I ask who you are now?"

I realise he wouldn't have seen the interview, but I don't have the appetite for reliving the entire tale again, because it won't end with one question. It never does.

"I'm promoting a new hotel based in Lapland, home to Father Christmas and his elves."

I catch his eye in the mirror. He looks bewildered, as if his latest passenger is on her way to a costume party. But it doesn't matter. I have done what I set out to do, and now it's time for the next chapter.

"I love Christmas. Especially as a kid. I used to get so excited just thinking about Father Christmas and the presents—"

He rattles on as I look out the window. The roads are still busy. The pavements still full of shoppers. Life goes on. You can't plan every part of your life. It evolves. It wasn't my dream to move to Lapland, but I became part of something, something bigger than me. I didn't believe I was important, but I made a difference and I understood now I was a somebody after all.

Acknowledgements

I have many people to thank for their help in getting this book published.

First, my wonderful family and friends—Amanda, Fiona, Glenn, Grace, Joy, Julie, Lis, Lisa, Marissa, Nicole, Patrick, Patrick-Kevin, Rachel and Suzanne, for being patient when I was busy and encouraging me to continue when I didn't think I should. Thank you for your thoughts on the cover and for listening to the rambling ideas of a middle aged woman.

Thank you also to my editor Pat Dobie, at lucidedit.com who helped me shape this book and to the team at ebooklaunch.com (Alisha and Mike)

And finally—For Paul. You are my biggest critic and my strongest ally. Thank you for allowing me to be the most successful person in our family.

About the Author

Amanda Miles is a nobody to everyone except her 19 year-old twins, husband, dog, family and friends. In her paid career she was a teacher. In her unpaid career she was a cook, cleaner, taxi driver, secretary, accountant, dog walker, costume designer, therapist, and school governor. She loves reading, pilates, walking the dog, watching tv and playing bridge and lives near London in England. She has written five children's books (a science based series 'Cell Wars') and more information can be found on her website.

www.amandamilesauthor.com

Printed in Great Britain
by Amazon

51309594R00193